The Cowboy Who Worked Late

A Forbidden Workplace Romance & Small Town Saga

Three Rivers Romance™
Book 4

Liz Isaacson

Reader Note

Hello Fabulous Christian Cowboy Readers! I'm thrilled you're back in Three Rivers with me!

This is a forbidden romance between Henry Marshall and Angel White. They work together at her family's boarding stable and ranch, where her daddy has instituted a strict no-dating policy...

This opens up the door for some sneaking around and some bending of the truth. Angel and Henry both work hard NOT to do that, and Angel is also dealing with a disabled brother, an ill mother, and an aging father.

All of my books address real life situations without fear or shame, because I believe we all make mistakes, our Savior suffered for all of us, and we can all repent, be healed, and come back to God.

So are you ready for true-to-life romance, family saga, and the small town goodness you might've come to expect from me?! I hope so! If you're new, you're in for a treat!

xoxo

~Liz

PS. For those of you who like a playlist for your books, this book has a song attached to it. *Slow It Down* by Benson Boone... I heard this song while driving and took a picture of the screen in my car so I wouldn't forget by the time I got home.

It's PERFECT for Henry and Angel, and you can listen to it **here**!

The Small Town of Three Rivers

Welcome to Three Rivers! There have been three complete series here already - Three Rivers Ranch, Seven Sons Ranch (Walker Brothers), and Shiloh Ridge Ranch (Glover Family).

That's 37 books. Loads of characters. I'm going to list them here, but you don't need to know them all comprehensively for this book. I just know some of you like seeing these amazing small towns and who lives here!

Three Rivers Ranch:

Frank and Heidi Ackerman - patriarch and matriarch. Frank died 15 years ago; Heidi is remarried to Malcolm Rust.

. . .

Squire and Kelly Ackerman

Son: Finn - 32
Daughter: Libby - 27
Son: Michael - 24
Son: Samuel - 20

Pete and Chelsea Marshall (Chelsea is Squire's sister, and they own Courage Reins, which is housed at Three Rivers Ranch)

4 sons:
Paul - 28
Henry - 26
John - 22
Rich - 19

Reese and Carly Sanders: They're the admins for Courage Reins, Pete and Chelsea's equine therapy unit at Three Rivers Ranch. They have no children.

Garth and Juliette Ahlstrom (former foreman; vet technician)

Son: Jake - 25
Son: Carson - 22

. . .

Cal and Trina Hodgkins (he's the full-time vet at Three Rivers Ranch)

 Daughter: Sabrina - 35

 Daughter: Abby - 27

 Daughter: Olive - 22

Ethan and Brynn Greene (they own Bowman's Breeds, which is housed at Three Rivers Ranch)

 Daughter: Carolina - 24

 Son: Tyson - 22

 Son: Bryan - 20

Beau Peterson (foreman at Three Rivers Ranch) and Charlotte Wisenhouer

 Son: Walter (6)

 Daughter: Michelle (3)

Bennett and Ellie Peterson (he's a cowboy, she works on the finances on the ranch with Kelly)

 Daughter: Joy - 10

 Son: Jaxon - 7

. . .

Tad and Sandy Jorgensen (he's a cowboy, she owns the pancake house in town)
Son: Nathaniel (Nate) - 22
Daughter: Helen - 19

Kenny and Taryn Stockton (he's a cowboy, she works for a local online newspaper in town)
Daughter: Joelle (Jo) - 21

Jon and Grace Carver (he's a cowboy, she helps Heidi run the bakery in town)

Andy and Lawrence Collins (he's a cowboy, she owns a clothing boutique in town)

Summer and Tanner Wolfe (he's a cowboy, she's a nurse at the hospital in town)

Gavin and Navy Redd - they own their own single-family ranch on the northeast side of Three Rivers

. . .

Boone and Nicole Carver (Squire's cousin) - they own and operate the full time veterinary clinic in town

Camila and Dylan Walker (he's a cowboy and an electrician, she owns a plumbing shop in town)

Seven Sons Ranch:
Momma & Daddy: Penny and Gideon Walker

1. RHETT & EVELYN WALKER
Son: Conrad - 23
Triplets: Austin, Elaine, and Easton - 19

2. JEREMIAH & WHITNEY WALKER
Son: Jonah Jeremiah (JJ) - 20
Daughter: Clara Jean - 18
Son: Jason - 17
Daughter: Emily - 15
Daughter: Hattie - 12

. . .

3. LIAM & CALLIE WALKER
   Daughter: Denise - 27
   Daughter: Ginger - 23

4. TRIPP & IVORY WALKER
   Son: Oliver - 34 (and married to Aurora Glover)
   Son: Isaac - 23

5. WYATT & MARCY WALKER
   Son: Warren - 20
   Son: Cole - 18
   Son: Harrison - 17
   Daughter: Rachel - 14

6. SKYLER & MALLERY WALKER
   Daughter: Camila - 20
   Son: Sawyer - 18
   Son: Gideon - 15

7. MICAH & SIMONE WALKER
   Son: Travis (Trap) - 19
   Daughter: Daisy - 17
   Son: Jensen - 13
   Daughter: Laurel - 11

. . .

Shiloh Ridge Ranch:

Lois & Stone (deceased) Glover, 7 children, in age-order: (Lois is now married to Donald Parker)

1. Bear — Sammy, wife

- Lincoln (27), adopted son
- Stetson (Smiles, 17), son
- Russell (Rock, 16), son
- Heather (14), daughter
- Sunnie (13), daughter

2. Cactus — Allison, ex-wife / Bryce, son (deceased) // — Willa, wife

- Mitch (28), adopted son
- Cameron (23), adopted son
- Kyle (21), adopted son
- Charlie (Chaz, 19), son
- Lynn (18), adopted daughter
- Melissa (15), daughter

3. Judge — June, wife

- Lucy Mae (33), step-daughter
- Birch (16), son

- Willow (13), daughter
- Linden (10), son

4. Preacher — Charlie, wife

- Betty (17), daughter
- Hank (14), son
- Daisy (11), daughter

5. Arizona — Duke Rhinehart, husband, living at the Rhinehart Ranch, just south of Shiloh Ridge

- Shiloh (16), daughter
- April (14), daughter
- Dwayne (12), son
- Dallas (8), son

6. Mister — Libby, wife

- Belle (14), son
- Marley (12), daughter
- Hazel (9), daughter
- Brantley (6), son

7. Bishop — Montana, wife

- Aurora (34), step-daughter and married to Oliver Walker

- Robbie (21), son
- Georgia (15), daughter

Aurora and Oliver have 3 children, who are Bishop and Montana's grandchildren:

- Jewel (7), daughter
- Laramie (Lara, 4), daughter
- Mason (almost 2), son

Dawna & Bull (deceased) Glover, 5 children, in age-order:

1. Ranger — Oakley, wife

- Wilder (18), son
- Fawn (17), daughter

2. Ward — Dot, wife

- Glory Rose (18), daughter
- Silver (15), son
- Flint (13), son

3. Ace — Holly Ann, wife

- Gunnison (17), son
- Pearl Jo (15), daughter
- Ashton (12), son

4. Etta — August Winters, husband

- Hailey (25), adopted daughter
- Joey (15), son
- Nash and Nellie (twins - 13), son and daughter

5. Ida — Brady Burton, husband

- Johnny and Judy (twins - 18), son and daughter
- Riggs (13), son
- Sonora (10), daughter

Bull and Stone Glover were brothers, so their children are cousins. Ranger and Bear, for example, are cousins, and each the oldest sibling in their families.

Chapter One

Henry Marshall walked at Gilligan's flank, watching the horse pick up and put down his front hoof. "There's still something wrong," he muttered to himself. He'd been trying to get the horse to take shoes for a couple of months now, but now that they were on, he wasn't walking right.

As a farrier, Henry had several tactics to try, and believe it or not, horses didn't all wear the exact same kind of shoes. This was the third—and lightest—set he'd tried on Gilligan, and they still didn't seem quite right.

Bard wouldn't be happy about that, but Henry could come up with another suggestion for the rescue horse the owner had brought home several weeks ago. He truly believed every horse deserved the best care in the world, and he marveled that he'd been able to find such a perfect fit for him in a career.

Not only that, but Henry hadn't been on a date since he'd started at Lone Star, and he let out a sigh that left his body with more contentment than ever before. He couldn't believe that, as he really didn't like staying home at night, and being alone in the evening was even worse.

But since coming to Lone Star, Henry had been busier than ever. Still learning a lot in his field, though he'd completed his coursework nine months ago. Meeting new suppliers, owners, farriers, and horses took a lot of his energy, and he thanked the Lord every evening for the connections he was making through Bard and Angel White.

He really liked his cabinmate, a man named Levi, and they were known to leave the ranch on Friday nights, but they just went to a restaurant, ate and talked and laughed, and returned to the ranch. Nothing scandalous, and Henry hardly recognized his life these days.

A year ago, everything had been so different. Henry himself had been wildly different, and as he looked back to Gilligan, a keen sense of gratitude overcame him. His momma had taught him to acknowledge the Lord in all things, especially when the feelings struck him, so Henry said, "Thank you for this good life, Lord," as he walked.

Gilligan looked at him as he spoke, and Henry lengthened his stride to catch the equine at his shoulder.

"This pair ain't for you, bud," he said. "I'm gonna take them off and put you in the pasture, okay?"

He put his hand on the horse's neck, and Gilligan crowded into him. He'd been underfed and overworked at his previous ranch, and Bard had taken him in an estate sale, along with a dozen other horses.

The horsemen at Lone Star had been rehabilitating them in the following days, weeks, and months, and because Henry's daddy owned an equine therapy unit, Henry had plenty of experience training and working with horses.

Gilligan had taken a shine to him, and only one other person could work with the horse—and that happened to be the worst person to work with Harry.

Angel White.

She'd been bringing her brother with her whenever she had to be in close proximity to Henry, something he'd absolutely noticed. He'd said nothing to her of it, and she even conducted his performance evaluations with the door open. He'd asked around, and none of the other men had to have their job skills, work ethic, or anything else critiqued where anyone walking by could hear.

Henry frowned internally, and Gilligan slowed and huffed through his lips. "Yeah, buddy, I feel the same way."

He'd not brought up the kiss from over a year ago now, and he wished God had not sharpened his memory of that moment, because he could relive it with precision any time he wanted. Asleep, awake, it didn't matter.

For Angel had kissed him back. He knew that, and he knew she knew it—which was probably why she didn't want to be in a closed-door room with him ever again.

He drew in a deep breath, getting a lot of horseflesh, the scent of fresh rain, and some notes of alfalfa as he prodded Gilligan to get moving again. The horse did what he wanted, and Henry had done more for the horses in his care than he'd ever done for any woman, for his siblings, even for his momma.

Most horsemen did the same, so Henry wasn't unique in that way. It simply surprised him, and he made a mental note to put it in his prayer journal that evening before he went to bed.

In the stable, he moved Gilligan back to the shoeing station, got the offensive shoes off, cleaned up his hooves, and turned him loose in the pasture with a few of his equine friends. Gilligan made no move to join them in the shade, where they snacked on the coolest grass. He was a bit of an outcast still, and maybe that was why Henry connected to him so deeply.

"See you tomorrow, bud," he said before turning to return to the stable. He had a standing desk in the facility—all the horsemen and farriers did—and he found Gilligan's file and entered the notes for that day's trial.

He pulled out his phone and texted Bard. *Those*

shoes on Gilligan weren't right. When can I come over and chat with you about another solution?

The older gentleman had retired completely from any administrative role at Lone Star, passing everything to his daughter, Angel. But he still liked to consult with his team leads on specific cases, and Harry and Gilligan qualified.

He wasn't glued to his phone the way Henry and others his age were, so he didn't expect Bard to answer immediately. He picked up the next folder, reviewed the notes for a pretty bay named Henrietta, and he went to retrieve her from her stall and get her feet back in shape.

Henry loved the fresh air he was privy to for his job. He loved the blue sky filled with puffy white clouds, and he loved the scratch of his gloves against his skin. He loved the view of his tools, the feel of leather along his arm, and the living, breathing animal at his side.

He chatted with Levi and a couple of other farriers throughout the afternoon, and by evening, he remembered he hadn't looked at his phone in a few hours. Bard had answered with, *Stop by whenever, son,* so Henry quickly texted back that he'd come by in the morning.

He then found several texts on his friends' group text. He appreciated his cousin for including him in the things he and his wife planned for their friends in Three Rivers, and Henry climbed the steps to his cabin and sat on the top one to read his messages.

I need a final count for game night on Saturday,

Edith Ackerman had said. Finn's wife. *Depending on who's in for sure will determine what game we'll have ready. We'll also make food assignments once we know.*

She'd added a smiley face and a heart, and Henry truly did feel like his friends in Three Rivers loved him.

We're in, Lincoln Glover had sent. He and his wife had been married for coming up on a year now, and Henry wasn't surprised at all to see his confirmation. Nor Dawson Rhinehart's. He and his fiancée would be there—and they'd be married in the next month.

Henry had enjoyed everyone's Valentine's Day pictures, and they'd all laughed when he'd sent one of him grinning next to a horse. He hadn't told them it was a male, but it hardly mattered. Everyone knew he wasn't dating anyone.

Oliver Walker had confirmed that he and his wife had a babysitter for their three kids and would be there. That made four couples, and Henry's internal frown started to form again. He'd brought a date to game night in the past, and sometimes he'd been paired with Dawson's brother. Sometimes Paul was his plus-one, but Paul had been dating someone for months now, and Henry expected to get a call from his brother any day now, telling him to clear his schedule for a summer wedding.

Not that Henry couldn't get home quickly. He could, and he wouldn't have to clear his schedule for anything. In fact, he and Finn had discovered that if

Henry took a couple of backroads, he could get to the ranch Finn owned, which bordered Three Rivers Ranch, where Henry had grown up and where his family still lived alongside Finn's.

No one else had answered, and as Henry started to text, in came Alex's message. *Nicki and I are going to the fertility clinic this weekend, so we won't be there. Hope it's fun.*

Henry's heartbeat jumped as if someone had thrown cold water in his face. He couldn't imagine wanting children and not being able to have them, and he backed out of the group text and sent one to Alex privately.

Praying for you and Nicki, brother.

Thanks, Alex said back. *We're meeting with an adoption counselor on Friday too. Nicki's not very happy about it, so any extra prayers for that would be appreciated.*

Why isn't she happy about it? Henry asked.

She wants a baby of her own, Alex said. *I think we should explore all options, so she agreed to go, but she's not too keen on adoption yet.*

Henry wasn't exactly sure of Nicki's age, but he knew she was quite a bit older than Alex, who'd just turned twenty-seven at the beginning of the year. She might be thirty-five by now, and Henry didn't know a whole lot about women, but he knew they couldn't have babies forever.

Prayers and good vibes for it all, Henry said. Then he

went back to his main menu and texted Brandon Rhine-hart. *Are you going to game night this weekend? Wanna be my date?* He added a laughing emoji, smiled in real life, and sent the text.

The main group string had several messages of condolences and *prayers coming* when Henry looked at it again. Brandon had not answered him, and Henry finally got up and went inside the cabin. The scent of baking bread met his nose, and he wasn't surprised to find Levi in the kitchen, an apron around his neck which had flour dusted down the front of it.

"You're baking," he said as he closed the front door behind him. "Trouble with Shad?"

Levi threw him a look made of poisonous darts and went back to cutting lines in the top of an unbaked loaf of bread. "He's completely wrong about the growth rate on Berniece. That horse needs new shoes every three weeks, and it irritates me to the bone that he makes me wait four. For no reason."

He bent and put the bread in the oven, then moved to the counter, where another pile of unformed dough waited. He slammed his hands into it and continued. "Today, her hooves were all overgrown around the nails, and I couldn't get them out. I took pictures and sent them to him, and he came running right over." He rolled his eyes and abused the poor bread dough. "It's been twenty-four days, so he got after me for starting early. It's unbelievable."

Henry pulled out the barstool and sat, surveying the mess that was bread-making. "I'm sorry, Levi. For what it's worth, I'm on your side. I'd re-shoe Berniece every two weeks if it were me. No sense in making anyone suffer. It's not like we can't afford it."

Levi's dark eyes flashed. "Right?"

Henry's phone buzzed, and he looked at it. *I'm out*, Brandon said. *I have a date this weekend.*

He grinned at his device. *Same woman as last week?*

Yep, Brandon said. *And I can't ask for prayers after Alex's thing, so I'll just say I can't come. Sorry, bro.*

It's fine, Henry said, though he certainly couldn't show up stag. Most games they played at these parties were for couples, and Henry wouldn't go alone. His heart ached to go home for the weekend, though, so he texted Paul and asked him. Then his cousin Libby. And even his brother Rich.

None of them could go—he couldn't believe he'd forgotten Paul was going to Hondo this weekend to meet his girlfriend's parents—and to add insult to injury, Edith messaged the group with, *That just leaves Henry. Are you in? Want to bring a date?*

He looked up at Levi, who'd gone quiet after his rant. "Want to go to game night with my friends this weekend?"

"When? Saturday?"

"Yeah."

"Yes," Levi said, and Henry confirmed that he'd be

there with "a friend." Satisfied, he set his phone aside for the evening, enjoyed the freshly baked bread with leftover chili from one of the cowboys from a couple cabins down, and kicked his feet up on the coffee table as Levi put on the Cowboy Channel and they found reruns of a rodeo out of Calgary.

He barely thought of Angel White, though the gorgeous blonde seemed to circle his mind whenever he started to get drowsy.

By Saturday, he couldn't wait for a day off, and since he didn't work Sundays or Mondays, he packed a bag with late afternoon sunshine shining through his window so he could stay with his parents for a couple of nights.

He heard the front door slam, and he called, "Hey, Levi, we have to leave in forty-five minutes." They'd planned to stop and get dinner in Stinnett before continuing on to his cousin's ranch for game night.

Levi didn't answer, and alarms rang through Henry's head when he heard boots running. *Running.*

He twisted toward his open door. "Levi?" He went that way and caught Levi's retreating back as he dashed into the bathroom.

A moment later, an awful retching noise filled the cabin. Henry's pulse leapt and lunged, and he stayed where he was as he asked, "Hey, are you okay?"

"No," Levi moaned.

Henry's weekend plans flew right out the window,

and he turned in a full circle. His packed bag waited for him, mocked him.

Levi moaned again as the water ran in the bathroom, and Henry moved to check on him. "I'm sorry, man," he said as he leaned over the sink and washed out his mouth. "I can't go to game night. I ate something that seriously doesn't agree with me." His skin was the pale gray color of a dry sidewalk, and his eyes seemed to sink into his face further than normal.

"It's fine," Henry said, though he now couldn't go to game night either. He wondered what his parents were doing on a hopping Saturday night on a ranch, forty-five minutes from civilization. How they lived so far out, Henry could not comprehend. "I'll just go stay with my folks. Let's get you to bed."

He put his hand on Levi's arm to steady him as he helped his friend into his bedroom. "There's loads of food here, and I'll let everyone know you're not feeling well, so they can check on you."

"Thanks, Henry," Levi said as he collapsed into his bed. He never made it, so the covers had been left where he'd flung them that morning and all he had to do was pull them over him, his eyes already settling closed.

Henry backed out of the room and went back into his, gathered his bag and his phone and went out to the kitchen. They had a group app for all the horsemen, cowboys, and farriers at Lone Star, and only the most important messages were meant to be shared on it.

This was one of those things, so Henry quickly typed out, *Levi isn't feeling well, and I'm headed to my parents' house for the weekend. Let's be sure someone comes by and checks on him from time to time, okay?*

That done, Henry needed to decide if he still wanted to grab something to eat in Stinnett, or maybe go all the way to Three Rivers and drive through somewhere there. Or he could make himself a sandwich here and stay for another couple of hours before he had to leave.

"Decisions decisions," Henry muttered as his phone lit up with affirmative responses that the others here would check on Levi for him. He was tired of making decisions.

He'd just opened the fridge when someone knocked on his door. "Come in," he called, because they never locked the door, and Henry knew everyone who lived and worked at Lone Star.

No one came in, and irritation snagged through Henry. "Just come in," he muttered as he closed the fridge and went to answer the door. He pulled it open with, "You just walk in around here." When he saw the heavenly being on his porch, he said, "Oh," and backed up a step.

Since he'd worked with Angel White for a while now, he could recover much quicker than before. "Hey, Angel," he said. "What can I do for you?"

"Levi is ill?" She looked past him like Levi might be making dinner, the joke on the entire boarding stable.

"Threw up a few minutes ago," Henry said. "Said he ate something bad at lunch."

"What did he eat?" Her blue eyes roamed around, finally coming back to lock onto his. Henry loved her eyes, and he couldn't name the exact shade of blue they were. Stunning blue. Was that a color?

Maybe for a nail polish, he thought, and it made him smile. "I have no idea."

But a very dangerous idea had just entered his mind. He'd learned so much in the past couple of years about himself, about self-control, about his temper. But apparently, he hadn't yet learned to stop his tongue from wagging out his thoughts, because he said, "What are you doing tonight? Levi was supposed to be my date for a game night, and I can't go alone."

Angel blinked her long eyelashes at him, and blinked some more, and blinked some more. He'd never stunned the pretty woman into silence, though if he'd wanted to, asking her on a date would've sat at the top of his idea list.

What a stupid thing to do, he chastised himself, but he couldn't recall the words now. So he waited to find out what the lovely Angel White would say to his game night invite.

Chapter Two

Angel White gripped her cellphone so hard, she feared it might break. Only two words screamed through her head: *Game night.*

Game night, game night, game night.

Game night?

Henry stood up a step from her, a tall, imposing figure with such a handsome face. Big hands too. That deep, sexy voice, which said, "We were going to get dinner in Stinnett. We could do that, or I could—you could—we could meet here and go straight to game night. It's at my cousin's farm in Three Rivers, so it's a bit of a drive." He took a quick breath. "A little over an hour."

A little over an hour, trapped in a truck with Henry Marshall. She wanted to go so badly, she almost started crying. At the same time, the rational, calm side of Angel's brain told her she'd been in desperate need of a break from this ranch for a month now. Anyone who asked her would elicit the same reaction.

Bottom line: Henry wasn't special.

He fell back a step. "Sorry I said anything," he said. "Can we forget it? Flint, Clay and Grady said they'd come check on Levi. I'll just cancel on game night and go see my folks." He pulled out his phone and started typing.

"...not going...to be able to...make it tonight..."

Angel slapped her hand over his phone, knocking it clean out of his hand. Henry yelped, and they both watched his device skitter across the floor. "What was that for?" He turned and moved a couple of steps to pick up his phone.

He looked at her, pure accusation in those beautiful eyes. "You broke my phone."

Humiliation streamed through Angel, and combined with her sheer exhaustion and ultimate desperation for a break from everything happening in her personal life, with her family, and on the ranch, an instant, emotional tornado spiraled into existence.

"I—" Tears spilled from her eyes. "I'm so sorry, Henry." She couldn't stand to look at him, but she couldn't move either. She covered her face with both of her hands and sobbed into her palms.

Henry said something, but the words couldn't penetrate her turmoil. She fell into the warmth and safety of his arms, and she distinctly knew the door had closed, sealing her in his house.

He sat her down on the couch and pressed in close to her. He said soothing things and put his arm around her. Finally, after what felt like a long time, but was probably only a few breaths, his voice reached her ears.

"...talk to me, okay, Angel? You're okay, Angel, and you can talk to me, okay?"

She lifted her head and lowered her hands. "I'm so sorry. I'll buy you a new phone."

"I don't care about the phone."

Angel looked at him. "What?"

"I can't believe I'm going to say this, because it's so something my daddy said to me five thousand times growing up." He flashed her a smile, and her curiosity about his family life, his past, his childhood rose up the ranks. "But Angel, I don't care about the phone; I care about you. Are you okay?"

"I am obviously not okay," she said, giving him a squinty-eyed look.

"Obviously," he fired right back. "But I mean, can I help you? I didn't mean to stress you by asking you to game night. It's—"

"I want to go," she blurted out.

His eyebrows rose, and Angel couldn't stand sitting

this close to him. Rather, she wanted to be closer, but she didn't trust herself. "I—"

She jumped to her feet. "I need to get off this ranch," she said, pacing away from him. Moving while she talked really helped get her brain to work better. "Things are so stressful right now, and there's so much going on with Trevor's doctor's appointments, and Daddy started coughing last week, and I have to get off this ranch."

She faced him and ran her hands through her hair. "So if you'll give me ten minutes to wash my face and get it fixed again, I'm ready to go."

Henry hadn't gotten to his feet, and he watched her from his perch on the couch. A moment passed before he said, "You can have nine minutes."

Angel blinked and then laughter bubbled up from inside her. She honestly could not remember the last time she'd laughed, and Henry had just given her a great gift. Excitement to get off the ranch—with him—flowed through her as the laughter cleansed her from the debilitating feelings that had brought on the crying.

"You might want to reconsider," she said. "I am very competitive at games."

"You might want to reconsider," he said. "It's couples game night, and we might have to do...things we don't want to do."

"Like what?"

"I honestly have no idea," he said. "My cousin and

his wife pick the game, but it's been made very clear that we need an even number of people for tonight."

Angel's chin quivered, but she wasn't sure from what. Another bout of crying? The thrill of going off the ranch with Henry? Pure desperation?

"I have to get off this ranch," she whispered.

"The clock's ticking," he said, and he did get up then and open the door for her. "Let me drive you back to your place."

She didn't protest, and Henry backtracked to get his truck keys. He opened her door for her, and he got her down the lane and around the corner to her house, which sat a hundred yards from her parents' homestead. Only thirty from Trevor's place, and fifteen from where their three full-time senior farriers lived.

"Six minutes," he said, and Angel flew from the truck. She could change her clothes, swipe on some deodorant, wash her face, paint some gloss on her lips, and grab some earrings and be ready to go.

Her heart pounded through all of it, and she had no idea how long she'd been inside her house before she yanked open the front door and flew out of it again. This time, she wore a pretty blue dress with white dragonflies flitting around on it, a pair of white sandals, pink lip gloss, and she carried a pair of silver hoops in her hand.

She stuck them in her pocket as she hurried across her porch, and she used the remaining walk to Henry's truck to run her hands through her hair and get it settled in the right place. So many pieces of her life felt fake, and Angel vaulted back into Henry's truck with his gaze stuck to her.

He had to see her—really see her—and that idea struck Angel's heart with pure fear.

"You look great," he said simply, and then he put the truck in reverse and backed out of the small parking area in front of her house.

"Thank you." She buckled and managed to get her earrings in. "Is my hair straight?" She faced him, her pulse like a gong being banged on over and over and over again. "It's not my real hair, and I need more than six minutes to make it look normal."

"It's not your real hair?"

"No," she said, when she could've said so much more. The truth was, she was going bald. Her. A woman. Her hair had thinned considerably in the past three years, and Angel had started wearing extensions right away.

However, those only broke the little hair she had, damaging it further. So she'd moved to wigs, and she'd settled on one that looked the most like her natural hair. She'd bought five of them, and she rotated them to make sure they could be cleaned, repaired, or replaced.

With horror, she realized she'd never told anyone she wore a wig. Not even her recent boyfriends had known. "Does it look okay?" she asked, reaching up to run her fingers through it again, trying to make sure the part sat right and the hair fell down correctly.

"It's gorgeous," Henry said, turning to look out the windshield again. He cleared his throat once and then twice. "Where do you want to go to eat?"

"Where were you and Levi going to go?"

"Stinnett." He glanced over to her. "There's a great little pub there. The Gas Light. It's not too loud this early in the evening, and the food is phenomenal."

"Pub food."

"They have great burgers and chicken," he said. "But they have amazing pizza too. And a really great mac and cheese." He seemed perfectly at-ease, and Angel started to relax too. "Great big salads with roast beef. That kind of thing."

"You've ordered a great big salad with roast beef from this pub place?"

"I've been with people who have."

"Women."

"Yes," he said.

"Are you seeing anyone right now?"

"If I was, I'd be taking them to the couples game night," he shot back. "Not my cabinmate." He glared at her. "Are *you* seeing anyone right now?"

She folded her arms. "No."

"Great. Neither am I. I haven't dated since I came to Lone Star, in fact."

"Why not?" From what Angel knew of Henry,

which admittedly wasn't much, he'd dated a lot during farrier school.

He shifted in his seat and looked out his side window. "Maybe I don't get off the ranch as much as I should either." He faced her and cocked one eyebrow at her. Almost as quickly, he softened. His grip on the steering wheel loosened, and he reached toward her.

But he pulled back before he made it even halfway to her, and Angel had no idea what she'd do if he tried to hold her hand. Or touch her. "I'm worried about you, Angel."

"I'm okay." She cinched her arms around her midsection and watched the landscape flow toward them and around them as he drove. "I just get overwhelmed sometimes. Don't you ever feel like you're just drowning?"

"Sometimes, yes," he said quietly.

Angel couldn't get air to go down the right way. Thankfully, it only lasted for a moment, and then her lungs and windpipe worked just fine. She breathed in, swallowed, and kept her gaze out the windshield.

"What do you do when you feel like that?" She felt him looking at her, but she steadfastly refused to meet his gaze.

"Honestly?" He sighed like she was asking him to cut off a hand and lend it to her for a while. "I'm a momma's boy. When I feel like I'm drowning, I go home to my momma."

Tears pressed into her eyes. "That sounds so nice, Henry."

"I'm really sorry about your mom," he said. In the next moment, before Angel could tell him it was okay, that she'd finally accepted that her mother wasn't going to get better, he slammed on the brakes.

"Holy horses," he said. "I forgot I'm not coming back here."

"Not coming back here?" Angel had just repeated the words, but they didn't make sense.

"I'm staying at my parents' until Monday."

"I can't do that."

Henry looked at her and cocked his head. "Can't you?"

"No," she snapped at him. "I look after Trevor, and I.... Daddy likes his eggs a certain way in the morning, and Mama can't light the stove anymore."

Henry reached for his phone, which rested in the cupholder. "I'll make sure your brother and parents are taken care of this weekend."

"Henry, no."

"Angel, by your own admission, you need a break, and my momma will feed you, let you sleep as late as you want, and my daddy has the sweetest therapy horses in the world. You can go play ball with them or go riding. Soak in the sunshine. Enjoy the big, wide sky over my family's ranch." He smiled at her, and Angel could admit that everything he said sounded absolutely wonderful.

Still, she hesitated. "I don't know."

"It's less than forty-eight hours," he said gently. "And I can see you need it." He ducked his head, his eyes on his phone but his hands absolutely still over it. "Will you let me help you?"

Angel closed her eyes and let herself go. "Yes," she whispered.

"Okay, then," he said. "I'm going to send a couple of texts, and then I'm going to call my momma." He stayed stopped right there on the dirt road as his fingers tracked over his phone. A minute later, he said, "Clay, Zane, and Derrick are going to make sure your family is taken care of. Only the senior farriers, your foreman, and the team leads know you'll be off-site for a couple of days."

Henry looked at her, and Angel's insides shook with nervous energy—and so much attraction to this man. "What did you say?" she asked.

"I told them you needed a break and that I was helping you get off the ranch for a couple of days. Asked them for some help with your brother and parents, and within sixty seconds, it's done."

Angel nodded and looked away from him. "Thank you, Henry."

"My word, I'm going to say something my uncle lectured me about endlessly." He gave a mirthless chuckle. "If you need help, Angel, say something. There are plenty of people willing to help you."

"I know." She sniffled and reached up to wipe her eyes. "I'm sorry, Henry. I swear I'm going to pull myself together before we get to your cousin's house."

"If you can't, that's okay too," he said gently. She'd seen him working with horses, and he was this polite and respectful and kind to them too. His quiet, almost dormant strength spoke to them, and just as easily to her too. "It's just game night, and everyone will survive without me. You just let me know."

She drew in a breath, trying to use the oxygen to fill herself with bravery and strength. "I want to do something fun, and game night with people our age sounds fun."

"Our age?"

She heard the teasing note in his voice, but she hid her smile. "Yes," she said. "I know how old you are from your application."

"Sneaky," he teased. "How old are you?"

"Twenty-eight," she said. And Henry would be twenty-seven this year. June, if she remembered right.

"That's pretty young to shoulder all you do."

She could only nod, because yes, she carried a lot of responsibility. "Trevor is seven years older than me," she said. "He was supposed to take over."

"He's a great guy," Henry said.

"I've seen you with him." Angel released the self-hug, glad when the tension in her muscles started to recede. "You're so kind to him. So good with him. I really appreciate it."

"Sure," Henry said easily. "I've worked with quite a few therapy patients through my daddy's equine unit. He's just a person."

"Yes, well, some people don't know how to deal with or talk to a disabled person."

"Mm, sure," Henry said again, and he made the turn onto the main highway, aiming the truck toward Three Rivers and not Amarillo. "Okay, we've got better service here. Let me call my momma. She can find you some pajamas and clothes for the weekend. She'll probably need to get a bedroom ready for you."

"If it's too much—"

"It's not." He cut her a look out of the side of his eye and tapped on the screen in his truck. A loud chirp filled the vehicle, and he said in a loud, clear, slow voice, "Call Momma Chelsea."

"Calling Momma Chelsea," his truck repeated to him, and Angel couldn't hide her smile this time. Oh, and now she knew his mother's name. She'd run into the woman when Henry had moved in last summer, but she'd deliberately kept all the doors between her and him closed, hoping her insane and intense attraction to him would diminish with time and space.

Sadly, that hadn't happened yet, and now she was currently riding in his vehicle, toward his cousin's house for game night, and then a weekend away at his parent's house.

"Henry, baby, hey," his momma said. "Are you still coming tonight?"

"Yes, Momma," he said. "And I need to beware you: you're on speaker with me and a friend."

"Okay," she said.

Henry looked over to her, and Angel had looked at him when he'd called her "a friend." She would not classify Henry as a friend, and she really didn't like him calling her that. Not because they weren't friends yet, but because he hadn't used the word *girlfriend*.

And why would he? The very thought was insane—and absolutely not allowed due to Lone Star's dating policies.

"Momma, my friend is a woman in desperate need of a break from the stables. But I forgot to tell her I was coming for the weekend, and she doesn't have anything. Not a toothbrush, a stick of deodorant, or any pajamas."

His mother stayed silent for a couple of seconds. "And I'm assuming she'll be staying for the weekend."

"Yes, ma'am," he said. "It's Angel, Momma."

"Oh, Angel." His mother's voice brightened, and Angel could only imagine what he'd told her. At least it sounded like they were good things. "Okay, so you're on your way to game night?"

"Dinner first," Henry said. "Then game night. Who knows what Finn and Edith have planned, but they've got that baby now, so I'm guessing we'll get to Three Rivers by like...." He hemmed and hawed for a moment and then said, "Ten-thirty."

"Okay," his momma said.

"Is that too late? We can leave early."

"Ten-thirty is fine, baby."

"Okay," he said. "Ten-thirty then."

"I'll make sure she has what she needs."

"You're the best, Momma."

"Thank you, Misses Marshall," Angel said, leaning toward the screen where a clock ticked up the length of the phone call.

"You're welcome, honey. See you two soon."

"'Bye, Momma." Henry reached out to the screen. "Love you."

"Love you, baby."

Henry tapped the screen to end the call, and he relaxed back into his seat. "That actually went better than I thought it would."

"Did it?"

"Yeah, well, I mean—yeah, she didn't ask a bunch of questions about why you're coming with me, if we're dating, etcetera, etcetera, etcetera."

"Will anyone assume that?"

"Honestly?" He sighed, and that combined with his rhetorical question made her adrenaline spike. "Yeah, my cousins and friends and siblings will probably assume we're on a date. But I'll just tell them we're not. It'll be fine."

Angel nodded, though everything inside her writhed and squirmed. "I mean, it would be okay with me if you just let them think we're on a date. You are taking me to dinner and everything."

Henry said nothing as he drove, the ride easy and smooth along the paved road. "I guess it feels like it could be a date."

"Sure," she said, mimicking him.

"But you can't date the men at Lone Star."

"Doesn't mean I don't want to." Angel sucked in a breath when she realized what she'd just said. She tried not to, but she looked over to Henry anyway. He wore a semi-stunned look on his face, and Angel wanted to wipe it away. Say something pithy about how she had a big crush on Levi or Clay or someone other than him. *Anyone* other than him.

"Okay," he drawled. "I just need you to answer a couple of questions for me. Can you do that?"

"Maybe," she said.

"I'll take a maybe." He cleared his throat and coughed twice. "One, when I inadvertently kissed you last winter, did you or did you not kiss me back?"

Angel balked at telling him the truth, but her parents had taught her not to lie. She'd been hiding a lot, and she couldn't carry another secret. "Yes," she said. "I did."

"Mm hm. Yes, you did."

She rolled her eyes, though every cell in her body told her to smile instead. "Is that it?"

"No," he said. "If I asked you out on a real date, would you say yes?"

"That's cheating."

"What does that mean?"

"You just want me to tell you I'll go out with you without you having to ask."

"It's against the rules at Lone Star to date anyone who works there," he said. "I *can't* ask you out, even if I wanted to—and I'm not saying I do."

"Then why does it matter?"

"Because a man would like to know if the incredibly beautiful woman he's had a crush on for seemingly ever would go out with him, that's why."

"I—"

"And because if she would, and she can feel this bubbling, sizzling thing between them, then maybe some rules need to be broken."

"Henry Marshall," she admonished. "You don't break rules."

"They're *your* rules," he said. "You could change them."

"They're my daddy's rules."

The truck traveled down the road, the signs for Stinnett coming into view. Angel sensed she'd lose him and the thread of this conversation once they stopped for dinner. But she didn't know what to say.

He'd just admitted to having a crush on her, and that made warmed honey ooze through her veins.

"I can feel this thing between us," she whispered.

"Mm hm. And?"

"And." She finished drawing in her breath and blew it all out noisily. "I'd go out with you if you could ask me to."

"Mm."

"You hum a lot."

"I just want you to know I heard you." He reached over and took her hand in his. Part of Angel wanted to protest, but she looked at him and saw the determined set of his jaw.

"Henry," she said, but she didn't have the words to continue.

"I'd break all the rules for you, Angel," he said, his voice soft and powerful at the same time. "But let's not deal with it this weekend, okay? You need a break, and me adding all this too your plate is selfish and unnecessary."

"Okay," she said, her emotions teetering on the edge of sanity again.

"Okay." He lifted her hand to his lips and gently pressed a kiss to the inside of her wrist. He said something else about the pub they'd be at soon, but all Angel could hear was the sweetest words a man had ever said to her: *I'd break all the rules for you, Angel.*

So she started praying that something could be done

about the no-dating rules at Lone Star. But that meant talking to Daddy about his policies, and he'd never been very open to her suggestions.

Not this weekend, she told herself. She deserved a relaxing, carefree break from the ranch, and that was exactly what she was going to do for the next two days.

With Henry Marshall at her side.

Biscuits and gravy, she thought-swore. *Dear Lord, don't let this be the biggest mistake of my life.*

Chapter Three

Henry pulled up to his cousin's house a couple of minutes early. But in his family, a couple of minutes early meant he was ten minutes late. Finn had the cutest little log cabin set against a beautiful Texas ranch landscape. He had a barn and a stable off to the right, but Henry couldn't see them now that he parked in front of the house alongside the other trucks that had already arrived.

He looked up to the log cabin with its front door right in the middle and two smiling windows on the side. He wondered what he'd find behind them. His friends, of course, his cousin, and they'd all welcome him happily with smiles and open arms. There would be good food and lots of laughter, and hopefully Henry wouldn't have to make too many explanations.

He glanced over to Angel. "You ready for this?"

"Sure," she said after taking a deep breath. She let it out as she continued to look at the house, and Henry noted that she would not look at him. He wondered what she was thinking, what explanations he'd have to give, and how she'd react to them.

Her blond hair and blue eyes accentuated her frilly dress. Henry found himself wanting this to be a real date. They'd had a great dinner with easy conversation because he'd deliberately kept it light. He asked her nothing about Lone Star, nothing about her dad, and nothing about her mama. He could tell she didn't want to talk about those things. In fact, those were the things that she was trying to escape.

Henry wanted to *be* that escape for her. "All right," he said. "Let's go in."

He got out of the truck and went around to help her down. But of course, Angel, in her strong-willed glory, opened the door before he got there.

"Hey," he said. "I can come help you down."

She glanced at him, finally. "I know, but I can get out of the car just fine myself."

"Yes," he said. "But it's what proper gentlemen do on dates."

She glared at him now, and he at least knew that she was feeling something inside. *Of course she is,* he thought to himself. *She has thoughts and feelings—a lot of them. That's why she sobbed into her hands right in front of you.*

Still, he offered her his elbow, and she laced her fingers through it while he pushed her door closed.

"All right," he said. "Don't get overwhelmed. There are only eight people inside. I'm related to some of them. Others I've just known for years, grew up with here in Three Rivers."

He glanced over to her as they started up the steps. "Did you ever come to Three Rivers growing up?"

"No," she said. "Not much. Maybe to the light parade for New Year's Eve. My family usually shopped in Amarillo. Sometimes we'd go up to Oklahoma for holidays and stuff. My granny lives up there."

Henry nodded, noting the bit about her grandmother, which she had not shared with him previously. "Three Rivers is a great little town. We'd go fishing, and hiking, and hunting. Of course, there's always work to do on the ranch."

"Always," Angel murmured.

Henry arrived at the front door and knocked. Then he opened the door without waiting for someone to tell him to come in. Everyone else was here, after all, and certainly, he didn't need to wait for Finn or Edith to come get the door. He entered and found all eight adults standing in the back of the house around the island, which was probably laden with leftovers, snacks, and desserts.

A baby shrieked, and Henry's eyes went over to the little boy sitting in a brightly-colored play seat. His arms flailed and his fists hit the plastic toys attached to the tray in front of him. Henry lit up then, because he could distract himself with a baby.

"Hey, you," he said, moving over to the little boy. "Angel, this is Theo." As he said those words, all conversation in the room stopped. All eyes came to him as he bent down and pulled Theo from the play seat.

He held the chunky baby boy who was blond, not so much like him, as Henry's mama had real dark hair. But both Finn and Edith both came from lighter stock than him, and Theo looked just like them.

He turned toward the kitchen, the weight of eight sets of eyes so heavy. Henry never had any problem talking to women. He'd never struggled introducing women to other people. In fact, he'd brought a complete stranger to Link's wedding—and that had been their only date.

"Guys," he said. "This is Angel White. Angel." He half-turned back to her. "This is everyone. I'll go around and say all their names, but I don't expect you to remember them. If y'all would just raise your hand when I say your name, maybe she'll be able to associate your face with your name."

He smiled as the little boy grabbed onto the edge of his cowboy hat. He pulled the hat off and took it away from Theo, then looked over to his friends again. Finn had come forward, of course.

"My cousin, Finn," he said. "He's married to Edith."

She raised her hand dutifully. Henry bounced the little boy. "This is their little baby, Theo. He's, what, nine or ten months now?"

"Ten," Edith said.

"Lincoln and Misty Glover are here," Henry continued. They both raised their hands. "Link works a ranch south of Three Rivers. It's quite a drive for him to get here, so we always appreciate when he decides to come up north."

Link chuckled and shook his head, and Misty simply beamed with all the strawberry-blonde radiance she possessed.

"And then we've got Dawson and Caroline," Henry said, smiling at the cowboy he'd known for years. "They're not married yet. Engaged, getting married in, what, two weeks? Three weeks?"

"Three weeks," Dawson said, glancing over to Caroline, a lovey-dovey smile on his face. She leaned her head against his shoulder, and it was very clear who they were, even though neither of them had raised their hands.

"Dawson and Caroline, wedding in three weeks," Henry said with a big smile. He handed Theo to Edith as the little boy started to fuss. She took him and soothed him, then put him right back in his seat, where she handed him a few pieces of cereal, which he went after immediately.

"And last but not least," Henry said. "We have Ollie

and Aurora Walker. Ollie works at a tech company over in the high-rise buildings in Three Rivers, and they have three little kids."

Aurora moved forward out of all of them and said, "Oh, it's so nice to meet you. You're Henry's boss, right?"

Henry had not conveyed that tidbit of information. He wondered how Aurora had known that. Of course, Finn probably knew, as did all of Henry's brothers, and Henry's aunt and uncle obviously knew. But he had not called Finn and told him he was bringing Angel. He'd only called his mother.

"Yes," Angel said, shaking Aurora's hand. "Henry and I work together at Lone Star." She glanced over at him, a fond smile on her face that he had never seen before. At least, not aimed in his direction. "He's a great farrier, one of our team leads."

"Is that right?" Ollie said as he came forward. "So great to meet you. Welcome to game night."

"We're just having snacks," Finn said, glancing at Henry. His eyes said so much more than his mouth, and Henry wanted to run to him, hug him, and say, *thank you for not making this a big deal.*

He just needed someone to come with him to game night, and Levi had been sick. Angel was not special, despite the fact that she would go out with him if he could ask. He didn't want to figure that out right now, so he clapped his hands together and said, "What are we playing tonight?"

He moved over to the counter to see what snacks they had, his taste buds dancing for something sweet. "Oh, I love these lemon bars." He took in the pan of beautifully baked bars, nostalgia hitting him hard.

"You like sour things in your desserts?" Angel asked as she stepped to his side.

"Yeah," he said. "Sweet and tart go great together, and this one's got a little bit of salt in the crust." He glanced over to Edith. "At least, if it's my momma's recipe, it does."

Edith smiled at him. "It's your mom's recipe."

Henry beamed at her. "Look at you, being all domestic with the baking."

She grinned back at him. "I can do it, sometimes. If I have to." She bumped him with her hip and added, "Come on, you guys. Now that Henry and Angel are here, let's gather around the table."

"We can bring the snacks over, right?" Misty asked.

"Sure," Edith said as she picked up a bowl of popcorn that had M&M's in it.

"Absolutely," Finn said. "Nobody can play games without snacks on the table." He turned to Angel. "I can barely stand to play when there are snacks."

"Hey," Edith said. "You like games."

"Do I?" Finn pulled out a chair and sat down, his eyes hooking into his wife's as he did.

"Absolutely you do," Edith said, her voice a bit on the grumpy side. "We host these game nights every quarter. If you don't like game nights, what are we doing?"

He laughed and said, "I like game night well enough. Like Link, I like getting out of my house at night."

Henry had always enjoyed that too. "Tell me about it," he said as he followed the others to the big dining room table. "When I was living in the dorms going to farrier school, I couldn't stand staying home at night. I had to get out of there."

Angel's piercing blue gaze fixed on him. "Ah, is that why you had to get out at night?" She rolled her eyes, half amused, half annoyed, and he wasn't sure what to make of it.

"Yeah," he said. "Those places were small, and man, some guys didn't like to shower right away." He shook his head as he pulled out a seat for Angel and nodded to it with his chin.

She dutifully came and sat down, and he helped her push her chair in before he took a seat next to her. "I had to get out of there. My spirit's a little restless. I don't like sitting home at night."

"It's really true," Finn said. "We could never get Henry to slow down. If we put a movie on and his mama said, 'Park it right there and watch this,' he would. But within ten minutes, he'd be up tying rope or looking for a pocketknife. Or he was always trying to do something on the computer."

Henry chuckled but couldn't deny it. He simply shrugged like this was normal. For him, it totally was.

"All right," Rory said. "We brought the game tonight, and y'all are gonna love it." She had something hidden behind her back, and she pulled it out and yelled, "Charades!"

Henry groaned along with several others. He hated charades, and he wasn't one who liked the spotlight on him.

"Well, it's not really charades," Ollie said as he took the box from Aurora. "You can draw it, you can act it out, you can do all kinds of things. You just can't say certain words, right?"

"Right," Rory said. "It's really fun to play in teams. Like, you can play with your partner, and everybody has to guess, and you try to get more than the rest of the group."

Henry had no idea what that meant, but he looked over to Angel. He sure did like the word "partner" when it came to her—as long as they were talking life partner and not something like *work partner* or *chemistry final partner*. He raised his eyebrows. "Charades?"

Angel grinned like she had just stepped onto the greatest stage of her life and was ready for it. "I love charades."

Henry could only stare at her. "You've got to be kidding me."

"I'm not kidding," she said. "Trevor and I would play

with my cousins when we were younger, and I always won." Henry would've found the competitive streak in her eyes, even if she hadn't warned him about it on the way here.

"All right," he said with half a laugh. "Let's see how this goes."

He sat back and listened to the others squabble about how to form teams and whether they could really do two-person teams, one person performing for another while the other eight people tried to get as many clues as them.

"That doesn't really seem fair," Finn said. "There's no way one person can get as many as seven other people."

"Yes," Rory said. "Because it's your *partner*. It's someone who *knows you* really well."

Henry raised his hand and said, "I think that's totally unfair for me and Angel. We're not even dating. We're not together. She's not my partner."

That once again brought all eyes to him. He glanced over to Angel, heat creeping into his face. "I mean, she came, because we both needed an escape from the ranch, and I knew I needed a partner to come tonight, or I'd have had to cancel."

"You could've come alone," Edith said.

Finn gave her a stern look and said, "No, this is a couples night."

"Well, he's come with Brandon before," Link said.

"What? Are they a couple?" He chuckled lightly. "I don't think so."

Henry pointed to him. "That's my point. But it's another person, and I would be at a disadvantage with Brandon too. He's also not my partner."

Angel sat there silently, her hands clasped neatly in her lap, looking like the gorgeous heavenly being she was. She didn't dispute that she wasn't dating Henry, that they weren't together, that she wasn't his partner, and that only made his frown deepen.

"All right, all right," Oliver said. "What about men against women?"

"Oh, I like this idea," Misty said.

"Yep, this is a good idea." Rory grinned as if she'd just won the lottery, and Edith edged her chair a little bit closer to Angel.

"I think we're going to wipe the floor clean with you guys," she said. "All right, you cowboys. Move to the other side. Ladies over here. Let's go. Everyone move."

Everybody shifted around until the five men sat on one side of the table, with their ladies on the other. Henry sat directly across from Angel, and he grinned at her with all he had. She smiled back, and she seemed to be twinkling like all the stars in heaven.

He sure hoped tonight and this weekend would be an excellent escape for her from the pressures and anxieties and worries of her professional—and personal—life at Lone Star Ranch.

Not only that, but Henry thanked the Good Lord above that he had been the one to provide this escape for her, and he hoped that when she needed another one, she would text or call him.

In fact, he made a mental note to check-in with her more often to make sure she was okay, so that if she needed even an hour off the ranch, *he* would be the one to drive her to Amarillo to get her favorite soda. Eat a hamburger. Or just go sit somewhere that wasn't Lone Star-owned, so that she could find the peace and serenity that she so richly deserved.

A couple of hours later, Henry couldn't stop laughing as he drove down the dirt road and around the bend toward his childhood home at Three Rivers Ranch. "I have never seen someone so animated during a game," he said, bursting into another round of laughter. "You should've seen yourself. It was incredible."

She laughed with him, and they'd been having a great time ever since they'd arrived at Finn's. Good food, ice cream, the best company, no awkward questions, and an amazing game.

"Hey, it was life or death," she said through her giggles. "We were only up by two points, and I knew you guys were gonna close in on that round."

Henry said, "Well, you cinched it with that last one.

You were standing up. I've never seen—you're a petite woman, but your arms were flailing. You almost hit Edith in the face, like, four times." He laughed again, really filling the cab of his truck with the sound.

Angel sucked in a breath and said, "Oh, I'm so embarrassed."

"Why?" he asked. "You don't need to be embarrassed."

"I'm too competitive. I was like this growing up too. And my daddy kept telling me, 'You have got to find a way to curb this because you're not gonna have any friends as an adult.'"

Henry grinned. "I really liked it. I think my friends really liked you too. Don't even worry about it. Nobody got hit in the head."

"Yeah," she said, and then she sighed happily. "Thank you, Henry. This was amazing."

A deep sense of contentment descended on him as he rounded the corner and the night sky brightened by some of the streetlights and house lights on the ranch. "Yeah, no problem," he said easily, because it was no problem. He'd had a great night too—dinner with a beautiful woman, game night with his friends. They all laughed with her, accepted her into their fold, chatted with her about her life, and enjoyed treats together. What was wrong with that?

"Well, here we are," he said. "This is Three Rivers Ranch. My daddy's place is right here on the right.

That's where I grew up." He paused before turning down the long driveway. "Big equine therapy unit right here."

He nodded forward to the huge glass-front building that was Courage Reins. "My daddy gets nonprofit funding from different organizations around the country, some even up in Canada. He helps veterans, people who have been in accidents, special needs children and adults. All kinds."

"They come for therapy?"

"Heck, sometimes I just like to go out there with the horses and play ball with them. Tell them all my troubles, walk around the fields with them." He quieted, thinking of his time with the therapy horses. He did love horses with his whole soul, and they were the best listeners on the planet.

"We can go out tomorrow if you want," he said. "My daddy will probably have appointments in the afternoon, but he doesn't do anything in the morning because they go to church."

Angel didn't say much for a beat or two either, and then she asked, "Do you go to church, Henry?"

He kept looking down the road toward the chicken coops and the long row of stables and the barn that he couldn't see, and the administration building for Three Rivers Ranch where he'd worked one summer with his uncle. Ah, Three Rivers Ranch.

"I have in the past," he said after a minute. "It's not a

priority right now. I'm still trying to find my feet under me at Lone Star, trying to figure out where I belong there, who my friends are, all that."

"You're friends with everyone," Angel said. "I've seen you. Everyone loves you."

"Well, that's not really true," Henry said. "Appearances can be a little deceiving."

She scoffed. "I don't believe that. You're charismatic, you're strong, you're kind, you're knowledgeable. What's not to like?"

"Maybe the part where I boss everyone around," he said with a chuckle. "It's fine. I know who I am. I'm trying to be the best version of myself. Levi and I get along real great, but he doesn't go to church, and I just haven't really found my way back there."

"Yeah, it's quite the drive," she said quietly.

"It is. You go with your folks, don't you?"

"Yes," she said. "Every week."

He looked over at her. "It doesn't sound like you really like it."

"It's fine," she said. "I mean, it's—yeah, it's fine."

Henry didn't know what that meant, and he didn't know how to press it further. He didn't want to press Angel anywhere right now. It was late. He told his mom they'd be in by ten-thirty, and it was ten-twenty-four. He needed to simply get down the lane, get Angel in bed, and then he could pace in his bedroom and try to figure out what to do after that.

"Anyway, another family friend who worked here at Three Rivers for a long time bought up some land on the left here. That's Bowman's Breeds. She trains barrel racing horses."

"Oh, that's wonderful," Angel said. "I did barrel racing for a year or two in high school."

"Did you?" Henry asked. "I would not pick you for the rodeo type of woman."

Angel laughed lightly. "That's why I did it for a year or two, cowboy."

Henry laughed with her and then, out of habit, put his blinker on to turn right. Feeling like a complete fool, he switched it off again and muttered to himself, "I don't know why I did that," and then made the turn to go down the lane toward his childhood home.

"My brother is down in the Hill Country," he said. "His girlfriend's parents live down there, and he's meetin' them this weekend."

"Wow," Angel said.

"Yeah." Henry took in the house as they drew closer. He wasn't sure why he'd told Angel about Paul. It didn't matter. He was simply supremely glad that he didn't have to deal with his brother—and Angel—this weekend.

"My mom loves stained glass," he said. "You can't see it right now, but in the morning, the front window and the front door have beautiful stained glass that my daddy put in when he built this house for her. It's real beautiful."

"Your daddy built this house for your mama?" she asked.

"Yeah," Henry said. "Yep. Before he even asked her to marry him, he started building it. Figured if he was going to live here, his best friend's sister might as well live here with him since he was in love with her and all." He grinned. "They have a beautiful love story. They're really fun most of the time."

"Yeah, they seemed nice when I met them when you moved in."

"You met them when I moved in?"

"Just your momma," she said. "I mean, I saw your daddy, but I didn't meet him. I still don't even know their names."

"Pete and Chelsea," he said quietly as he came to a stop in front of the closed garage. "Momma will be up waiting for us. I don't know who else will be. Daddy gets up real early, and the other kids aren't even living here."

"Okay," Angel said.

Henry got out, not even bothering to go around and open her door this time. He moved to the back passenger seat to get his overnight bag with his clothes and toiletries. He looked up into the night sky as Angel's door slammed.

"Dear God," he whispered. "Please don't let this be a disaster." He didn't know what else to ask for, but he figured that was good enough. He probably would have to give his momma and daddy a lot more answers than he'd given his friends, but not tonight. He could at least buy himself a few more hours before he would find himself out in the stables bright and early with his daddy.

But for right now, he met Angel at the front of his truck, took her hand, squeezed it, and then, as he entered the house through the kitchen entrance, he let go of her hand and softly called, "Momma?"

She rose from the couch, her face illuminated with the blue light from her phone. Henry reached for the light and snapped it on. His mom grinned and said, "There you are," in the most pleasant, kind voice ever. Henry loved coming home. In fact, there was nothing he liked more, and he hoped Angel would be able to feel the comfort, peace, and love of his parents while she was here with him this weekend.

Chapter Four

Angel woke in someone else's pajamas, but they felt like her own. The bed had been comfortable, soft, and warm, piled with pillows just the way she liked. She had no idea what time it was, as the sun hadn't quite risen yet, but the light coming in through the wide-slat blinds, which she'd closed last night, held more gray than gold.

It had to be getting close to morning. She kept her eyes closed as she rolled away from the window. A sigh passed through her body at the thought that she didn't have to get up and get out to the stables to check on everyone today. She didn't have any meetings. She didn't have to go make sure Trevor could get the milk out of his fridge for his oatmeal. She didn't have to go fry the eggs for her daddy. And she didn't have to go sit by her mom's bedside and tell her everything that had happened the day before.

Now, she had some great stories to tell her mama. Angel smiled to herself as she thought about telling her about her "date" with Henry last night. *Oh, it wasn't a date,* she reminded herself. But it so was—dinner and games, an amazing time talking and laughing with a man. It was definitely a date, even if she couldn't define it as one. Even if she had to tell her mama a little white lie and say that she'd only gone out with a friend.

Henry wasn't even a friend. She wasn't even sure she liked him, though she was definitely attracted to him. Angel was still getting to know him as more than a farrier, more than a man who went out with a lot of women, and more than the man who kissed her last year for no reason.

He did have a reason, she reminded herself, and she decided a long time ago not to hold grudges against people. She had to, or she'd have a list a mile long to carry around with her. She thought of her granny and how she'd taught all her grandkids that whenever they had a problem with someone, they should write the person's name on a slip of paper and put it in their shoe. Then, they could walk around all day on that person and feel like they had the upper hand over them.

Angel had heard similar advice when she took some business classes about interviewing. She was there as the person doing the interviewing, but the class had been more about those preparing for an interview. The instructor had said to wear something that nobody could see, something that only you knew about—your little secret. Like a special pair of underwear, a special necklace, or a ring, something that really meant something to you, so that you could have the confidence going into an interview and sitting across from someone that you really wanted a job from.

Angel had never done either of those things, because she didn't believe she was better than anyone else. She didn't believe Granny did either. Granny just held grudges, and eventually God would soften her heart. Granny would take the name out of her shoe, shred it up, and go make things right with that person.

Angel had seen her do it over and over. In fact, she'd witnessed her daddy doing the same thing. Maybe he didn't wear names in his shoe, but he'd stomp around like an angry cat who'd been cornered, starved, and skinned. Then, when God finally got to his heart, it would be softened, and Daddy would come around.

She was a little bit like both of them, but she tried not to be. She really wanted her men at Lone Star to respect her and treat everyone with kindness. She wanted them to know that she cared about them individually, that they belonged to the same team, that they all needed to raise and care for the horses the best they could.

Horses meant the world to Angel, and she would not

stand for any of them mistreated or uncared for. And none of the men who came to Lone Star stayed for long if they didn't subscribe to her culture and her methods for how to treat horses—and that extended to the people who worked there.

Henry was an exemplar of both, and she really did like him. She could admit it to herself in the growing-lighter gray light of the bedroom that wasn't hers.

The scent of coffee met her nose, and Angel decided she better get up. She rose early most mornings, and she hit the ground running. Today, she didn't have to do that, so she stood slowly and stretched.

Last night, she hadn't worried too much about the pajamas that Henry's mother had laid out for her. Now, she glanced down and found they were a silky, light purple, one of her favorite colors.

She wasn't sure she could just pad down the hall to get a cup of coffee in her pjs. At her house, she would have, and she had to believe that Henry and his family were just as casual in their own home as she would be in hers.

So she tiptoed over to the door and opened it. A light beamed down the hall from the kitchen, and she hitched her bravery in place, pulled her shoulders back, and stepped toward the kitchen.

When she arrived, she found the big room empty, which wasn't that surprising. The clock on the stove said six-forty-four, and surprise stamped through her that she'd slept that long. Her alarm usually went off at five-thirty, but she'd silenced it last night when she'd finally made it to bed around eleven.

Henry's momma had been up and waiting for them, and she'd given Angel another hug that had almost broken her. If she hadn't gone to dinner with Henry, and then had such a great time with his friends at game night, Angel would've collapsed into sobs again.

But she was a little stronger last night, after having some of her own spirit fed. She'd made it all the way to the bedroom, she'd brushed her teeth with a brand-new toothbrush provided by Chelsea, and she'd changed into these pjs.

She'd noted the clothes Chelsea had gotten for her, and then she'd fallen into bed. And she'd slept all... night...long. Angel couldn't remember the last time she'd slept that long, without tossing and turning, getting up to use the bathroom, or simply lying awake.

"What a blessing," she murmured to herself.

She poured herself a cup of coffee, found the sugar and cream sitting on the counter, doctored up her caffeine the way she wanted, and went back to the bedroom to get her phone.

Henry had texted. *I went out to feed the horses with my daddy. I should be back around 7:30 to make break-fast. If you're starving before then, Momma put some cereal out on the counter.*

No emojis, and she'd never gotten any from Henry.

But as Angel re-read the text, she wondered what it would be like to have a heart sitting right after his last word.

I should be back around 7:30 to make breakfast. If you're starving before then, Momma put some cereal out on the counter. <3

Yes, that heart would be amazing there.

She wanted someone to send her a heart emoji. She wanted to know that someone loved and cared about *her*.

Shaking away the negative feelings of loneliness and desperation, she took her phone and her coffee back into the kitchen. She sat at the little table that faced the back window and looked out over the ranch. From here, she could see fields for miles with horses dotting them, grazing already in the morning sunshine. Angel loved nothing more than this type of environment, and she could only imagine growing up here.

"Feels a lot like Lone Star," she said, noting yet another similarity between her and Henry. For her daddy had built their house for her mama too, just like his had.

Another round of surprise marched through her when she realized neither her mama nor daddy had texted her. Daddy hadn't asked who was going to run roll call. He hadn't asked who was going to make his eggs. He hadn't asked why she left and where she was going.

"Fascinating," she whispered to herself. He did love Henry Marshall, and Angel figured that Daddy probably trusted him to take care of her wherever they were going. "Or," she muttered to herself. "Perhaps Henry texted him and told him."

That only made her curiosity brighten, but she didn't get up. She wanted a slow start to the morning. She wanted to sip her coffee with nothing more to do.

She'd seen social media posts from people she'd known in high school. Some married now, maybe had children—women like Rory and Edith who had babies.

They got to do whatever they wanted all day long. They could go for a walk with their friends at eight-thirty in the morning if they wanted. They could go to lunch with their girlfriends.

They didn't have to live and die by the clock. They didn't have to run payroll. They didn't have to live with over two dozen men, aging and disabled parents and siblings, and over two hundred horses who needed constant care.

Angel shoved the thoughts out and replaced them with ones of gratitude. "I love my life," she whispered. "I have a very good life. It's the life I want."

And in so many ways, it was. She adored horses. She loved Lone Star. She loved her parents. She loved having fields like these here at Three Rivers.

She also wanted a family. She also wanted someone

to take care of her. She wanted to break down into sobs and have someone who would take her in his arms and say, *Shh, my angel. It's okay.*

Tears touched her eyes, and Angel sniffed and wiped one away quickly. She did not want to cry in the next two days. She wanted this to be a healing time for her. She wanted to smile and laugh. She wanted to walk through the sunlit fields, and she wanted to be with horses.

She couldn't do any of that in her pajamas. So she got up, and as she turned to put her coffee cup in the sink, having only drunk half of it, she heard footsteps coming down the hall.

She arrived at the sink just as Chelsea entered the kitchen. "Oh, good morning, Angel," Chelsea said with a bright smile. She had dark hair that hung down past her shoulders and almost olive skin, but that could have been a suntan as well.

"Good morning," Angel said. "Thank you so much for everything. I really appreciate it."

Chelsea looked at her with such knowing eyes, and Angel wasn't sure what she saw. Angel was very good at hiding how she felt, and she simply waved back at Henry's mom and said, "Henry said he'd be back at seven-thirty to make breakfast."

"Yeah," she said. "My husband always makes break-fast on Sunday morning." Chelsea smiled as she poured herself a cup of coffee, her eyes trained down on the mug. "It's a luxury I've gotten used to. He's a much better cook than I am, and he taught all the boys."

"How many boys do you have?" Angel asked.

"Four," Chelsea said with obvious pride in her voice. "Henry is the second oldest. Paul is our oldest, and he works here at Courage Reins with Pete. Then we have John, who's down at Baylor finishing up his senior year. He'll graduate in a couple of months. And Rich, who just went to Amarillo with a few friends for college." She threw a smile at Angel without truly looking at her and turned toward the island where she also put sugar and cream in her coffee. "What about you, dear?"

"I just have the one brother," Angel said. "He's seven years older than me, and he lives on the ranch with us."

"That's great," Chelsea said. "Henry says you run the ranch."

"Yeah." Angel blew out her breath. "Yeah, I do." She hugged herself and looked out the window. "Trevor fell off a horse five or six years ago, and he has a traumatic brain injury and limited use of his legs."

"Oh, I'm so sorry," Chelsea said, lifting her eyes to meet Angel's fully. "I—I—Henry didn't tell us that. I didn't know."

"It's okay," Angel said, though she needed a second, stronger skin to keep all her emotions inside. "He's real good with horses still." She flashed Chelsea a smile. "Once we get him in the saddle, he can get 'em to do whatever he wants. He trains cutting horses and sells them."

"That's fantastic," Chelsea said. "A good cutting horse is hard to come by, and worth his weight in gold."

"That he is," Angel agreed. "I think I'll go get dressed and go out to the stables. Is that all right?"

"I'd wait until after breakfast," Chelsea said. "Henry said he was going to take you over to the therapy stables and get the horses out there."

"Yeah," Angel said. "He said you guys might have clients this afternoon."

"You could come to church too."

Angel gave her a closed-mouth smile. "I'll talk to Henry about it."

Chelsea nodded, resignation flashing across her face. She obviously knew Henry wouldn't go to church with them that morning. Angel wasn't sure if it upset her or if his momma had just accepted it.

"What time will y'all be back?" Angel asked. "We could make lunch."

Chelsea gaped at her. "Oh, honey, Henry doesn't make lunch."

Angel laughed lightly. "Well, he's twenty-six-years-old and has managed to keep himself alive this long."

Chelsea added her giggles to the conversation. "Yeah, he likes going to the grocery store and getting food from the bars there. He can put together eggs and bowls of cereal. But lunch for everyone?" She shook her head and laughed more fully. "Not one of his strong suits."

"I organize and help prepare dinner three times a week for all of the men at Lone Star." She swallowed and added, "I could do it."

Chelsea started shaking her head before Angel even finished speaking. "Absolutely not. You're our guest. You don't need to make lunch for us."

Angel didn't want to argue because she also didn't want to make lunch. She thought it polite to offer, and she would have done it. But Chelsea had said no, and Angel wasn't going to push her on it.

"Okay," she said.

"We'll probably go eat with my brother and his family," Chelsea said. "His daughter's in town so that she can introduce her boyfriend to all of us."

"Oh, that's great," Angel said. "Is this Libby, the woman whose clothes I'm wearing?"

Chelsea grinned and nodded. "That's right." She glanced down at Angel's purple pajamas. "I'm glad they fit."

"Me too," Angel said. "Is it just Libby and her boyfriend?"

Chelsea took her first sip of coffee. "No, Finn and Edith will probably come. They want to meet Libby's boyfriend too. Sammy lives here on the ranch. Mike's away, and he didn't come home. So there'll be a small crowd. We'll just wander over to the homestead and eat over there after church sometime. Kelly's a real good cook."

"That's great," Angel said, not sure she wanted to join that crowd.

"My mom owns the bakery in town," Chelsea said. "So she'll come out with her husband." She flashed a tight smile and let her eyes dance away. "They'll bring pastries and desserts. It'll be fun."

"Okay," Angel said. "It does sound fun." She glanced down the hall. "I guess I'll go get dressed."

Chelsea nodded her out of the room, and Angel quickly put on Libby's jeans and a green floral tank top that was a little bit too bulky for her smaller chest.

Then she spied her wig lying discarded on her nightstand. Pure horror snaked through her as she realized she'd just had an entire face-to-face conversation with Henry's mom without her hair.

She reached up with both hands and planted them on her scalp. She had so little hair, but a lot of it was on the top. Maybe Chelsea hadn't noticed. Angel scoffed at her ridiculous thought.

"How could she not have noticed?" she asked out loud. Chelsea hadn't said anything, but she'd definitely noticed. Angel snatched up the wig and moved over to the full-length mirror to put it into place.

At least Henry hadn't seen her.

Angel hated her hair, and she hated how easily it went under the wig cap and how little of it she could see beneath the nylon. She fitted the wig over it and clipped the clasp in place. It pinched for one moment, and her head got hot for two seconds, and then it went back to normal.

This was her normal. She wore a wig every day. She wore it up in a ponytail when she worked outside in the hot Texas heat and down when she went to church.

She looked at the dress she'd worn here, folded neatly on the bed that she'd already made. She slipped her feet into the boots that Chelsea had provided for her. They fit pretty well. She went down the hall where she heard the sound of male voices.

That meant Henry and his daddy had returned. The hummingbird wings in Angel's pulse picked up. She took a deep breath just before she exited the hallway and saw Henry with his parents, both of them standing at the counter, their backs to her as they faced him. He stirred something into his coffee.

"She's just a friend, Momma."

"Is she?" his mom challenged. "She's really pretty, Henry."

"Yeah, she is," he said. "That doesn't mean she's my girlfriend." He glanced up to his mother but didn't look over to the mouth of the hallway.

Angel faded against the wall, pressing her back into the drywall behind her.

"Are you dating her?" his daddy asked.

"I just answered that question," Henry said. "I told

you in the stables as well. I'm not dating her. She's not my girlfriend." He heaved a heavy sigh, and Angel wished she stood beside him and could hold his hand and squeeze it to give him strength. "She needed help."

Angel didn't want to hear this. She did not want to hear what Henry thought of her. She did not want to know what he saw when she broke down in front of him. She didn't want to know his opinion of her family, of her parents, of her brother. She thought it might break her further if it wasn't exactly what she hoped to hear. And to be honest, she didn't even *know* what she hoped to hear.

"What do you mean, help?" Chelsea asked.

"She carries a lot for Lone Star," Henry said slowly, thoughtfully. Angel had heard him speak like this to other cowboys too, about horses and the schedule of their shoeing, and the different ways that they could take care of the equines that lived at Lone Star.

"I don't know exact specifics," he said. "I told her we didn't have to talk about it this weekend, and we haven't talked about it. But I knew she needed help. God told me she needed help, and so I invited her to come with me. I thought maybe a couple of days away from all of her heavy responsibilities would help her."

Angel's heart melted at his words, and she stepped back down the hall, making her steps really loud, then turned around and came back. She entered the kitchen, and all three of them looked at her.

"Hey," she said as brightly as she could, everything on the inside wavering. She looked at Pete and then Chelsea and then Henry, where her gaze landed and locked. "I can help with breakfast."

Henry moved toward her. "Not necessary," he said. "Daddy never lets anyone in the kitchen to help him when he's making breakfast on Sunday."

He grinned at her, his eyes scanning down to her boots and back. "How are the boots?"

"Great," she said. "Just fine."

"Have you had coffee?"

"Yes," she said at the same time his momma said, "She had coffee."

Henry looked at his mother for a moment and then turned back to Angel. "Do you want to go out to the stables after breakfast?"

She nodded, not quite sure why she was so nervous with all of them watching her. "I don't think you've met my daddy yet," Henry said as he moved to her side instead of standing in front of her. "Daddy, this is Angel White. She's my boss at Lone Star." He said the last couple of words with plenty of heaviness in his voice.

"Angel," Pete said with a smile as wide as the Texas sky and as bright as the Texas star. "So great to meet you. Welcome to our home."

"It's so lovely here." She turned toward the blue door. Henry had said the sunlight would hit that door in the morning, and she'd be able to see the beautiful stained glass. She turned toward it fully. "The stained glass is amazing. I love it."

She faced Henry and his family again, and she found Henry's smile just as wide as his daddy's. "Thank you," Pete said. "We do love that door." He put his arm around his wife. "Don't we, hon?"

Chelsea smiled at him. Angel could see the pure love they had for each other, and she really wanted it for herself. Her mama and daddy looked at each other like this too, and her heart throbbed at the thought that perhaps she and Henry could have this kind of love one day.

"We can go sit out on the front porch," Henry said. "Until breakfast is ready." He didn't touch her, but he looked at her with pure questions and desire in his eyes.

"Sure," she said. "That'd be great." She wanted to reach out and hold his hand, but she had just listened to him tell his parents that they were not dating, that she was not his girlfriend.

She didn't think that would be a very "just friends" kind of thing to do. So she started toward the front door while Henry muttered something to his parents behind her. When she made it to the front porch, she took a big, deep breath of the air here at Three Rivers Ranch, feeling it cleanse her lungs and fill her soul with more strength than she'd had in a long time.

"Thank you, Lord," she whispered just as Henry stepped out onto the porch next to her. She turned to face him as he closed the door. She grabbed onto him and hugged him tightly against her. "Thank you, Henry," she said, her voice wavering but not breaking.

He wrapped her up in a tight hug too, and Angel thought if she could just have one of these every day, or even every time she felt like she couldn't go on for another moment, she would be okay.

Chapter Five

Henry could hold Angel in his arms for a good long time. He stood at least six or seven inches taller than her, which meant she could lay her cheek against his chest right where his heart beat, and he could fold his arms around her shoulders, enveloping her in his embrace. He did, and he'd gladly do it as many times as she wanted him to.

He wasn't sure what he needed to be thanked for. It was his momma who'd done everything. But he didn't mind. Angel wasn't crying, which was a good sign, and she only clung to him for two more seconds before stepping back.

She drew in a deep breath and said, "I sure do like your ranch here, Henry."

"I do too," he said. "I mean, I left almost the moment

I could, and I don't want to take this place over, but it's really nice to come home to when I need a breather."

"Your parents are great," she said as she moved over to the chairs. A little round table sat between two of them, and she sat down and started rocking back and forth.

Henry simply watched her because he'd seen his momma and daddy bring sweet tea and lemonade out here to this table and rock in the evening shade many times. He'd never thought that would be his reality because he'd never wanted to stay at Three Rivers Ranch.

He wasn't the oldest, number one, and Paul was much more of a cowboy than Henry. He didn't like crowds, he didn't mind a long drive to town. He wanted peace and quiet, wanted to work outside, and wanted to look out every window in the house and see cows or horses.

Henry didn't like cattle ranching nearly as much as anyone else, but he'd take a horse any day over any person. *Maybe not Angel*, his mind whispered, and Henry had never felt like that about a woman before.

"Are you going to sit down?" she asked.

Henry moved over and took his place in his daddy's chair. It rocked back with his weight and then moved forward again. He hadn't brought out his coffee, and he'd only had two sips, but he was keyed up enough to sit with Angel for the morning.

"Daddy'll probably make pancakes," he said. "He puts fruit in them. Is that going to bother you?"

"What kind of fruit?" she asked.

"Apples," he said. "Sometimes he shreds them. Or blueberries. Depends on whatever Momma got at the store."

"Did they plan it?" she asked quietly.

"I don't know," Henry said. "Maybe."

"My parents did. Daddy would make a list for Mama to go to the store, and she'd get whatever he wanted. For the cowboy dinners, for our Saturday morning breakfast that we had growing up."

"Did your daddy cook too?" Henry asked.

"No, it was usually Mama. Daddy did all the cowboy dinners," she said. "Mama did all the family stuff."

"I see," Henry said.

"Your momma says you know how to cook," Angel said.

He looked over to her. "My momma says?"

"Yeah, I talked to her for a couple of minutes this morning," Angel said.

"Mm." Henry drew in a breath, and he saw no reason to hide the fact that he actually could cook. "Daddy taught all of us how to take care of ourselves, how to make meals, how to clean up. He had four boys, and he wanted Momma to be taken care of when she got older. He wanted us to know how to take care of our wives."

Henry didn't know what else to say because he'd literally never seen himself with a wife before. He'd just barely started to settle down into himself and start thinking about a real future.

He'd been so focused on his farrier education that he hadn't given much thought to almost anything else.

But now he heard the whisperings of the wind, and in them, maybe the low voice of the Lord telling him that he was ready. That it was time. That he could live in a cabin on a ranch just like Finn, with a wife and a baby, and maybe like Ollie and Rory, he could have three or four kids.

He didn't know what to say next because the feelings streaming through him sounded loud in his head, drowning out his other thoughts. Angel may have said something to him, and he wouldn't have heard it.

The silence between them felt nice. The silence on the ranch had always calmed Henry, for this place felt like a being of its own that stood wider than him, that had bigger wings than him. Here, he could lean his head against the pulse of God, and God would wrap him in His arms just the way he had Angel.

He let out a slow breath, everything in his life slowing down just the way he wanted it to be. "I thought after breakfast," he said. "We could go over and play ball with one of the horses."

"You keep saying that," Angel said. "But I don't know what it means."

"Well, my daddy trains the therapy horses," he said. "They play ball with some people. We roll them the ball; they kick it back. Sometimes we ride while they kick the ball. No matter what, the horses are meant to work with people wherever they are. To heal them—mind, body, and soul."

"I've never done equine therapy," Angel said.

"I like it," Henry said. "I've done it several times. It's best when paired with a real therapist, like a human therapist. I don't always do that, but my daddy requires it of his patients." He let a path of silence go by, and then he said, "I know how to train them. I think we'll work with one of his new horses this morning."

"What's his name?" Angel asked.

Henry let out a low chuckle. "You're gonna love this."

"Am I?"

"Yeah," he said. "She's got a name a lot like you."

"Did you name a horse Angel?" she asked dryly. "Haven't heard that before."

Henry laughed outright then. "My daddy usually acquires horses after they're done working. Sometimes he buys them and trains them as therapy horses, but typically, they're older horses who've served a good life on the ranch, and they're ready for a slower pace of life.

They're good horses, easily trained, have great personalities, that kind of thing."

"We have some horses like that at Lone Star," Angel said.

"Sure do," Henry said, nodding. "So most of the horses, as you can imagine, come to us with names already. My daddy didn't name her."

"Ah, I see."

"This one's name is Nevaeh. It's heaven backward."

Angel looked over to him, and Henry smiled, wondering what she saw on his face, wondering what ran through her head. The woman was an enigma, as she never let too much show. In fact, that was why Henry had been so alarmed when she'd buried her face in her hands and sobbed on his front porch. He'd never seen Angel do anything like that before. He'd never seen the woman cry. Anger, sure. Frustration, absolutely. Irritation—he seemed to irritate her just by being in her presence. Except for right now.

"Nevaeh," she repeated. "I like that."

Henry looked away, out into the yard, past the emerald grass to Bowman's Breeds across the street, down to his aunt and uncle's place. "I don't hate it," he said. "I'm not usually one for kitschy names."

"Your horse is named Stormchaser," she said.

"Yeah, it's not kitschy," he said. "She's great. She chases storms, just like a storm cloud. Totally makes sense."

"Well, Stormcloud would make more sense," she quipped.

Henry could tease her about the horse names at Lone Star, but they usually came with their names as well. Angel had her own horse too, and she'd been named Starlight. Henry could probably make a joke about that, but he didn't. And he kept his hands to himself too, though he really wanted to hold her hand.

The scent of bacon made his nose twitch and his stomach growl. "I'm gonna go see if Daddy needs any help."

"Okay," Angel said, making no move to get up and go with him.

Henry returned to the house and found his daddy tipping bacon out of the pan and onto a paper towel-covered plate. "Need any help?"

"Yes, you can warm up the syrup," Daddy said.

Henry walked through the living room toward him, hoping all the awkward questions and conversations had been had. Then maybe he could enjoy today and tomorrow before heading back to work.

"I've got the griddle hot. When we make pancakes, we'll want to eat 'em hot. Momma," he called down the hall.

Daddy looked up and met Henry's eyes. So much was said between them in that moment that Henry came to a stop. He'd been working so hard for his momma and daddy to be proud of him. They'd paid for a four-year college degree that Henry was never going to use, and guilt gutted him every time he thought about it. He'd paid his own way through farrier school, scrimping and saving to make ends meet, calling and texting and emailing anyone he had to for jobs.

His momma had sent him money over the years, but Henry wasn't sure if Daddy knew about that or not.

Daddy was a questioner, and Henry hated answering his questions. Henry always wanted to have a good time growing up, and he had a lot of girlfriends. That made his parents worry. The older he got, the more he realized that they just wanted him to be safe. They wanted him to be kind. They wanted him to work hard.

They wanted him to be a good man. A good cowboy.

Henry got his feet moving again, and he picked up the stout syrup bottle and put it in the microwave. He set it for one minute, and turned to face his father, who'd gone back to whisking the pancake batter.

Momma hadn't come back down the hall yet, and Henry should probably go get Angel from the porch. But instead, he moved to stand right next to his daddy. He leaned into him and said, "I love you, Daddy."

His father stopped his breakfast prep, as he had many times over the years, to give Henry his full attention. "I love you too, son," he said. "Momma and I are real proud of what you're doin' at Lone Star."

"Thanks, Daddy."

"What's the next step for you?" Daddy asked.

"I don't know. I'm a team lead there. My apprentice-ship is up at the end of May. A lot of men stay on for another year or two. It's a good place, with excellent master farriers."

Daddy went back to the batter. "How much more do you think you can learn from them?"

"I don't know," Henry said again. "I mean, I don't know what I don't know, right?"

"Sure, right." Daddy opened the drawer to get out a measuring cup. "Do you see yourself working for someone else your whole life? Shoeing their horses?"

"Yeah, Daddy. That's what farriers do. They shoe someone else's horses."

"Yeah, you know what I'm asking," Daddy said, a tight clip to his voice as he poured the first pancake onto the hot griddle. It sizzled, and Daddy was such an expert that he got twelve of them down before Henry could even say a word.

"I've thought about opening my own business," Henry said. "It's different than working somewhere like Lone Star. There, I have a job everyday. I have a place to live, and people who know me. People I like. People who can step in in an emergency. Horses I know, and horses I like."

Part of him wanted to set his own hours, run his own life. But he also liked the stability somewhere like Lone Star provided.

"If I start my own business, there's more travel. I

have to find somewhere to live, and I have to drum up my own jobs."

"Yep," Daddy said, offering nothing else.

"So I don't know," Henry said. "My apprenticeship isn't over yet. I don't know what Lone Star will even offer. Sometimes they don't let men stay on."

"They'll let you stay on," Daddy said. "You moved to team lead within the second week you were there."

"Yeah," Henry said. "And I've haven't moved up to captain yet."

"Well, you might," Daddy said. "There are other men in those positions who've been there longer than you."

"Yeah, that's true."

The front door opened, and Angel entered, drawing all of Henry's attention the way she did every time she came close to him.

"Pancakes are down," he called to her. "I was just comin' to get you."

"I can smell them," she said. "Smells real good, Mister Marshall." She wore a sunny smile on her face, and though the clothes didn't quite fit her—Libby was a tiny bit bigger than her—she still shone with radiance and beauty.

"We're gonna go work with Nevaeh after breakfast," Henry said. "Is that okay?"

"Sounds perfect," Daddy said, passing the spatula to

Henry. "Henry, you flip these. I'm gonna go check on what Momma's doing."

Daddy left the room, and Henry stared at the griddle. He'd flipped pancakes before, but Angel came to his side, easily plucking the utensil from his hand.

"I'll do it, cowboy," she said. "You just gotta watch for the bubbles."

He stood beside her while she flipped the pancakes, and he wasn't sure why that was so hot and so sexy, but it was, and he felt himself falling for her, which so couldn't happen. Not with the current rules at Lone Star.

He wasn't going to ask her to change them. He told her he wouldn't talk about it this weekend, and he wouldn't.

He put it in his pocket for later. Maybe on the drive home. Maybe the next day. He wasn't even sure when he'd see Angel once they got back to the boarding stable. He leaned in, inhaled the scent of her hair, her skin, her shoulder, and said, "I sure do like you, Angel."

He stepped back because his parents came in, and Henry wasn't going to say more than that.

"I can't believe horses know how to do this," Angel said. "Look at her just kick it back to me."

Henry chuckled and watched as Angel reached

down to receive the exercise ball. "Maybe it's something we can offer to the cowboys on the ranch."

She straightened, and even though Nevaeh kicked the ball back to her, she didn't bend down to stop it. She just let it bounce against her knees softly. "Henry, we're not an equine therapy unit."

"I know that," he said, something stinging in his chest at her tone. "But it's one horse. I bet your mama would like it. Your daddy, maybe. Trevor would love it for sure."

"I know Trevor would love it." Angel's expression hardened, and Henry wasn't sure what he'd said wrong. "You don't know my brother," she said, turning away from both Henry and Nevaeh.

"Can we ride her?" she asked, her eyes sweeping the arena in front of them. Daddy had built a huge indoor arena where he did classes and horseback riding lessons, as well as the equine therapy.

"Outside or inside?" Henry asked.

"Outside," she said. "Is there a path we could take that won't take too long? We need to have her back on time. She needs to rest before the afternoon appointments."

Henry gathered his courage and stepped over to Angel, not getting too close. She could definitely tell he was coming, and she glanced over to him, then quickly looked away.

"There's a short path over to the river," he said.

"Nevaeh's not working this afternoon anyway, so it doesn't matter if we ride her."

"Okay," Angel said. "I'll get her saddled."

"I can do it," Henry said.

"I can do it too, cowboy." She trailed her fingers along the top of the ball, got it to bump along the dirt with her as she walked toward Nevaeh. "Come on, Nevaeh," she said in a much more chipper voice. "Let's get you saddled for a ride."

Henry watched her go because he could saddle a horse in two seconds flat, and he knew Angel could too.

He wasn't sure what he'd said wrong, but he wanted to make it right. So he let out a sigh and followed her, a silent prayer in his mind, in his heart, for God to give him the right words to say.

I need to bring her closer to me, not further away. She doesn't have anyone. That thought struck through him like someone hitting a gong. *She doesn't have anyone.*

The truth was, Angel was surrounded by people. Lots and lots of people. But no one took care of her. She took care of all of them. She took care of every cowboy. She took care of her mom and dad. She took care of Trevor. So if Henry could find a way to take care of her, he was going to do it.

He found her in the tack room, and he said, "This is her stuff right here," handing her the saddle. He then moved to get some for Cinnamon, the horse he would ride.

Within five minutes, she swung up into the saddle, and Henry did the same next to her.

"I'll just follow you," she said.

"Okay," he said, and he set off toward the south, toward the river.

It ran between this ranch and Finn's place, and Henry thought that might be a talking point that they could get to when they finally got there.

Nevaeh and Cinnamon seemed to know their way, and Henry barely steered, barely held the reins, and barely held his thoughts back. After a few minutes, the overwhelming urge to apologize to her came into his mind. He pushed against it; he hadn't done anything wrong. Henry had always pushed against apologizing and admitting something he'd done wrong, but in the end, he always did it.

So after another few minutes of the Lord needling him and needling him to the point of irritation, Henry looked over to Angel and said, "I'm real sorry about what I said about Trevor."

She rode a step or two behind him, and he had to twist to look at her. "Okay?"

"Okay," she said. "You didn't say anything wrong."

"You got upset," he said.

"Upset's the wrong word," she said.

"Okay, then tell me what you got."

"I don't know," she said. "It's just irritating. Nobody knows what it's like to take care of Trevor except for me, because I'm the one who takes care of Trevor."

"I know that," Henry said. "That's why I offered the equine therapy. Because then someone other than you could take care of Trevor."

"You?" she asked.

"Yeah," he shot back. "Me. What's wrong with that?"

Angel looked like she might say something else, and then she clamped her mouth closed and pressed her lips together.

Yeah, he thought. *Nothing's wrong with that.*

He faced forward again because he didn't want to fight with Angel. He tipped his head back to absorb the sunlight, and he let Three Rivers wrap him in a hug and steal away all of his frustration, his irritation, his loneliness—anything that wasn't good for him. He simply let it go and bled it out into the land in front of him. When he opened his eyes again, he said, "I really am sorry. I don't want you to be upset with me, or irritated, or frustrated, or anything."

"Okay," she said. "I'm not."

"Okay," he said.

When they got to the river, Angel jumped down, threw the reins over a pole, and walked right to the edge of it.

"It runs fast in the spring," he said. "Not so much right now."

She didn't respond but instead just gazed into the water. A little trickle ran through the stream bed that would get much bigger and faster in the spring. They didn't get much snow in the Panhandle, but some, and it stayed up in the hills until it melted, usually in another month or so. Henry sidled up beside her, feeling reckless and brave, dangerous and strong all at the same time. He threaded his fingers through hers and held on tight. She wasn't a limp noodle, and she held his hand back, just the way she'd kissed him back a year ago as well.

He wasn't going to kiss her now, and he didn't even look at her. Instead, he watched the water too, marveling at the way it moved when it wasn't alive. "Would you come to Caroline and Dawson's wedding with me?"

"Yeah," Angel said without a pause at all. "That sounds real nice."

Henry breathed out, realizing that he hadn't truly been breathing on this first half of the ride. "Great."

He released her hand and stepped away. Even when she looked at him, he didn't look back at her. He wasn't sure what life was going to be like when they returned to Lone Star. Out here in the wilds of Three Rivers, he could ask her out. She could say yes.

They could come to Three Rivers, and they could go on a date.

But when they got back to Lone Star, what would they do? How would that go over with Bard and with the other cowboys? To Henry's knowledge, the no-dating rule at Lone Star had been in place for years, decades maybe.

No one asked Angel out. No one tried to break it. And here he came, doing exactly that.

What would people think of him?

His heartbeat stuttered at him because he wanted to have purpose in his life. He wanted the things he did to matter. And he wanted the people around him to like him. Angel and Bard had a strong culture of teamwork at Lone Star. There was no "I." There was only "we."

They had roll call every single morning for a half-hour. Angel led it now, but Bard had in the past, and sometimes some of his master farriers. They told stories about horses that they'd rescued. They inspired the men there to love and care about their jobs, the horses, and each other.

When she came back and picked up the reins for Nevaeh and got back in the saddle, he mounted Cinnamon again, and they started the journey back to the center of the ranch. He hoped that she would find peace here, that she would find strength she could take back with her.

And maybe then they could have a conversation—the hard conversation—about starting a real relationship that other people knew about.

Chapter Six

Angel heard the back door slam, which meant Henry had just come outside. He moved down the steps and started toward the trampoline where she already lay as dusk encroached on the amazing day she'd had here at Three Rivers Ranch.

"All right," Henry said as he climbed up onto the trampoline. He kicked off his boots the way she had, and she lay on her back with her hands crossed across her stomach as he crawled toward her, bouncing with every move.

"Sorry." He chuckled. "Sorry, sorry." He held something out to her, and Angel looked toward him.

She took the cup of rice pudding. "I've never bought this at the grocery store before."

Henry grinned. "It's amazing. I know you think it's not going to be amazing, but it's amazing. My granny owns a bakery in town, and even she says it's better than her rice pudding. You're gonna love it."

Angel wasn't so sure, but she managed to rip off the top and pull out the little plastic spoon that had been affixed to it. "All right," she said. "I guess I'm doing a lot of things today that I wasn't sure I was gonna enjoy."

"I guess so," Henry said as he lay down beside her. He'd suggested they come out to the west side of the farm where the trampoline was. He said he and his brothers would often sleep out here—they'd put up tents, whatever they needed to do just to get out of the house and enjoy the weather and each other after a good, hard day after harvesting or working with horses. It faced west so they could see the sunset, and since there were no mountains obscuring their view, the sun hadn't quite kissed the horizon yet.

Angel never took time to watch a sunset. She hadn't been on a trampoline in at least two decades. She hadn't had rice pudding since the last time she visited her granny in Oklahoma, which was going on a couple of years now. A pang of nostalgia and missing hit her, and she told herself she needed to get up to Oklahoma to see her granny sooner rather than later.

Gramps had died a few years ago, right around the time Trevor had fallen from a horse, so none of them had made the trip up to his funeral. Granny said it was totally fine, no big deal, and they'd all gone to visit once Trevor had gotten out of the hospital. But Angel didn't have time for more casual visits the way she used to. Not anymore.

You could make time, she thought, though she wasn't entirely sure that the voice was hers. Sometimes she needed to be chastised by the Lord, and perhaps this was one of those times. Perhaps Henry was right, and she didn't have to be on the ranch all day, every day.

Nobody had called today; there had been no texts, no emergencies, no pictures of dead horses or dead men. Everything was just fine without her. She wasn't sure if she liked that or not, as it made her feel even more unsettled. As she took her first bite of the rice pudding, she glanced over to Henry.

"Do you ever feel just utterly replaceable?" she asked.

He sighed as he pulled the spoon out of his mouth, his tongue darting out to lick his full lips. Angel glanced away quickly because she'd already started thinking about kissing him. And that would not do.

In truth, she wasn't sure what would do and what wouldn't. What would her father do if she started dating one of the cowboys at Lone Star? He wasn't in charge anymore. She was.

What if she was willing to put up with the drama? What if she was willing to work with someone who had broken her heart or whose heart she'd broken?

Daddy had made the rule many years ago, because he couldn't stand drama. There had been some in the past when they'd had some female trainers and farriers. But Angel didn't employ any women right now. And she'd never really wanted to date any of the cowboys at Lone Star.

Until Henry.

"Yeah," he said. "I mean, I'm the second son, and Paul is perfect." He sounded a little bitter about it. "I mean, he's not perfect, but he *seems* perfect. He doesn't argue with my parents the way I do. He got great grades in high school and even went to college. I passed. I made it by, because I'm not really a school person. And then John is my next younger brother. He was like the prince of everything. He was on the football team. He was in student government. He got a scholarship to Baylor. It was like Momma and Daddy could just skip over me. Go from Paul to John and be just fine. They didn't need a Henry."

Angel didn't like the sound of that at all. "They didn't need a Henry?" She stuck her little spoon in her rice pudding and reached over and took Henry's hand in hers. She brought it to lay flat against her stomach and curled hers over the top of it. "I think everyone needs a Henry."

Henry drew in a sharp breath, and Angel wasn't sure if it was born from emotion, or surprise, or something else entirely. "That's a really nice thing to say."

"Well, it's true," she said. "I'm not just saying it. Everyone needs a Henry. Lone Star would be lost without you. You lead the summer internship farriers with kindness and power. All of the horses love you. My daddy thinks you're the greatest farrier we've had in years."

"I'm not a master farrier," Henry said.

"So what?" Angel said. "You still have value every day. Today you do. You showed me an amazing time. You helped me get out of my head. You helped me slow down." She took a breath and watched the golds and oranges turn into bruises—purples and pinks and deep blues. "Sometimes I have a really hard time slowing down."

Henry adjusted his hand, threaded his fingers through hers. "I do too," he said. "I'll help you slow down anytime you need it, Angel."

She nodded, and the movement of the trampoline probably told him that, so she didn't have to say anything. The sun dipped lower. She took another bite of the rice pudding on her baby-sized spoon.

"This is really good," she said.

"See?" Henry said with a chuckle. "I'm not a liar, that's for sure."

Angel did like that about him. He was honest. He spoke his mind, sometimes in a fiery, passionate way. When he got fired up, it was something important, and everyone around him stopped to listen.

If he said nothing, it wasn't that big of a deal. If he said his opinion and didn't bring it up again, also not a big deal. But if he would go back and forth with someone and continue on an issue, trying to solve a problem, then it meant something to him, and Angel really needed to pay attention to what those things were.

"How's Gilligan's shoes?" she asked.

Henry let out a frustrated sigh. "Nothing's working on him," he said. "That horse deserves good shoes, and I'm gonna put together something for your daddy. I was gonna go see him last week, but it didn't quite work out."

"What are you going to propose?" she asked. "I think you've been through every shoe on the market."

"Yep," Henry said. "But they're doing amazing things with 3D printing these days, Angel. And I think we can make a custom pair of shoes for every horse with a 3D printer."

"3D printed shoes?" she asked. "That's not going to last."

"You'd be surprised what they can create," he said. "I've been doing some research on it, which is why I didn't go talk to your daddy yet. But I hope to have something new for him this week. If I can get on the computer at some point. Maybe tomorrow night when we get back."

"Interesting," she said, really impressed with Henry's out-of-the-box thinking. "3D printed shoes."

"Yeah," he said. "They're really amazing. You can print anything 3D now. There are all kinds of printers. You can print on doors and garage doors and stickers for cars. You can cut things out. I mean, the engineering school that I was in, we did tons of stuff with 3D printing."

"What engineering program did you do?" she asked.

"Industrial engineering," Henry said. "I have a degree in it and everything."

"I didn't know that about you."

"Yeah, we used 3D printing a lot. We would use it for the construction of things, to do models, to see if something would resist weight, all of that kind of stuff. And I've played around with a lot of it, and I really think we can make horseshoes."

"Will they be made out of metal?"

"No," he said. "Not metal. That would be too heavy, and I'm not sure we can have a 3D printer that could do something like that."

"Yeah, seems a little strange."

"Yeah. So I'm thinking something maybe more lightweight, that's real thin, that you might not even notice. Right now, I'm working on the materials. I'm going to put a presentation-type proposal thing together. If you'd like, you can come to the meeting when I'm ready."

"I'd like that, Henry."

"Great." He took a breath, his passion for the 3D printing clearly evident. "I'd like that too."

Angel looked to the western sky as the sun steadily sunk into the horizon, which swallowed it up inch by inch until it was half sun, and then only the very tippy top, and then nothing.

Henry sighed. "There's nothing better than a Texas sunset."

"There sure isn't." Angel couldn't remember the last time she'd taken the time to watch the sunset, and she sure was glad that she'd done it tonight. She had no idea what she and Henry would do tomorrow, what time they would leave to get back to the ranch, or any of it. But right now, it didn't matter. Right now, she had rice pudding, the gorgeous rays of the sun shooting up from beneath the land, and Henry's hand in hers.

For right now, that was enough.

Chapter Seven

Finn Ackerman walked into the farmhouse through the back door, tossing his gloves on the table beside it before he did. He expected Edith to be in from her she-shed by now. She didn't write very often during the day, but she was on a deadline with her editor and needed to get this book done in the next couple of weeks.

Finn's half-sister, Libby, had been dating a man named Rusty Jackson for the past several months, and she finally decided that he was worthy enough for her to bring home and introduce to the family. However, she didn't want to overwhelm him with the enormity of people at Three Rivers Ranch, something Finn really understood.

There were a lot of cowboys working his family ranch. Heck, just his mama could be overbearing by herself, though he loved her dearly.

So Libby brought Rusty to the ranch on Saturday and introduced him to Momma and Daddy, Grams and her new husband, and Uncle Pete and Chelsea. On Sunday, they had lunch together.

She wanted to do something a little less formal, with fewer people and off Three Rivers Ranch, so she'd asked Finn if she could bring Rusty to meet him and Edith for lunch today. Since Henry was in town, she'd invited him and Angel too, but Finn wasn't actually sure if they were going to come.

"Hey," Finn called. "Anyone here?"

No one answered, which meant Edith was still out in her writing shed. It didn't matter. She'd gotten a recipe from Momma and put something in the crockpot last night so that it could slow-and-low cook all night and this morning. All they had to do was shred some lettuce, chop up some tomatoes, get out the tortillas and cheese, and they'd have burritos.

Finn washed up in the sink, going all the way to his elbows because he'd been fixing fences and moving chickens that morning. A minute later, he had just gotten the tomatoes out of the basket when Edith walked in.

"Oh, hey, baby," she said. "You're here."

She carried Theo on her hip, and Finn grinned at the little boy and took him from her.

"Hey, baby," he cooed at his son. "What are you

doing with Mama out there?" Theo had red cheeks, no smile, and a little blank look in his eyes.

Finn guessed that he had just woken up. "Did you just get up from your nap?" he asked. "Were you being good for Mama so she could write?"

Theo once again just stared at him as if he'd never heard Finn's voice before, never learned English. Finn leaned down and kissed his son on the cheek. "You're the best boy. Let's put you with your toys for a minute so Daddy can help Mama get lunch ready."

He started to move into the living room just as the front door opened, and Libby walked in.

"Hey," she said brightly. "We're here."

"Come on in." Finn detoured away from the play-seat where they put Theo when they couldn't hold him. He could sit up on the floor just fine by himself, but he tended to crawl around and get into things Edith didn't want him to get into.

Finn moved over to Libby and gave her a side hug. She was the oldest child of Momma and Daddy, their first biological child, born when Finn was eight years old. She was headstrong and confident, responsible and hardworking, smart and beautiful, and Finn loved her with his whole heart.

"Hey, Libby," he said, hugging her tightly with Theo semi-mashed between them. "How are you? How was the drive over?"

"It was great," she said. "It really is faster on horse-back. It's incredible."

A man crowded into the doorway behind her, and Finn backed up so that they could come into the house properly.

"This is Rusty," Libby said, reaching for him and taking his hand in hers. She smiled at him with all the glory of the sun and stars, and Finn saw that she was in love with him. He prayed desperately that Rusty would be just as in love with Libby as she was with him because she hadn't had the best luck with men.

Libby looked over to Finn, something bright and hopeful in her expression. "This is my brother, Finn."

Finn stuck out the hand that wasn't holding his son. "Hey, Rusty," he said. "Welcome to Legacy Ranch. It's great to meet you."

"It's great to be here," Rusty said. "This part of Texas is so beautiful."

Finn didn't hear that too often, though it was true, and he grinned at the man. "It is beautiful here right now," he said. "It's starting to green up a little bit. You're here at a great time before everything gets a little bit too brown."

"It's great," Libby said.

"It is," Finn said. "That's why I bought a place here."

Rusty looked at Finn, then at Libby, a smile on his face, in his eyes, and emanating from his very soul.

Oh boy, Finn thought. *He's in love with her too.* That

settled his heartbeat back to its normal rhythm. He hadn't talked to his parents about Libby at all, and he wondered if Momma or Daddy would say anything. He wondered about their impressions of the man.

Rusty was taller than her by quite a few inches. He had dark hair and a neatly trimmed beard and mustache, and a cowboy hat on top of all that. He looked like Libby's cowboy hero, the one that she'd been dreaming about for years, and trying to find, and making witty quips about. Finn really hoped that he was The One.

"Come in, come in," Edith said. "Why are y'all standing in the doorway?"

"Yeah, come in," Finn said. "I was just putting Theo down to play."

"I'll take him," Libby said, and she eased the little boy out of Finn's arms easily.

"We're having burritos today," Edith called. "Or you can make a shredded pork salad with chips. We have all the toppings. Come on in."

She had guacamole out, sour cream on the counter, shredded cheese. She'd chopped up the tomato that Finn had gotten out, and she had a knife slicing through the lettuce as he entered the kitchen to help her.

He got out the bag of tortillas and set them on the counter, got down a stack of plates, and brought the chips over from where they sat waiting next to the fridge. He'd never really envisioned himself as an entertainer, but he hosted his friends for game nights, and he had the ranchers for lunch twice a year. He enjoyed going to the other lunches that were held at Shiloh Ridge Ranch, the Rhinehart Ranch, or over at his brother-in-law's place, Coyote Pass.

Questions about Alex and Nikki weighed on Finn's mind. They were supposed to be coming home today, but neither Finn nor Edith had heard anything about their appointments in Amarillo.

They'd met with an adoption counselor on Friday, and Finn knew they'd had an appointment with a fertility doctor at a clinic in Amarillo this morning. His heart worried over them, because Nikki was eight or nine years older than Alex and already in her mid-thirties. She desperately wanted children, and it felt like the clock was really ticking against her.

"I love a good burrito," Rusty said.

"It's one of his favorite foods," Libby said.

Finn looked up, a hint of surprise moving through him. "Are you serious?"

"Yes."

"Did we really nail it?"

Rusty grinned. "You really nailed it. I love burritos."

"That's great news," Edith said. "We're lucky when we get things just right."

"Must have been a prompting from God," Rusty said, and that jerked Finn's attention to him too. He looked at Libby, and they had a whole conversation without saying anything. She ducked her eyes and looked at Theo as he reached for her hair.

"No, no, no, baby," she said as she pulled her hair out of his grip.

"He just woke up," Edith said. "He's coming into consciousness still."

Theo made a shrieking noise then, and threw one of his fists into the air. Libby laughed and dodged away from him so she didn't get punched.

"You can put him in his play seat," Edith said, and Libby turned to go do that.

"He's going to be walking soon," Libby said.

"Yeah, no kidding," Edith said. "Then we'll have to put a leash on him to take him out on the farm."

"I grew up at a place like this," Rusty said. "My mama and daddy worked it with just two other cowboys. And us kids."

"Oh yeah?" Finn asked. "How many kids in your family?"

"There's three of us," Rusty said. "I'm the oldest. And I got two sisters who are still living at home, helping Mama with our egg business and the jams and jellies that she sells."

"Oh, she sells jams and jellies?" Edith asked. "You guys are in southern Oklahoma, right?"

Rusty nodded. "Yep, that's right, just across the Red River. We could probably stand on one side of it, spit, and hit Texas."

Finn laughed because that was true; Oklahoma wasn't that far away. He wondered if Libby had told Rusty that she was set to take over the ranch here, and he wondered when she was going to do it. He thought it would be last year, but she'd stayed in Oklahoma, and nothing had been said so far this year. But it was only the end of February.

"Is Henry coming?" Libby asked.

"I don't know," Finn said. "I haven't heard from him."

"Is he dating Angel?" Libby asked.

Finn shook his head. "He staunchly says he's not."

"No, he's not," Edith said. "He needed a plus one for game night. And apparently, she needed a night off the ranch."

Finn moved the big bowl of lettuce so it sat in the row with the other toppings. "Right. She needed some time away from Lone Star. That's a big boarding stable that she owns and runs, and so they came for game night. They're going home later tonight. At least, that's what I thought."

Libby nodded as she sat down at the bar. "I saw Paul this morning. He said meeting Brielle's parents went real well."

"Oh, that's great," Finn said. "I haven't talked to him yet either." He didn't really have a reason to call up his cousins and chat, other than they were family.

"Yeah, he came over for a little bit so he could meet

Rusty." Libby leaned into him as he put his arm around her and stood behind her on the side. Finn thought they were so cute, but he ducked his head to hide his smile.

"All right," he said. "What's the news from Oklahoma?"

Libby sighed and folded her arms on the counter in front of her. "I started talking to Tyson last week."

"Oh yeah?" Finn asked, his heart now booming like a big bass drum in his chest. "About what?"

"About leaving Sunlit," she said.

Finn pulled open the bag of corn chips. "Finally going to do it, Libby?"

He couldn't see Libby as he turned to put the cutting board in the sink, but when he faced her, she wore a determined look on her face as she nodded.

"I'm going to do it. I'm staying through harvest at Sunlit, and then I'm going to make the transition to Three Rivers."

"So, like October?" Finn asked.

"My last day is going to be Halloween," Libby said. "Then I'll come back to Three Rivers. Daddy's going to start teaching me all the things I need to do around here. Probably take a year or more, and then he's going to move into semi-retirement."

Finn knew all of this, of course. He'd talked to his father about it, talked about having a place on Three Rivers Ranch, but Finn had wanted his own ranch. "That's great, Libby," he said, genuinely meaning it.

"You belong there. You're going to do amazing things with that ranch."

She looked up to Rusty and said, "I hope so. It feels like a really big responsibility."

"Well, that's because it is," Finn said. "It's hundreds and hundreds of acres with over a thousand cattle. You've got three operations there, and you employ two dozen people. It *is* a big deal."

"Thanks," Libby said. "That makes me feel so much better."

Finn grinned at her. "But you've been running a big-deal ranch for years, Libs. How many acres is Sunlit Plains?"

"Seven hundred and forty," she said.

"Yeah, seven hundred and forty," he echoed back to her. That was a huge ranch, not something to be trifled with.

"But we don't do cattle."

"It's about the same," he said. "And you're not going to be doing it alone. Daddy's still going to be there, and he's a full-time vet. And Beau is an amazing foreman, and they've got fantastic cowboys. You've got nothing to worry about."

Libby smiled too, though the edges of it trembled with anxiety.

"Let's eat." Edith folded her arms and looked at Finn, always giving him the ability to call on somebody to pray. Since it was just the two of them right now, it was either him or her. So, not much of a choice. But now he could look at Libby or Rusty.

Before he could say anything, the door opened and Henry said, "Knock, knock. Are we too late for lunch?" He entered and stepped back out of the way and let Angel enter first.

She was a beautiful, blonde woman with hair that went down past her shoulders and bright blue eyes. Today she wore a pair of cut-off shorts that seemed a little bit too baggy around her knees and a tank top the color of violets.

Finn had known Henry his whole life, and while he was older than the other man, he'd heard plenty of stories while he was serving in the military of Henry's dates in high school and the type of women that he liked. And oh, Angel was right up his alley. All blonde, blue-eyed, fair-skinned, bright smile, and strong-willed.

Finn hoped he could rope her in somehow and make her his. He wasn't sure if Henry could, though, because Henry had never been the type to want to settle down.

Maybe for the right woman, Finn thought, and he went to tell his cousin that of course he wasn't too late for lunch.

Chapter Eight

"Just take it," Henry said, his voice one that she might attribute to a grizzly bear. "She's not going to take no for an answer."

Angel looked at the huge tote of food that Henry's mother had put together for her. "We really don't need all this, ma'am."

"Well, half of it is Henry's," Chelsea said. She flipped over to the pantry. "Oh, I forgot to get the chocolate-covered pretzels. Henry *loves* chocolate-covered pretzels."

"Momma," he said, "I can buy my own chocolate-covered pretzels."

She whipped the bag out of the cupboard. "But do you have any at your house?"

"Not right now, Momma," he said in total resignation.

"That's what I thought." She put them on top of the other containers, bags of chips, two loaves of bread, and two thermoses. Chelsea looked at the tote, then looked at her son, and then looked at Angel. "I know you don't need this. It just makes me really happy to give you food."

She glanced over to Henry. "Besides, Kelly made most of it, and she's a really great cook."

"We'll take it," Angel said, looking into her eyes and seeing so much of her own mother there. Momma had spent many years feeding and caring for others. It was really what she loved, what she enjoyed doing. And if Angel had brought home a friend and said even half the things Henry had said to his parents, she would load them up with a tote of food as well.

Angel gave her a soft smile and said, "Thank you, Mrs. Marshall. I'm happy to take it."

Chelsea beamed with all the sunshine in the world, all the moonbeams, and every single particle of light that could come from a star. She stepped over to her son and grabbed him in a hug. "Oh, I love you so much," she said, her voice pitching up to cover her emotion. "You call me when you get back to the ranch, okay?"

"Okay, Momma," he said. "It's paved roads all the way. We're gonna be fine."

"I know you're gonna be fine. I just like to know that you're home."

"I'll give you a call when we get there." He looked at

Angel for only a brief moment, turned, and picked up the tote. "All right, Angel. Let's hit the road."

The clock sat just past four, which meant they'd get back to Lone Star by dinnertime. Angel wasn't sure how she felt about that. She kind of wanted to sneak back onto the ranch in the dead of night and pretend like no one knew she'd gone to Three Rivers with Henry.

At the same time, she'd have to face her momma and daddy and Trevor and all the cowboys sooner rather than later. She wondered if they would notice a change in her.

She wondered if she'd changed in just two days' time. She sure felt better, more settled, less like she was about to burst into tears at any moment, less like she might claw someone's face off if they asked her the wrong question.

Because of course, on the team at Lone Star, there were no wrong questions. Everybody asked what they needed to ask, and they had leaders to guide everyone with the correct attitude, the right techniques and procedures.

So Angel didn't have to answer a lot of questions. She wasn't sure what put her in such a terrible mood that she couldn't even answer texts, but sometimes she felt like if she got one more text, it would cause her to implode.

Henry started for the front door, and Angel turned to go with him right when Chelsea grabbed onto her.

"Oh, you get a hug too." She pulled Angel into her chest. "You're such a sweet woman," Chelsea whispered into her ear. "I don't know what-all you have going on, but I can see some weight in your eyes. And I'm going to pray that God will send you some relief and help you carry some of that burden."

Angel didn't know what to do other than hold her. When Angel finally stepped back, she said, "You give the best hugs in the whole world."

Something inside her crumpled, as if someone had picked up an empty plastic water bottle, smashed it flat, and then pulled it back to normal. She blinked a couple of times, the few tears that had gathered in her eyes going right back in. "I haven't hugged my mother like that in a long time," she said. "Sure feels nice."

Chelsea pressed one hand over her heart and said, "I'll pray for your mama too."

"Thank you, ma'am," Angel said, and then she turned to follow Henry before she could start crying again. Strangely, as she left through the side door, she didn't feel like crying. She didn't feel like even talking about her mother would push her over the edge. She didn't feel like she was about to lose her mama the way she had many times in the past.

She'd texted both of her parents by now. After all, she'd been off the ranch for forty-eight hours, and they needed to know she was alive and okay, doing well. She'd sent them some pictures of her and Nevaeh, she'd had Henry take some pictures of them playing with the ball, and she'd sent those as well. They both responded positively and said that the ranch was doing fine. They missed her and they'd see her when she got back.

When she got in the passenger seat, she pulled out her phone and texted her daddy. *We're on the way, should be there within the hour.*

Henry put the food in the backseat and then climbed in behind the wheel. "Everything all right?"

"Yep." She looked up, turned toward him, and gave him a full smile. "I really like your mom and dad. Thank you for inviting me this weekend."

"Anytime, Angel," he said easily, and Angel could tell he absolutely meant it. "You know the way now. You can come anytime you want."

She scoffed and looked away as he put the truck in reverse to back out of the driveway. "I'm not going to come without you," she said.

"Oh, are we going to talk about that?" he asked, his voice pitching up all innocent when it wasn't innocent at all.

"Talk about what?"

"Oh, come on," he said. "Are you going to do that?"

She gave a light laugh and shook her head. "I suppose we should talk about it."

"Why don't you define *it* for me?" he said.

"Why don't *you* define *it* for *me*?" she fired back.

"Holding hands," he said. "How about that? How

about you hugging me, telling me thank you twenty-five times a day, saying how much you liked my family? I mean, if we'd been dating, if we'd gone to dinner a few times, and maybe I'd kissed you, this could be the weekend I took you home to meet them. Like it was for Libby, bringing her boyfriend home to meet her family."

Angel had known Henry for a long time, a couple of years now at least. He'd done a summer internship two summers ago, and he'd been an apprentice at Lone Star for almost a year. She'd known him before that too, as her father had done quite a bit of training at the farrier academy Henry attended, and she'd gone with him several times.

"I see your point," she acknowledged. "But we haven't gone to dinner a bunch of times. We haven't gone to the movies. We haven't kissed."

"Well, technically the last one isn't true."

She could hear the smile in his voice, and she didn't even need to look over at him to see it. Oh, that blasted kiss. If only Angel didn't think about it every night before she went to bed.

"You know what I mean," she said.

"Yeah, I know what you mean," he said. "Because trust me, when I kiss you for real, we're both going to know it, and we're going to know what it means."

She whipped her attention to him now. "You think you're going to kiss me again?"

"I'd like to," he said in a brave, bold voice. "I think

the rule about no dating at Lone Star is a little anti-quated. And I think you have the power to change it. Your daddy's not in charge anymore. He doesn't have to deal with any of the drama at Lone Star. You do. And if you're the one dating, it's your drama."

He gripped the wheel hard, released it, and turned to go around the corner that would lead them back to the highway. Angel watched the landscape. It wasn't all that different than at Lone Star.

"I can also see that point," she said. "But you know my daddy, right? You've talked to him lots of times."

"Yes," Henry said. And he had a guardedness in his voice, which meant he knew exactly what Angel was going to say next.

"He's not the easiest man to convince to do some-thing he doesn't want to do," she said.

"I can see that," Henry said. "But you've made new rules since you've been in charge."

"Yes," Angel said. "And each one of them took hours of consultation with my father." She crossed her arms across her middle, hoping that she wouldn't say too much. "I love Daddy," she said. "I love him with my whole heart. He is a frustrating and irritating man to work with sometimes, but whenever I have a prob-lem, I go to him and I talk it out. He never leads me wrong."

"I got a daddy like that too," he said quietly.

"Going to him and telling him I want to change this

rule would require me to tell him who I'm interested in," she said. "I don't really do that with my parents."

"You haven't introduced them to a boyfriend?"

"Not in a long time," she said. "No one ever made the cut to bring home for dinner."

"Not even that guy I saw you with in the grocery store a couple of years ago?"

Angel shook her head. "We only dated for six or seven months."

"Why did you break up?" Henry asked.

Angel looked over to him, putting every fiery star she had in her gaze. "Because you kissed me, Henry."

He came to a stop at the stop sign. All he had to do was turn right and get on the highway, but he sat there. Angel saw no traffic coming, but Henry made no effort to even look.

"Because I kissed you?" he asked.

She couldn't bear the weight of his gaze. Those powerful eyes and dark beard. He seriously was the most handsome man she had ever met.

"Yes," she said. "Because you kissed me. And I realized how much I liked it and how much I wanted to go out with *you*. And it didn't seem fair to keep going out with Caleb."

The resulting silence smothered her. Angel couldn't believe what she had just admitted.

"Is this why you do my interviews with the door open?" he asked.

"Yes," she clipped out.

"Well, that's gonna change." He made the turn and accelerated quickly, pushing Angel back into her seat, and she realized he was upset, maybe even angry.

"What's wrong?" she asked.

"You've liked me for a whole year, and you've said nothing?"

"You haven't said anything either," she shot back.

"There—is—a—rule," he clipped out. "And I follow the rules because I need this apprenticeship to graduate."

"You got the apprenticeship," she said crossly. "You're going to graduate." She worked up the courage to look at him again. "I have an idea," she said in a much softer voice. "This might sound crazy."

"What?"

"After we watched the sunset last night, I stayed up for a while thinking about us. I'm gonna pray about the situation again tonight. And maybe you can too."

Henry looked over to her and swallowed. He looked nervous and anxious and also, yes, angry. "All right," he said. "Spit it out. My word, we've got to start saying what we mean to each other."

Angel smiled at the exasperation in his tone. "Is that what we've got to start doing?"

"Yes," he said. "Are you holding back with me on things at Lone Star too? Anything with the horses?"

"No," she said. "I talk about the horses."

"So it's just your own feelings you don't talk about."

"Yes," she said. "No. I talk about my feelings. I've literally just told you I've had a crush on you for a year."

"Yeah, well, mine goes back longer than that, sweetheart," he said.

Angel rolled her eyes, blinked, and looked away. "Yeah, well then who needs to start talking first? Me or you?"

"You do," he said. "You've got an idea."

"Yeah." She drew in a long breath, trying to get her tangled thoughts to line up. She didn't want to fight with Henry. She liked holding his hand. She didn't need to talk to her father about the rule. Or did she?

She was in charge. Why did there need to be a no-dating rule at all?

"Do you think any other cowboys would want to ask me out if there was no rule?" she asked.

"I have no idea," Henry said. "But if they do, I will seriously rearrange their faces."

Angel burst out laughing, because she was not expecting him to say that. He did not join her. He growled. "I'm not kidding, Angel. I don't want you going out with anyone but me."

Angel heard the dark, possessive tone of his voice, and it didn't bother her. She felt wanted and needed, desirable and seen. "What if," she said. "We leave the rule in place? That way no one else thinks they can ask me out."

"I'm following," he said.

"What if we don't say anything to Daddy quite yet, and when we do, we do it together? Because I don't really want to talk to him by myself. He really likes you, and I think if we get to know each other more and start dating, there might come a point where, when he looks at us, he can tell that we really care about each other."

"I really care about you right now," Henry said quietly.

"I know," she said. "I care about you too. But I don't know you. I feel like we need more time to get to *know* each other."

"That's what dating is, right?" he asked.

"That's what dating is. So I'm thinking maybe we just keep it a secret."

"A secret," he repeated.

"For now," she qualified. "Nothing has to change, and we'll find ways that we can be together that aren't obvious. I mean, you go to town with Levi. Why can't we just go to town together?"

"Angel," he said. "If we are seen going to town every weekend together, everyone on that ranch is going to know what's going on by the second weekend. They're not stupid."

"I know," Angel said. "I just meant like, you're going to town for groceries, and I drive myself."

"No, we're not driving ourselves to Amarillo and

meeting there for some clandestine date. That's not happening."

Angel huffed out a breath. "Fine. It's a stupid idea."

"It's not a stupid idea," he said. "It's a fine idea, but we need to...finesse it a little bit."

"Finesse it a little bit," she said.

"Yeah," he shot back. "Just like trying different pairs of shoes on horses. This is like that. We'll try one thing, and if that doesn't work, we'll try something else."

"Yeah, but in the meantime, people could figure out that we're dating."

"Dates can happen in a lot of different ways," Henry finally said. "We don't even have to leave the ranch."

"You think so?"

"Number one, I know you'll want to leave the ranch. You *need* to leave the ranch every week, Angel—but it's not for me, and it's not with me." He glanced at her. "It's just something you need to do to take care of you."

She couldn't look at him, but that had never stopped Henry from talking. "No one expects you to work seven days a week without a break."

Angel scrunched up her face and pressed her teeth together. She wanted to say, "I know," in a bratty voice, but the truth was, she didn't know. She did feel like Lone Star would fall apart without her, and the past couple of days had proven to her how replaceable she was.

"I don't like feeling unneeded," she said.

"I'm right there with you, sweetheart," Henry said. "But that doesn't mean you have to work yourself into the ground."

"Okay," she said. "I hear you."

He reached over and took her hand in his. "I'll help you slow down when things feel too hectic," he said. "I'll help you carry some of the load."

She nodded, and Angel relaxed into the drive from his family ranch to hers. He pulled down the lane toward Lone Star, a familiar weight settling over her shoulders. She did love this place, with its rolling landscape, green fields, and oh, she could smell the horses before the stables even came into view.

Henry went past the farmhouse and around the corner, pulling in front of her house only a few seconds later. He put the truck in park and looked at her.

"I won't say thank you twenty-five times a day."

He grinned, then burst out laughing. "That's what you've been worked up over during the drive?" He shook his head as he chuckled and got out of the truck. She followed him into her house, him carrying the big tote right to her kitchen counter like he'd been here dozens of times in the past.

He had not.

Angel almost didn't want to close the door—which was why she hadn't been able to do his performance interviews with the door closed either. Shutting herself into tight spaces with Henry made her fantasies about kissing him again—for real, this time—dance to life.

He unloaded food into her fridge like he lived there, and left other things on the counter. Finished, he finally looked at her, still standing way over by the front door. "You think I'm gonna bite?" he teased.

"No." But kind of.

He laughed, walked over to her, and drew her straight into his arms as if he was a mother hen and she the little chick that needed guidance. She felt so small and so safe inside the circle of his arms. She wrapped her arms around him and hugged him tight.

"I'll see you tomorrow," he said. He bent his head down and brushed his lips from her earlobe down to her jaw. "Okay?"

She looked up at him from beneath the brim of his cowboy hat until she nodded. "Okay," she said.

He left her house with the rest of the food, and Angel wasn't quite sure what to do with herself now.

I better go see Trevor and make sure he's okay.

Her brother might have questions about where she'd been and who she'd been with, but Angel didn't mind telling him. In fact, if Trevor didn't ask, Angel was simply going to tell him so that she could get the teeming things inside her out, get them laid down where she could see them, and maybe even have her brother help her understand what all of this meant.

Chapter Nine

Instead of heading straight back to his cabin, where Henry desperately wanted to get so that he could think through all the things that he and Angel had done and talked about in the last two days, he swung by Shad's house instead.

Shad Roundy was one of the master farriers at Lone Star, and he was an excellent horseman. He could read horses better than anyone Henry had ever seen, except maybe Bard and his own daddy. And he was a real team leader.

Henry wasn't sure why Shad had a bee in his bonnet over Berniece, and he still felt like he should stop by and say something. All the master farriers at Lone Star had their own cabins, so Shad lived alone. If he was married, his family would have been able to live there with him, the way Ford's did. But Shad wasn't married, and as far as Henry knew, he wasn't even seeing anyone.

"I wonder if he would ask Angel out if he could," Henry muttered to himself, instant jealousy and darkness spreading through him. He did *not* want Angel to lift the no-dating rule because he absolutely did *not* want anyone else to ask her out. He'd never heard a rumor or whisper of anyone liking her in a romantic way. But he'd never let on as much either.

He stopped by the back passenger door and grabbed the bag of chocolate-covered pretzels out of the tote his momma had sent. No, he didn't have any at home, and yes, they were his favorite treat. But he had to take something to break the ice between him and Shad. Up the steps he went, where he rapped on the door.

Shad was the morning master farrier, which meant he got done at three o'clock and was always home for dinner, so Henry wasn't surprised to hear him yell, "Come in," a moment later.

Henry went right in and grinned at the man who sat on the couch wearing reading glasses as he held the Bible in his lap. So he was probably in a good mood—or at least a calm frame of mind.

Henry held up the bag of chocolate-covered pretzels. "My momma sent you a gift," he said, because he was not going to claim credit for the pretzels when they were his mother's.

Shad set aside his scriptures and got to his feet as he removed his reading glasses. "Wow," he said with a chuckle. "That's amazing." He moved over and took the pretzels from him. "How are your parents?"

"They're great," Henry said. "Yeah, they're doing just great." He put his hands in his back pockets and waited for Shad to take the pretzels into the kitchen. He set them on the counter next to the fridge and turned to face him. With about fifteen feet separating them, Henry decided he better just go for it.

"I wanted to talk about Berniece," he said.

Shad's expression hardened instantly. "Yeah, Levi said something to me."

Henry nodded. "Yeah, he sure did. And he's not happy, and you're not happy, and Bard has a rule that we don't go to bed angry."

"Yeah, I know about Bard's rules." Shad folded his arms as he leaned back against the counter.

"And I know Levi's probably not going to say anything more to you about it. And I've been really thinking about it. And I really think that I've been prompted to come here and say something. So here I am."

"She's an old horse," Shad said.

"She still deserves good shoes."

"Berniece takes a size that's hard to get," Shad said.

"Then let Levi order in bulk," Henry said. "I'll take

Berniece. You don't even have to manage her anymore. I'll do it."

Shad considered him, not quite angry but not happy either.

"I'll get her the shoes she needs," Henry said. "But that horse needs to be re-shod every two weeks. Her hooves grow fast. She gets abscesses, Shad. Levi has to dig the nails out, which causes pain. It goes against everything we do here at Lone Star. You have to see that."

Shad nodded once, his jaw tight.

"I know you've got a lot going on with the new horses we've gotten in and all the boarding that's coming up in March. They filled us up real full, and I can take on Berniece, because I know it's a problem for you and Levi. And if it's me and Levi, then it won't be a problem."

Shad said nothing, but Henry, with his mouth that never seemed to stop running, kept going. "I'm meeting with Bard this week anyway about Gilligan's shoes, and I can talk to him about Berniece then."

"You're meeting with Bard about Gilligan? Why?"

Henry didn't want to go above Shad. But he didn't have to run everything past Shad. The master farrier above him was Clay, and Henry should run everything about every horse past him....

His rebellious streak immediately bumped against such an idea. He swallowed, trying to get his pride to go down, trying to get the words he wanted to retort to retreat. When they finally did, he said, "Yes, sir. I'll talk to Clay before I go in. Angel wants to be there too."

Shad's eyebrows went up. "Angel wants to be there?"

"Yeah," Henry said, barely managing not to stutter over the word. "I talked to her a little bit about Gilligan when we were in Three Rivers this weekend. She said she'd like to be in the meeting with me. It's something new that we haven't done here at Lone Star before, and since she's in charge now, she wants to be there."

Shad once again didn't say anything, and Henry would have killed to be able to get inside the man's mind and know what he was thinking about him and Angel. Maybe nothing.

"How was she this weekend?" Shad finally asked.

Henry didn't know what to say, because he didn't know how Shad thought Angel should be. He wasn't sure what persona Angel had been putting forth to him, and how Shad had perceived it. He didn't want to say anything bad about Angel or make her feel weak or inferior if his words got back to her. She was their boss, after all, and she wouldn't like him talking about her to Shad in the slightest.

"She...." He stopped and considered his words. "Is very busy here," he finally said. "And it's a lot for her to carry sometimes. At least I think so. I don't know her that well; that's just the gist I got."

Shad nodded. "She works too hard, and that's gonna catch up to her."

Just because Henry agreed didn't meant he had to keep talking about Angel.

"I'll talk to her about passing off some of what she does," Shad said. "She doesn't have many friends, so if you can help too, I'm sure it'll help."

"Okay," Henry said, and he thought his voice sounded semi-normal.

Shad sighed and pinned Henry with his steady gaze. "I know we all just want what's best for that horse."

Henry nodded quickly. "And if there's anything I can do to get it, then I'm willing to do it."

Shad came toward Henry and stuck out his hand. Henry took it as Shad said, "You're a good man, Henry. I want you to take Berniece. Talk to Clay and Bard about her. See what we can come up with."

Happiness surged through Henry that he had been able to say what he needed to say without saying too much, without throwing Angel under the bus, and without making Shad feel like he wasn't good enough.

"You're a good man too, Shad. I really enjoy working with you." They shook hands, and Henry left the cabin.

When he finally got back to his house and took in the tote, he called, "Levi, my momma sent food!"

"Oh boy," Levi yelled from down the hall. He came out a moment later drying his hands with a towel Henry's momma had once sent home with him too. "I knew your momma would send food, and I was just praying I would be well enough to eat it."

He wore a huge grin on his face, and he didn't seem like he'd been sick at all. "Well, Bard sent over a cleaner, and they wiped everything down with antiseptic. So hopefully you won't get sick at all. No one else has, and I think it was really a twenty-four-hour bug."

Henry put the tote on the counter and started pulling out bowls of soup and packages of crackers and plastic containers. Levi picked one up and said, "Oh my word. Is this the spinach Alfredo lasagna?"

Henry laughed. "Yep, that's her special spinach Alfredo lasagna."

Levi grinned and hugged the container to his chest. "I love your momma so much."

Henry laughed again, because he loved his momma too, and he was so glad that she'd sent food for him and Angel.

And as Levi prayed over their dinner, Henry added a small prayer for Angel, that she'd learn how to let go of some of the responsibilities in her life. Then, she wouldn't have to carry such a heavy load.

He also prayed for himself, selfishly asking the Lord to make it possible for him and Angel to find discreet, meaningful ways to be together and get to know one another better. *Dating things, if it be Thy will. Right here on the ranch, where no one knows about them.*

And with those prayers spoken in his heart and

mind, and Levi's big voice saying, "We're so grateful for Henry's momma and this food," Henry closed out his prayer with an "Amen."

Now he just had to pay attention to Angel and make sure she didn't spiral down as far as she had a couple of days ago.

Chapter Ten

"How are you feeling now?" Trevor asked.

"I feel good," Angel said, though the weight of Lone Star had already fallen back onto her shoulders. She looked up as her brother put a plate of food in front of her. "Thanks, Trev."

He smiled at her and watched as he used his hand canes to go back into the kitchen to get his own food. He picked up the plate and then just used one cane on his way back to the table.

"You're moving really good today," Angel said.

"Yeah," Trevor said. "I didn't work at all today. Took the day off."

Alarm bells rang through Angel. "You took the day off today?"

Trevor grinned as he sat down, the affair kind of clumsy and noisy, but Angel was used to it. "Yeah,"

Trevor said. "I had a bad headache last night, so I didn't train with Cutter today."

"Oh," Angel said. "Are you feeling better then?"

"Yeah," he said. "Took some medicine, a hot shower, and then a nap. I feel great." He picked up his fork and stabbed it into the pile of mashed potatoes on his plate.

Angel looked at her own food, which was a barbecued chicken breast, mashed potatoes with country gravy, and corn on the cob, and she wondered why she thought Trevor couldn't take care of himself. It may not be gourmet food or fine dining, but the man ate just fine. He had money to buy groceries, and all he had to do was get a ride into town to pick them up. Angel often took him or just picked up his grocery order when she went to town.

"This looks great, Trev," she said, her voice catching in her chest. Thankfully, it didn't make it up to her throat where he could hear it.

"Why don't you tell me what you have going on?" Trevor picked up his corn and took a bite. He held incredible strength in his lower back, abs, chest, and arms. He had to move his whole body that way sometimes, as his injury had left his legs less than able to support his weight. Trevor still did physical therapy every two weeks to improve his range of motion and strength. He would never be able to walk without some sort of assistance, but he wasn't wheelchair-bound either.

Angel took a bite of her own mashed potatoes. "I went to Three Rivers with Henry Marshall."

"Yeah," Trevor said around his mouthful of food. "He texted all of us; we all know that." He didn't seem alarmed by that. He didn't seem like anything shady was going on, and Angel relaxed into her plan to perhaps just keep Henry a secret for a little while.

You have to finesse it, she told herself, echoing Henry's words in her head. She didn't know how to do that with Trevor. Heck, she didn't know how to do it at all. She looked at her brother, pure vulnerability streaming through her. She loved him dearly, but she didn't have to hide anything from him.

"I like Henry Marshall," she said.

Trevor looked up from his dinner, his eyes widening with every nanosecond that passed. "You *like* Henry Marshall?"

Angel nodded, picked up her knife and fork, and focused on her own food. Trevor's gaze wasn't quite the level of Daddy's, but she still couldn't hold it very well.

"I like him," she said. "Like, I want to go out with him. I want to hold his hand. I want him to kiss me. I *like* him." She couldn't believe she even said the word "kiss" to her brother.

She especially didn't like how, out of her peripheral vision, she saw Trevor wipe his hands and his face and lean back in his chair. "Well, what are you going to do about that?"

"I don't know," Angel said. "I'm talking to you about it. What would you do?"

"What would I do?" Trevor asked. "I don't know what I would do."

Angel let out a huff, scarfed down a bite, and stabbed through a piece of chicken that she cut. "Let's say that I hired somebody to work out here, a girl that you really liked. She's a really good farrier. She leads the team well. You thought she was the most beautiful woman in the world. What if you wanted to go out with her?"

Trevor folded his arms. "We don't have any women working here right now."

Angel glared at him. "But what if we did? And you liked her?"

Her brother looked at her, searching her face—for what Angel had no idea. She put the food in her mouth so she wouldn't say anything else. Like she'd already held Henry's hand, and he'd already kissed her, even though that hadn't been a real kiss and it had happened a year ago.

"Pick up your fork," she said. "Eat." She cut off another piece of chicken, a slow anger simmering inside her. "Is it so shocking that I like a man? That I want to go out with someone?"

"No," Trevor said quickly, and he did pick up his utensils and start to eat. "It's not shocking at all, Angel.

It's just...one of the guys here." She heard the level of insecurity and incredulity in his voice.

"Yeah," Angel said. "I mean, where else am I going to meet men?" She looked over to him. "Heck, I barely leave this place. And when I do, it's just to run errands. It's to pick up medicine for Momma or get groceries. It's to go into the farrier academy and attend meetings, teach a class, or do internship selections. I don't ever go hang out with people my own age. The people my own age are off-limits to me. And I'm just wondering what you think. Like maybe...."

She trailed off, trying to get the right thing to come. "But what if they weren't?" This time, she had enough mental capacity to put a little bit of potatoes on the fork with her chicken. She took that bite, and she looked at Trevor, the question hanging in the air between them.

"You're going to talk to Daddy about the no-dating rule?" he asked.

Angel really didn't want to do that, but she didn't see a way around it. "I don't even know if anything between me and Henry will happen."

"Does he like you too?" Trevor asked.

Angel shrugged one shoulder, though she knew the answer to that question was yes. "I think so."

She focused on her food again, using it as an excellent distraction. "I had a real nice time with him this weekend," she said. "It was an escape that I needed."

"You work too hard around here," Trevor said. "Everyone knows it."

"Will you lead roll call tomorrow?" she asked.

Trevor pulled in a breath, and she looked at him. "Me? You want *me* to lead roll call?"

"Yeah," she said. "I want someone else to start taking over roll call, and I think you can do it." She occasionally had others lead roll call, but not often. "Who did it when I was gone?"

"No one," Trevor said. "We just didn't have it."

Angel shook her head, displeasure and irritation bleeding through her. "See, that's not okay. We need to have roll call every single day, and what if I have a headache?" She gave Trevor a glare. "What if I can't make it out there by seven a.m.?"

She stabbed at her food again. "There needs to be someone else to lead this ranch when I can't."

"I agree."

"Great," she said without missing a beat. "Then I want you to lead roll call."

"I don't really know what's going on with the farriers," he said.

"I don't either," Angel said. "I would text Shad." She raised her eyebrows, a clear challenge in the movement. "In fact, why don't you just text Shad and ask him to do the business at the beginning, and you'll do the inspirational or training part? And then I can talk about schedules. One person doesn't have to do everything."

She caught the surprise in her brother's expression, and it flowed freely in her veins too. "I know this is new," she said quietly. "But I think it's time for something new." She pushed her potatoes around her plate, wishing she was hungrier.

"Henry's momma sent a lot of food for us," she said. "I'll bring you some in the morning."

"Okay," Trevor said. "And okay on the roll call, Angel." He reached over with his fork and tangled it up with hers, starting a little pushing war in the potatoes that made her smile. He'd done this when they were younger, when Daddy lectured them too much, when she wanted to go to prom but didn't know how to bring it up.

She laughed and looked at him. "Okay, Trevor."

"Are you okay?" Trevor asked. "Because you don't seem okay to me, Angel. And you're real good at hiding it from everyone, but you can't hide it from me. And if you start dating Henry, you're not going to be able to hide it from him either."

Angel already knew about Henry's eagle eyes. She'd already revealed a lot to him. He already did see her— the real her, the Angel behind the walls, behind the straight-line face, behind the schedules, behind the roll call, behind the public façade.

Henry already saw *her*.

"Yeah," she said. "I'm doing okay, now that I've had a little break."

"I'm glad," Trevor said. "But what else do we need to change?"

Angel took a deep breath and sliced off another piece of chicken. "Not this chicken, I can tell you that."

Trevor grinned back at her. "I even made the barbecue sauce myself," he said. "It's Granny's recipe."

"We need to go visit Granny," Angel said.

"Yeah," Trevor agreed. "We haven't been there in a while." He scooped up another bite of food, and Angel got herself to take one too.

"I'm not Daddy," Angel finally admitted. "I can't do things the way Daddy did. He has a lot of good systems in place for hiring farriers, for how we get things done around here, and our culture, and I want to keep all that. But I'm not Daddy."

She simply couldn't take another bite, but she looked at the glistening corn on her plate. "I can't work eighteen hours a day with no breaks. I'm so lonely." She looked at her brother, and she knew he saw her too. "I need time away from the ranch. I do want to date Henry. So I'm going to need more help. Maybe another foreman."

She dropped her head again, and this time, when Trevor reached over, it was to cover her hand with his. "Then we'll hire another foreman," he said. "Maybe even Henry. Move someone up from one of the team leads, those who are already ingrained in our culture. It's part of our motto. We promote from within."

"Yeah," Angel said. "What about you?"

Trevor pulled his hand back, already shuttering off his own vulnerability. "I'm too slow for that, Angel. Besides, I don't work with the farriers. I train cutting horses."

"You only work with one horse at a time." Angel knew that. And he had two men who helped him. That was their whole job, to take care of his cutting horse and him.

"Okay," Angel said. "I'll start going over the team leads and see who's appropriate." She looked at her food, put another bite in her mouth, and started to feel more settled. After swallowing, she asked, "Can I sleep here with you tonight?"

"Anytime you want to," Trevor said.

"Do you think it will look fishy if I promote Henry?" she asked. "I don't want the other men to think I'm favoring him. Especially when they find out that we're dating."

"Are you dating?" Trevor asked.

"No," Angel said. "But if we do—let's say we do—and I promote him, then what?"

"What if you promote him first?" Trevor asked.

"Did anyone seem like it was weird that we were gone together this weekend?"

Trevor looked at her blankly. "I don't think so. I didn't hear anything."

Angel nodded, her thoughts becoming more and more wild as they raced around. They tied knots in her head, and she decided she didn't have to know or decide anything tonight. "Thanks for dinner, Trevor."

"Any night you want to come over, Angel," he said. "You're always welcome here." She nodded because she knew that was true. She helped her brother in the morning get ready for work. They always went to roll call together. After roll call, she went back to her parents' house and helped them while everyone else got to work. By eight-thirty, she was fully entrenched with ranch work. She was lucky if she was home before seven.

As Angel finished her dinner, she knew absolutely that she'd spoken true. She wasn't her father, and she couldn't keep doing what she'd been doing at Lone Star for the past year. Something had to give, and she didn't want it to be her.

They'd both finished eating, but neither of them got up. Angel finally looked over to her brother again. "Just say what's on your mind."

"I'm a little nervous about it," Trevor said.

"Yeah, you think I wasn't nervous to come over here and tell you I have a crush on Henry Marshall?" She gave him a wry smile that broke the ice between them.

"All right," Trevor said. "At the risk of sounding like Daddy, I'm gonna give you some advice."

Angel nodded in tight little bursts. She loved her father, and she went to him for everything. She always wanted his advice. And the truth was, she'd always relied on Trevor too.

She listened to him when he spoke, because he said things straight from his heart. No judgment.

"You gotta stop running away from what you don't want," Trevor said. "And go toward what you do." He nodded just one time, his jaw tight. "We don't run away from problems. If there's something that needs to change, we figure out what that thing is, and we work toward it. That's what Daddy would do—that's what Daddy *taught* us to do."

Angel swiped quickly at the corners of her eyes, which had started leaking tears. "You're right," she said. "I know you're right." She tipped her head back and looked up to the ceiling. "I guess I just don't know what I should be running toward."

"You'll figure it out," Trevor said. "You already know some of it."

"Yeah," she said, with a heavy sigh. "I guess I do."

"You can ask God tonight," Trevor said.

"You think I haven't been asking Him?"

Trevor chuckled. "I bet you have, but sometimes when there are a lot of other loud things in the world, God is hard to hear." He covered her hand again, and Angel met his eyes. "And Angel, you know I love you to death, but I think your life has been really loud lately."

This time the tears slipped down Angel's face, because Trevor had spoken true. Her life was loud. She had so much going on all the time. Things to do, people to talk to, orders to put in, jobs of her own, errands to run, schedules to make, men to hire. Henry had told her he'd be there for her if and when she needed to slow down, when she needed things to be a little quieter. Right now, that was exactly what Angel needed.

"All right, Trev," she said. "You're right. I'll figure it out."

"I know you will," he said. "If there's anything I can do, let me know."

"Well, you're going to run roll call for the foreseeable future," she said. "Even if that means you ask Shad or Flint to do it. I don't care. You're in charge of roll call for now."

Trevor nodded resolutely. "I can do it, Angel."

"'Course you can," she said. "I trust you, Trev." And she realized as she said those words that she'd been severely lacking on the trust front. She didn't truly trust Trevor until now. She needed to trust. Trust the men on her team. Trust everyone who worked at Lone Star. Trust her brother. Trust her parents. Trust herself, and most of all, trust God.

Maybe she'd fallen away from doing that. She wasn't sure. She'd known her brother would help her iron out the things inside of her or help her see what she needed to do.

She got up and moved over the two steps to hug him. "Thank you, Trev. I love you to bits and pieces too." Then she cleaned up the dinner he'd made while he texted, supposedly with Shad and others about roll call.

And because Angel didn't want to go to sleep alone in her house, she helped Trevor get in bed and then she moved into his guest bedroom, pulled back the comforter that probably hadn't ever been used, and climbed into bed.

Run toward what you want, she thought, echoing her brother's advice. But the real question was: What did Angel White really want her life to be?

Chapter Eleven

Henry didn't see Angel at roll call. Shad got up on the mounting stool she normally stood on to give the day's announcements, inspirational message, training, and special assignments. He glanced around the crowd of men who'd gathered for roll call like they normally did on any given Tuesday at seven o'clock in the morning.

Angel wasn't hard to find, because she was the only woman there. She currently stood across the crowd from him, her back leaned against the shed, her arms folded, and her eyes on Shad.

Henry should be listening too, but he couldn't bring himself to do it. He wanted to edge through the crowd of men, go to Angel's side, and ask her if she was okay. She looked okay. She wasn't crying. She didn't have an angry expression on her face.

But oh, Henry knew this mask and what it hid.

He did pick up the fact that Shad said they'd have four new horses coming in that day, and he would be giving special assignments for those assigned to greet them. He expected them to know the horses' names and have their stables prepared by the time they arrived.

Henry looked away from Angel then, because if he had to lead a greeting today, he needed to be ready.

"Now we'll hear from Trevor for our inspirational message and training," Shad said, and he got down off the stool. Henry's heart beat a little bit faster as Trevor shuffled forward and started to step up onto the stool.

He couldn't believe the man could do that, though he had two men standing right there, balancing him. With his limited mobility, Trevor should not be climbing up anywhere. Not only that, but Trevor had never spoken at roll call before, and a buzz ran through the men. Everyone seemed to know this felt different, looked different, and absolutely was different.

Levi had told Henry last night that they hadn't had roll call while Angel was gone, and that had surprised Henry too. She had asked Shad or Clay or Flint or Justin —the foreman at Lone Star—to run roll call before. Not often, but they'd done it, so he'd been surprised to find that no one had stepped into the role while she'd been gone.

It also showed him how reliant everyone at Lone Star was on Angel White, and Angel White alone.

Trevor started by reading an email from one of their boarding clients, who claimed that their equine was restless at home after he'd been housed at Lone Star for a couple of weeks. The owner, a man named Lane Rickson, had started to go out to the stable more and more often.

"He said," Trevor said as he held his phone in front of him. "It took me a couple of weeks of this extra attention and care before Central Park settled down, and I realized it was because of the excellent care and attention you gave to my horse while he was at Lone Star. He now expected that, and he was upset that I'd simply put him in the stable and then let him out into the pasture the next morning.

"He wanted more. He wanted me to brush him down for longer. He wanted me to talk to him. He wanted special treats, and he wanted new shoes. When I provided those things—along with more time with him— he settled right back into his calm, gentle self.

"It was a real testament to me about how much you care about the horses that you board at Lone Star. They're not just another body with four legs, more work, shoes that need to be done, things that need to be brushed, fed, watered, and exercised, but that you really care about them there. And I really appreciate that. I can't wait to bring Central back, and I tell everyone that if they need somewhere to board their horse, to go to Lone Star."

Trevor handed his phone to Flint, who stood right in front of him, with his other helpers right behind him.

"That's the kind of service we provide at Lone Star," he said. "If you're not feeling it today, talk to someone you trust, and get feeling it. These horses *are* our livelihood; we *do* care about them. We want every single one of them to go home feeling like they were spoiled while they were here with us.

"Our full-time residents need extra special care. If you're walking by one today and you feel like you have something to say, say it to 'em. I know the horses can't talk back," he said. "But they love being talked to, so don't ever hesitate to tell them things. They're some of the best listeners I know, and they're a lot like God in that way. They can hold any burdens for you, so you don't have to.

"Everything we do at Lone Star is about excellence," he said. "We provide excellent care for our horses, and we take excellent care of the humans who bring them to us. Let's not forget that today."

"Amen, brother!" someone yelled from the crowd. The fire of good hospitality burned in Henry's soul too.

"All right," Trevor said, and he twisted to get help getting down. "I'm gonna let Shad give you the assignments for today." It took a minute for him to get back to solid ground, and everything seemed stilted and clumsy, the way things were with Trevor. Henry loved him in that moment for his ability to put his disability on display.

Henry needed to be more like that. He tended to bottle everything up, hide everything that he felt was a flaw or that others wouldn't like, only put forth the best parts of himself.

Shad retook the stand, blue folders in his hand now. Blue meant arrivals. "We have welcome packets today," he said. "We have a horse coming at nine o'clock, one at ten-thirty, one at eleven, and one at four."

He surveyed the crowd, a very serious expression on his face. "Our ten-thirty and eleven appointments are really close together.

"I expect those stables to be ready, and I'm assigning a team of three to those horses, so we have everything done on time."

Henry gaped at him. It took at least an hour to get a horse settled at Lone Star. Sometimes they had to settle the owners too, as horses could be so fickle sometimes. And Shad was saying they needed to be ready for two horses within thirty minutes of one another?

"We want every guest who comes to Lone Star to feel like they're the only horse here, that we prepared just for them. That's what our welcome packets are for," Shad continued. "The nine o'clock crew has four people on it since you only have ninety minutes to prepare. There are notes in here—we've had this horse before.

"We know who he is, we know what he likes, and we

want his stall prepared appropriately. We're giving this horse to Henry as team lead and his crew, and the fourth person I need over there with him is Copper."

Henry nodded, and Copper, who stood far closer to Shad, took the packet. "It's Gentry Michaels," Copper called out in his heavy Texan drawl. "And Pure Country."

Henry's muscles relaxed. He knew Pure Country; the horse loved him. He could get him off the trailer and settled in his stall in no time. Henry's crew started to move over to him, the two farriers he oversaw, and then Copper joining them as well. Henry took the packet from him as Shad announced who would take the other horses, and he wasn't surprised that Ford got the ten-thirty horse. He was one of the three master farriers here, and he could handle any equine.

Levi got the eleven o'clock horse, which was a great honor for Henry's cabinmate, and he grinned over to him. The four o'clock horse went to Nathan, a good farrier Henry had known for years in the academy.

"All right, guys," Shad said. "Let's make Tuesday the best day this week." He clapped his hands one time, and everyone clapped back once at him. He got of the stool, and roll call ended.

Henry flipped open the folder as his guys gathered around him. He pulled out the picture of the owner, Gentry Michaels. "We've had Gentry here before," he said. "Been here three or four times since I've been at Lone Star."

He handed the picture to the man next to him, a talented farrier intern named Jake, who'd come from Henry's academy too. "Memorize his name, make sure you know what he looks like. There's information there about his wife, his family, what he's doing."

The next sheet showed a picture of Pure Country, Gentry's horse. He was black and white like a cow, with a long black tail and mane, a black face, and a white patch across where the saddle went.

"This is Pure Country," Henry said. "He likes butterscotch candies more than strawberry candy, so let's make sure we've got those in our pockets. He doesn't need a halter to get off the trailer; we can just back him out with a rope. He doesn't like to go into the stall right away, so we'll put him in the exercise ring first. He's a little keyed up when he comes; usually the exercise will calm him down. We could probably put him in the pasture with Susan and Tea Time," he said, naming some of their calmest full-time horses. "So, Caleb, I want you to be in charge of the exercise ring and the resulting pasture that he'll be in."

"Yes, sir," Caleb said.

"Copper, you and I are gonna make sure the stable's ready for him. He always goes in the same one, number twenty-seven. He likes shavings more than straw, so we need to check it. I don't know who's in twenty-seven right now, but they might need to be moved. He likes it because it has a wider opening over the door. He's quite a tall horse, and it gives him more headroom."

"Yes, sir," Copper said.

Henry looked at Jake, who still held the photo of Gentry. "Do you think you want to take on meeting Gentry today?"

Jake looked up at him, his eyes wide and afraid. "I've never met an owner before," he said.

Henry nodded and clapped him on the shoulder. "Everyone has to do something the first time."

Jake swallowed. "Where will you be?"

"Copper and I are on stable crew," Henry said, which was the lowest ranking crew member for greeting a horse. It was the thing the horse saw last, though it was important. Every step along the way was important.

But greeting the owner was something the boss did. Moving the horse, getting him off the trailer, and settling him somewhere where the owner could see he was going to be taken care of was something really talented men did. Men the owner really trusted.

Cleaning the stable, the owner didn't even see. So Henry and Copper wouldn't even meet Gentry today.

"Copper and I'll just be behind the scenes," Henry said. "Or I can come with you to meet him and let you lead." Now that he thought of it, that was probably the wisest move. "That's probably what we should do," he said. "I can be there to shake the man's hand. He knows me. Pure Country knows me too. And then I can just stay out of the way so that you and Caleb can get the experience that you need."

Caleb nodded, his expression resolute. "I can do it, boss," he said.

"I know you can," Henry said. "I know you can too, Jake. That's why you're on this team. That's why we got Gentry and Pure Country. They're both easygoing. It's a great time for you guys to step up into a different role."

Jake nodded as he swallowed. "I can do it, boss."

"Yep, let's do it."

Everyone had their assignments. And even though Jake's right now was to go away and study the profiles, make sure he knew everything about Pure Country and Gentry, and he didn't really have much to do until this horse showed up in an hour and a half, Henry knew that every detail in that folder would be memorized before Gentry pulled onto the ranch.

He'd given himself stable duty because he needed something to keep his hands busy and his mind off Angel. Once they had Pure Country settled for the day, Henry would be back to his farrier rotation, and he'd find folders sitting on his standing desk with his charges for the day.

Angel usually walked around and handed those out, but today, he wouldn't be surprised if Shad, Ford, or Clay did it. And he secretly smiled to himself that she was already doing less now that they'd returned to Lone Star.

This distraction in the stables worked for a little bit, but Copper certainly didn't need instructions on how to move a horse, clean and prep a stable, and get things ready for a new boarder. He wasn't a farrier but one of the more senior horsemen who worked with horses every single day, moving them, exercising them, caring for them, inspecting them, feeding and watering them. He knew every horse at Lone Star, same as Henry, and he worked fast, efficiently, and quietly so Henry's mind was free to wander wherever it wanted.

And he wanted to think about Angel. He needed to see her, find out how her night had gone. Simply breathe in the scent of her skin. He wasn't quite sure how to do that, and she hadn't texted him at all since he'd dropped her off last night.

Was the ball in his court? Could he text her and ask about lunch or dinner? Or about meeting him in the afternoon shade of the eastern barn so that they could talk for a quick minute?

"I'll get the name tag," he said to Copper, and he headed toward their supply room down at the end of the row. They made a name plate for every horse who came to Lone Star, even if they'd only been there once.

Pure Country, of course, had been boarded here more than once, and when Henry found his name plate, it held seven stars. That meant he'd been here eight times—once to get his name plate made, and one star for each of his seven subsequent stays.

When a horse stayed with them ten times, they got a permanent star on their name plate in silver, and Henry couldn't wait to tell Gentry that he only had one more stay before Pure Country got his silver star.

Once he'd hung Pure Country's name on stall twenty-seven, Henry pulled out his phone and tapped on Angel's name.

Of course, he had texted the woman many times over the past ten months since he'd been here at Lone Star, but he'd never had trouble with words with women. He always knew what to say, what questions to ask. His work was quick, and his mind sharp, and he could change directions at any time. He could read any room and any situation in less than a second and pivot on the spot.

He found himself standing in the stable in the middle of the aisle, outside stall twenty-seven, staring at his phone, at a complete loss for what to say. He finally tapped out a message and sent it, hoping it wasn't the lamest thing on the planet. Then he sighed, shoved his phone in his back pocket, and went to find Jake so that they could go over how to greet an owner before Gentry arrived.

He had plenty of time to stew over Angel before he saw her, and he could only pray she wouldn't think his message was the lamest thing she'd ever gotten.

Chapter Twelve

"It was nice." Angel sat down at the table with her momma and her daddy. "Henry grew up on a really nice ranch in Three Rivers," she said. "Well, it's quite far outside of Three Rivers, kind of like we're outside of Amarillo. If I could get in an airplane and fly there, it's probably straight east of here. About thirty minutes is all, but we have to go south to the highway, across and into Three Rivers, and then all the way north. So it really took about an hour and a half to get there."

Neither of her parents said anything, and honestly, Angel wasn't sure what she thought they might say. "You look good today, Momma," she said, and she smiled. "Daddy got your pills all weekend?"

"Yes," her momma said. "He did just fine." She wasn't wearing her oxygen today, which was a good sign. She had a problem with her lungs, where they didn't take enough oxygen from the air she breathed to maintain a high enough oxygen concentration in her lungs and her blood.

So she wore oxygen whenever she moved around too much, and Momma didn't like sitting and doing nothing. She didn't leave the house much anymore, though. But Daddy had gotten her a walker with a seat, and she could always be found cooking, counting, sewing, crocheting, or knitting.

Angel didn't know how many baby blankets she had in the closet down the hall, but she sent one of those and at least two jars of preserves or jams or jellies or grape juice to every woman she heard of having a baby. Everyone getting married got a blanket and preserves too, and sometimes Momma just called the cowboys to her house and started handing out jars of jam.

Angel looked up as her father sat down at the table with a big bowl of cubed watermelon. "Shad went and picked up our groceries yesterday," he said in his usual gruff manner. "This watermelon is actually pretty decent."

It had taken a lot for her dad to give over the shopping to the grocery store. He grumbled about how no one could pick out produce or meat the way he could and that he might get something that he actually didn't want, but then he'd have to take it and pay for it. Angel finally convinced him that it was far easier to put in an order in over the phone or on the internet and just let her drive to town to pick it up. She didn't have time to take him hobbling through the produce section to knock on the end of every watermelon.

"It looks good," Angel said as she traded her spoon for a fork so she could stab a chunk. She put it in her mouth, the watermelon cold and sweet and juicy, and she moaned as she nodded. "Yeah, this is great, Daddy." She smiled at him. He flashed a quick grin at her in return, but something seethed just below the surface. Her phone chimed with the sound that she had assigned to Henry, and her pulse went wild.

Surely Daddy and Momma would know that was Henry, and that Angel had a mega-crush on him. *Not a crush*, she thought. *A craving.*

Daddy looked at her phone too, and it took every ounce of Angel's willpower not to reach out and flip the device over. She wasn't sure what Daddy saw, but Henry's name flashed before her eyes. His text started with, *I hope you're having*, and then it blipped away.

"How was your weekend with Henry?" Daddy asked, every word calculated and measured. He scooped up a forkful of his eggs and ate them.

"She already said it was good, dear," Momma said. "Weren't you listening while you cubed the watermelon?"

Daddy was always listening, so Angel wasn't surprised to find him nodding.

"Yeah, I guess I just wanted more of a report." His blue eyes bore into hers. "A *personal* report."

Angel swallowed, because she knew what her father wanted to hear, but she didn't want to say it. She glanced over to Momma and reached for her hand. She folded her fingers across her momma's and tucked them underneath. "If you must know," she said crisply. "I was so completely overwhelmed with everything that I do around here that when I got Henry's text about being Levi being sick, I went to check on him. I thought I was fine; I really did, Daddy."

She really wanted him to understand, but Daddy never seemed to be harried or overwhelmed. "But I ended up—" Angel's voice gave out on her, because she didn't want her father to hear the emotion climbing its way up her throat.

Her parents loved her; she knew that. Daddy had trusted her with the entirety of Lone Star. She could tell them.

"I broke down in front of him," she blurted out. "Okay? I carry so much around here, Daddy, and I can't do it anymore. It was so nice to have two days off, where someone else fed me, and someone else told me what to wear, and I got to sleep as late as I wanted."

She took a big breath and pulled her hand away from Momma's. "I needed a break, and Henry saw that, because I sobbed my eyes out in front of him. And he whisked me away. That's it."

She wasn't ready to admit her feelings for Henry, not to her parents. A conversation about changing the rules at Lone Star was one she wasn't ready or willing to have within twelve hours of returning to the ranch.

"I talked to Trevor last night," she said. "We both agree that I can't keep doing what I've been doing." She ducked her head and looked at her cereal, which had gone soggy. She wouldn't eat it now, and she didn't care.

"I want to promote someone else to a second foreman," she said. "I carry too much, and I'm not you, Daddy." Her voice broke on the last word, shame, regret, and guilt filled her. "I've tried to be." She shook her head, feeling the long ends of her wig brush her shoulders. "But I can't keep doing it. Trevor can see it; Henry saw it; surely you can see it too."

She lifted her head, pulled her shoulders back, employed her faith—just the way her parents had taught her—and looked at him as she said, "God told me too. I'm not you, and I don't *have* to be you."

Daddy gave her a soft smile and took her hand. "Of course you don't need to be me, Angel. I'm sorry if that was the implication that you got—that I expected you to do all I did."

"Maybe it's a burden I put on myself," she said. "No matter what, I need help. So I'm going to have an open promotion period, where anyone can submit an application to move up the ranks."

"Sounds good," Daddy said.

"Someone who's passionate about horses and their care, who understands our culture. I already asked Trevor, but he doesn't want to do it." She glanced over to Momma. "We have team leads that I could pick from, but I'm also considering our master farriers."

"Can't be a master farrier," Daddy grumbled. "They're too important to the farrier team."

"We have team leads on the horsemanship side too," she argued back. "Our foreman is a horseman. Copper's ready to become management, and he could move up. There are others to move into his role."

Daddy had been retired for a full year now, and she knew more about the day-to-day operations at Long Star than he did.

"So you're thinkin' you're going to take someone from the horseman side?"

Angel thought of Henry quickly. "Either side," she said. "I think a farrier could be an excellent foreman. In fact, it's probably what we should do."

"Why's that?" Daddy folded his arms, and that wasn't a good sign.

Angel wasn't going to back down now. "Because, if I'm running toward what I want, and that's to maintain what we have built here—without me having to do everything—we already have a foreman from the horseman side."

She held up one hand, palm out. "He knows the horse care. He organizes all of their care, and I handle all the farriers. But what if I promoted a farrier to foreman too? And we had one from both sides."

Up came another hand. "And both sides have proper management, which would leave me to manage far less." She pressed her palms together, her fingers lining up and pointing toward the ceiling. "I might even be able to get back to doing some private horseback riding lessons—you know, stuff I used to really enjoy."

She looked over to Momma, and found her smiling for all she was worth. "That's an excellent idea, don't you think, Bard?"

Daddy looked like he'd eaten lemons for breakfast instead of scrambled eggs. He grunted, which Angel took to mean, *Probably a good idea.*

He blinked a couple of times and asked, "What are you running toward?"

"I just said it." She lowered her hands, sure her vision was crystal clear.

"Say it again."

"I want to maintain what Lone Star is and has," she said, "But I can't do it by myself. So, if we want to maintain the excellence in farrier care, *and* we want to be the most excellent boarding stable there is within a five-hundred-mile radius, then I need more help.

"I need people who can lead the people under them the way *I* would do it. So, I want to promote from within. I want both sides of Lone Star to have representation—horsemen and farriers." She used her hands to show both sides, and then she pushed her palms together, her fingers pointing up toward the ceiling. "And then me and Daddy, we're at the top. We're the ones going 'How are the farriers doing? How are the horsemen doing?' and we get reports," Angel finished. "But I'm not the one passing out the folders."

Daddy nodded, his lips pressed together. They twitched, and then turned up into a smile.

"Henry, or Clay, or Levi can pass out the folders."

"I think this a real good idea, Angel."

Relief sagged through her, more than she'd even thought it would. "Really, Daddy?"

"Yes," he said. "It'll be a different kind of management for everyone."

"Yeah," she said. "But we have good men here. And if I'm wrong, then I'll fix it."

"I believe in you, Angel," he said, some of the best words Angel had ever heard.

She squeezed his hand. "Thank you, Daddy." She got up and cleared away their dishes, leaving Momma and Daddy to talk with her not so close. Of course, they could talk with just their eyes, but Angel kept her back turned to them as she noisily cleaned the dishes and put them in the dishwasher.

When she returned to the table, she found Daddy sitting in her spot next to Momma, and they'd clearly been talking. She took Daddy's place at the table and said, "So, I'd love some advice on who you would move to foreman and how we would then shift things around. Looks like we might have two promotions that we're going to be doing."

"Maybe more," he said. "Maybe you need more team captains, new team leads. If you had more people in management, that would free up some of what you do as well."

"Yeah," she said. "I have been feeling like we need a new scheduler." She swallowed, not sure she should keep speaking. "In fact, I feel like we need to have our schedulers who schedule the arrival of our horses be the ones who then meet the owners when they come, so they can say, 'Hi, I'm Justin, and I spoke to you on the phone two days ago about Cloudy White. Welcome to Lone Star.'"

"So you're gonna have people who make the schedule be the greeters?" he asked.

"Yeah," she said. "Why not?"

"That's a lot of scheduling," he said.

"Yeah," she said. "So we hire someone to schedule things, and we move our current scheduler to a...a Welcome Greeter." She made up the title on the spot. "Someone who makes the confirmation phone calls two days before, like we already do, and is also the one who greets that specific owner at the gate."

"That will require a lot of new training," he said.

"We already have team leads who know how to do

that," she said. "So maybe they can make a few phone calls on the days before they become greeters."

"We don't typically assign greeters until morning-of."

"So we'll change that," she said, firing right back. "Things can be changed, Daddy. We can implement new systems. Our culture is good. We have good people willing to step up. Either we trust them, or we don't. And I think we should trust them more by giving them more time to prepare than the morning-of for a new board coming in."

She exhaled angrily. "Heck, Henry had to have a stall, an exercise ring, and his crew ready within ninety minutes of roll call this morning. That's almost not okay. It's almost asking too much of those men."

"Maybe," Daddy said, which was his way of saying he'd think about it, and maybe Angel was right, and maybe she wasn't. Daddy could admit when he was wrong. It just took him a while to get there.

"I'm going to start sketching it out," Angel said. "I had Ford pass out the farrier assignments this morning. That's another thing I don't need to be doing. And I don't want to do it anymore. I'm going to rely on our three master farriers who already know what horses need to be done and when and who knows those horses to make those assignments and drop off those folders."

Daddy simply looked at her, neither confirming nor

denying that he'd even heard her, but she knew he'd heard her.

"Okay. Sketch it all out, Angel. I'd love to see it. And then let's have a meeting with the new foreman and our master farriers and see if we can figure it out."

"Okay," Angel said. "I'm going to make a shortlist of those that I think would be great to move into a foreman position from the farrier side and what the ripple effect of that might be."

"All right," Daddy said.

"All right," Angel parroted back to him, and then she got to her feet. "I'll be in my office for a bit this morning, working on that."

"You've got your phone," Daddy said, and that was his way of saying, *If I need you, I'll text you.*

Angel forced herself to make it all the way to her office in the blue and white barn that she'd painted herself before she looked at Henry's text. It said, *I hope that you're feeling good today. Let me know if you need anything.*

Of course, she wasn't going to let him know that she needed anything, because Angel didn't do that. If she got too close to him, he'd know just by looking at her. But Angel did press her phone to her heartbeat and sigh, because it sure was nice to have someone checking up on her, asking how she was. Surely he'd noticed that she hadn't done roll call this morning. She'd felt his eyes on hers, and she'd looked his way just as he glanced away from her back to Shad.

She tapped out a quick message to him. *Just talked to my momma and daddy about the weekend.*

He started typing a response almost instantly. *I'd love to know how that went. You want to meet this afternoon?*

She stared at his text. "Meet this afternoon?" she asked out loud. "Where would we meet this afternoon?"

Maybe over by the East barn, he suggested. *It's real shady in the afternoon. A couple of cowboys put chairs there. We can just sit and you can catch me up on what your momma and daddy said.*

Then Angel did one of the most surprising things she'd ever done. She allowed her fingers to type whatever they wanted. *All right. I'll meet you there at three.*

Henry came back with, *Sounds good, Angel. See you then.* And this time, he put an emoji that made every organ inside Angel's body melt into a puddle of goo. *All right, Angel. See you there. <3*

Angel arrived in the shade of the East barn ten minutes before three. Henry wasn't there, and she paced the length of it, wondering why in the world she'd agreed to come here.

"Why are you even here now?" she asked herself out

loud. Four camp chairs stood in a semi-circle right in the middle of the patch of shade of the East barn. Men obviously came here to take a break and chat. She and Henry could be happened upon at any time, and then what would people think? Surely he wouldn't warn them away in private texts, because that would also alert them to their budding relationship.

"It's not a relationship," she muttered to herself. But she wanted it to be, and that was the real problem. She made it to the edge of the shade again, then turned back just as Henry came around the corner.

"Oh, hey," he said easily, as if meeting a woman in the shade of the East barn at three o'clock was an everyday thing.

That almost made Angel angry. She didn't respond, and he held up something in his hand.

"I brought you an oatmeal cream pie."

Everything tight in Angel loosened. "You brought me an oatmeal cream pie?"

He granted her that grin that lifted higher on the left than the right, and it made him look so sexy, so handsome, and so devilish at the same time. She moved toward the middle of the barn as he did, and he handed it to her.

"Yep," he said. "I just stopped by my house to check on something, and I grabbed a couple. Figured you might want one. I know you like them."

"You know I like them?" she asked.

"Yeah," he said with a shrug. "I mean, when you set out that Thanksgiving Day picnic a few months ago, you emptied box after box of them into a bowl." He gave a light laugh, and Angel couldn't look away from him.

He'd watched her empty the oatmeal cream pies into a bowl?

"And then I noticed that you pulled back two or three, tucked them in a box, and hid them behind the bags of napkins. I figured you liked them."

"I do," she said, ripping open the package. "If my house is empty of oatmeal cream pies, I go immediately to the store."

He laughed and said, "I'm like that with red licorice and Doritos." He grinned full-force at her. "Now you know one of my dirty little secrets: I'm addicted to nacho cheese Doritos."

She laughed with him, really enjoying the fact that he could give her that release. That this was such an easy, casual place for her to be, on a lazy Tuesday afternoon, after a great weekend and then hard conversations with her parents.

She took a bite of her oatmeal cream pie as they settled into the middle two chairs in the shade of the barn.

Finally, Henry looked over to her. "Well, how'd it go?"

"I didn't talk to them about us," she said.

"I didn't think you would."

"I told them that things need to change, that I can't do everything that I've been doing. And I spent most of today sketching out different positions, maybe new captains, new team leads, and another foreman. A whole bunch of stuff like that. We're going to go over it this week and try to figure out some adjustments inside our personnel so that I'm not shouldering so much."

Henry reached across the arm of the camp chair and took her hand in his. "That's amazing, sweetheart," he said. "I'm really glad you're doing that."

"Me too." She took another bite of her oatmeal cream pie, and since they weren't that big, she could usually eat them in three or four bites. He let her finish, and then he took her trash and tucked it in his pocket.

"Trevor did roll call," he said.

"Yeah." She brightened, both in body and spirit. "He did a great job too, didn't he?"

"Yeah," Henry said. "He sure did." He chuckled. "I was a little worried about him being up on that stool, but he did all right."

"Yeah," Angel said. "I'm going to have Justin build him a platform that has a railing to hold on to when he's up there."

"So he's gonna be doing roll call for a while?" Henry asked.

"I put him in charge of roll call indefinitely," Angel

said. She cut a glance to Henry, noticing that he watched her with an open mouth. "I'm capable of change."

"I didn't say you weren't," he snapped, closing his mouth. "It's just...you haven't changed anything since you took over for your daddy."

"I know," she said. "Which is why I'm a complete basket case and have kind of broken down several times in the last year. It's time for a change. I was just stubborn to see it until now."

"Until me?" he asked.

"Oh, don't give yourself too much credit." She swatted at his chest as she giggled. As she sobered, she nodded. "Yeah, Henry, until you."

She looked at him then, and Henry reached across the small space between them to cradle her face. "I don't mean to be a problem for you, sweetheart."

"You're not," she whispered, her eyes dropping to his mouth. "You have a unique way of helping me see things that are right in front of me."

"Is that a good thing?" he asked.

She nodded. "It's not a bad thing."

"I'm gonna kiss you now," he whispered. "Unless you stop me."

Angel closed her eyes instead, and the anticipation of kissing him was almost more than she could bear. Her heartbeat vibrated through her body, and every skin cell heightened to the potential of being touched by him.

It seemed to take forever until his mouth met hers, and then everything ignited, almost like an explosion. Angel kissed him back, receiving his stroke and hoping that he would kiss her, kiss her, and kiss her for a good long while.

Chapter Thirteen

Henry had not come to the East barn to kiss Angel. However, he wasn't going to complain about kissing Angel. She kissed him back, just like she had last February, but this time was so much better.

Oh, so much better, as she actually wanted him to kiss her, she'd known it was coming, and the passion between them felt like hot lava exploding out of Mount Vesuvius.

Henry told himself to stop, that he was kissing her for too long, but he couldn't make himself do it. Her lips tasted like apples and cool water at the same time, and the way her fingers moved into his hair, dislodging his cowboy hat, made his skin prickle with pleasure.

He finally got control of himself enough to duck his head, breaking their kiss. He leaned his forehead against hers and took ragged breath after ragged breath. She did the same, and Henry didn't want to open his eyes and break the moment.

"I guess we're doing this then," he whispered, and it wasn't a question.

"I guess so," Angel whispered back. She moved, causing Henry to lift his head and open his eyes. Reality rushed back. Oh, he wanted to sink into that fantasy of kissing Angel over and over. Now that he'd done it, and it was real, he had such a better experience to relive than he'd had before.

He reached for his cowboy hat, which had fallen to the ground, dusted it against his chest, and settled it back on his head as he cleared his throat. He sat back in his chair the proper way and took her hand in his again.

"I didn't come here to do that, you know."

"I know."

"I'm real happy you talked to your momma and daddy," he said. "I'm real glad there's going to be some changes around here for you."

"Thank you, Henry."

He took a deep breath, wondering what to do next. With any other woman, he would ask her to dinner and do some reconnaissance to figure out her favorite place, so he could provide the perfect first date for her.

Henry excelled at the perfect first date. He excelled at dating in general. But this was something different. This didn't feel like real dating, though in his heart and mind, it absolutely was.

Then Angel did something awful. She voiced Henry's worst question. "What next?"

He released the breath in his lungs, wondering how to answer. "Indeed," he said. "What do you think we should do next?"

"What would you normally do next?" she asked.

"I'd ask you to dinner," he said. "Take you out somewhere real nice. Have a good time. Try to kiss you again."

She shook her head but grinned too. "I don't think you'd have to try very hard, Henry."

"Well, that's good to know." He looked out over the fields in front of them and said, "I would like to go out with you. A real date. Not a fake weekend together."

"I'd like that too," she said. "I'm not sure when it will happen, though."

"I can be patient," he said.

"Can you?" she teased. "Is that one of your strong suits?"

He burst out laughing because no, patience was definitely not one of his strong suits. "Not if you ask my daddy," he said with a chuckle.

Angel grinned at him too, and he leaned over and brushed his lips across her cheek. "I have to go, sweetheart. I told Levi I'd help him with the four o'clock delivery. And I've still got another horse to shoe after that."

"Okay," Angel said, her voice sounding small and far away.

"I'll text you," Henry said. "Maybe I'll call you or something. We'll keep in touch a lot more than we did before."

"You better," she said.

"We'll find a time we can go out," he said. "Where it's not a big deal, where there won't have to be major explanations."

"Okay."

She nodded, and he took her face in his hand again, this time with fingers on one side of her chin and his thumb on the other. "We'll find a time, Angel," he said. "I promise."

"Okay," she said again.

Henry leaned down and matched his lips to hers one more time. He didn't hold on, didn't stroke for all he was worth, didn't try to get every last ounce of Angel the way he had last time. He simply gave her a kiss, glad when she received it.

"I'll talk to you later." And with that, Henry pulled himself away from Angel and escaped the shade of the barn. Heat filled his body, and not just from the sun that now touched his skin, but from all that had happened in those ten minutes in the shade.

His mind buzzed with thoughts. She was hiring new people, creating new positions, and he wondered if he would be one of them. He wondered what the other men would say if they knew he'd been kissing her in the shade and then got promoted.

A sick feeling descended into his gut. *Surely she won't promote you if you don't deserve it*, he thought. He didn't want to move up the ranks like that. He wanted to move up because Angel thought he was worthy of moving up, of being a captain. He didn't want to do it because she liked him.

Pushing those thoughts aside, Henry went to do his job. He helped Levi bring in the last horse for the day, and then he went and found Tesla to shoe. When he got back to the cabin, Levi had just opened the microwave to pull out some reheated meals.

"Your mom's lasagna," he called as the door closed behind Henry.

"Bless you," Henry said. "I'm going to shower first."

"Yep, I'll heat it up for you while you get dressed." Levi settled at the table with one bowl in front of him and one waiting on the counter to be heated up for Henry.

"Thanks, Levi," he said, and he really meant it. He loved Levi and loved living with him, and he loved that they took care of each other. He wanted to tell Levi about the upcoming restructuring, but he knew he shouldn't. So he kept his mouth shut. He showered, then ate, and then he pulled out his folder on 3D printing.

Levi settled in front of the TV, and Henry joined him, bringing his lap desk with him as he often did. If he didn't have a project he was working on, he'd journal through his thoughts at night while they watched game shows and sitcoms.

Tonight, while Levi blurted out answers every now and then during *Jeopardy*, Henry went through his notes on 3D printing from college many years ago. He never thought he'd use that education in industrial engineering as a farrier, but he'd been wrong. He had a few phone calls he needed to make, and he made notes of those. He wrote down the materials he wanted to ask about, and about the time Levi started yawning, Henry closed his folder.

"What you working on?" Levi asked.

"3D horseshoeing," Henry said.

"3D what?" Levi asked.

Henry grinned at him. "Sorry, that came out wrong. I'm tired."

"Yeah, you've had a busy few days." Levi pinned him with his gaze. "How was going home? You never did say."

"I said," Henry said. "It was great. My mom took great care of us. We had a really relaxing weekend."

"I'm glad," Levi said. "It was a little wild Angel not doing roll call today, wasn't it?"

"Yeah," Henry agreed, because it was. "I'm glad she's letting Trevor step up, though. He's a good guy."

"True," Levi said. "He knows a lot about horses. Not much about farriers, though."

"No," Henry said. "But he's right. And they want

Lone Star to have a certain culture. He can definitely deliver that, so Angel doesn't have to do it."

"I liked that email he read."

"Yeah," Henry said with a laugh. "Because you took care of Central Park. So it was like a direct compliment just for you."

Levi laughed and said, "So what? Everyone needs a direct compliment every now and then."

Henry nodded, suddenly sober. "You're so right about that, Levi. Everyone *does* need a direct compliment about them, about what they've done, about who they are, every now and then."

Henry wondered when the last time was that he'd paid a compliment like that to someone around him. He told Jake that he'd done a great job, welcoming Gentry to the ranch, but was it a direct compliment about what the man could do and his abilities, or was it just a good job? Henry wasn't sure. He reached for the journal he kept underneath the coffee table and pulled it out.

"I'm going to bed," Levi said.

"I'm right behind you," Henry said. The TV switched off, and Levi padded down the hall, leaving Henry in the living room with the kitchen lights shining behind him. He quickly wrote down his ideas about compliments, and he made a list of all the people he saw on a daily basis.

He could definitely start to do more in building their morale and helping them know and understand that their contributions to Lone Star were seen, if not by Angel, Bard, and Trevor, then by him.

He snapped his journal closed and headed down the hall to his bedroom. Henry wasn't the type to always kneel down at his bedside and pray. Most of the time, he was so tired he collapsed in bed, got his covers exactly how he wanted them, and then remembered that he needed to thank the Lord for the day he'd had.

So then he'd pray in bed, his eyes closed, his thoughts grateful, and he believed that God counted those prayers. But tonight, Henry stepped out of his usual routine.

He knelt down, folded his arms on his bed in front of him, and closed his eyes. This type of formal prayer wasn't his favorite thing to do, and he had no idea what to even say. He'd had a pastor once who'd said, "God wants to be talked to right out loud," and Henry hardly ever did that. Only over meals, probably.

Most of his prayers stemmed from his heart, murmured through his mind, or got uttered quickly in a state of emergency. They weren't heartfelt, out-loud conversations with God, hardly ever.

"Dear Lord," he said. "Help me to know how to pray." He figured he might as well start there. His momma and daddy had taught him as a little kid, but again, Henry had been out of practice for a while. Everything in the room seemed to come to a standstill, and

Henry felt the presence of the Lord more powerfully in that moment than he ever had in his life.

"I'm really grateful for a good weekend," he said. "Really grateful for good parents and a momma who takes care of me and all those around me by sending food. I'm grateful Angel and I had a chance to get away, and I'm real grateful that something started there. I don't know how to navigate this ground. I'm going to need a lot of help. I don't really want it to be a secret, but I can understand why it needs to be for now."

He rolled his neck from side to side, feeling it pull in an almost uncomfortable way. "To be honest, Lord, this thing feels a little bit forbidden." He sighed, almost angry with himself. "Fine, it feels exciting too. Okay? I'm excited about it. I like this woman. I think she likes me. I feel more settled now. I don't feel as wild and as young. And yeah, it's exciting to be in a secret relationship that no one else knows about."

He felt himself settle out of that wildness he'd just spoken of. "But I don't want to be a liar. I want to work hard. I want to do good. I want my life and my work to matter. So if there's anything that I need to do, if there are different things I need to say or different paths I need to go down or something I need to study, I ask for Thy help in guiding and directing me to those things."

Henry ran out of words, something that rarely happened to him. So he closed simply with, "Bless my momma and daddy. Bless Paul, John, and Rich. Bless everyone here at Lone Star. Amen."

There was no resounding "Amen" to come behind it from the congregation or his family at mealtime. Henry held very still and tried to listen for choirs of angels who would add their seal of approval to his prayer. He didn't hear them so much as he felt them, especially in the presence of his granddaddy, who had passed away more than fifteen years ago. He didn't carry the Ackerman name, but he *was* an Ackerman, and he wanted to do good. He wanted to make his momma and daddy proud, and his grandma and grandpa proud, and Three Rivers proud.

Henry finally climbed into bed, snapped off the light, where he finally got to relive his amazing outdoor kiss with Angel as he drifted off to sleep.

* * *

The following day, Henry paced in front of his standing desk, his phone pressed to his ear. "Yeah, all right, Charles," he said. "I understand."

"I know it's not what you want to hear," Charles said.

"No," Henry said. "It's not, but I understand. I get the limitations of things. It's not like it's your fault. I'm just a little frustrated."

And frustrated he was. It streamed through him like

white river rapids racing down a hill toward their final destination of a waterfall, where he would be drowned at the bottom. "Thank you for your time, Charles. If you think of anything or anyone else I can talk to, give me a call."

"Yes, sir," Charles said. "Always good to talk to you, Henry."

His frustration eased a little bit, and he said, "You too, Charles. Have a good day." The call ended, and Henry used his willpower to keep from throwing his phone against his desk and then stomping away like an angry badger.

Instead, he gently set his phone on his desk, sighed, and took his head in his hands, running them through his hair as he looked down at the jumble of notes on his desk.

None of it had to do with a horse that needed to be shod. All of it had to do with 3D printing and the limitations they had with the materials they could use. It turned out some of the lighter metals that he wanted to try simply broke under 3D printing. There weren't printers advanced enough to do that, and the layering techniques that the metal had to go through with blacksmithing caused the shoes to be brittle and hard. They still wouldn't work for Gilligan, and Henry felt like he was back to square one, trying to shoe horses in the Dark Ages.

"Shoes would only last five days," he muttered to

himself, circling the big number five he'd scrawled on the notebook in front of him. There was no way he could take a proposal to Bard and Angel about having to get 3D printed horseshoes every five days.

It would take that long just to cut them all and weld them all together. So they would need a full-time person making shoes just for Gilligan, and that so wasn't reasonable or feasible.

"No way," he muttered again, and he slammed closed the folder of his notes. Various pages stuck out the sides in a jumbled mess, and he carefully tucked them all in and arranged them so they were all standing up straight like soldiers.

He put the folder on the shelf under his desk and looked at the brown one there. That meant he had a horse to work on. He always had plenty of work to do around the ranch, but part of their commitment to excellence was to find a way for every horse to be cared for individually, to have their personal needs met, and for their owners to know that Lone Star was the only place that was going to provide the quality service that their horse deserved. And that included shoes for Gilligan.

Failure streamed through Henry now as strongly as the frustration had just a moment ago. In times like these, he wanted to call his momma and be reassured. Talk to his daddy about what he should do next. So Henry picked up his phone, picked up his head, and tried to pick up his spirits as he texted his father.

Need some advice, he said. *Working with a horse named Gilligan, and I can't find a pair of shoes that he likes.* He spelled out the trouble the horse had with his back frog and how he needed something really light and really soft. He sent that text and quickly followed up with, *I've been exploring 3D-printing options and nothing that I've found so far will work. Do you have any contacts or anyone I can talk to about shoes for a horse like Gilligan? Let me know.*

Henry navigated over to his text thread with Bard as he told him that he would like to set up an appointment sometime this week. It was already Wednesday. He started a new text thread with both Angel and Bard in it, and said, *I've hit a roadblock with the 3D printing for shoes for Gilligan, so I don't need to meet with you quite yet. I'm still working on some possibilities and exploring some other options. Let me know if you want me to bring in what I've got, but it's not much. It's not a solution that we can do, and I don't have another option for Gilligan at this time.*

Henry hated sending that text, but he did it anyway because it was his job. Then he picked up the two folders he had to work on that afternoon, and he headed out of the stable, where the desks were, to get his next horse. That horse also deserved excellent care, and he could hold secrets just as well as Gilligan or any other horse.

So Henry set aside his cares and troubles over the

3D printing, and the fact that he and Angel had no plans to meet up again that day or the next day or ever again, and he focused all of his attention on making sure that Cocoa-Mocha felt like the king of all equines.

When he finished, he texted Angel privately to find out if he could see her that night, and if they could have another clandestine meeting somewhere here at Lone Star.

Then he prayed she'd say yes, because he really needed something to look forward to.

Chapter Fourteen

JJ Walker trudged up the stairs, the backpack on his back feeling heavier than it had when he left that morning, though he had turned in a couple of the library books he'd borrowed for his midterm. He really wished this building had an elevator, but it didn't. Sometimes, JJ really wished he hadn't decided to come to Amarillo State College at all. At the same time, his life had been completely stagnant at Seven Sons Ranch, which his father co-owned and still worked eighty hours a week.

JJ was named after his dad. The two J's stood for Jeremiah Jonah, and he felt like he had a lot to live up to. He did. The Walker name really meant something, and the seven brothers that comprised the family, along with their wives and all their kids, had taught JJ that. One of his uncles, Uncle Tripp, had adopted his wife's son,

Oliver, and JJ grew up hearing, "Walkers are winners. The Walker name means something, son," from everyone in his family—all the men, Grandma and Grandpa too.

Walkers are winners, he thought. The family motto his momma had put into place had started as a joke, but later on, whenever JJ didn't do that well on a math test, or he didn't make the football team as a junior, or he wasn't ever sure what his life was going to be, his momma would take his face in her hands and say, "Remember, JJ, Walkers are winners."

JJ didn't feel like a winner right now. It was the beginning of March, and the last of his midterms were done for now. He still had two more months of school before finals, and then he wasn't sure what he was going to do. He'd come to Amarillo with Rich Marshall, who'd already said he was going back to Three Rivers to work his family's ranch for the summer.

JJ didn't want to go back to work the ranch until he knew it was what he was going to do with his life. And right now, he had no idea what he was going to do with his life. He liked to work with his hands, he knew that. So he'd taken some computer classes, and he was really good at pulling apart machines and putting them back together. Maybe he could be a mechanic. He'd started looking into some of those classes, but he hadn't taken any yet. He wasn't great at math, and he didn't like to sit down and read like his daddy.

He'd cook if he had to, so he'd managed to keep himself alive these past several months since he'd left his parents' house. But a lot of that had to do with the other two men JJ and Rich had moved in with.

Noel Tyler and Tate Reynolds. JJ had connected to Tate the most, as Tate felt a little lost and adrift as well. He didn't know what to do with his life any more than JJ did. They'd taken a few classes together this semester, just to be there for each other through the homework and projects.

Everyone these days was real big into group work, and JJ hated it. But with Tate in his classes, he had someone to talk to, bounce ideas off of, and who'd do his part of the work.

He reached the third floor and pushed out of the stairwell, feeling hot and sweaty, though the true heat hadn't reached the Texas Panhandle yet. Still, his breathing came quick, though JJ wasn't one to just sit around and do nothing. He also didn't get up and run or lift weights in the morning. Merely walking around campus seemed to be enough to keep him in shape just fine.

His stomach growled, as it was near dinnertime, and he started to pray that perhaps Noel had brought home something from the pizza parlor where he worked, or Tate had been struck with a brilliant idea for something to make for dinner that night.

He turned the corner to go around his apartment,

where only two doors sat right across from each other. He instantly came face to face with a beautiful woman standing there. The closer he looked, the more he realized that she was *not* very old, maybe not even a woman yet.

She turned toward him, and JJ came to a complete stop. He'd been out with girls before in high school. He'd been to prom. He'd had a girl he went with for a little while, sneaking kisses at school around the corner by the band room, and maybe even out on the ranch that his daddy and momma didn't know about.

But this girl—and she was definitely a girl—and if she wasn't, she was a freshman for sure, was different. She had long, auburn hair that bordered on brown and blonde at the same time, with that hint of red in it. She painted her lips with something soft and glossy and pink, and JJ licked his just to make sure he still had a pair of lips. She seemed just as frozen as he was, but something inside him told him to get moving.

So he did. He took a couple of steps forward and asked, "Are you lost?"

There were two apartments in this hallway, and they both housed four men each. He'd never seen a woman over here, in fact, and he wondered what to do next. He couldn't just fit his key into the lock and walk away. Not if she needed help.

The cowboy gentleman inside of him wouldn't allow

him to do that, so he paused just out of arm's reach of her.

She swiped angrily at her eyes. "I don't think I'm lost," she said, her voice quivering the littlest bit. "I think my brother lives here."

Oh, boy, JJ thought. "Who's your brother?" he asked, his heartbeat pounding along in time with the way her eyelashes fluttered. She was definitely trying to hold back tears, and JJ wasn't sure what to do with crying women on the best of days, and today wasn't the best of days.

"I just got separated from my family," she said. "We agreed to meet at his apartment."

"Okay...who's your brother?"

She sniffled, her chin wavering, and JJ decided to move this conversation somewhere less awkward. "I'm in there," he said. "You want to come in and get a drink?" He moved closer to her, catching the scent of something smooth and clean and floral—and he sure did like it.

She didn't answer, and JJ did fit his key in the lock and opened the door. "You can come in, if you want," he said. "We'll figure out who your brother is and where he is." The interior of the apartment didn't smell too bad, though sometimes it could smell like dirty laundry or sweaty shoes. Four men lived there, after all.

JJ appeared to be the only one home right now, though sometimes his roommates hid out in their rooms.

"I'm fairly sure we have orange juice," he said. "And

water, of course. Probably some chocolate milk. Rich likes that." He wasn't sure if the woman had come inside with him, and if she had any brain cells at all, she wouldn't.

He turned and looked over his shoulder and found her hovering in the doorway. "If your brother lives in this apartment or the one across the hall, I probably know him. I can just call him for you."

She nodded, her eyes darting around the apartment. "His name is Tate," she said, and that made bombs go off in JJ's mind. His heart plummeted to the soles of his cowboy boots.

Of course this was Tate's younger sister.

The moment she'd said his name, JJ could see all the pieces of his best friend in her face. Tate didn't have as much red in his hair, and he kept it shaved short anyway.

He'd seen pictures of Ruby, but her hair hadn't been down. She competed as a gymnast, and her hair was always slicked back.

"Sure," JJ said as nonchalantly as he could with his pulse galloping through his veins like wild stallions. "You're Ruby Reynolds."

Her gaze came to his then. "You know me?"

JJ gave a strained laugh that surely sounded like a serial killer about to attack. "No, but Tate's shown us some family photos." He gestured to the tiny dining room table. "He lives here. This is his apartment."

"It is?" Relief washed through her face, and JJ moved over to the fridge.

"You want water, juice, milk? We've got it all."

"I'll take some juice," she said, and he wasn't sure why that made him so happy, only that orange juice was his favorite drink of all time. If he could mix soda pop with it, that only doubled the happiness quotient.

He pulled out the carton of orange juice and a bottle of Sprite. "You want a little soda mix-in?"

"There you are, Ruby," someone said outside his field of vision.

JJ turned back toward the door, holding the juice and the pop. A woman, clearly Ruby and Tate's mother, entered the frame and took Ruby into her arms.

"You can't be wandering off like that."

"We agreed to meet back at his apartment." Ruby sniffled against her momma's chest. "You guys left me in the museum." She straightened and glanced over to JJ, and his hands had turned totally slick.

Maybe because of Ruby's presence. Maybe because the soda pop bottle had already beaded with condensation. No matter what, the bottle of Sprite slipped from his hands, and his ninja-like reflexes abandoned him in his moment of greatest need.

The soda pop hit the floor with a horrifying, loud, plastic *thunk!* against the linoleum. Suddenly, everything about his apartment was dirty, dingy, and downtrodden. They did have cleaning inspection next week, which meant they hadn't tidied up in a while, and all of these thoughts ran through his mind as the bottle bounced up in slow motion.

It tipped toward Ruby and her mother, hit the floor again with a less impressive thud that still managed to pop the lid right off.

Soda sprayed toward them in all its fizzy glory, and both women shrieked and held up their hands to shield their faces.

JJ stood there with the orange juice carton in his hand, completely humiliated and staring as clear soda dripped from Ruby's hands and her mother's elbow.

"Hey, hey."

JJ recognized his best friend's voice, and Tate added, "What is going on here?" as he arrived in the apartment too. He scanned his momma and sister from feet to face, his eyes widening.

Ruby shook her hands of the offensive, sticky soda while her mom simply blinked with wet eyelashes. JJ could only stare, but thankfully, something kicked at his brain that told him to move, to act.

He set the orange juice on the counter and spun to get a towel from the handle on the stove. "I'm so sorry," he gushed as he stepped toward Ruby and her mother. "I didn't mean to drop it."

JJ's cowboy boot came down in a puddle of Sprite, and oh, it hadn't had time to dry into a sticky mess. He slipped, his balance getting thrown completely off.

This cannot be happening, he thought. He threw his arms out to try to catch himself so he wouldn't embarrass himself further.

Tate lunged through his momma and sister, his arm reaching for JJ's. He grabbed onto him and said, "Whoa, whoa, cowboy, I got you."

They righted themselves, thankfully, and JJ looked straight into Tate's eyes. "Your sister's looking for you," he said needlessly.

Tate grinned and laughed. "Yeah, brother, she's right there."

Foolishness filled JJ, and he was so done with today.

"Did you meet her?" Tate stepped back to Ruby's side and put his arm around her. "This is my little sister, Ruby. Rubes, this my best friend, JJ—Jeremiah Jonah—Walker." He grinned like they'd all have birthday cake later, but if he knew what ran through JJ's mind, Tate might feel differently.

"And my momma," Tate said. "Louise." He looked at her too. "Daddy's coming up."

As if summoned by his son's words, another man came into the apartment—their father.

JJ had already made a complete fool of himself, and he wasn't going to stick around and flirt with Ruby, wasn't going to try to get her number, nothing. He'd put her straight out of his mind, because she was nowhere near old enough to date him.

He was almost twenty-two, and she hadn't even

graduated from high school yet. So he stepped forward and with his towel-less hand, he shook hands with everyone, feeling all of the stickiness on Louise's and Ruby's hands.

He retreated to get some cleaning wipes while Tate led his family into the living room, where they settled down to chat about Ruby's college campus tour. JJ got himself out of the room as fast as possible, mentally grumbling to himself about how he had the worst luck when it came to almost everything.

He headed to his bedroom and closed the door, paced to the window and back, and then told himself, "Walkers are winners," under his breath. "Things like this happen, JJ. It's not just you."

He sank onto his bed when some of his nervous energy had finally abated, tossing his cowboy hat behind him. With midterms done, he had the weekend ahead of him without being on the work schedule. But as laughter floated down the hall from the living room to his ears, he couldn't help but think that God had cursed him nonetheless by bringing the gorgeous—and completely unavailable—Ruby Reynolds into his life too soon.

Chapter Fifteen

Caroline Thompson stood at her front window and watched the sky lighten and darken every few seconds. Clouds rolled across Three Rivers, and they moved through her soul too.

"It's going to rain tomorrow," she muttered to herself.

"What did you say?" her sister asked.

Abigail had come from Colorado Springs for Caroline's wedding. Her mom and dad had come too, as had her brother. Belle still lived here, of course, with her daughter, Judy. Caroline had enjoyed having her family in town for a few days. They'd all met Dawson. He'd taken them around on the Three Histories tour, something he'd done for Caroline last fall.

They enjoyed themselves, visiting the ranches, museums, and parks surrounding Three Rivers. But her wedding was tomorrow, and they'd planned an outdoor event in mid-March at the Rhinehart Ranch. The house she and Dawson would live in had been finished two weeks ago.

Dawson had moved in and had been living there by himself for a fortnight. Caroline was eager for this next chapter of her life to begin, but she didn't want it to start with a thunderstorm.

"Dear God," she prayed to the window, to the wind outside, to the gray sky, to the Good Lord Above. "The wedding will really only be a half-hour. Thou can calm the seas for Jesus to walk on. I know Thou can clear the skies for half an hour for my wedding."

Someone yelled from behind her. The door leading into the kitchen slammed. She turned away from the window and went into the kitchen to find Belle there, lifting her recyclable grocery bags onto the counter.

"Whew. That wind is no joke today," Belle said.

Caroline's frown deepened, moving all the way into her toes as she went to help her sister unload the groceries.

"Zona is staging True Blue just in case we need to move inside," Belle said without looking at Caroline.

Caroline wanted to pull a move Dawson often did. When he didn't like the conversation, he'd grunt, he'd glance, he'd think, and then finally, he'd say something. It was a good recipe for how to deal with something so that he didn't say something he would regret later, and Caroline employed it now.

She grunted; she glanced at Belle; she went back to unloading grapes and lettuce and cherry tomatoes while she thought about a proper response. She didn't want to get married in True Blue, the Glover family barn at Shiloh Ridge Ranch. Lincoln and Misty had gotten married there, as well as a whole host of Link's aunts and uncles. It was a beautiful facility, Caroline could admit that.

Big space. Easily decorated. Full kitchen. Very rustic, and perfect for cowboys. Caroline could have all of that. But it had nothing to do with her and nothing to do with Dawson.

She wanted to be married on *his* ranch with his hens, his crows, his dog, and his family. She wanted to be part of the Rhinehart legacy. And she would be tomorrow when she took on his last name. She wanted to do it at his ranch, silly as that may be.

They didn't have a nice indoor facility with space for a large number of people. And the Rhineharts, being old Three Rivers blood, knew everyone in town. Heck, the entirety of the Glover family would come from Shiloh Ridge.

Finn and Edith, and Alex and Nikki, and a whole host of cowboys from Three Rivers Ranch. Golden Hour Ranch was owned by Brit Bellamore and he and his wife were coming, as well as his three kids and their spouses and families.

The cowboys took care of each other around Three Rivers, and Dawson had been working with many of them for decades. And if not Dawson, then his daddy. Caroline was old enough to know that a wedding wasn't just about the bride and groom.

"What about...?" she started to ask, but she couldn't finish. There was nowhere on the Rhinehart Ranch that could house three hundred people. Absolutely nowhere.

"I'm just going to pray that there's no rain," she said. "I only need it not to rain for thirty minutes right in the middle of the day. Surely God can do that."

Belle looked at her, a nervous tic of apprehension in her eyes. "I'll pray for the same thing."

Belle was going to stay in Caroline's house. In fact, Belle had been healing and recovering from her divorce over the past year and a half so well that she was nearly in the position where she could purchase the house for herself. She was going to work on that after the wedding, but for right now, she was renting it from Caroline for only what it cost to pay the mortgage.

"Auntie C, look at my dress!" Judy said, and Caroline turned around to find her niece standing there in a beautiful, pale yellow dress.

"Oh, it's so beautiful." Caroline crouched down to hug her niece. "Do you think you can wrangle the hens?" They had planned for the hens to wear little collars around their feathered necks, tied with twine that would go to one main piece that Judy would hold as she walked down the aisle with the hens. She was the only flower girl as Abby's kids were a little bit older and would simply walk with the family.

"I can do it," Judy said. "I've been practicing real good."

"That's great." Caroline smiled and straightened and stepped into her mother's arms. "It's going to rain tomorrow, Mama," she whispered.

"Oh, it's not going to rain," Mama said. "I've been having a good long talk with both Mother Nature and God, and it's going to be fine."

Caroline wanted to believe her, so she held on to her shoulders in another long, tight squeeze, and then she stepped back. "All right," she said as she drew in a deep breath. "Belle just got back with the groceries, and that means we need to get started on the feast."

Dawson and his family would be dining at Caroline's house tonight. He was bringing Brandon, Duke, and Arizona, and their four kids would come, of course, as would Wade and Abby. Two families coming together for one final meal before they were all officially joined.

Caroline had such a vision of what her wedding would be like, with the crows hopping down the aisle ahead Dawson, and Judy leading the hens after the wedding party had marched their way to the altar.

Dawson had included his friends and family

members in the wedding party, but Caroline hadn't asked any friends to be in the wedding party except those that were married to Dawson's cowboy friends. Only her family would walk in the wedding party.

Judy would follow with the hens. Then the crows, if they could be properly enticed with the right shiny things. Dawson would walk down the aisle with Ruffin at his side, and then Caroline and her daddy would come last. She could just *see* it playing out, with gorgeous rays of sunshine tickling the tent that they could hopefully put up in the morning—if the wind wasn't too strong.

Though Caroline owned the house, Mama moved into the kitchen and whipped out her recipe cards. She handed the funeral potatoes to Belle, the artichoke dip to Caroline, the walking taco dip to Abby, reserving the spiced apple tarts for herself.

"This is a tight space," she said, and Caroline almost bristled at the near criticism of her house. "But I believe we can do this." She looked at Caroline and Abby with pursed lips. "You two don't need to be in here for a few minutes. You can do your dips at the table and then move out. Belle and I have more work to do, and we'll be in the kitchen."

"Sounds good, Mama," Caroline said, because she didn't want to argue. She was happy to have her sisters and parents here.

"What are Danny and Daddy doing?" Belle asked.

She cut a glance over to Caroline that looked a little furtive, something secretive. Caroline watched her, on high alert now. "They're doing something at the house."

"Something at the house?" Belle asked, echoing Caroline's thoughts. "What does that mean?"

"I don't know," Mama said, clearly flustered. She turned away from everyone and started washing her hands at the sink. "Daddy said they had to go up to the ranch today to help Dawson with something at the house."

"The house is brand new," Caroline said. "What could they possibly have to help Dawson with at the house?"

Not only that, but everybody in the family had already taken a tour of Rhinehart Ranch, as well as the new house that Dawson had paid Bishop and Montana Glover to build. It was a beautiful house with five bedrooms, a home office, high-end finishes, and big, clear windows so that Caroline could see the world beyond.

"I don't know," Mama said. "That's what they told me, and that's where they are. Frankly, they're out of our hair, so it doesn't matter what they're doing."

Oh, it mattered to Caroline, but she decided not to push it. She met Belle's eyes; Belle had plenty of questions there. Caroline simply shook her head oh-so-slightly, and resignation entered Belle's expression.

"All right," Belle said. "But we need some yard work

done here at the house too. They're not going to leave without helping me with that, are they?"

"It's on their agenda," Mama said somewhat crossly. "Now let's get going. Abby, come help peel these potatoes before you start that dip."

Abby dutifully moved into the kitchen, though she was nearly forty years old and certainly didn't need to be bossed around by Mama. Caroline gave her a smile and squeezed her forearm as she went by.

"Thank you for coming, Abby."

"Of course. Brett's got the kids in town at a movie, and they'll be back later." She looked over to Belle. "They can help with the yard work too." Belle said something else about that, and Caroline collected her bowl of ingredients and left them to talk.

"I'll work out on the picnic table," Caroline said as she moved toward the back door. "Then I'll be out of the way for a while." She stepped outside. The wind wasn't warm, though the sun had come out for this moment, and she set down her bowl and ran her hands up and down her forearms, finally cradling them around her elbows.

Danny had brought out the folding tables, but he hadn't set them up. Caroline started to count in her head how many people would be at dinner tonight. Ten from the Rhineharts. Eleven from her family.

"Twenty-one people," she murmured, "Almost a fifty-fifty split between Rhineharts and Thompsons."

It was a beautiful thing trying to merge two families, two lives, and Caroline really hoped that she could do it this time. All at once, she knew she could. It took both partners to be committed, and Dawson was her perfect match, her One True Love. He was kind and understanding, and she was willing to change. She couldn't wait to start her new life as a Rhinehart and a permanent resident of Three Rivers.

But as the sunlight flickered away, as clouds moved in, Caroline looked up to the sky and prayed one more time, "Please, God, I just need thirty minutes."

Chapter Sixteen

Dawson Rhinehart didn't like all the bodies in his barn office. It was barely big enough for him to sit at his desk, step over to his whiteboard, move his sticky notes around, and house a filing cabinet. Today, everything had been put away. Dawson's whiteboard didn't hold any sticky notes. His ledgers, notebooks, and computers were all closed and stowed away. For today, he was getting married, and by tonight, he and Caroline would be on the first leg of their road-trip-honeymoon.

He'd be gone for the next eight days, and a lightning bolt of anxiety flashed through him. "My tie's too tight," he grumbled, and Duke turned toward him.

Brandon had also come into the barn office, and Daddy was expected to arrived at any moment. Four grown men in the barn office, and Dawson felt like he was about to suffocate.

"Your tie is fine." Duke put two fingers under the collar. "Look how much room you've got. It's fine." His eyes met Dawson's, and he said, "It's okay to be nervous, but don't miss out on today."

"I'm not going to," Dawson said crossly.

"Well, you're totally grumpy," Duke fired back. "You think Caroline wants to see your growly bear face as she comes down the aisle? I can guarantee you she doesn't."

Duke was just as grumpy as Dawson, as evidenced by the lecture he'd just spewed. The truth was he was right. Dawson didn't want to feel like this on his wedding day. He turned toward the little window above his desk and looked outside.

"Did it stop raining?" he asked.

"I'll go check," Brandon said.

Dawson had woken to rain on his new roof that morning. He'd made breakfast through it. Caroline had shown up twenty minutes early with a somber look on her face. She really wanted to get married outside. Dawson wanted to do whatever he could to make his lovely bride's dreams come true.

So he, her daddy, her brother, Duke, Brandon, and her sister's husband had set up the tents that morning. Zona and Belle had started setting out chairs and decorating them according to their plans.

Because Arizona came from the Glovers, who had plenty of money, she'd found some last-minute rentals that she wouldn't reveal the price of, and she'd paid to have them installed from the back of the barn to the wedding tent in the pasture.

It was only about twenty feet, but if it rained, those extended tents would keep the ground dry and allow them to have the wedding outside. Guests might get a little wet if it was raining when they came and parked, but they'd be dry once they made it into the barn. Everything was covered after that.

Zona had found heaters somewhere, and Dawson had given up trying to ask her how much everything cost and when he could pay her back. "Nonsense," she'd said to him. "You don't need to pay me back. We're family, and this is your wedding."

He loved his sister-in-law so much. She'd been so good to him and Brandon over the years, and she'd tamed Duke. She raised good kids, and Dawson hoped April would have a good time at the wedding.

Caroline had been extra-kind to her over the months, as April came around Dawson often. She'd said she was worried she wouldn't be able to, but Dawson had assured her Caroline wouldn't mind, and that April could still pop by whenever she wanted.

The door opened, and Dawson expected either Brandon or Daddy to come in, but instead, he heard "Uncle Dawson," in April's voice. He turned toward her. She wore a pretty green dress the color of sagebrush, almost gray but definitely still green.

Caroline had chosen blue, yellow, green, and pink

for her colors. "I can't decide on just one," she'd said. All the girls in the family, in the wedding party, wore a different color, and Dawson thought it looked like a field of wildflowers, just like the dresses Caroline liked to wear.

She'd been wearing a flowery, flowing dress for breakfast, and then she disappeared into the farmhouse where her mama and sisters and Dawson's momma and sister-in-law would all prepare. She'd do her final staging in the barn as that was where the aisle started—right at the back where the big double doors could be opened to the ranch beyond.

"What's up, little miss?" he asked.

"Grandpa says it's time for you to come over. We're lining up."

Dawson's pulse practically attacked him, but he nodded. Duke looked at him, grabbed him, and pulled him into a hug. "You are so ready for this. You are gonna make her so happy."

Dawson had never really thought that he would do anything for Caroline. *He* felt like the lucky one.

"Let's go." He stepped out of the barn office and down onto some extra mats that someone had put down, which was a brilliant idea because then he didn't have to walk in the mud.

The ranch would be mucky in spots, but he hoped they'd gotten the tent up soon enough to keep things mostly dry. Daddy had mowed the aisle right down to the dirt almost, and a certain buzz filled the air that also seemed to crawl right into Dawson's bloodstream and make him more excited than he'd been before.

He went into the barn, scanning for Caroline, but he didn't find her. A whole mess of people stood by the doors in the back—the family wedding party.

Brandon should be off getting the crows to do what they needed them to do. Nobody had any idea if Rocks and Nugget were even around today. They certainly wouldn't come under a tent. They were wild animals, so Dawson wasn't sure how he was going to get them to hop down the aisle the way Caroline wanted them to.

He heard the warbling of chickens, which meant his hens were here, but he couldn't find Judy to see if she had them leashed the way they'd planned. She'd practiced a couple of times, and it really was the cutest thing Dawson had ever seen—his five favorite hens tied with twine and walking along, bobbing their heads behind a little girl.

"Where's Ruffin?" Just as he asked, Daddy appeared at his side with his dog.

"Hey, Daddy." Dawson melted right into his father's arms. "I'm really doing this."

"You're really doing this," Daddy said. "And it's about time." He grinned at Dawson, and turned him toward his mother to hug.

"I love you, Momma," he said.

"Oh, I love you too, my precious boy."

Then Daddy took her arm and tugged her away from Dawson. "We have to go up to the front." Everybody shifted that way, in fact.

Dawson would exit the barn last. Not quite—Caroline would come after him, but her daddy was spying to make sure that Dawson was all the way out of the barn and walking toward the aisle before she would come in.

"All right," Duke said, waving his arms above his head and employing his loud voice. "All right, everyone, we're about to get started. Everyone get in line. Please, get in line."

Dawson swallowed. He tugged on the ends of his jacket sleeves, putting them right in place. His tie still choked him, but he didn't reach to adjust it. He said, "Ruffin, right here," and the dog stayed right by him.

Duke turned and opened the double-wide barn doors, and all the energy of the guests came in from outside. It flooded the barn, nearly knocking Dawson back. The love and support of the people who'd come to see him get married was incredible to him. He'd always thought of himself as a small piece, a tiny little cog that no one ever really noticed, both here on the ranch and in the greater community of Three Rivers.

Sure, he showed up and helped when there were disasters, when houses needed to be fixed, when food needed to be brought in, when extra hands, extra shovels, and extra smiles were needed. Dawson always showed up, but he'd never really thought anyone noticed or, frankly, cared.

Of course, he had friends in Lincoln and Misty, Alex and Nikki, Finn and Edith, Mitch Glover, and Henry Marshall. Combined with his family, they made up his wedding party. Caroline hadn't asked anyone from work, claiming she wasn't that good of friends with them, and instead, had only her family walking in the wedding party. They started to move out, all of them pairing up or grouping up and walking down the aisle together.

Belle went last after she bent down and said something to Judy. Judy turned and looked at Dawson, and he held up the five fingers that they'd agreed on, then four, then three, then two, then one. When he dropped his hand, Judy turned and took the first step out of the barn. To his great relief, the hens followed. Their warbling went with them, their small clucks, their little guttural noises, their heads bobbing. Oh, how Dawson loved them.

"It's our turn next, Ruffin," he said, but he wanted to give Brandon a chance to get the crows there. Caroline *really* wanted the crows, and Dawson *really* wanted Caroline to be happy.

So he moved through the barn until he stood at the double-door entrance, and he looked at all of the people who had come to the wedding. They smiled at Judy. They pointed. People snapped pictures.

Then they looked to him. He put a smile on his face.

The love and gratitude, brotherhood, and camaraderie he felt for everyone there overwhelmed him. He sure was glad that Duke had told him to pay attention, to be present, to enjoy this day. This was his *wedding day*, after all, and he aimed to only have one of those.

Down at the altar, which had been a saddle horse that he had upholstered and then Caroline had pinned flowers to, the pastor waited. All of the chairs had flowers pinned to the white clothes covering them, and flowers hung from the tent poles as well.

Dawson suddenly understood why Caroline wanted to get married outside so badly. It was so much better than an indoor wedding with the fresh air, the green pasture, and all of the blooms that really represented Caroline. The ranch itself represented Dawson, and bringing them together like this formed a union between the two of them that was as physical as it was mental, emotional, and spiritual.

He found his parents down in the first row on the left, Caroline's mama on the right. As he watched, Brandon came in from the back of the tent, holding a string of silver beads in his hand. Both Nugget and Rocks flew in and landed on the altar. Rocks wanted the beads, of course, and Brandon let him take them. Nugget just wanted everyone to know that she was there, so she cawed, and several people cried out in surprise. Dawson laughed.

His crows had come. Caroline would be so happy.

With the birds in place, he stepped down the aisle, Ruffin right at his side. With every move he made, he felt sure he would disintegrate into ashes or dust or the ground would disappear beneath his feet. He almost felt like he existed outside of his body. But he kept going, kept walking, and he arrived at the altar, where he hugged his momma and daddy again, reached out and patted his crows, bent down and touched the top of Ruffin's head, and then looked back down the aisle.

Caroline stood there now, and Dawson pulled in a tight breath. Tears came instantly to his eyes. She had come.

Of course, he hadn't expected her not to be there, but it was still awe-inspiring and breathtaking to see her standing there. Her dress, as white as it was, also bore blooms in as many colors as Dawson's eyes could comprehend. They seemed to be sewn under the lace, so the colors were muted, pastel, soft, and beautiful—the exact epitome of Caroline herself.

She clung to her daddy's arm. She'd curled and clipped up her hair. Her eyes met Dawson's. She smiled, sparkled from her inner beauty, and she too took step by step until she reached her family. She hugged her mom and all of her sisters, and then she turned to Dawson and took his arm.

Just like that. A movement so simple and yet so meaningful it stole his breath all over again.

"This is the most beautiful dress I've ever seen," he

whispered to her. "You are the most beautiful woman in the world."

She simply hugged his bicep and leaned into him, her eyes falling closed in one moment of bliss. Then they turned to face the pastor.

Pastor Patrick Knowlton—Willa Glover's brother—smiled warmly at both Dawson and Caroline. The guests behind him settled into their seats, into respectful silence, the only sound the rushing of the wind as it intensified.

Dawson tensed, because they really only needed a few more minutes to get the I-do's said. Rocks hopped over to Caroline and held up his claw clutching the silver beads.

"I see you, buddy," she whispered, her voice made of pure fondness.

Dawson's heart pounded as he lifted his eyes back to Pastor Knowlton, his arm securely around Caroline. The weight of the moment settled over him, a blend of awe and reverence. Every bit of his love for her radiated from his chest, mingling with the joy and excitement of their friends and family gathered around.

Pastor Knowlton smiled warmly. "We are gathered here today to witness and celebrate the union of Dawson Rhinehart and Caroline Thompson in holy matrimony," he began. "This is a sacred moment, a pledge of love and partnership, witnessed by family, friends—and animals

—" He nodded to the crows and over to the still-warbling hens. "And God."

Dawson's dropped his hand to Caroline's as he absorbed the pastor's words. The steady rhythm of her heartbeat pulsed against his arm, grounding him in the surreal-ness of the moment.

"I just wish to say this one thing." He took a moment, and Dawson couldn't even imagine how many weddings Pastor Knowlton had performed. A lot. "A marriage is multi-faceted. There aren't just two sides to every story; there are an untold number of feelings, words, emotions, thoughts, and conversations. Nurture your love with patience, understanding, and unwavering commitment."

He looked with some urgency from Caroline to Dawson and back. "Let your bond be rooted in mutual respect and open communication, and may your shared faith guide you through all of life's seasons, whether they are filled with rain and hail, or sunshine and flowers." He nodded with a smile to Caroline's dress.

"Dawson," Pastor Knowlton said, his voice steady and kind. "Do you take Caroline Denise Thompson to be your lawfully wedded wife, to have and to hold, in sickness and in health, for richer or poorer, in joy and in sorrow, to love and to cherish, from this day forward and for all the days of your life?"

Dawson swallowed hard, emotion choking his voice as he managed to say, "I do." He locked his eyes locked onto Caroline's, wanting to be right there in front of her today. She smiled at him, her eyes glistening with unshed tears, and he seriously thought his heart might burst in that moment.

"Caroline," Pastor Knowlton continued. "Do you take Dawson Wade Rhinehart to be your lawfully wedded husband, to have and to hold, in sickness and in health, for richer or poorer, in joy and in sorrow, to love and to cherish, from this day forward and for all the days of your life?"

Caroline's voice came out clear, unwavering. "I do."

Pastor Knowlton nodded to Brandon, who stepped forward with a small pillow bearing the rings. Rocks took one look at it and hopped that way instantly. "That's right," Brandon whispered. "Take it to Daws, buddy."

The crow plucked one ring from the pillow, but he couldn't get both. After a couple of tries, and some audience members starting to twitter with laughter, Dawson extended his hand toward the crow.

"One at a time is fine, Rocks."

The crow looked at him with his beady eyes, and Nugget took the moment to caw throughout the tent. The wind picked up again, ruffling everyone's feathers.

Rocks, thankfully, dropped the ring into Dawson's palm, and he flipped Caroline's ring in his fingers before slipping it onto her finger.

"With this ring, you're mine," he said softly, gazing at the glittering diamond and aware that Rocks had gone back to Brandon. "It is a symbol of my love, my faithfulness, and my commitment to you."

Caroline wiped at her eyes and tried to get Rocks to give up Dawson's ring. But the crow wouldn't do it. He didn't make much noise, but he cawed and took flight, sending a murmured cry through the crowd—and pure fear through Dawson's bloodstream.

"Rocks," he barked at the crow, and Ruffin added his voice to the conversation. That only caused Nugget to bark back at the dog, and the wedding guests were outright laughing now.

Dawson felt way too hot, and he looked at Caroline, who wore a somewhat stupefied look on her face. "Hey, you wanted the crows," he said.

Thankfully, Brandon brandished another string of beads, this one bright gold, and Rocks dropped the comparatively boring wedding band in favor of that fake string of beads. Caroline looked at the ring on the ground, and Judy swooped in to rescue her.

"Here you go, Auntie C." She handed the ring to Caroline, who smiled prettily at her niece.

"Thank you, baby." She held his ring, and his hand trembled as he held it out for her. Her touch landed steady and sure against his skin, nearly burning him. "With this ring, I'm yours and you're mine," she echoed. "It is a symbol of my love, my faithfulness, and my commitment to you."

Dawson sure liked the weight of the silver band

around his finger, and he took Caroline's hand in his again. His left hand with hers, both of their rings sparkling though the light had definitely turned a shade of gray that meant nothing good.

Pastor Knowlton placed a veined, seasoned hand over their joined two. "By the power vested in me by the state of Texas, and by God, I now pronounce you husband and wife. Dawson, you may kiss your bride."

Dawson leaned in, capturing Caroline's lips in a tender, loving kiss. The crowd erupted in cheers and applause, and Dawson heard Nugget and Rocks cawing loudly as if in approval. The hens clucked mightily, probably startled by the applause and all the yeehaws. Even Ruffin barked and barked.

He smiled against Caroline's lips, pulling back to gaze into her eyes. "It's a real zoo around here," he quipped, and she tipped her head back and laughed.

As they turned to face their guests, Dawson somehow heard the first drops of rain against the tent. He glanced up though they'd be protected, and couldn't help but smile. Caroline's prayer had been answered in the most poetic way. They started down the aisle together, hand in hand, as the drizzle became more earnest.

By the time they reached the barn, the rain had turned into a downpour, the drops landing loudly against the taut fabric of the tent. Laughing, they ran the last few steps, ducking inside to more applause. The guests followed, cheering and laughing as they sought refuge from the sudden storm.

Inside the barn, safe and dry, in the middle of everyone who knew and loved him—and who he knew and loved—Dawson pulled Caroline into his arms. "We did it," he murmured against her hair, his heart over-flowing with love and joy. "I love you, darlin'."

She looked up at him, her eyes shining with love, with relief, with happiness. "Yes, we did," she whispered back. "And it was perfect. Absolutely perfect."

The sound of rain pounding on the barn roof became a comforting backdrop as they stood there, surrounded by the warmth and love of their friends and family. Dawson knew in that moment that this was just the very beginning of a beautiful life together.

Chapter Seventeen

Misty Glover closed her notebook as the last class in her "Raising Independent Children" course ended. She smiled around at the other ladies who had attended with her, only a handful of them, for the past eight weeks. This was the third parenting class that Misty had taken and completed. As she hugged the instructor and said goodbye to her friends, she wondered if she needed to take any more.

Of course, she didn't know everything about how to raise a child, and she knew that actually having another little human being to take care of was different than just studying about how to do it.

She left the community center, got situated in her SUV, and started the car. She needed a moment to run through what the rest of her day would be, as her birthday was this weekend.

They had celebrated Link's while Mitch was in town for Dawson and Caroline's wedding, but Misty hadn't wanted to combine their birthdays this year. It was fine last year when Sammy took charge and really wanted to make everything special. But Misty wanted to start her own family traditions with Link.

She'd asked if they could have a private birthday party at the Top Cottage for her and invite only his immediate family. So that was what she'd planned; she and Sammy had started working on a menu together.

She had a few things to get at the grocery store on her way back to the ranch. She enjoyed living at Shiloh Ridge more than she'd anticipated. Even though it was quite far from the city of Three Rivers, it was like a bustling little town all by itself, with ten or eleven families living there, cowboys paired up in cabins, all the animals, and of course, Link's horse and dogs.

As she did after every parenting class she'd taken, Misty sat in the car, bowed her head, and prayed.

"Am I ready to be a mom?" she asked.

Her own mother had been such a disaster. Misty was still trying to forgive her, and she continued to work through some of the issues that had come from her childhood trauma. Every other time, after twenty-three other classes, Misty had felt like she wasn't quite ready.

Today, the Spirit whispered to her, *It is time.*

Misty's eyes popped open as a rush of adrenaline filled her chest. Link had deferred to her over when they would have children, and she'd wanted to wait and make sure that she was ready, that they could handle it, that they were solid in their relationship.

She wanted some time with just them. She'd had it—nine months. A small, jealous part of her wanted more. She wanted Link just to herself. She wanted all of his attention, because he was so good at giving it to her. He excelled at making her feel loved and cherished and adored. He took such great care of her. If they had a baby, his attention would be divided, as would hers.

And a tiny part of her didn't want that.

Then, a louder voice whispered, *A child will be part of Link. You'll have more of Link to love.*

And besides, they might not be able to have a baby right away anyway. Alex and Nicki hadn't been able to.

Misty left the community center, got her groceries, and returned to the ranch. She wasn't all that surprised to see Sammy's old truck parked in front of the Top Cottage, with Link's momma still sitting behind the wheel. Misty smiled at her and waved as she parked next to her. She got out at the same time Sammy did.

"How long you been here?" she asked.

"Oh, two minutes," Sammy said. "The dust has hardly settled."

She nodded as she moved to the back of the SUV. "I got the groceries."

"I've got a bunch too," Sammy said, and she met Misty at the tailgate of the SUV. "Happy birthday, my darling girl," she said, and pulled her into the sweetest, most maternal hug Misty had ever had.

She loved hugging Sammy, as Sammy was so extraordinary at showing Misty specifically how valuable she was and how much she loved her. Misty could go to her for anything, just the way she should have been able to go to her mother.

Sammy stepped back and said, "How was your class?"

Misty nodded, her breath sort of whooshing out of her nose as her emotions made her mouth and jaw and tongue so tight. When they finally released, she said, "It was good."

Sammy nodded and didn't ask anything further, and together they took their groceries in, making a couple of trips to get everything. After all the ingredients sat unpacked on the island countertop, Misty looked at the vast array of things they needed to make her preferred birthday meal.

"This is a little bit over the top, isn't it?" she asked.

"It's your birthday," Sammy said, as if over the top could never happen on someone's birthday. "Absolutely not, and Etta is bringing the cake in a couple of hours."

"Oh, that's great," Misty said. Etta had been baking birthday cakes and wedding cakes for everyone in the family for a long time, and she never told anyone no when they needed a special dessert.

"All right," Sammy said, "I'm going to start on the

chili, since that needs to go the longest, and you're going to...?" She looked over to Misty, her eyebrows raised.

"I'm going to do the potatoes for the fries," Misty said. She wasn't making anything fancy because she wanted some of her favorite foods, and that was a chili dog and chili cheese fries. Growing up, she'd counted herself lucky to have had a can of chili and a single hot dog for her birthday.

Now, of course, Sammy would make homemade chili with a family recipe, and they had all-beef hot dogs from the best butcher in town. Sammy would put together her famous broccoli-craisin-apple salad to go with it, and today she was going to show Misty how to make the famed Glover family peach punch.

When the birthday cake arrived, it would be the perfect celebratory meal for Misty. She thanked the Good Lord Above that He had led her to this town, and specifically this family, so that she could be healed, and held, and shown what real families looked like.

* * *

"Thank you so much for coming." Misty hugged Heather and then Sunny, Link's younger sisters. "You guys be careful out on the fence tomorrow."

"We will," Heather promised. They left the house after their parents and older brothers. Misty and Link went out onto the porch with them and waved good-bye to his family. Darkness had already settled over Shiloh Ridge, and since Misty had gone to class today and then spent the afternoon cooking, then the evening entertaining, a certain measure of tiredness entered her body. But it was the kind of exhaustion that sparked from an amazing day of laughter, love, and good times.

She put her hand on Link's chest and said, "Thank you, baby," before she returned to the house.

"I didn't do anything," he said.

"You have a great family," she said.

He came into the house behind her and closed the door. Misty's heartbeat thundered up and down her throat and then behind her eyes. Link slid his hand along her waist and down her hip, then up to her stomach as he hugged her from behind.

He murmured, his mouth right at her ear, "What does it feel like to be thirty-three?"

She held on to his arms and leaned back into his strength of his chest. "Feels like thirty-two."

Link chuckled in her ear, his lips right there touching her skin below her ear and then moving down her jaw. She turned in his arms and looked up at him. He gazed down at her, waiting for her to say what lingered in her mind. He was exceptionally patient and very good at making her say what she sometimes didn't want to. She drew in a breath. The words sat there, but they wouldn't come out.

"Want me to kiss you tonight?" Link asked softly.

Misty nodded. Link leaned down and touched his lips to hers, no more questions asked, a soft, almost seeking kiss, as if he could find what she wanted to say that way. His touch grew in passion, and of course, Misty wanted to be with Link that night. But she had to tell him first.

He's not going to be upset, she thought. She pulled away and pressed her cheek to his. "I finished my last parenting class today," she whispered.

Link simply nuzzled her closer and kissed her neck.

"I think I'm ready."

He pulled back almost instantly, almost as if her skin and hair had caught fire. Palpable shock flowed from him, and his wide eyes broadcast it through their house. "You're ready?" he repeated. "For what?"

"To have kids," she said. "I think I'm ready to have a baby."

Link blinked one time, and then a smile filled his whole face. "That's fantastic," he said.

"Are you ready?" She fiddled with the collar on his shirt, doing up one button and then undoing it again. "I mean, do you feel ready to be a dad?"

"I don't really know," he said. "I don't feel like I'm not ready."

Misty nodded and looked up at him again. All of the fears, the worries, the knots, everything that just wasn't right, became flat. She'd always calmed in his presence.

She *was* different from her mother. She was *not* going to be the type of mother hers had been.

"I want a baby," she said.

Link kissed her again, this time with all the wild, rough passion he did when he made love to her. "All right," he whispered. "Let's go make a baby."

Chapter Eighteen

Mitch Glover got off yet another plane in Amarillo. He felt like he went back and forth between Texas and Virginia quite often. In fact, this ticket had been free, because he'd used his airline loyalty miles to pay for it.

Of course, Daddy would pay for anything Mitch needed, including a cross-country move at the drop of a cowboy hat if Mitch said he wanted to come home to Three Rivers tomorrow. Daddy would make it happen.

Mitch would fall down dead if Daddy wasn't already waiting for him on the curb, and he moved expertly through the airport, picked up his bag from one of the carousels, and stepped outside. He imagined what a busy place like an airport might sound like, with luggage clunking along metal claim stations, people talking, high heels clicking along the floor, family members laughing as they met up after a while apart.

Mitch couldn't hear any of it, but it sure wasn't hard to miss Daddy's truck. King cab, with an extra-long bed, double-wide wheels in the back. He stepped out of it and walked around the hood, already signing as he came.

Happiness filled Mitch in a brand new way, as he'd been in a real struggle with himself, his life, and God for the past few years.

You're early, Daddy said as he stepped into Mitch and hauled him against his chest for a hug. Mitch wanted to say, *You're still here before me*, but he had to wait until he stepped back so he could use his hands. Daddy smiled at Mitch, who imagined him to be laughing.

Yeah, I'm still here. He picked up Mitch's bag, took it to the back of the truck, lifted it up, and then opened the passenger door for him.

Mitch found his younger siblings lined up in the back seat. Chaz, who'd graduated from high school last May, and Lynn who would in a couple of months. Finally, his youngest sister—Melissa—waved for all she was worth, and Mitch waved back, signed hello, and allowed the goodness of his younger siblings to fill him front to back, top to bottom.

What are y'all doing here? he asked, though it was Spring Break in Three Rivers too. Momma had been teaching them sign language since they were born, so they could communicate with him. A wave of gratitude flowed over him for such a good mother.

They all started signing at once, and since Mitch had been living at and working for a deaf academy, as well as taking more advanced sign language classes of his own, he'd gotten so much better at his own language.

He laughed, kept up with their individual conversations, signing to one teenager and then another.

Daddy got two new dogs, Chaz said, completely selling out their father without having to say a word that Daddy could hear.

Mitch laughed again. *Of course Daddy got new dogs*, he said. *Is there room for Liberty back there?*

Yes, there was room for Liberty, as Daddy had just opened Chaz's door to let the hound up. She jumped up, and in total non-hearing-dog fashion, she licked his younger brother's face while the girls grinned and grinned.

Daddy said something, but Mitch only caught part of it as he wasn't facing him fully and Daddy hadn't signed. Chaz interpreted, *We're going to stop and get burgers for everyone on the way back.*

Sounds great, Mitch said. *Airplane food is gross.*

At least you've been on an airplane, Chaz said.

Don't worry, buddy. You'll get on an airplane someday. He turned around and faced the front when his father got in the car. Since he couldn't hear the conversations around him, he didn't usually like riding in the car.

He wasn't sure if the other kids were talking, and right now, he didn't have the energy to try to keep up. So he simply enjoyed the ride back to Three Rivers, where they got oodles of burgers and fries—way more than they needed for their family.

That should've been his first clue that it wasn't only going to be his immediate family at the Edge Cabin. In fact, Daddy didn't even go out to the Edge. He turned left at the top of the hill, just under the arch announcing their arrival at Shiloh Ridge Ranch, and parked in front of True Blue.

Mitch looked over to him, and Daddy made the sign for *Sorry. I should've told you. Everyone wants to see you.*

I was just here three weeks ago, Mitch said. *Everyone saw me then.*

He wasn't sure why, but he wasn't prepared to be the center of attention for one hundred people this afternoon. He just wanted to have something good to eat, take in the view at the Edge, and lie down to play a couple of games on his phone.

The Edge Cabin burst at the seams with the number of people who lived in the small space. But April had arrived, and Daddy had a couple of rooms made up in the barn for anyone who wanted to be by themselves. Then Mitch wouldn't have to sleep on a bunk with Chaz beneath him.

Uncle Judge arrived, and he got out and retrieved several boxes of pizza from the back of his truck. So this had to be some sort of come-as-you-are, fast food event. Mitch got out and helped his daddy with his dog, the teens, and the bags and bags of hamburgers and French fries.

They went inside the barn, where Uncle Bear set down six pink boxes of doughnuts. More Glovers arrived, all of them with junk food or fast food. Nothing high-end and nothing homemade, which seemed so odd for the Glovers.

Confusion ran through Mitch, and he automatically looked for Link or Gunnison or Wilder. They'd be able to tell him what was going down here this afternoon. He found Smiles looking his way, and he signed, *What's happening here?*

Smiles smiled, something he was very good at. He was very easy-going, go-with-the-flow, laid-back type of cowboy, and Mitch sometimes envied him for that. *There's no school today*, Smiles said. *Teacher work day before Spring Break, so Momma and Aunt Oakley decided we should have a movie afternoon with as much junk food as possible.*

Mitch smiled too, because that so sounded like Aunt Sammy and Aunt Oakley. His own mother bustled out of the kitchen, searching the crowd, and when she spotted him, she burst into a quick jog toward him.

Mitch, baby, she signed, her whole face aglow. *You*

made it. She hugged him as if she hadn't seen him in years, and Mitch held onto her too.

He didn't teach on Fridays, and Whispering Paws—the deaf academy and dog academy where he worked—had Spring Break next week. He'd decided to come for the whole week, and he had a special appointment on Monday that he hadn't told anyone about yet.

It weighed on his mind and heavy in his fingers, and he pulled his momma away from the group and said, *I need you and Daddy to come with me to an appointment on Monday.*

Momma immediately detected a change in Mitch. *What is it?* she asked, her smile disappearing and her hands moving slower.

I have a meeting with a real estate agent, Mitch said. *He's going to show me a few pieces of property for something I'm thinking of doing.*

Momma blinked a couple of times. *What are you thinking about doing?*

He glanced over as someone came toward him. Link. Love filled Mitch, and Link looked between Mitch and his momma, clearly understanding that he'd interrupted. *Sorry,* he signed. *Sorry, I'll come back.*

No, no, it's okay, Mitch said quickly. He faced his momma and grinned at her. *I'll tell you and Daddy about it tonight.*

He didn't wait for her to say okay before he turned to Link and grabbed onto him. He'd seen his cousin just three weeks ago too, but there was something different about this trip. Mitch realized it was him. *He* was different on this trip than he'd been the last time he'd come to town.

God had told him to do whatever he wanted with his life. He'd asked him, *What do you want to do, Mitch?* And Mitch hadn't known.

He'd been angry; he just wanted God to *tell* him what to do. But the Lord wasn't going to do that, so Mitch had started thinking about what he wanted to do with his life, what he wanted his life to be. What could he do so that every morning when he got up, he would be excited to do it?

He never wanted to feel the weight of his job in his shoulders, or moan and groan about having to do his work that day. Slowly, over the past several months, Mitch had sketched out a plan for what he wanted. The problem was, he had no idea how to execute plans as big as his. When he got down on his knees and told God that, his Heavenly Father had said, *You do it one step at a time, Mitch.*

One step at a time.

Mitch didn't know which step came first in starting a deaf academy that would teach children of all ages—preschool through high school—sign language and how to speak out loud. He would need trained professionals for that, and he had no idea how to find them and get them to come to Three Rivers.

He needed land, he needed facilities, he needed on-campus housing. Just the fact that he thought he was going to build a *campus* of any type in Three Rivers was absolutely ludicrous. And yet, Mitch had called a real estate agent to take the first step.

Finn had given him the man's name, and Jerry Bozeman had scheduled some time on Monday morning to show Mitch three building lots in the area. Empty patches of land that could be the homesite of Mitch's dreams.

He wanted part of his facility to be a training arena for dogs, so those students at his school could have a hearing dog when they left. Or, they could take the canines home at night to help them with their communication in their families.

He wanted to offer community sign language courses, so that hearing people who had deaf loved ones could speak with them. Deaf children, teens, and adults deserved a language-rich community with both those who couldn't hear and those who could.

He wanted community courses on cochlear implants and ways to support the deaf community, provide inclusive services for the deaf, and more. All of that started with education for all people, hearing, deaf, and everything in between.

He envisioned part of his academy to be a training breeding ground for hearing people to become licensed and professional interpreters. Then, they could go out into the world and provide excellent service for the deaf community as they needed help with their doctor's appointments, to get their driver's licenses, to fill out forms for college, apply for a job, anything that a hearing person did that was *so simple* for them.

They could speak and ask questions, and someone could answer. Done. Mitch couldn't do that. He was severely limited in his communication, and he felt bundled and bound inside his own body. He hated typing out everything he wanted to say, and he would fight for more inclusivity and accommodations for the deaf in the world.

As he'd sketched out his plans, his academy had grown several limbs. He knew he wouldn't be able to do them all at once, but again, he only needed to do one thing at a time. And right now, apparently, it was movie-junk-food-afternoon. Mitch folded himself into the Glover embrace, flopped down on the beanbag with Wilder and Fawn, Uncle Ranger's kids, and ate anything anyone passed to him.

When Monday morning came, Mitch drove with his daddy in the passenger seat and his mom in the back to meet Jerry Bozeman. They went to his office first, where Mitch used Momma as an interpreter to talk to the real estate agent, asking a few questions about the lots, their availability, the zoning laws, and the permits he might need to build a campus.

Jerry showed him aerial views of the lots he had selected to show Mitch that day. He told Momma, who told Mitch, that they were all viable options for the type of academy he had described. For the amount of land he needed, and the water rights he required, and they were all plumbed and ready for electricity as well.

While Mitch's academy would serve a nonprofit in one sense, providing interpreters and hearing dogs for the deaf, it would also be a commercial enterprise, a school where people would pay to send their kids. Mitch would need to pay his employees and himself. He had to have a way to make money.

"All three of the lots do this," the real estate agent said, and Mitch read his lips. "They're already zoned, and the proper permits have been filed."

Mitch nodded. *I don't know if I'm ready to buy a piece of land*, he said. *I just want to see what there is.*

"Well, there are some great opportunities here," Jerry said, looking right at Mitch. "Some of these properties sit on the market for years, because they're specialized, and they're waiting for the right business to come in."

So you won't be upset if I waste your time this morning and just look?

Jerry smiled and shook his head. "I won't be upset. This is what I do. You might see something you really like, and you might learn what you don't want. That's why you look."

Mitch nodded, reassured that he wasn't doing something he shouldn't be doing. Together, the four of them got up and left the real estate office.

Jerry drove this time in his SUV, and Mitch sat in the passenger seat with his parents in the back. No one spoke to him, and his nerves balled in the back of his chest behind his lungs, pushing the air out faster than he could bring it in.

The first lot was on the west side of town, close to Aunt Dot's landscaping company. Beautiful land existed out here, and Marcy Walker also had her crop-dusting business, Payne's Pest-free, on this side of town. Several other industrial enterprises lined the south side of the road, but this parcel of land sat on the north side.

They accessed it on a new road that had been well-maintained, and Mitch gazed over it before turning to face Jerry. "It's forty-two acres," he said. "I think that's more than enough for your academy and some on-campus housing." He glanced over to Momma. "Have you worked with an architect at all?"

Mitch shook his head, and he pulled out his phone to make a note for himself. He probably should talk to an architect or someone who could design something for him based on what he envisioned in his mind for the academy.

"That might be a good idea," Jerry said. "They might

tell you how much land you really need. Based on what you told me in your email, I figured forty acres or above."

Mitch nodded. *This is a nice location.* He looked at his father. *What do you think? We're kind of close to town.*

Daddy said nothing, not with his hands or his mouth. His eyes sure said plenty, though. Mitch looked across the land, but it was hard to assess forty-two acres with a single glance.

Daddy did the same and finally looked at him. *This is a nice location.*

Momma smiled and said, *It would be great here, Mitch. It's out of the way. It has a nice road. You could do good things on this piece of land.*

I was kind of hoping for more of a ranch environment, he said, and Momma spoke to Jerry.

"We've got a piece of land like that," he said. He continued speaking, but Mitch didn't catch it. Instead, Momma signed to him, *They have a piece of land like that.*

Mitch nodded and said, *Let's go see that one.*

They drove across town, this time to the north and east, up near the rich estates where rodeo celebrity Wyatt Walker lived in a gated community. The hills here made for a more mountainous, rural area. They pulled up to a dirt road and went down it until it ended in what looked like a dirt cul-de-sac, then they piled out of the vehicle.

"This one is fifty-seven acres," Jerry said, waiting until Mitch looked square at him. "It is a little bit more remote, and it's on the east side of town, which is generally equated with being higher-end."

Mitch nodded because that was true. Three Rivers definitely had communities, some of which were poorer and older than others. On this northeast side, it was hillier, more remote, and the communities newer and nicer. The houses here cost far more than in town, and Mitch wondered if that was the vibe he wanted for his academy. He wanted it to be elite but not elit*ist*.

The real estate agent spoke with Momma and Daddy, and Momma conveyed all that he said to Mitch.

This is a great piece of property. The management group that owns it has been trying to sell it for a year, and it's going nowhere. I don't think anyone's looked at it in six months. So again, you don't need to be in a rush. They're looking for something beautiful to be built on this side of town and are a little picky about who they'll sell to.

Mitch nodded as he gazed east, the morning sun painting the land into a color he'd call golden warm. *It's a nice piece of land*, he said. Because it was, but was it *his* nice piece of land?

They all piled back into the truck and drove south along the highway where Uncle Preacher had gotten in a terrible accident many years ago. They continued south past the turnoff that went to Golden Hour Ranch and

Seven Sons Ranch, and they drove so far south that Mitch was sure they'd passed Shiloh Ridge too.

Are we even in Three Rivers still? he signed to Momma.

She asked Jerry, who shook his head. *No, this other piece of land is a county property.*

Mitch wasn't sure what that meant, so he looked at his father. *Just means it's not in an incorporated city, son.*

What about water and electricity? Mitch asked.

"You pay to the county," Jerry said, explaining to Momma and Daddy that it was still plumbed with electricity and water, but payments would go to a county's system instead of Three Rivers. Mitch nodded once he'd gotten the information from them.

They came up on the land, and it was definitely more remote. Mitch hadn't seen a house, ranch, arch, or turnoff in at least ten minutes. He wasn't sure how he felt about that. Anyone coming to the academy would likely have to go through Amarillo, and this was at least a two-hour drive from that airport. Maybe more.

It's remote, he said as he got out, not looking at anyone. It definitely was remote. There weren't as many trees, the land was flat, and it looked completely barren and uncared for. Mitch suddenly had the urge to be the one to bring it to life, to make it an oasis for the deaf community, as he often felt alone, desolate, and uncared for.

"This one is the largest parcel," Jerry said. "It's

ninety-seven acres and has a stream that runs through it, which is kind of nice. It needs a lot of work, and that's why it's on the market for the price it is—the cheapest one, but with the most land."

Mitch nodded. He looked at his daddy and said, *It's really far away.*

Daddy nodded and looked around as he signed. *You said you wanted it far away.*

Yeah, Mitch said. *But I'm not sure I want it this far away.*

Well, he's given you three really different pieces of property, Momma said. *It gives you an idea of what's available around Three Rivers.*

Mitch couldn't argue with that. *That's true,* he told his momma. *Thank you so much, Mister Bozeman.* He shook Jerry's hand, counting on his mother to voice his words for him. *This has been really great. I know it's a lot of driving and we've taken your whole morning. I really, really appreciate it.*

"No problem," Jerry said. "This has been really fun. I don't often sell land."

No? Mitch asked, cutting a glance over to his father. The wind out here pulled at their cowboy hats, and Daddy had one hand pressed to the top of his head.

"No," Jerry said. "Usually farms and ranches."

A new idea pranced through Mitch's mind. *What about me taking over a farm or a ranch? You think that could be converted into an academy? It would already have buildings.*

Jerry sat thoughtful for a moment and then said, "It's actually a possibility. One of the more luxury ranches would have a huge lodge-type house on it. That might be somewhere you could house children, and they probably would have a generational house where you could live on-site. Something to think about."

I bet they'd be far more expensive.

Jerry nodded, not even trying to cover up that fact. "Yes, far more expensive."

Mitch looked over to his momma to follow the conversation through her hands instead of lip-reading. *How expensive?*

She asked the question to the real estate agent while Mitch waited. She got the answer and turned to Mitch. *Some of the top-end luxury ranches go for two or three million dollars around here.*

But they're private, right? Mitch asked, and Daddy conveyed the question this time.

"Yes, they're private, remote, and beautifully maintained."

Mitch's throat closed over the fact that he might spend millions to build this academy. *I think maybe I'd like to see some of those.*

"Sure," Jerry said once Daddy had told him what Mitch had said. "How long are you in town?"

I fly out Friday.

"Let's meet on Thursday. That'll give me a couple of days to find what you're looking for, and I can take you around to some properties then."

Sounds great, Mitch said. He shook Jerry's hand again, and they all got back in the car. So many things teemed inside of him. He just wanted to start flailing his arms and spew them all out into words, but he contained himself while they made the long drive back to the real estate office.

He shook Jerry's hand again, and then he and his parents piled back into his truck. He still couldn't talk to his momma and daddy as he drove, but as soon as they got back to the Edge, they got out of the truck, and Mitch started talking and talking and talking.

Chapter Nineteen

I NACH, Angel texted as she got back behind the wheel of her SUV. Over the past month since she and Henry had started seeing each other, they'd devised little ways to communicate secretly. If someone else saw either of their phones, they wouldn't know what their cryptic messages meant.

INACH meant *I need a cowboy hug*. It also told Henry that Angel was on her way to town, where he should be already.

He had been tasked that morning to go to town and pick up their supplies—a whole load of feed, some tools they had taken in for repair, and more. He was not expected on the ranch until evening. When Angel had discovered that, she'd urged her brother and father to put in their grocery orders, claiming she was out of cream for her coffee and all of her oatmeal cream pies. She simply *had* to go that afternoon. She'd told her daddy, "I just need a break from this place," to get him to order faster. That excuse had started working with everyone in her life.

Now that she'd started to restructure some things, she hadn't done roll call in a month—five or six weeks, actually. But she had gotten up last Friday and announced that there would be more positions opening up at Lone Star.

She'd said she wanted a farrier to apply for the job of a foreman position—and that this new position would co-foreman with Justin Owens, who already ran the horseman side of things.

She'd met with Justin previously, and he was ready to work with someone, help her with the interviews, and go through the applications with her.

She'd announced they would be promoting into three new captain positions and three new team lead positions that didn't currently exist. She was looking for two welcome greeters—new positions that also didn't exist. That made eight new positions on the ranch, plus the foreman.

Nine new positions, and Angel's vision went a bit blurry at the thought of it all. She barley had twice that many men working at Lone Star right now.

The buzz in the group that day had been astronomical, and Angel had hidden in her office for the rest of the day. In the subsequent days, applications had been coming in, and Angel filled her time scheduling meetings, talking to Justin, and laying out applications. She liked to see them all side by side as she considered certain personality traits and skills.

Applications were due by five p.m. today, but she didn't have to be present to take them. Men could put them on her desk, give them to Trevor, hand them to Justin, or leave them at the house.

So she sent a text saying she would be off the ranch for the afternoon, getting groceries in town. If anyone needed anything, they could let her know. Often, a cowboy would need a dozen eggs here and there as they ran out, and she expected to get several texts as she drove to Amarillo.

Her phone beeped with Henry's text, and she glanced at it. It said, *I got you*, with a smiley face. She loved how he added emojis to his texts since she'd told him she liked it.

They'd met several times in secret locations around the ranch, once earlier this week in her office with the door closed. Henry had pressed her there and kissed her for a good long while before she said, "I didn't ask you here to kiss me."

And he'd said, in his lilting teasing-cowboy tone, "Oh, I'm sorry. I thought that's why I came."

She warmed up just thinking about it. She *had* asked him to come. She had wanted to kiss him, but really, she wanted to know if he was going to apply for any of the positions.

"Absolutely," he'd said. "I'm going to apply for all of them."

"Okay," she said. "That's good."

"That's why you called me here?" He kissed her again. "I really think you called me just to kiss me."

And so they did that for a while, and then Henry slipped out, leaving Angel breathless and hot. She'd taken a walk out on the ranch for a good long half-hour so she'd have a reason to be sweaty and red-faced.

Now, she made the drive to town and parked on the side of the grocery store in the shade. She did have pickup orders to get, and she checked her phone. She had five or six items she needed to run into the store to get for the cowboys at Lone Star, but really, she and Henry were here for a date.

She'd once seen the cowboy filling up plastic clamshell containers of food from the hot bar and the salad bar here at the gourmet grocery store in Amarillo. She liked their food too, and when he suggested they meet there one day, Angel started trying to figure out how to make it happen.

Their little secret relationship had definitely been finessed. She'd suggested to Henry to come this afternoon to get all their supplies, pick up their feed, and get their tools, and he had taken it and run with it.

She didn't see the big farm truck that Henry had

driven. He was picking up a lot of feed today, as well as salt blocks for the horses, and he wouldn't be driving his personal vehicle. She turned off her car and started to get her purse together, stick her phone in, and take her sunglasses off. Then she turned to get out of the car.

Someone stood in the space between her car and the one next to her, and she grunted in surprise, her adrenaline high and her fight reflex up immediately. A man's hand wrapped around her wrist and pinned it against the car. He leaned down and kissed her.

And oh, Angel knew this kiss. She knew the shape of this mouth. She knew the taste of Henry Marshall.

She relaxed into the kiss as Henry's arm swept along her waist and brought her flush against his body. They stood in public, so he didn't go on too long. When he pulled away, he said, "Took you long enough to get here," in that devilish, flirtatious tone that he'd perfected.

"I texted you when I left," she said.

"Yeah, and I mapped you the whole way." He drew her into his chest and whispered, "Here's your cowboy hug, sweetheart."

She wrapped her arms around him, pressed her cheek to his pulse, and enjoyed the way they fit together. They hadn't had too many serious conversations yet. They were only six weeks into a secret relationship that no one else knew about. Angel hadn't even brought it up with Trevor again.

"You good?"

"Yes." Angel exhaled. "Thanks, baby." She looked at him, and Henry cupped her face in one of his big hands.

"You're calling me baby now?"

Angel smiled at him. "Don't tell me you don't like it."

"I do like it," he said. "I want you to say it again."

Angel absolutely would not say it again. Not right there. Not just because he told her to. She pressed her palm against his chest to get him to back up. "I'm starving. Let's go eat."

He chuckled and gave her room. She moved out of the doorway of her car, closed the door, locked it, and they went into the store together. They both went down the bar, filling their clamshells with whatever they wanted.

The grocery store had tables in the back corner where they could sit. A few people sat there, but no one Angel knew, thankfully. She didn't expect anyone from the farm to catch them. When she sat down with her soup and her salad, Henry slid onto the other side with his hot food and salad too.

"Are you going to text your momma?" she asked.

He whipped his phone out. "Yes, ma'am." He snapped a picture of the veggies, his thumbs then flying over his screen. That done, he set his device aside and picked up a plastic fork.

"I started making a new employee handbook," she said, forking up a slice of cucumber with her lettuce.

"Is that so?" He took a bite of his teriyaki chicken and rice. "What's going to be new about the handbook?"

"New rules," she said. "Some new procedures for our welcome greeters, that kind of stuff. All the new positions, what they do, the teams, scheduling, and new roles on the ranch."

He swallowed and kept his gaze on his hot lunch. "You going to take out the rule about not dating on-site?"

"Yes," she said. "It's already out."

"Have you showed it to your daddy?"

"No." She stabbed a grape tomato doused in ranch and put it in her mouth. Henry looked up at her, barely meeting her eyes from underneath the brim of his cowboy hat. She knew what he wanted, but at the same time, she wasn't ready to give it.

"Everyone will know eventually," she said. "The new employee handbook is going to come out at the same time as the promotion announcements."

He said, "And what do you think cowboys will think when they find out we've been kissing, and you promoted me?"

"I don't know," she said. "And who says you're going to get a promotion?"

"Maybe I won't," Henry said, "It all feels knotted up." He leaned back in the booth. "I'm just going to shoot straight with you, sweetheart."

"As if you haven't in the past," she said dryly.

He didn't smile. He'd hitched a mask in place she

couldn't see through. "If I get a promotion, I want to get it because I'm good. I want to get it because of my merit. I want to get it because I deserve it, not because I'm your boyfriend."

"Of course," Angel said.

"If I don't get a promotion, it's because I didn't deserve it, I'm not ready, or there are more qualified men on the ranch. Not because we're breaking the rules, and I'm your boyfriend."

She nodded. "It is a little bit knotted, isn't it?"

"It's completely twisted up," he said. "Who's picking all the promotions?"

"Me and Daddy and Justin for some, and me, Trevor, and Daddy for others."

"So you're gonna have other opinions besides yours when you look at my application?"

"Yes, sir," she said.

He nodded. "Okay. Then I'm gonna stop worrying about this. I'll let it go."

"Okay." She marveled that Henry could compartmentalize like that. He could let things go and stop worrying about them once he knew the parameters of how things operated. She wished she could be a little bit more like that, but she wasn't.

"I'm starting horseback riding lessons again." She took another bite of her salad. "I'm real happy about that."

"I am too, sweetheart." He gave her a nice smile. "That's great. I think you'll enjoy that."

"Were you ever at Lone Star when I did the lessons?"

"No, ma'am," he said. "I think that was before my time."

"It probably was." They ate a little bit more, and then Angel looked at him and said in the boldest voice she had, "I want another date on the calendar."

"All right," Henry said easily. "What do you want to do?"

"I want to find a way for us to finesse a night out on the town," she said.

"It might be hard for us to both be gone in the evening."

"I want dinner at a nice restaurant, and I want to go to a movie or a show with you. And I want you to buy me dessert after."

Henry chuckled. "You're not demanding or anything."

She laughed too. "You can plan the date. But I want to go *out* with you."

"We are out right now," he said.

"We're at the grocery store," she said. "And you've done a ton of errands, and so have I."

"We're still out."

"Yeah, I guess," she said. "I guess I just want something...." She trailed off, but Henry seemed to be able to read her mind.

"Romantic. You want something romantic. You want me to be your boyfriend, and you want me to act like it."

She read his eyes, nothing wavering there. "Yeah," she said. "That's what I want."

"Alrighty," he said. "I'll start working on it."

"What are you going to do?" she asked.

"I don't know," he said. "But we'll work it out, just like we worked out this afternoon."

She nodded. She'd finished eating, and so had Henry. They cleaned up their clamshells, and Henry took hers from her to take it to the trash.

When he returned to the booth, Angel had just gotten to her feet. "You got stuff you gotta get here, sweetheart?"

"Yeah," she said. "Some cowboys called in last-minute things."

"Me too," he said. "I'm out of chocolate-covered pretzels and red licorice."

She laughed. "You and your obsession with red licorice."

"As if you don't have an obsession with oatmeal cream pies," he said.

"That was my excuse to come to town," she said with a giggle. "So we have to make sure we get a bunch of those." Another text came in, this one from Trevor, and she looked at it and added, "Oh, Trevor forgot to put butter on his list."

Henry grabbed a cart, and they walked around the grocery store together, putting items in that they or the cowboys at the ranch needed. It felt like a very domestic thing to do, something Angel would do with a partner, a spouse.

As she and Henry checked out, she gave him a furtive glance.

He gave it right back to her. "What's that for?"

"Can grocery shopping be considered romantic?" She threw a look toward the cashier, but she seemed engrossed in weighing the green grapes she'd gotten for Shad.

Henry swept his arm around her and pulled her into his side. "Of course it can be." He kissed her temple and then her cheek. He took the change from the cashier and started toward the door with their groceries.

Angel followed him, and stood back as he loaded her groceries into the back of her car. "I have to text to get the pickup orders." She looked at him, wishing they'd just arrived at the grocery store. "I don't want to go so soon, but I've got stuff in the car that needs to be in the fridge."

Henry took her face in both of his hands and kissed her again right there in the parking lot. "I'm gonna come over tonight."

"You're going to come over tonight?"

"Yeah," he said. "I'll make sure no one sees me. Once I get in your house, no one will know I'm there."

"What are you going to tell Levi?" she asked, still trying to think through the excitement of his kiss and what he'd said at the same time.

His face looked blank for a moment, and then strong determination came into his jaw. "I don't know," he said. "But I'm going to come over tonight." He kissed her again, his lips sliding down and touching her neck.

"Because I miss you, Angel. And I want to see you every day. I want to talk more about what you want your life to be, hear more about your horseback riding lessons, and find out if you want to have kids, or if you want to stay at Lone Star, or if you've got other big dreams and things that I can help you achieve."

She sure liked the sound of all of that. She threaded her fingers through Henry's hair and guided his mouth back to hers. She kissed him this time, and Henry let her lead the way, stroke for stroke. When she pulled away, they stayed close, their breath mingling.

"I would love a slow evening with you at my house."

"We do need to slow down," he said.

She wasn't sure if he meant the amount of kissing they did or if life was just hectic right now. For Angel, she was implementing a lot of changes at Lone Star. She had a lot of work in front of her before she could estab-lish the nine new positions that would alleviate a lot of her stress.

"Yeah," she said. "I need you to help me slow down tonight."

"I'll be there," he said. "I don't know when, okay? But I'm gonna be there."

"Okay." With great difficulty, she took herself out of his arms and got in her car. He pushed the cart down the long row to where he'd parked the big ranch truck, and Angel sighed.

Yes, they'd just eaten from a salad bar in a grocery store, and they'd only walked around and bought a few things, but it had felt intimate. It felt like something friends did, something she'd do with someone she trusted, someone she could just walk around casually with and be comfortable with.

Angel needed that level of comfort and friendship in her life, and she had just pulled out of the stall when she got a text from her momma that said, *If you're still at the store, I need more canning lids for strawberry jam.*

Angel let out a sigh, pulled back into her parking space, and went to get the canning supplies. She could weather anything today. She could wrestle any challenge to the ground. She could shoulder anything—because Henry was coming over tonight.

Chapter Twenty

Henry sat on the top step of the porch at his cabin, his eyes on his phone, as the sun sank in the west. The day turned dusky, then darker and darker, and would eventually be night. Henry hoped he could then slip away and walk over to Angel's. He often sat on the front porch or on the front steps and texted, so this wasn't a new activity for him, and Levi shouldn't suspect anything.

And it so happened that his family text string had gone off the rails. Momma had just found out John's graduation date, and of course, she wanted everyone to come celebrate him as a Baylor graduate. Paul had already said he'd be there. Rich would return home from Amarillo State for the summer, so he'd be living in Three Rivers, and he would go with Momma and Daddy to the graduation. That, of course, left Henry.

He swiped over to his calendar and looked at it. John's graduation was on a Friday, but Baylor was hundreds of miles away. He would need at least two days off to be able to attend, and he might be able to be back by Monday.

"Could be three days off," he said to the deepening darkness. Not that it really mattered. Angel would give him the time off; it was a family thing, not just him going out, getting drunk, or losing track of time.

After he'd left the grocery store this afternoon, he'd gone by the farrier academy to get his own graduation packet. It was due next week, and Henry would make another trip to town to drop it off. *I have my graduation date too*, he texted. *May 21.*

A few weeks after John's, so his parents should be able to come, and he wondered if John would be able to. He'd gotten an internship with a company that made horse trailers, and he knew it started pretty quickly.

That's great, Momma said. *I'll put it on the calendar right now. Daddy and I will for sure be there.*

I can be there too, Rich said.

I'll be there, Paul said. And, of course, that just left John. He'd been texting a few minutes ago, but he didn't chime in right away, and Henry didn't really mind if his brother missed the graduation.

I understand schedules are tight and weird, he said. *If everyone can't come, it's not a big deal.* They'd all come to his college graduation, as he'd been the first in their family to earn a college degree. He didn't expect them to come for his farrier certificate.

They're rearranging a bunch of stuff here at Lone Star, he texted next. *I've applied for a captain position, as well as a foreman position, as well as a welcome greeter position that doesn't even exist right now. Angel's doing a lot of restructuring. I'm expecting her to make some announcements in the next couple of weeks.*

That's great, Daddy said. *We'll pray for you.*

Henry lowered his phone and looked out into the night. It hadn't quite turned all the way dark yet, but his eyes took a moment for them to adjust from the light of his phone to the blackness beyond.

He sure liked that his daddy had gone right to *we'll pray for you* when Henry had told him about the opportunities here. And that tickled his compliment bone, the one he'd been trying to exercise more and more since his conversation with Levi weeks ago.

Who else can we pray for? he texted his family. He'd been trying to find people around him that he could help, people that needed lifting up, and he figured he could extend that to his family.

Paul answered, and as Henry read the message, a blip of surprise moved through him. *I'm planning to propose to Brielle soon,* he said. *I'm real nervous about it, so I could use some prayers for that.*

Momma sent five praying hands, and John said,

Wow, you're gonna propose to Brielle? with five question marks.

Henry kind of felt the same way but not really. Paul and Brielle had been dating for almost a year now. He tapped out of the family texts and moved over to one with just Paul.

Why are you nervous about asking her to marry you? he asked.

Her family has a ranch in the Hill Country, Paul said to just Henry. *Brielle's the oldest, and she's kind of always thought that she would take it over. But I've got Courage Reins and all the things I do with Three Rivers, so I'm a little nervous that she might not say yes because she doesn't want to live on that ranch with me.*

Henry hadn't known that Brielle had a ranch and that she might inherit it in the Hill Country. He assumed that she'd move to Three Rivers with Paul, that they'd find a house in town or find a way to build a house out at the ranch, and that they'd live there while Paul ran the equine therapy unit for Daddy.

Henry's lungs had no idea how to keep breathing, but his fingers managed to type out, *Wow. That is something.*

Yeah, Paul said, and Henry could hear the dejected tone in the four letters.

I'm sorry, brother, he said. *I'll pray for you and Brielle both to have a clear mind.*

Thank you, Paul said. *I think that's what we need.*

I know you'll figure out the right thing to do for you, Henry said. *You're real smart like that, Paul. Don't forget that.*

Paul called, which didn't surprise Henry all that much, and he said, "Hey, brother," as he answered the phone.

Paul said nothing, which spoke volumes, and Henry's own throat worked with emotion. Finally, Paul said, in a slightly nasal voice, "Thank you, Henry. I really needed to hear that."

"That you're smart?" Henry asked.

"Yeah," Paul clipped out.

"Why do you think you're not smart?" Henry asked.

"Well, I'm not graduating from Baylor," Paul said in a normal tone. "I didn't graduate in industrial engineering, and I'm not about to get my farrier certificate. In fact, I'm the only one who didn't go to college at all. I just work the ranch."

"There's no 'just' about that," Henry said softly. "I know loads of men who work ranches. They're really good at it, and it means something to the people they serve and the work they do."

"Yeah," Paul bit out again, clearly inside his head on this issue, and Henry wasn't sure how to help him.

"Well, you're the smartest person I know," he said. "Whenever I'm wondering what to do, I think, 'What would Paul think? What would Paul do? How would Paul handle this?'"

"Oh, that's just not true," Paul said.

"It is," Henry said. "You lead with a level head. You always say the right thing, and you always do what you're supposed to do, even if you don't want to."

"Do you think that includes leaving the ranch and going to the Hill Country to be with Brielle?" Paul whispered.

Henry didn't rightly know, and the stars that had started to come out certainly didn't hold the answers. He took a breath of the night air, wishing the night would cool off, but it probably wouldn't. "I don't know, Paul. I wish I did, but I don't know."

"I don't either," Paul said. "I told Daddy about it a couple of days ago. I think he's totally stumped; I don't think he knew what to do at all."

"Yeah," Henry said. "Because I'm not there. John's not there, and Rich is kind of...." He didn't know what to put there that wouldn't be demeaning. He loved his younger brother.

"A party animal," Paul supplied. They both laughed, and Henry decided that summed up Rich pretty well.

"Yeah," he said. "He's young still. That's what he is. He's young still. Needs time to grow up."

"Yeah," Paul said. "But Daddy's not sure he has time. He's ready for someone to start taking over right now, so he can move into semi-retirement the way Uncle Squire's gonna do by the end of this year."

"Yeah," Henry said. "I heard Libby was coming back."

"Yep," Paul said. "She's got everything worked out with her job in Oklahoma. She's going through the paperwork, and she should be here before Thanksgiving."

"That's amazing," Henry said, and he had no desire to return to Courage Reins or Three Rivers and make it his permanent home. He thought about Angel, and there was no way she would ever leave Lone Star. She'd already taken it over. Anyone she fell in love with and married would live right here at Lone Star with her.

But do they have to? Henry wondered, and he wasn't sure why his mind had come up with that question, nor was he sure how to answer it.

"Momma's texting again," Paul said. "She really wants everyone at John's graduation, and she wants everyone at yours."

"I know," Henry said. "I'll talk to Angel about it tomorrow. In fact, I can talk to her about it tonight." His nerves suddenly itched at him to get off these steps and over to Angel's. "I've got to go."

"Yeah," Paul said. "It's getting late."

"Yeah," Henry said, as if he was going to go to bed next. "I'll talk to you later, brother. Love you."

"Love you too," Paul said, and the call ended.

Henry got to his feet, stretched out his back and his legs, and then texted Levi. *Family stuff is crazy right now. I'm gonna go for a walk for a little bit. Don't wait up for me. I'll see you in the morning.*

Okay, Levi said. *I'll leave the light on. I'm going to bed now.*

Okay, Henry said.

Anything I can do about the family stuff?

No, Henry said. *But thank you, Levi.* And he meant it, because Levi was a good friend and a good man, and if he could help Henry, he would. Henry had talked through some of his other familial problems in the past, and Levi had helped him have a level head going into certain situations and conversations with his daddy.

Now, Henry tucked his phone away and moved into the darkness, away from the cabins, away from the lights coming from the cabin. The stables had automatic lights that came on when someone got too close, but Henry had been walking the line between the cabins and the stables, testing how close he could get before the lights flashed on.

The alley was about twenty feet wide, and if he just stayed in that area, he could walk in the darkness, no one would see him, and he could get to the back of the farmhouse that way. Angel just lived another jog down the road from there. He'd walked it a few times now, planning on surprising her one night.

Tonight was that night. Outside the grocery store, he'd kissed her deeper than he ever kissed her before, and she'd kissed him back. When Henry said they needed to slow down, he meant physically. He didn't want to get himself into too much trouble. And he and Angel had really only been dating for six weeks, despite the fact that he'd known her longer than that.

He crept up to her back door, knocked a few times, hoping she was still awake. Cursing himself mentally, he pulled out his phone to send her a text when the door opened, and light spilled out onto her back deck, haloing her from behind.

"Henry," she whispered.

"Sorry, I meant to text you," he whispered back.

She pushed open the screen door, and Henry slipped inside. She sealed them in and locked the door, which felt very dangerous and very off-limits to Henry.

She didn't wear her usual jeans and tank top, nor her cowgirl boots. In fact, Henry saw her bare feet, when he hadn't seen before. At his parents' house, on that lazy Sunday where she'd worn his cousin's clothes, she'd worn socks.

She wore a pair of loose, blue pajama shorts with a matching tank top, and she looked like she might head outside and sit in a chaise lounge to get a suntan. Perhaps she wore a bikini underneath her clothes, and she'd take those off so that she could get every inch of her skin a golden brown.

Henry shoved the thoughts away, recoiled from the images that entered his mind, and licked his lips as he looked at her. "How're you doing tonight?"

"Good," she said, staying across the kitchen from him.

"The deadline for applications is over." He didn't know what to do with his hands. He wasn't sure why he was so nervous. But the fact was, he'd only been in her house once before this, and for some reason, this first, forbidden meeting in her house had brought some nerves to his chest.

"Yeah," she said. "It seems like everyone applied."

"That's good," Henry said, though his competitive streak reared up. "That means you've got a good, nice culture here."

"Yeah," she said. "I'm not unhappy with it. Lots to choose from."

"Everyone?" he asked.

"Almost everyone," she said. "Caleb's finishing up his apprenticeship, and he's decided he's not going to come back."

"Oh," Henry said. "When do I need to decide that?" With everything else going on, he hadn't even thought about staying on at Lone Star or moving on.

"I'm going to go over all of that in the interviews," she said, tension all over her face. "Normally, I'd do that in May, but there's no reason to have two interviews so close together."

"Mm hm."

"Do you have any idea what you might do?"

Every door in his life felt like it stood wide open

right now, and Henry couldn't add his future at Lone Star to the mix. "No, I'm not sure."

"Well, your apprenticeship will be up at the end of May," she said. "We'll write you a real good letter of recommendation if you have somewhere else you want to go or if you're starting your own place." She cut off when Henry reached out and touched his finger to her lips.

"I don't know what I'm doing, Angel," he said. "There's no other place. I'm not going to start my own business. I've just got a lot going on right now and haven't thought about extending my apprenticeship here."

She nodded, and Henry dropped his hand. "You want some coffee?"

"No, ma'am," he said. "I'll be up all night. Already got a lot of thoughts in my head keeping me awake."

"You do?" she asked. "Like what?"

Henry hooked his thumb over his shoulder. "Can we maybe go sit down?"

"Yeah, sure," she said, and she seemed nervous too.

Henry took her hand and started to relax. He led her into the living room. He sat on the couch and pulled her down onto his lap. "It's sure good to see you, Angel." He nuzzled the tip of his nose against her cheek. "I didn't mean to kiss you so strongly this afternoon," he said. "I apologize."

"It's fine," Angel whispered.

"Yeah, I know," he said. "But I minded it. It's not something we should be doing."

"Okay," she said.

Henry sighed. "I don't think the 3D horseshoes are going to work."

"No?" She took off his cowboy hat and set it on the top of the couch, then she brushed her fingers through his hair.

Henry closed his eyes and enjoyed the sensation of her touch. "No," he said. "Everyone I've called says it can't be done. I even asked my daddy for help with Gilligan's shoes. He's got a master ironsmith who does custom shoes for horses, and I'm going to meet with him next time I go to Three Rivers."

"When is that going to be?" Angel asked.

"I don't know," Henry said. "My brother's graduating from Baylor at the end of the month, so probably then."

"You're graduating in May too," she said.

"Yeah," he said. "Six or seven more weeks. I just got the packet today. Momma's got it on her calendar. Everyone will come."

"You don't sound happy about that," she said.

"I am," he said. "My family's just...my family. You've got one. You know how they are."

"Yeah," she said. "They're awesome, but they're a little complicated sometimes."

"Exactly." He touched his mouth to her jaw and then her neck. "You sure smell good."

"Hm mm."

Henry smiled at her adoption of his humming. "I didn't get an 'I need a cowboy hug' before I came over."

"Maybe I didn't need one," she said.

Henry opened his eyes and looked at Angel, the moment sobering and lengthening. "What if we fall in love, but I don't want to live here? Then what?"

Angel's eyes widened and she blinked rapidly. "What do you mean?"

"What if we want to get married?" he asked. "I know it's real early. I don't need you to be thinking about that. But what if we do?" He took a big breath. "I think it would be great if you lived off-site," he said. "It would give you more distance from Lone Star, and we could commute in."

"You want to buy somewhere else and commute in?"

"Yeah," he said. "It's something I've been thinking about. I might talk to my cousin Finn about finding a place. He's got a one-man operation."

"You want to buy a *ranch*?" she asked, incredulity in her voice. "Henry, baby, if we get married, Lone Star *is* our ranch."

"It's *your* ranch."

But if you're with me, it's your ranch too," she said.

"But that doesn't mean we have to live here." He

brushed her hair back, noting that she still wore her wig. "Can I take this off?"

Panic paraded across her face, then everything relaxed, and she said, "Okay, I'll do it." She reached up and pressed something, and when she brushed her hair back, the wig came right off. She wore a wig cap underneath. Henry had seen those because his momma had used them in the past.

"I just don't have very much hair," she said. "It grows in real thin, and I look bald in some places."

"Hm." He reached up and pushed the wig cap back, loosening her hair. He brushed his fingers through it. It was silky and soft, like corn silk, and she was right. There wasn't a whole lot of it.

"Medical condition?" he asked.

"I got pneumonia when I was eighteen or nineteen," she said. "My hair never grew right after that."

He pulled her head down and kissed her on her forehead and then kissed her on the top of her head. "You're beautiful no matter what."

Angel smiled at him, and she leaned her head against his shoulder. Henry didn't know what else to say. He'd already brought up *marriage* and where they might live if that happened, and he figured that was enough for tonight. With all the graduations weighing on his mind, and Paul possibly moving to the Hill Country, Henry simply couldn't think about anything more. So he held Angel in his arms, and he slowed all the way down until only the two of them existed in this small living room, in a house, on a ranch, in the Texas Panhandle.

Angel lay softly in his arms, and when she breathed in deep and then let it out slow, he realized she'd fallen asleep. He loved that, because it meant she had also slowed down enough, and she was comfortable enough with him, that she didn't have to be on high alert. She didn't have to be on alert at all.

Henry's disappointment over the 3D printing of the horseshoes melted away, all the stress of his calendaring and scheduling, and the worry over perhaps getting a promotion here at Lone Star—none of it mattered.

Only the woman in his arms mattered. Henry stood as carefully as he could so that he didn't disturb her, and he carried her down the hall to her bedroom. She stirred slightly as he tucked her in, then she went right back to sleep.

Henry tiptoed out of her room. He wasn't sure if she pulled her bedroom door closed all the way or not, so he left it open a few inches and snuck back into the night.

The sky spanned forever above him, pricked with starlight. Henry allowed all of his questions to come out, and he murmured them as he took the fifteen-minute walk back to his cabin.

"What's the right thing for Paul to do? Can John really come to my graduation? Should Angel and I make our relationship public? How will things go over when the new employee handbook comes out? Who are she and Justin and Bard going to pick for the promotions? What should I do with my life? Should I stay on for another year? Should I start my own farrier business? Should I try to find a place of my own to live in and commute to Lone Star if I stay?"

Everything came out, and Henry let it because the night was so big and so wide that it could absorb whatever came out of his mouth. God felt the same way to Henry. He was so big and so wide, and He could take anything Henry threw at Him.

His front porch light activated as he stepped close enough to his cabin, and Henry murmured one more thing: "Lord, light the path ahead, and I will follow it."

Chapter Twenty-One

Angel bent over the whiteboard in her office. It had been covering her desk for the better part of the past two weeks. She and Justin had made nameplates for every man working at Lone Star, and she'd started moving them into new positions.

"If we move Copper to a welcome greeter, will he still be able to keep up with his duties in the stables?" She didn't look at Justin as she asked, and he came over to her desk with a cup of coffee.

She straightened and took it, and he said, "Yeah, Copper's great. He'll have no trouble keeping up, even as we move into summer."

She took a sip of her coffee, wondering if her choices would hold. She had been relying a lot more on her intuition, making moves, and then taking those decisions to the Lord at night.

293

She prayed every morning over breakfast with Momma and Daddy that she would have a clear mind and eyes to see, and that she would meet the needs of the men at Lone Star who had embraced the culture. They lived for it and wanted to be there.

"I think our welcome greeters are great," Justin said. "Shad's going to do fantastic as a farrier foreman. Caleb will be amazing in your captain position here."

Angel nodded and said, "Hm," just like Henry did. Caleb would be their first all-horseman captain, as in the past, all their captains had been farriers. The farriers dictated what horse care needed to be done, and then the horsemen carried those out.

She and Justin had agreed on Cedric, Jake, and Nathan as new team leads, which would fill those three positions—*if you hadn't moved Henry and Ray to captain positions*, she thought.

That had created two more vacancies for team leads. She'd given them to Thompson and Miles, both interns this year, who showed incredible promise. Henry and Ray would move into two of the three new captain positions, as well as Thane, another horseman who had never held a leadership position before. As she'd studied his application, she'd seen a fantastic horseman, worker, and person He was in his mid-thirties, so he wasn't new to this, and he'd come to them from another farm when it had closed.

She took another sip of her coffee and looked at the whiteboard. "I'm not sure what else to move."

"We haven't moved names on this thing for three days." Justin grinned at her and turned around so that he faced the door and she faced the window. He looked out the side of his eye, because sometimes it was better if people didn't make direct eye contact with Angel.

"Angel, I think this is it. You're obsessing over it a little bit. It's time to just make the announcement."

She nodded and said, "I'll tell Trevor I'm ready for Monday." A nest of bees grew in her stomach instantly, but that also could have been hunger pangs, as Angel hadn't eaten since that morning.

"All right," Justin said. "You've got contracts to generate, don't you?" That was his not-so-subtle way of saying *stop obsessing over this. The lineup is final.* He walked out of her office, gently closing the door behind him.

Angel studied the whiteboard for several more moments, as well as the names on the side who hadn't been moved into any of the new positions. The nurturing, caring side of her wanted to give every man at Lone Star an opportunity for leadership and advancement. She knew it wasn't possible, just like she knew she couldn't hire every farrier at Sherman Academy.

She turned away from the whiteboard and went to sit at her temporary desk, which was a four-foot-long folding table that Henry had set up for her last week. Her computer sat there, as did her printer, and Justin had been right. She had contracts to print.

She'd seen no need to duplicate the work of interviewing everyone at Lone Star to find out if they were going to stay for another year—something she'd normally do in two or three weeks—when she was already interviewing everyone for these new positions on the ranch. So she'd asked everyone a month early, and she told them all to let her know by yesterday.

And they had. So, yes, today she had new contracts to generate, even though they wouldn't be signed for another six weeks. She wanted to hand every man moving into a new position a welcome folder with their job descriptions, their teams, and their new contracts. Since she'd had to move people into team leads and captain positions, as well as appoint a new foreman and her welcome greeters, she now had eleven new packets to generate.

Justin and Daddy had gone through the teams and mixed everyone up so that everything would be brand new and shiny starting on June first. Angel simply had to input the names of who would be on what team, and of course, she'd spent the last month laboring over the new employee handbook, which now included brand new job descriptions for welcome greeters as well as a farrier foreman. That wouldn't be back from the printer for another month, but she could print individual pages for those specific jobs.

She still hadn't brought up the no-dating rule with Daddy, and she hadn't shown him the employee handbook before sending it to the printer. "Justin saw it," she muttered to herself, but he had made no comment on it.

Angel's printer whirred every few minutes as she finalized documents and printed them. She needed a much longer table, but she managed to put together Shad's foreman folder as well as the welcome greeter folders before someone knocked on her door.

"Come in," she called. She stood at the table, stuffing folders for Zane and Copper, so she could easily turn and see who was coming in. Henry entered, a bright smile on his face, matching the way his white cowboy hat tipped up into a grin as well.

"Hey, sweetheart," he said, all the swagger in the world in his voice and in his step. "You realize you're missing dinner, right?"

Angel blinked at him. Surely she hadn't forgotten that tonight was one of their three weekly dinners where they fed everyone.

"What day is it?" she asked.

Henry laughed and said, "Thursday, baby." He took her into his arms, but he hadn't closed the door, and an alarm bell rang through Angel.

"Henry," she whispered, "The door's open."

"Hm. It sure is," he said as he leaned down and inhaled the scent of her skin along her neck. "And everyone's at dinner except you." He raised his head and looked at her. "Well, and now me."

He pressed his lips to hers in a closed-mouth, chaste kiss. "Do you need to finish up? Can I help you with something? Everyone's wondering where you are."

Angel could stand in the circle of his arms for a good long while, but her stomach did tell her that she needed to eat. And she could print out the team lead and captain positions tomorrow.

"I can come now," she said.

Henry reached over and turned off her computer. "Great, let's go." He held her hand for the few steps it took to get out of the office, but then he dropped it as he led the way outside, and down the path to the backyard of the farmhouse.

Sure enough, tables had been set up for the thirty people who ate there three times a week, and the combined scent of pulled pork, barbecue chicken, and smoked brisket rode on the air.

At least the catering arrived, she thought. *Without any help from you.* She'd ordered the catering, of course, and she did love Chuckwagon Dinners and their smoked meats and delicious Texas sides they brought once a month.

"There you are," Levi said as Angel arrived at the table where Henry had obviously been sitting.

"Found her working," Henry said, and he flashed a smile that didn't look too flirty or too romantic or like they were anything more than friends.

Angel smiled at the men sitting there and said, "Just lost track of time. I'll go grab some food."

On her way to the long table that held all the proteins and side dishes, her stride got interrupted as someone whistled through their teeth. The loud, shrill noise cut all the conversation, and Angel turned to find Justin standing on a chair.

"Now that everyone's here," he boomed, graciously not looking over to Angel. "I just want everyone to know that roll call is going to start fifteen minutes early tomorrow. Please be gathered in front of stable one at six-forty-five instead of seven. Miss Angel will have a lengthy announcement about the new positions here at Lone Star, and anyone moving into a new role will receive the information they need at that time."

He grinned at her then, and Angel suddenly felt like the entire world's eyes had landed on her.

"All right," Justin said, clapping his hands. "Get back to eatin'."

All the cowboys in the group clapped back at him, the slapping sound of it hanging in the silent air. Angel stood there for a moment, and while a few conversations broke out and the energy in the air had definitely doubled, she felt like she had been stripped of all her clothing and now stood naked in front of everyone who worked at Lone Star.

Not only that, but she'd have to go back to her office and get the packets printed and ready for tomorrow morning—fifteen minutes early—or she'd have to get up really early to finish that work. Irritation burned through her as she caught Justin's eye, his grin wide as he came toward her.

"You're mad, aren't you?" he asked with a chuckle, but he certainly didn't care if she was.

"Who says I'm going to announce the leadership positions tomorrow?" she grumbled as she headed toward the food table once again.

"I just did," he said. "Because I knew if I didn't, you'd obsess over it for the whole weekend, and you don't need to do that." He'd become firmer with her since she'd been to Three Rivers, since she'd talked to Daddy about getting new positions, since she'd told Justin that she needed another foreman on the farrier side and had asked him to help her staff more leadership positions at Lone Star.

She'd been grateful for all of that, as he was several years older than her and had plenty of experience in barn management and equine care.

She didn't confirm or deny that she would obsess for the next three days until Monday morning, and she figured a Friday morning roll call was as good a time as any to announce the leadership roles. They still had roll call on the weekends, but they all worked a reduced schedule. And with the new positions in place, she wouldn't have to work hardly at all on the weekends.

"Those new positions don't start until June first," she reminded herself. She still had six weeks of carrying everything at Lone Star. But suddenly the load wasn't so heavy, because she really was bringing on an excellent team to help her, to take Lone Star into the future, and to ensure that the boarding stable would continue to provide excellent care for men and equines alike for many years to come.

She got her food and returned to the table where Henry had saved her seat. She sat between him and Caleb. Everyone around her went silent, and Angel stared at her potato salad as she pushed it around on her plate, finally stabbing a chunk. She looked up and said, "It's done, guys. It's decided."

That seemed to break the ice, and Henry said, "Yeah, of course it is. And no matter who you picked, Angel, we're going to support them—and you."

She looked at him and found the utmost sincerity in his eyes.

"That's right," Levi drawled from across the table. "Everyone here is deserving. Whoever gets the positions, we'll all rally behind them."

"Thank you," Angel said quietly, though that had been the culture that she, Daddy, and her granddaddy before him had cultivated.

Henry went back to his phone, and Levi said something to Copper down the table. Angel glanced across to Levi. With Shad moving into the farrier foreman position, that left one of their three master farrier positions open, and she and Justin had chosen Levi for it. He had been a full-time skilled farrier working with apprentices at Lone Star for two years now, and while it might be a little bit early to advance him, as Angel looked at him and he gave her a healthy smile, a warm blanket settled around her shoulders, letting her know that she'd made the right choice.

Two seats down from him sat Zane, another full-time farrier. She'd moved him to a greeting position, and she'd had to promote somebody else from captain into that position. That would be Brent Howsman. She glanced down the table toward Henry's side but didn't see Brent.

So many changes, she thought, and another flutter of nerves winged its way through her body. *It's going to be fine*, she told herself as she finished her potato salad and moved to the brisket.

"Here you go," Henry said. He placed a bottle of barbecue sauce in front of her. "You like the sweet kind, right? Or is it the spicy?" He looked down the table. "Hey, Copper, hand us that spicy sauce."

"I like the sweet," Angel said. "It's fine." She waved off the spicy sauce just as her phone dinged. She'd set it next to her plate in its usual place so she could glance at it whenever it went off. If she needed to answer, she'd pick it up.

Heat filled her face, zooming from her toes up her legs through her torso and straight to the back of her mouth when she saw Henry's name there and the letters *INACH*.

That had started out as code for "I need a cowboy hug," when Angel needed him to slow her down, help her, or simply be in the same room with her to soothe her.

It had morphed to "I need a cow*girl* hug" whenever Henry wanted to come to her office, or he'd figured out a way for them to meet off-site.

In the past week or so, it had morphed into simply an acronym that meant "I'm coming over tonight." She supposed they could have changed it to *ICOT*, but they hadn't. And Angel didn't dare look at Henry, just in case her face had turned to the color of poppies.

She flipped her phone over and clued into the conversation happening next to her. She didn't have to contribute to it to be more present, and she did want to be present. These family-style dinners three times a week fed the culture here at Lone Star. The men here really did support each other. And it was really hard to have misunderstandings go on for too long or people who didn't get along super well when they ate together three nights a week. That didn't mean everyone got along spectacularly, and Angel feared that with her shake-up, she may have teamed up people that would cause some discomfort in the beginning. Angel had gotten comfortable with being uncomfortable, and she expected her men to do the same.

Something popped into her mind, and she turned to Henry and said, "Oh, your leave of absence is approved for your brother's graduation."

"Great," he said. "Thanks." He'd be gone Thursday through Monday next week, and he'd invited her to go to John's graduation with him. Angel hadn't known how to answer initially. She wanted to be with Henry off the ranch. But showing up to such an intimate family event?

She wasn't sure how she felt about that. Henry had said he had not told his parents that they were dating, and when she challenged him with, "Well, what are you going to tell them when I show up for John's graduation?" he'd remained silent.

They both knew that couldn't happen, even if they wanted it. Angel's mind shifted to his graduation. He hadn't asked her about coming yet, and she wondered if he would. She and Daddy sometimes attended the graduation at Sherman Academy, especially if they had an intern there who was becoming a master farrier, which took quite a few years.

Flint was getting his master's certificate this year, and in fact, he wasn't returning to Lone Star come June. He had another job opportunity in Central Texas, and he was taking his family and moving there. She could perhaps use that as a reason to go to Henry's graduation this year, but she kept that tucked under her tongue for now.

Angel managed to eat her dinner, and then she headed back to her office with snakes slithering through her bloodstream to get the last several packets ready for tomorrow morning's announcement.

Chapter Twenty-Two

Henry and Levi walked over to roll call by six-thirty the following morning. They clearly weren't the only ones nervous and early. At least half the cowboys that lived and worked at Lone Star had already arrived. They stood around in clumps of two or three, most of them not talking, but every once in a while, one of them would say something and the others would nod or agree. Then silence would descend again.

Flint had built a proper stand for Trevor that didn't have steps, but instead, a ramp. The man could get up that far easier, and he had something to hold onto the whole way.

"This is terrible," Levi muttered, just as he had last night at dinner. Henry had gone to see Angel last night, but he'd made a promise to himself with every step of the fifteen-minute walk that he would *not* ask her for any of the names of the men in new positions. He didn't want to know if he'd gotten one. He didn't want to know if Levi did. Well, he did, but he didn't want to ask her, and he hadn't.

Six-forty came and then six-forty-four, and finally six-forty-five arrived. Trevor moved awkwardly up the ramp to start roll call, his helpers right there next to him and Justin at his side as well. The current foreman of the ranch stayed on the ground and folded his arms, making his biceps and shoulders look beefier than they already were.

He was an excellent horseman with a decade of age and experience on Henry. He was the barn manager at Lone Star, and Henry reported to him about his horses, but he'd never really worked with the man outside of that capacity. Bard and Angel obviously trusted him, and because they did, Henry did too.

Trevor started the day by saying, "Thanks for showing up on time. We know a lot of you are real nervous about today's announcements, and we're not going to prolong things and make them harder for you. Angel is just finishing up a few things in her office, and then she'll be right out. I've asked Justin to give you a little insight into how this process went and some behind-the-scenes knowledge of the decisions that were made." He looked down to Justin, who finally put a smile on his face.

"It's a great Friday morning, men," he called, and he

clapped his hands once. Everybody clapped back at him, including Henry, and plenty of feet shifted left and right. Henry could barely swallow. His nerves assaulted him, and he wasn't even sure why. He'd felt like his interview had gone well. He told Angel he was going to come back for another year, and she said she'd prepare his contract, that they'd be glad to have him.

He'd celebrated with his family on the group text string they shared, and he expected his momma to have a little gift for him when he went home for John's graduation next weekend.

"All y'all have been here for at least a year," Justin said. "Some of us a lot longer. If you know Angel White at all, you know that she pours everything she has into this place, into this job, into your lives, into her family's life, into the land, into the horses. The only reason she's announcing the jobs today is because I made her. Otherwise, she'd have endured three more sleepless nights before she finally did it on Monday. No matter what you hear, you're valued here. Every one of you." He paused and surveyed the crowd, the emotion streaming plainly across his face.

"You all have skills to contribute, even if you're just now coming up on your year mark, even if you haven't graduated yet, even if you don't get promoted. Everybody here has value because *you're here*, and just getting here means you're in the top echelon of horsemen and farriers in the world. Don't forget that."

Trevor started to move down the ramp, where he hugged Angel when he reached the ground. She held at least a dozen folders in various colors in her hands, and Henry could only stare at her as she went up the ramp to the small platform. She reached over the railing and handed all the folders to Justin, and she swallowed as she looked out across the others standing outside stable one.

She wore her usual blue jeans, steel-toed boots, and her tank top this morning bore the color of bright, ripe apricots. Her wig sat clipped perfectly in place, and Henry swore the sunlight glinted off her glossed lips. His heart beat faster because she was so pretty and so perfect, and he wanted to be the one for her.

He also really wanted a new position at Lone Star. He hadn't been able to admit it to himself until that moment. But as Angel cleared her throat and said, "Justin's right, you know," Henry could admit that he didn't want to be a team lead anymore.

The next logical step for him would be captain. He had no grand aspirations of skipping that position and going to foreman. Though he supposed he could be a welcome greeter or, if one of their master farriers got moved into a higher position, he could become one of those. His mind whispered to him that he was not a master farrier yet, and in fact, not even a licensed farrier for six more weeks.

Even if Bard liked him, even if his work was exceptional, the best Henry could hope for was captain, and hope for it he did.

Angel could make speeches if she had to. Henry had heard her do it before. But today she let the country stillness drape over all of them for several long seconds. Then she said, "I really value all of you here at Lone Star. I appreciate your time in coming to interview with me, your honesty, your integrity. And just each one of you for who you are. I'm not going to make you suffer any longer. Anyone who gets a folder today is going to be asked to stay after this meeting, which is why we started a few minutes early. We'll still be done at seven-thirty, and everyone will be moved on to their daily jobs by then. Remember that none of these positions begin until June first, including any increase in wage, the title that you might have after your name, and your duties between now and then. Justin and I will meet with each of you, and we expect you to meet with your new teams."

She swiveled her head left and right, her eagle eyes missing nothing as a murmur rose through the men. "That's right," she said. "Every single person will be on a new team. From today forward, your team leads and your captains and your foreman—your *new foremen*— will reach out to you and let you know that you're on their team. And those of you who get leadership positions today, that needs to be done by noon. So you'll have an extra job. And hopefully, we're going to give you an extra fifteen or twenty minutes this morning to do it."

She cleared her throat again and held out her hand. Justin put the only green folder in it.

"Without further ado," she said. "Most of you won't know your new position. But a couple of you do. Our higher-ups already know because today for them is going to be busier than usual." She opened the green folder and said, "So everyone welcome your new foreman on the farrier side." She looked up, her blue eyes blazing and her smile filling the whole sky with warmth and sunshine. "Shad Roundy."

Applause burst out, and Henry added his clapping to it, trying to get some of the nervous energy out of his system through his hands.

"Shad's gonna be great!" he yelled to Levi standing next to him. "What a great choice." Levi's smile rivaled Angel's as he clapped and then whooped and hollered with everybody else.

Shad's face bore a bit of ruddy color as he went forward and took the folder from Angel, accepted a handshake and a half-hug from Justin, and faded to the side to stand with Trevor.

Justin passed Angel the only yellow folder, and everyone instantly silenced. "With Shad moving into a foreman position," she said. "That leaves a hole in our full-time master farrier trio." She paused, looked at the closed folder, then continued with, "I'm pleased to say that Shad's position is going to Levi Johnson." She looked right at Henry—really, she looked right at Levi, who stood next to Henry. The crowd erupted again, and Henry turned to Levi and could only stare at him.

"You knew about this, didn't you?" he yelled over the crowd. Levi finally laughed, shook his head, and grabbed onto Henry in a hug. Henry pounded him on the back, offering his congratulations before Levi jogged through the crowd to get his yellow folder.

Justin handed her a purple folder, and everybody instantly quieted again. "It's with a heavy heart that I need to inform you that Flint is going to be leaving us this summer. He's going to take his family and move to another ranch just outside of Austin," she said. "That leaves a hole in our full-time apprentice leaders. And with Levi moving into a master apprentice position, we have *two* people that we need to move up into these leadership positions."

Angel handled herself with grace and power, and she beamed radiance out into the crowd. "Owen and Ranger."

Applause burst out again, and Henry joined in, cheering for Owen and Ranger, who were great farriers. They'd graduated a few years ahead of him, and they'd be great in the apprentice management positions.

"Now I want to do team leads next," Angel said. "These men are all farriers, and they'll lead a team of two horsemen and one farrier, which makes a team of four. Our captains will do the same thing: two farriers, two horsemen on every team."

Justin handed her a pile of blue folders, and she didn't open them or consult a list. "Your new team leads are Cedric, Jake, Nathan, Thompson, and Miles." Henry glanced over to the nearest man to him, who happened to be Nathan.

"That's five," he said as he started to clap along with everyone else. Angel had only announced *three* team lead positions a few weeks ago—why had she called five names? The men went forward and collected their folders, moved off to the side, shook hands, hugged those around them. The crowd in front of Angel was starting to be smaller than the one to the side of her.

"We have new captain positions," she said as she accepted a handful of red folders. "Thane, Ray, Caleb, and Henry."

The air left Henry's lungs, leaving plenty of room for gratitude to stream in. Had his name really been called? It had, if the way Caleb beamed over to him and said, "Let's go, boss," and took off toward Angel.

Again, Henry's mind cataloged that she'd called four names when she'd only announced three positions. But he realized now why—he was no longer a team lead. Someone had to take his place. She'd announced three captain positions but called four names, which meant somebody who was a captain would be doing something else. Henry couldn't keep up with the buzz, the energy, the handshakes, the smiling, and Angel had two more folders anyway.

"And lastly, we have our two brand-new, welcome greeter positions," Angel said, holding orange folders in her hands now. The breeze kicked up, but Henry had never known a more perfect spring day.

"I'm thrilled to have two of our very best cowboys, one from the farrier side and one from the horseman side, taking the lead as the public face of Lone Star." She smiled out at everyone, held up the folders in her hand, and said, "Zane and Copper."

The crowd erupted again. Henry was impressed by those who didn't hold a folder in their hands at all, at the way they cheered for their colleagues, at the way they smiled though surely some of them felt only disappointment.

Justin was out of folders, which meant the promotions had ended. Angel handed out the folders to Zane and Copper and got down off the platform.

Justin called, "That's it, folks. We'd like our new positions to stay here and have a chat. Everyone else, you're free to go." Henry held the red folder in his hand, every cell in his body vibrating. He stayed for the meeting, flipping open his folder and seeing that he would be working with Grady, one of their full-time men over apprentices, as the other farrier on his team, and then two horsemen, Creston and Wick. His heart fell slightly because he didn't get along super great with Creston, but he put a smile on his face, noted their phone numbers, and paid attention as Angel said she and Justin would be meeting with each group of men one day next week to go over questions, concerns, and other things as they moved into their new positions at the beginning of June.

Henry quickly sent the three texts to his team, got responses of high-fives, thumbs-ups, and *can't wait.* Then the meeting broke up.

He definitely had work to do that day, but he furtively moved toward Angel's house. She'd likely come in the back door, and he slipped around to the front porch and texted her, *Come see me out front of your house when you get a minute.*

On my way, she texted back. Henry looked up and across the dirt lane to the fields beyond. Pure happiness moved through him, and he tilted his head back and said, "Thank you, Lord, for giving me a captain position." He could thank Angel and Justin too, but only one of them with a kiss.

Angel came out her front door a couple of minutes later, and Henry jogged up the steps, laughing. She grinned and giggled with him as he grabbed onto her and twirled her around.

"Is this joy about your promotion?" she asked.

He set her on her feet and ran his hands through her hair. "Sure is, sweetheart," he said. "Thank you for taking a chance on me."

"You're a good farrier, Henry," she said, planting

both palms against his chest. "When are you going to start believing it?"

"I don't know," he whispered. "Maybe in June." He kissed her then because every amazing promotion needed to be sealed with an amazing kiss.

Maybe he kissed her for too long or maybe too deeply, but when he heard a door slam, he came to his senses and pulled away. Angel jumped back, and she looked past him to her front yard. Henry turned and looked that way too, every ounce of blood in his body turning to ice as her daddy stared at him from the front corner of his pickup truck.

Bard let out a long, huffing sigh and then went around to the passenger seat to help Trevor get down. Trevor wore pure astonishment in his expression when he faced the house, and Henry wished he had chameleon skin so he could fade into the siding of Angel's house and simply disappear.

Chapter Twenty-Three

"I should go," Henry murmured as he moved past Angel. She agreed, but she wanted him to stay. The look in Daddy's eyes told her Henry absolutely should not stay. Henry went down the steps and met Daddy and Trevor where the cement met the grass. They paused, their eyes locked, the silence so thick Angel could cut it.

Henry ducked his head, muttered something, and hurried around the corner of her house, leaving Angel to face her family alone.

She looked at Daddy just as he looked at her, and a firestorm burned in his gaze. He assisted Trevor through every painstaking step up to the porch and said, "We brought breakfast," in a horribly low, gruff voice.

He continued past her toward the front door, which he opened and held for Trevor, and then went in without waiting for her. Someone had filled Angel's lungs with sawdust. That was why she couldn't breathe. That was why she couldn't speak. She hugged herself and looked out into the blue sky on this brand-new day that had been going so well—a great announcement, lots of energy on the ranch, an amazing kiss from Henry.

Frustration pulled through her, and she turned around and entered her own house. "Daddy, I'm almost thirty years old," she said to her father's back as he went into her kitchen. She hurried to follow him.

"It's nothing serious." As soon as she said that, she heard her own mistake. One, Daddy didn't believe in dating if it wasn't going to be serious, and two, every nerve ending in her body screamed at her that what she and Henry had was definitely serious.

"I mean...." She stopped in the doorway of her kitchen and exchanged a nervous glance with Trevor. "I like him, Daddy."

"How long has that been going on?" Daddy growled.

"A few months," she said, and she cleared her throat, needing the whole truth to come out. "Since I went to Three Rivers with him in February."

"That's only *two* months," Trevor said. "Not that long."

"Right," Angel said, seizing onto the words. "Not that long."

Daddy said nothing as he reached into the brown

paper bag where he'd packed their breakfast. "There's a rule here, Angel."

"I took the rule out of the new employee handbook," Angel said, swallowing. Daddy looked at her, and now he wore the surprise in his expression.

"You took the rule out of the new handbook?"

"Yes," she said. "*I* run Lone Star now, Daddy, and I think it's okay if people here want to date."

"You just gave that man a promotion," Daddy said.

"*You* signed off on all the promotions," Angel said. "I didn't make the decisions myself. Justin helped. You helped. Henry's deserving. He didn't get it because he's my boyfriend."

She balled her fingers into fists, then strode across the room to help her dad get breakfast out. She didn't know what else to say because everything she'd said was true. She was an adult. She'd only been dating Henry for a couple of months, and she had removed the rule.

"This doesn't affect you," she finally said as she scooped the last spoonful of eggs onto Trevor's plate. She took her brother his meal and returned to get hers, meeting her father's eyes again. "I *really* like him, Daddy. He's a good man."

Daddy couldn't argue with that, and he didn't even try. He simply grunted, picked up his plate, and took it to the table. Angel followed him and sat down, feeling like the chair might break at any moment. She shot a look over to Trevor, who gave her an encouraging smile, and said, "The announcements went really well this morning. Energy is real high on the ranch."

"Sure is," Trevor boomed, and Daddy threw him a glare too. To her surprise, her brother laughed.

"Come on, Daddy," he said. "Who do you think is gonna take over Lone Star if Angel doesn't start having kids?"

She pulled in a breath, which sent a chunk of scrambled egg down her throat. She started to cough and wheeze and gasp, and Trevor laughed even harder. "I've got no prospects," he said through his chuckles. "I haven't dated anybody since my accident. If Angel doesn't get married and have kids, it's going to be the end of this place."

Angel cleared her airway by taking a big drink of orange juice. She glanced from Trevor to Daddy. "Henry and I haven't talked about kids or marriage or anything like that yet," she said. "It's been two months."

"Daddy met Momma and married her within two months," Trevor said dryly.

"It was four months," Daddy drawled, and that set Angel giggling too.

She managed another couple of bites of breakfast before everyone sobered and she looked at her father again. "What are you going to do?"

"I'd like to talk to Henry," he said.

"Daddy, less than a week ago, you told me he was

your top choice for captain." She cocked one eyebrow and took another drink of juice.

"Yeah, well, that's before I knew he was kissing my daughter," he said.

"That doesn't impact his work at all," Angel said. "It only makes him more loyal to us." She hated using Henry as a business asset, but Daddy could at least understand that. He nodded and said, "I'm still going to talk to him."

"Fine," Angel said. "I'll text him and tell him that you'd like to meet with him."

"I have the man's number," Daddy said slowly. "I'll text him myself."

Angel wanted to lunge for his phone and throw it against the wall to break it. "Daddy," she said with as much courage and patience as she could. "I really like this man, and I have very little opportunity to meet men off the ranch."

"Everyone should know," Daddy said.

"And they will," Angel said. "But you're not going to tell them. That's something that Henry and I get to decide." She threw another glance to Trevor, though she didn't know what her brother could do to help her.

"When the new employee manual comes," she said, seizing onto the idea. "I'll tell everyone. There is no longer a no-dating rule at Lone Star, and that Henry and I are together."

"When's that going to be?" Daddy drawled.

"Another month," she said. "It's going to be fine."

He didn't say anything else, and breakfast concluded in stony silence—clearly waiting another month was not fine with Daddy.

Daddy helped Trevor stand, and they left with Trevor saying plenty of non-verbal things with his eyes. The moment the front door swung closed, Angel whipped out her phone and texted Henry.

Daddy wants to meet with you. He was not happy. I think I managed to delay him from telling anyone or making an announcement or embarrassing us until the employee handbook comes out.

Oh, boy, Henry sent back. *I'm real sorry, Angel. I didn't mean for that to happen.*

Angel sighed. She honestly wasn't sure what she wanted to have happen. *Maybe it's okay,* she typed out. *Maybe now that he knows, we don't have to be so secretive. Maybe we can just start hanging out and holding hands and everyone will get the hint.*

Henry called, and instead of saying hello, he said, "No, that's not gonna work for me."

"Not gonna work for you?" she repeated, throwing his attitude right back at him.

"Angel, we're not just going to start pretending like we just started dating and hope other people catch on," he said. "This requires an announcement—either from you, or Trevor, or Justin, or Shad, or your dad...but I think it should come from *us*. Us, *together*."

Angel heard the power in his voice. She heard how passionately he felt about this. And she had to say she didn't disagree. So she said, "Okay...but I'm not ready."

"That's fine," he drawled. "I did want to ask you if you'd come to my graduation in a few weeks."

Angel once again hesitated, but Henry seemed to have none of that inside him.

"Do you think you might be ready to make our announcement before then? Then we could attend that together. I could tell my parents about us."

"Maybe," she said. "Let me get through this next week of getting everyone settled into their new roles, and then we'll see where we are."

"All right," Henry said. She didn't detect any degree of disappointment, though. "Well, I guess I'll see you when I see you then."

"Yeah," she said, and the call ended. She immediately texted him, *INACH*, and Henry texted back, *INACH* <3

It didn't mean everything was okay between them. In fact, Angel doubted very much that it was, but Henry spoke his mind with her, and she spoke hers with him. And she had to believe that somehow it would be okay— if Henry could make it through the conversation with her daddy without losing his cool—or his job.

Chapter Twenty-Four

Henry looked at the full moon and decided it was the biggest star in the sky and that he could wish on it.

He did so silently from the back porch of his cabin instead of on his way to see Angel that night. He thought it wise to maybe put a little bit of distance between them until after he'd met with her daddy.

Pure anticipation drove through him, for he had no idea what Bard would say to him. At the bottom of Angel's steps that morning, he'd said, "Your daughter is a beautiful woman, sir," and then he'd left before Bard could rip his arm off and feed it to him.

He hadn't heard from the man yet, and he wondered if this was part of Bard's strategy to torture him to death —or until Henry showed up at the farmhouse with his hat in his hand, apologies streaming from his mouth, and promises to break up with Angel.

She hadn't said what she'd told her father that morning when he showed up with the scent of bacon emanating out of a brown bag, and Henry hadn't asked.

She'd gotten his leave approved for next week, and his family had all cheered for him. He said he'd be there Thursday morning, bright and early, where he'd leave his truck at Courage Reins, load into his daddy's truck, and they'd all immediately head for Waco.

Momma didn't like leaving anything to chance, and though John wasn't graduating until Friday, she wanted to be in town with plenty of time the night before. Henry sighed as he sank into a patio chair and watched as clouds passed in front of the moon, dimming the light.

His phone brightened with a text, but Henry didn't want to look at it. Angel had messaged that she needed a cowboy hug, and he texted the same thing back. But he'd since told her he didn't think he should come tonight. She'd accepted his text without argument, but that didn't mean she liked it. Or maybe she did. Henry wasn't really sure right now.

He knew one thing: their relationship was only two months old, and he sure didn't want to cap it now before he had a chance to really know if he could fall in love with her and she could fall in love with him.

Henry had been in plenty of relationships that didn't

make it past the first date. He had some that had made it a month or two, and he'd had a few that had made it to six or seven months. None longer than that.

Almost all of that was his fault, he knew, but he also acknowledged that he'd changed. His phone bleeped out another text, and Henry sighed in irritation as he looked at it. He found a photo coming up, and as it crisped and came into focus, he saw his brother's handsome face full of stars and sunshine, joy and happiness.

A pretty woman with dark hair pressed her cheek to his, and she held up her left hand with a glinting, glittering diamond taking center stage.

Henry's heart stopped completely for a moment, then fell to his bare feet and rebounded back to his chest in the most painful way possible.

Paul had just gotten engaged.

Save the date for November tenth! Paul said. *Brielle are getting married that day!*

Henry swallowed, not really jealous, but totally jealous at the same time. Thankfully, happiness poured in over that a moment later, and he lifted his phone to answer.

HOLY COW, he typed in all caps. *SHE SAID YES!* He added a few exclamation points, one of the rare times he thought more than one should be used, in reply to his brother.

He wanted to ask if they had decided where they

were going to live once they got married, but he wasn't sure if she was still with Paul and if it was a sore subject or not. Last time he'd asked about it, Paul said he was just going to try to get through the proposal before he brought it up again.

Surely she wouldn't say yes if they didn't have a plan, Henry said to himself, but he didn't know that. He didn't know Brielle, as he'd never met the woman.

Paul texted, *You can meet her when you come next week for John's graduation.*

Can't wait, Henry said, though all that did was remind him that Angel had told him she would *not* be coming to his brother's graduation.

And really, it had been stupid of him to ask anyway. Stupid, and foolish, and out of complete desperation had Henry asked Angel to come to John's graduation with him. He'd known she wouldn't be able to, but the thought of going alone had been more than Henry could handle in that moment.

He'd texted her that he needed a cowgirl hug, but since she lived alone and he did not, he always made the trip to her house to talk through the things which bothered him. She'd slowed him down, gotten him out of his head, and then sent him on his way with a kiss goodnight.

The truth was, Angel White rescued Henry on a daily basis. Whenever he felt like he was drowning in dirty water, she appeared to pull him out. When she felt like that, Henry knelt on the side of the pond and reached for her to bring her back.

He wasn't sure if he could fall in love in two months or not, but the feelings he had for Angel were definitely stronger and bigger and fiercer than any he'd had for anyone else in the past.

I can't wait to meet her, Henry told Paul.

Are you bringing anyone to graduation? Paul asked, and the fact that did that told Henry how pathetic he really was. Henry had taken women to family functions, game nights, and friends' weddings on first dates. He simply didn't want to attend anything alone, ever.

But again, he had started to change in the past year since he'd come on at Lone Star. He could be alone now. In fact, sometimes he craved being alone. Like right now, as he sat on the back porch while Levi finished up a load of paperwork for his new job.

Levi would be moving into Flint's cabin in another five or six weeks, and that meant Henry would get a new cabinmate. That brought a flutter of nerves to his gut, and he wondered if life would ever just be steady, even, and predictable. Where he would have peace of mind that every day he would wake up with the people he wanted to be with, work with the people he wanted to be with, and go to bed with the people he wanted to be with.

Only if you get married, he thought. All at once, he realized why marriage was so spectacular. He didn't have to worry about a cabinmate then, or if they'd get along, or if he'd be annoyed if the man shed his boots by the front door or if he left food in the fridge so long that it molded and stunk up the whole house.

In a marriage where he was committed to his wife and his wife to him, they would work through any problems they had *together*. And Henry suddenly wanted that more than anything.

He thought of his momma and daddy, and then Bard and his wife Justine. He'd seen them together too, and they were sweet and kind and clearly best friends. He tapped away from Paul's text, suddenly realizing why Bard hadn't texted him.

He wanted Henry to come to him. The man would probably be in bed by now, but Henry texted anyway. *I'd love to come talk to you about Angel*, he said. *Tell me when a good time is, and I'll make it work. I am leaving next Thursday to go to my brother's graduation, so I'd like to do it before then, if possible. I don't want anything weighing on me or anything between us for too long.*

He read over the words, thinking of Bard's rule of not going to bed angry with anyone on the ranch, and he wondered if Angel had changed that in the employee handbook or not.

And it became apparent that Bard lived by the rules he'd expected his cowboys to, because he responded with, *Come by tomorrow for breakfast*, when he should've been in bed a couple of hours ago.

Henry's pulse hammered as he tapped out a reply. *Don't you and your wife eat breakfast with Angel?*

Yes, Bard said. *But she wasn't real keen on me talking to you alone. And I figure you're both adults, and we can have an adult conversation.*

Yes, sir, Henry said, because he *could* have an adult conversation. That settled, he didn't feel like he was breathing pond water anymore, and he went inside to find that Levi had left the light on over the stove for him but had gone down the hall to bed.

Henry did the same, and he closed his door and fell to his knees in front of his bed. "Lord," he prayed, "I feel slow of speech like Thy servant Moses. But I know that You gave him the words he needed, and I'm begging You to give them to me tomorrow when I meet Angel's parents...as her boyfriend."

The following morning, Henry attended roll call as usual, and he noticed that some men had grouped up differently than before. He still stood with Levi, sipping a to-go cup of coffee that he'd gotten from the machine in stable three.

Justin made that every morning, and the man was a good coffee maker. He didn't see Angel anywhere as he listened to the announcements, as Trevor went through their inspirational message, and as the day's work began. But the moment that Levi turned and left his side, she seemed to materialize out of nowhere.

"Hey." She wore a hoodie this morning, and she tucked her hands into the front pocket of it. It had rained a little bit overnight, and the sun hadn't come out that morning, making everything above the emerald-green fields and pastures gray and white and dreary.

"Morning." He turned toward the farmhouse, glad when she fell into step beside him. "Tell me what I'm walking into here."

"I don't rightly know," Angel said. "Daddy said he wanted to meet. I'm surprised I got invited at all."

"Hm." It didn't take long to make it to the farmhouse, and with Angel with him, he didn't even knock. She just opened the door and said, "Morning," and expected him to follow her inside.

He did, closing the door behind him. He'd been to this house many times as he'd met with Bard for various horse issues and other work-related business. They'd remodeled the farmhouse, so the living room flowed right into the kitchen, where Bard turned from the fridge with a pitcher of bright pink liquid.

Henry's knees weakened on his next step, and his legs almost buckled underneath him. But he managed to keep walking. Angel's mama wore an oxygen tube in her nose, and the steady hum and hiss of the canister as it pumped pure oxygen into her airways almost comforted him.

"Morning, ma'am," he said to her. Justine, who had always been kind, squeezed his hand and gave him a smile.

"Chocolate croissants are almost done," Angel's daddy said, and she came to a complete stop.

"I'm not making scrambled eggs this morning?"

He put the grapefruit juice on the table and said, "Sit down. The chocolate croissants are almost done."

Henry saw no choice but to sit down where a bowl of cubed watermelon, pineapple, and cantaloupe already waited. Trying to put forth his best effort, he pulled out a chair for Angel and looked at her. She threw him a menacing glare but took the seat, and he sat next to her, Bard on his immediate left and Justine down on the other end next to Angel. Sure enough, the chocolate croissants came out a moment later. Bard put the hot tray from the oven right in the middle of the table.

"They're supposed to sit for five or ten minutes," he said as he pulled his chair back. "I reckon that's enough time for us to talk." He sat and surveyed everyone at the table, and it was very clear that he was going to lead the conversation.

After several long seconds, Angel made a scoffing sound and said, "Daddy, this is ridiculous."

"How long have you been dating my daughter,

Henry?" he asked as he reached for the fruit bowl and spooned some chunks of only pineapple onto his plate.

Henry refused to look over at Angel, though he really wanted to borrow some of her strength, to lean on her the way she leaned on him sometimes. "A couple of months, sir," he said. "We talked about it first when I went home for Three Rivers that time in February."

Bard nodded, and Henry decided he'd passed some sort of test. "Anything before that?"

Henry swallowed, not sure if he should bring up the incident from last year. He figured his conscience would be clear if he did, and so he said, "Well, I did something real stupid a year or so ago," he said. "When Angel came to Sherman make the announcements for apprentice-ships and internships—"

"Henry," she interrupted.

"No, I'm going to tell him," he said, feeling his lungs expand and then collapse. "I was really angry that I didn't get one. See, I hadn't gotten her email from the day before, and I went to talk to her about it, because I didn't have a position anywhere and I was desperate. I needed an apprenticeship to graduate."

He realized his tongue had run away from him, but he didn't know how to stop it. Surely Bard could under-stand the desperation a man would have after four years in farrier school, and all he needed was an apprentice-ship to graduate.

"When I was talking to Angel, and it became clear that I *had* gotten the apprenticeship—the only one Lone Star had offered—which I was real thankful for, sir. Real grateful. I've loved being here, so much that I'm coming back next year."

"Yeah, we'll see about that," Bard said.

Henry's vision flashed black and then white before the kitchen came into view again. "My job is in jeop-ardy?" he asked. "For dating Angel?" He couldn't handle the pressure now descending through his shoulders. It mixed with that same desperation he'd felt in the apprenticeship meeting last year. "Sir, she's a grown adult and so am I. She barely gets off this ranch."

"Henry," she said again, softer this time.

He turned to look at her, hearing something signifi-cant in her tone, and he tried to figure out what she was trying to say to him with her eyes. But something inside him told him that he needed to stand up for her, and himself, and this relationship.

It *meant something* to him, and he wanted Bard and Justine to see that. He looked down to her momma. "She takes care of everything around here. All the cowboys, all the farriers, all the land, all the schedules, Trevor, you guys. She goes to church every week. She's awake at the crack of dawn, and she's staying up late to get various things finished. And I have to admit that I'm part of the problem with that. I've been trying to leave her place by nine-thirty so we can both get a good night's rest. I've been trying to be real respectful of her time. Real respectful of her as a woman."

He reached over and took her hand the way his daddy taught him. "I sure do like your daughter, sir." He switched his gaze back to Bard. "I *like* her. I like spending time with her. I like talking with her. And yeah, I like kissing her. We've only been dating a couple of months, but in my mind, we're headed toward something serious, something long-lasting. A real commitment. Something that could be beautiful and wonderful and forever."

Beside him, Angel sniffled. But Henry wasn't done talking yet. "So last year when I found out about the apprenticeship, I was just so excited. And I can admit maybe I was a little bit of a player back then. I really started to change the most when I came to Lone Star in the summer." His voice cracked because his friendship with Bard was real to him, and the mentorship that Bard had done for him meant a great deal to Henry.

"Anyway, I grabbed onto her right there in the conference room at Sherman Academy, and I kissed her. I shouldn't have. I know that. It was just my way of celebrating in that moment."

Bard blinked. "Kind of like this morning when you showed up at her house and kissed her on the front porch after you got your promotion?"

"Yes, sir," Henry said quickly. "Kind of like that. Except this time, Angel and I are dating, and she's not with some other guy." He chuckled lightly and glanced over at Justine. She wore a smile now, a soft look around her eyes, and Henry felt like maybe he'd scored some points.

"That's all?" Bard asked.

"Yes, sir," Henry said. "I came on last summer. Nothing happened. Angel and I have worked together just fine. We've been friendly, but."

He cut a look over to her. "I wouldn't call us friends. Until the day Levi got sick. I sent that text and Angel showed up, asked about him, and completely broke down. I offered to take her home to Three Rivers with me, and things really started then. I confessed my crush on her, and you know what, sir? She told me that she would go out with me if there wasn't this no-dating rule. So we decided that we would...kind of bend the rule a little bit. We'd see each other when we could. We'd find private moments."

"You've been sneaking around, you mean," Bard said.

"Only a little, Daddy," Angel said. "Nobody got hurt. It's not that big of a deal."

Henry wasn't sure Bard saw it that way, but he figured he'd said everything he needed to say. And it'd been about five or ten minutes. So he reached for the spatula and scooped up a chocolate croissant. He put the first one on Bard's plate, the second on Justine's, and the third on Angel's. That only left one for him.

Henry put it on his plate, turned to Angel, and said, "You want some fruit salad, baby?" as if he ate breakfast with her parents every day. As if he'd start calling her "baby" in front of everyone at Lone Star. All three of them gaped at him.

"Oh, do we need to pray first?" Henry asked.

Angel's face broke into a smile, and she laughed. "Yeah, cowboy," she said. "We usually pray first."

Henry looked over to Bard, who gave him a single nod that Henry took as total acceptance of his relationship.

"Angel says the two of you are going to handle telling the other cowboys about your relationship," he said.

"Yeah," Henry said. "That's right, we are."

"When?"

"When Angel's ready."

She didn't give further details, and Bard didn't ask. Justine said grace, and Henry lifted his chocolate croissant to his mouth, moaning when he got the flaky pastry and the chocolatey goodness all in one.

"I wish you could come in with me," Henry said almost a week later. His packed bag sat in the backseat of his truck, solo. Angel had met him on the side of his house, and since he lived on the end, they'd taken a risk that no one would see them. He'd attended roll call as usual, but he needed to get on the road in the next ten minutes to satisfy his momma's timeline.

"Me too," Angel said as she rested her cheek against his pulse. He held her, brushed his fingers through her hair, and gently tipped her face up to kiss her.

"I'll miss you while I'm gone," he said.

"It's only a few days," she said.

"I'll call you tonight. We'll be down Waco, and I'll find a way to sneak away."

"You aren't going to tell your parents about us?"

His eyebrows went up. "You think I should?"

"Well, my parents know now," she said. "And who are your mom and dad going to tell? Someone here on the ranch?"

He grinned at her. "No," he said. "They don't know anyone here on the ranch."

She smiled back. "Exactly," she said, and then Angel matched her mouth to his again.

Henry could kiss her for a long time, but he pulled away, resettled his hat on his head, and said, "I'll call you tonight."

He got behind the wheel of his truck and drove away from Angel, which happened to be one of the hardest things he'd done in the past couple of years. It felt odd to think that, to know it, to feel it deep down inside his chest. And he wondered once again what it would feel like to be in love.

Maybe this weekend, he could ask Paul about it.

He could talk to his momma and daddy about Angel.

Maybe when he visited Three Rivers, everything would once again be reset, and he'd know exactly what to do and when to do it when he came back to Lone Star next week.

Chapter Twenty-Five

The pinch in Henry's lungs loosened as he went around the corner and his childhood home, the big Courage Reins building, and the beauty of Three Rivers Ranch spread before him. He did love this place, and the longer he stayed away and worked somewhere else, the more fond he became of it when he returned.

He turned down the long driveway and pulled out of the way so he didn't block Paul or Daddy. Paul had decided that he would drive himself and Brielle to Waco. He had invited Henry to ride with him, but Henry wasn't sure what he was going to do.

He needed to have a serious conversation with his momma and daddy, but he didn't want to do it with Rich in the truck. Perhaps he could find a way to get his youngest brother to go with Paul and Brielle, and he would go with Momma and Daddy.

He'd barely dropped from his truck when his family streamed from the farmhouse. "There you are," Momma said, and while she surely didn't mean to make him feel like he was late, that was exactly what she accomplished.

"I'm not late," he said. "We're not leaving for ten more minutes."

"We're loading up now," Daddy said, and he handed Momma her canvas bag full of who-knew-what. She brought it on every trip they took, and Henry had seen her pull books from it, crochet yarn and needles, and even puzzle books. She liked to have her hands busy in the car, and it took seven hours to get to Waco.

"All right," Henry said, and he turned to get his bag out of the back seat. Rich helped Daddy load the cooler into the back of his truck while Paul put his bag in his vehicle.

"Who you ridin' with?" Henry asked Rich, and his youngest brother shot a look over to their momma.

"I'm gonna go with Paul," he muttered. "Don't feel like riding with them."

Henry shouldn't have felt relieved that someone else in the family didn't always get along with Momma and Daddy exactly right, but he did. He grinned and said, "Great. I'll go with Momma and Daddy, so they don't have to go alone."

"It's fine," Momma said. "You boys do whatever you want." She was used to being the only female in their family, and she lifted her chin high. "I can handle myself." She pinned Rich with a steely glare. "And Rich, if you can't handle an adult conversation, then you need to figure out how to do that. Maybe going with Paul and Brielle will help you."

"I heard you the first time, Momma," Rich griped, and he stomped around Paul's truck, tossed his overnight bag in the back of it, and climbed in the passenger seat. Paul looked at all of them with wide eyes and said, "Don't worry, I'll talk to him."

And of course he would. Paul was steady and strong and rational—and he usually got along great with Momma and Daddy.

Henry added his bag next to the cooler and helped Momma lift hers up. "You can really ride with them too," she said.

"Don't need to," Henry said. "Besides, I want to talk to you and Daddy about something."

Daddy paused at the corner of the truck and looked at Henry. "About what?"

"Not right here," Henry growled at him, lifted the tailgate, and then helped Daddy pull back the cover so that their stuff wouldn't get rained on, blown around, or dusted as they drove to Waco.

He sat in the back seat while his parents got situated in the front, and they let Paul lead out. Henry didn't say anything until they reached the highway, and then he said, "It's real good news about him and Brielle. They sure seem happy."

"You haven't met her yet, have you?" Momma asked, her mood completely different now.

"Not yet," Henry said. "But I'm sure there's gonna be plenty of time for us to get to know each other." He and Paul had both been invited to the next luncheon here in Three Rivers, but with Henry taking this time off, he didn't think he was going to be able to make it.

Dawson would host in June, and that would be an easier drive, as Henry could take the back roads south to the southern ranches instead of having to come all the way into town and then go north again.

Of course, not everyone could make it to every luncheon. And Henry didn't own a ranch here in Three Rivers, so he already felt out of place. Alex did, Finn, Paul, Dawson, and Link, and he was happy that they'd formed a little crew of men their own age, doing similar things with their family ranches that they could talk to each other about and support one another.

His daddy had always had his best friend—Uncle Squire—and they had a whole host of cowboys at Three Rivers they could rely on. It reminded him a lot of Lone Star, except Three Rivers Ranch raised cattle and Lone Star boarded horses.

"You better start talking," Daddy said. "It's a long drive."

Henry glanced up to the rearview mirror and found his father watching him, not the road. "I'm thinkin'."

"Makes me nervous when I know you got something

to say, and you're not saying it." Daddy looked away, but everything about him remained relaxed, comfortable.

Henry wished he could experience all of that in this moment. "You really don't trust me at all, do you?" He chuckled, and added quickly, "I know you do."

"Of course we do," Momma said.

"I just said I know you do," Henry said. He heaved in a breath and then let it all blow out. "Listen. This is not a big deal. It's nothing serious or anything." He rolled one shoulder that had been aching since a particularly tough re-shoeing a couple of weeks ago.

"I mean, it *is* serious. It's not nothing, but it's not like I'm moving across the country or anything like that. I'm still going to graduate, so you guys can relax a little bit."

The wheels kept rolling, and Henry tried to get his thoughts lined up.

"So this is a woman thing," Daddy said, no question mark in sight.

"What makes you think that?"

"Well, if it's not school-related and it's not job-related—we already know you're staying at Lone Star for another year—it's gotta have something to do with a woman." Daddy's piercing eyes met his in the rearview mirror again, and Henry held them this time.

"Yeah, all right," he said. "I'm dating Angel White." Just like that, the confession came right out. He didn't trip over his tongue. He didn't feel nervous about it. He wasn't embarrassed.

"I told you he was dating her," Momma said, swatting at Daddy's shoulder.

"I wasn't when we came," Henry said, just for clarification. "That's about when we started."

"I thought there was a no-dating rule at your ranch," Daddy said.

"There was," Henry said. "But Angel's in charge now, and she changed it."

"Hm." Daddy hummed, and Henry realized for the first time that he'd picked up his humming habit from his father. He loved his father, he did, but he had worked to become his own person inside the parameters of what his parents had taught him.

And he'd never realized about the humming.

"Why is that a bad thing?" Henry asked. He didn't understand why everyone seemed to think he and Angel together were a bad idea.

"She's your boss," Daddy said. "Whether there's a rule or not. It's awkward. It's complicated. Makes everything harder."

"Does it?" Henry asked, genuinely confused. "Because being with her doesn't feel hard. Talking to her isn't hard. Seeing her isn't hard. In fact, it's *easier* because we're right there together. I don't have to drive forty-five minutes to Three Rivers to see her, the way Paul does to see his fiancé, or thirty minutes to Amarillo to meet up with some girl in college."

His chest felt like someone had wrapped him in

rubber bands. "She's a year older than me, and I don't get why everyone thinks this is a big deal." He realized that he'd spewed out all kinds of things, and both his momma and daddy did him the courtesy of sitting silent for a moment, and then another, and then a whole minute.

The silence in the truck smothered him, and despite the speed at which Daddy drove, Henry pressed the button to roll down his window. A horribly loud whooshing noise entered the truck, along with the summer heat, and Henry immediately put his window back up.

"Who else thinks it's a big deal?" Momma asked.

"Well, Bard does," Henry said. "Obviously, he's the one that instituted the no-dating rule. And you know what? Angel is the only woman at that ranch, so that rule was made specifically so that she wouldn't date the cowboys at Lone Star." He scoffed and looked out the side window, "Which is utterly ridiculous. Who does he think she's going to meet, and when? She works fifteen hours a day at that place, and then falls down dead at night."

He shook his head, wishing he hadn't gotten so frustrated so fast. He took a long breath through his nose and held it for a moment, trying to infuse some reason into his mind.

"Well, he must have a reason if he doesn't want the cowboys dating his daughter."

"Yeah, he doesn't want cowboys dating his daughter," Henry said. "That's it, Daddy. That's the reason. He thinks it's a distraction. He thinks it causes drama."

"Well, it might," Daddy said.

"Yeah, it might," Henry could admit. "But so far it hasn't."

"It's only been a couple of months," Daddy said.

"Yes, exactly," Henry said. "It's only been a couple of months. But you know what? You and Momma didn't date that long, and we see each other all the time—and I've known her for years, so it feels like we've been together longer."

"Are you feeling serious about her already?" Momma asked, her voice tight and airy, as if she was trying to pretend like she didn't care.

"You know what, Momma?" he said. "I am. I know you guys think I'm a total wild bull, moving around from woman to woman, thing to thing, but I'm really not. I did a whole degree at Amarillo State, and now I've done an entire farrier program. I know how to stick with something, and I've grown up a lot since being at Lone Star."

"No one thinks you're a wild bull, Henry," Momma said.

Henry looked over to Daddy, but he kept his eyes on the road. He'd served in the Army with Uncle Squire at Henry's age, and he adored horses with his whole soul. He was softest when with an equine, and Henry had some of his best conversations out in the barn with his dad.

"I like her," he said again.

"That's great," Momma said.

"And she seems to like me too," he said. "And I really don't understand what people see when they look at me and they look at her and they think, 'Oh, there's something wrong here.' Doesn't feel wrong to me."

Daddy shifted in his seat in that way he did when he had something he wanted to say and wasn't sure how to get it out. Henry gave him the space to think and organize, and finally Daddy said, "If it doesn't feel wrong, Henry, it's probably not wrong."

Henry wasn't sure why he'd needed that reassurance, but he had, and he specifically needed it from his parents. From Daddy. He started nodding and couldn't stop. "Thank you, Daddy," he said. "I'm not a total moron."

"No one thinks you're a total moron," Daddy said at the same time Momma said, "Stop saying stuff like that, Henry."

Henry sighed and watched the landscape roll by. No, he didn't really believe his parents thought he was stupid, but things got piled up and felt so...weird sometimes. "I just...sometimes it's hard when you feel like every decision you make is being questioned. I don't like feeling like that."

"No, I can't imagine you do," Daddy said. "No one does. We've all been there, though, son. There was a time in my life when I literally questioned every single thing I was doing. Should I stay at this ranch? How do I get these nonprofits going? Heck, I lived in a tent on the side of an unfinished house during a terrible storm, and let me tell you, I questioned everything then."

"That was just you being bull-headed, by the way," Momma said. "You could have stayed at the homestead just fine."

Henry grinned because he'd heard this part of his parents' love story before. Momma had built Daddy the website of his dreams to make-up with him, something Henry found very sweet—and which obviously Daddy had too.

"It's just that Justine and Bard didn't seem too happy either," Henry said. "And I'm trying to figure out why, what you guys see that I don't."

"Oh, so they know?" Daddy said.

"Yes, sir," Henry decided he didn't have to humiliate himself by saying he and Angel had been caught kissing. "Angel's in charge now, Daddy, and she's changing the employee handbook. There is no rule against dating at Lone Star anymore. And we're going to make an announcement together to all the cowboys there. We're grown-ups. We can handle this."

"Of course you can," Daddy said. "And Henry, you're a really good grown-up."

Momma nodded along with him, and Henry once again found that he needed this specific reassurance. He needed their vote of confidence, even though the people giving it to him loved him no matter what.

"Thank you," he said. "Like you said, Daddy, it's early. It's new. It's been two months. Who knows what will happen? All I know is I want to keep dating her. I want to keep getting to know her. I want to keep being with her."

"That's sweet," Momma said. "I'm so glad, Henry." He was too, mostly because the conversation was out now, and he wouldn't have to stew over it for the next seven hours as they drove to Waco.

They all seemed to realize the conversation had run it's course, and after a couple more miles, Henry asked, "You guys know what Paul and Brielle are going to do after they get married? Where they're going to live?"

"They haven't decided yet," Daddy said.

"What are you going to do if Paul moves to the Hill Country?" Though he sat in the back, he saw his father's grip on the steering wheel tighten, his jaw mirroring the movement.

That meant he didn't know. Henry decided not to push it. He also didn't volunteer to come back to Courage Reins. John wouldn't, he knew that, but Rich might, and Henry just wanted to see how things would play out before he threw such a hairpin into his own life.

"All right," Momma said. "Can we talk about something a little more fun now?" She turned all the way around in her seat and looked at Henry, her eyes aglow.

"What's that?" he asked cautiously, an inkling of what she wanted to talk about in his mind.

"Your graduation party," she said with pure glee.

Henry groaned. "Momma, I don't need a graduation party."

"Yes, you do," she said, her smile faltering slightly. "Everyone needs a graduation party when they graduate."

His aunt Kelly, who ran Three Rivers Ranch steadfastly and perfectly alongside his uncle, loved parties and loved planning them. By the gleam in Momma's eye, she'd been partners in crime with Aunt Kelly for far too long.

"I already graduated from college once," he said anyway, knowing this fight would be lost.

"Well, you have that nice ranch where you work," Momma said. "It has tons of space, and we'd like to get to know Angel a little more too. We could just do a picnic at your cabin and invite all the men."

"Lone Star already feeds all the men all the time," Henry said. "And we'd need more room than a single cabin."

"Great," Momma said without missing a beat. "Then we'll sponsor this dinner. There's got to be other men there graduating."

Henry couldn't lie and say there weren't, so he simply gazed at his mother, feeling all the fondness and all the love and all the sacrifice that she'd done for him over the years and said, "All right, Momma. I'll talk to Angel about it."

She grinned, clapped her hands together, and said, "It's going to be so great, Henry." She turned around and faced the front again. "Do you want me to order those meatball subs that you like from Papa Kelsey's?"

Henry's mouth watered, because he could use a meatball sub right this moment. "Yeah, sure, Momma. That would be just fine."

"Is Angel going to come to your graduation?" Momma asked next, and Henry felt exactly the way Daddy did when he squeezed the steering wheel and pressed his jaw together. He didn't answer the way Daddy did.

And Momma said, "Oh, I see."

What she saw, he wasn't sure, but he didn't put anything past her. "It depends," Henry said. "On whether or not the men at Lone Star know we're together by then."

Momma hummed this time, and for some reason, that tickled Henry's funny bone, and he chuckled. That broke the mood in the truck, and Daddy reached to turn up the volume on the radio. Country music played through the cab, and Henry settled back into his seat for the long drive, bringing up his phone so he could text Angel that he'd told his parents about them.

It went decently well, he told her. *Though they didn't*

seem happy about it in the beginning, same as your parents.

I'm glad you told them. Can't wait till you get back to the ranch.

Henry couldn't wait for that either, and he sent her *INACH* <3, and she sent him the very best text in return: *I got you, cowboy* <3

Chapter Twenty-Six

Angel shimmied and shook, pulled the dress up over her shoulders until she could reach the zipper. She missed it a couple of times, and then managed to grab it and bring it up. She smoothed her hands down the front of her body and looked at herself in the mirror without her wig. She didn't look half bad.

Henry had once told her that his favorite color on her was purple, so today for his graduation, she wore a lavender dress with big, splashy, golden horses running across it. It felt fitting for the graduation at Sherman Academy, where this year three farriers who worked at Lone Star had earned certificates or degrees.

She and Daddy didn't attend graduation every year, not even when they had men graduating who worked on the ranch, so she hadn't known if she'd be able to go this year just for Henry. The employee handbooks had been delayed, and they had still not made any announcement about their relationship, and that hadn't helped.

Then, like she did with most things, Angel had gone to her father to talk it through. In the end, he'd gotten her to admit that yes, she wanted to attend this graduation. Yes, just for Henry.

So he'd made the decision that they'd attend, and Angel appreciated her father for carrying some of that load.

She turned away from her reflection and picked up her wig cap to finish getting ready. She definitely sensed some growing unrest inside Henry over the lack of a dating announcement, but he hadn't brought it up again. They'd continued sneaking off-site to meet, or he'd come over to her house late at night the way he had been.

With only one more week until June first hit and everything got mixed up, new farriers came on for the apprenticeship positions, and the summer internship positions began, Angel felt like her life was about to blow up one more time.

You have help in place this year, she told herself. But everyone, literally everyone, would be new at their job—including Angel—and she simply wasn't sure how it would all play out.

She clipped her wig in place, slipped into her heels, and grabbed her purse before she left the house. Down the road a bit and around the corner, she came to the farmhouse where Daddy sat outside in his rocking chair, a book in his hand.

Angel sweated as she climbed the steps and said, "I should have driven over; it's way too hot already."

Daddy smiled at her, a brief gesture that only lasted a moment before it floated away. "It's pretty warm today." It had been warm in the Texas Panhandle for a while now, and Angel had lived here her whole life. But that didn't mean she'd gotten used to it.

"How's Momma this morning?" she asked as she sat in the chair her mother had once relaxed in.

"She's doing fine," Daddy said.

Angel let the silence sink into her soul. While her mind ran away from her, she carefully went through her shoulders and her back, trying to relax her muscles. "You sure look nice this morning," Daddy said.

"Thanks." Angel threw him one of his type of smiles: brief. "I can't believe Flint is going to be gone next week."

Flint was married and had three kids, and he'd been working as a master farrier for fifteen years, ten of those here at Lone Star.

"A lot of change is happening next week," Daddy said, and the tension and stress that Angel had just relieved tightened up her muscles again.

"Should we go?" she finally asked.

Daddy set aside his book and got to his feet. "Yeah, let's go," he said, almost like he was marching into battle instead of going to see their friends, employees, and loved ones earn something significant. Angel didn't comment on it; she let Daddy drive off the ranch and toward Sherman Academy.

"Do you ever miss it?" she asked as the tires bumped over the gravel road.

He glanced over to her, but she didn't have to clarify what "it" was. Daddy had taught at Sherman Academy for many years while running Lone Star. Angel did guest lectures every now and then, and she'd done a class or two in the past, but nothing for a couple of years.

"They asked me to teach this fall," she said. "I got an email about it yesterday."

"Is that right?" Daddy asked. "What are you going to do?"

"I don't know," Angel said. "I don't love teaching." And she didn't. She liked being outside. She liked organizing schedules. She loved being with horses. "Depends on how many riding students I can get, I guess. I'd rather do that."

Daddy grunted, which meant, *It's not always about what you want to do.*

Angel knew that having a presence at Sherman Academy ensured that Lone Star got insider information about the best farriers in their program. They got access to their grades, could read the reports on their strengths and weaknesses, and they could try to get the best men to come to *their* boarding facility.

"I'm going to do that guest lecture at Amarillo State," she said. "For the equine care and agricultural sciences program."

"That's great," Daddy said. "It's good to stay in touch with Herb."

"Yeah," she said. "He said they've got an unusually large crowd of students graduating this year who'll need jobs next year."

"Good," he said. "We always need people who know what they're doing with horses." And that was true. Justin and Shad couldn't be the foremen and barn managers forever. New men would have to move into those positions eventually.

The conversation stalled, and Angel's worries did too as they continued to drive to the academy. They held their graduation in a huge horse arena with stands all along the side, and Angel had not been back to Three Rivers since February, but she knew Henry had told his parents and his family about their relationship. So she automatically started looking for Chelsea, a new set of snakes growing in her gut. She had not even *thought* she might have to introduce her father to them today. How had she missed that?

"I don't want to climb up too high," Daddy said, and Angel started looking along the first couple of rows where she might find two seats.

In doing that, she spotted Chelsea's dark hair and her bright red lips. She drew in a breath; she hardly made any noise, but Chelsea seemed to hear it, turned toward her, and zeroed in on her. Recognition lit her face, and she tugged on her husband's arm.

Chelsea pointed at Angel, and she saw no way around it. Henry's family sat about twenty yards to Angel's left on the third row, and there was plenty of room beside them.

"Daddy," she said carefully. "Can we sit by Henry's parents?" She didn't look away from Chelsea as she asked, and Daddy must have clued in on that.

He looked toward them too and said, "All right."

Angel lifted her hand in a wave, and Chelsea pointed to the bleachers next to her. Angel nodded and held up two fingers to indicate that they just needed two seats. She helped Daddy up to the third row, and they started walking down.

"How are you, dear?" Chelsea asked when Angel reached her. She took her into a hug and did a little shimmy. "Oh, it's so good to see you again."

"Thank you, ma'am." Angel wondered how Henry had felt walking into her parents' house the morning after she'd made the promotion announcements. Did it feel like the sky might fall? Had he wondered if he'd make it out alive?

"You remember Pete," Chelsea said as she leaned back so Angel could see him.

"Yes, of course. Hello, sir." She shook his hand.

"This is my daddy, Bard. Daddy, these are Henry's parents, Chelsea and Pete Marshall."

Pleasantries got exchanged, along with handshakes, and everybody sat down. Chelsea pushed on her husband's chest, and he leaned back. "These are our other boys. Rich is our youngest. John is just older than him, and Paul is our oldest. That's Paul's fiancée, Brielle, down on the end."

Angel nodded and smiled at all of them. "It's great to meet you," she said as she leaned forward to see them all. They all had hair in various shades of dark brown, and Angel catalogued that Henry's was by far the darkest out of the boys. "Henry talks fondly of you all."

"Does he now?" Paul said with a smile, and Angel wasn't sure what to make of that.

"He's real glad you could come, John," Angel forged ahead. "He said you might not be able to with your new job this summer."

"Yeah," John said with a pleasant smile. "It worked out okay. Here for the weekend." He had a good air about him, and Angel couldn't quite remember where he'd traveled from, probably near the Dallas-Fort Worth area.

She glanced over to Daddy, feeling like she sat on spikes instead of a flat bench. She looked out to the arena, where the dirt had been swept away to reveal the hard-packed earth underneath. Chairs had been set up in rows, and a stage had been erected with Sherman's colors—red, white, and blue, to match the Texas state flag and the United States flag.

A general buzz rode in the air, and Angel breathed that in, trying to calm herself. She had attended graduations here before, and they didn't take long.

Music started to play, and the graduates began marching out. Not very many women went into being farriers, but Angel caught a few of them wearing the bright royal blue robes that all the men wore.

"There's Henry," Chelsea said, pointing off to her left. "There he is, Pete. Do you see him?"

"I see 'im," his daddy said.

Angel saw him too. He wore his white cowboy hat, and he found his momma easily, who frantically waved her hand, and he returned the gesture.

When he saw Angel sitting there, she lifted her hand just up to her shoulder, and the smile vanished right off his face. It rebounded quickly, and he waved to her as well, then followed the line to where he sat in the second row.

President Wilson got up and spoke for a few minutes, and then someone who was earning his master farrier certificate, a man named Winston Bauble, spoke for about ten. After that, they started calling graduates' names in alphabetical order.

Angel whistled and cheered for Cedric Davis, one of the apprentices who worked at Lone Star. And the closer Henry got, the harder her heartbeat pounded. She wasn't even sure why. She simply liked being here, being able to celebrate with him, being in this special moment with him.

Though he stood a good hundred yards away from her, she sure did like him. She couldn't wait to talk to him, lay in his arms, and ask him what was next in his life. Did he have any big dreams? Did he want to open his own boarding stable or his own farrier business?

She was pretty locked in at Lone Star, and he knew that, but she'd been thinking more and more about living off-site since he'd mentioned it.

Why couldn't she do that? She didn't have to live in that cabin. She could commute into work every day. Some of their interns and even their full-time apprentices did that, as they didn't have room for everyone to live on-site.

They'd offered two apprenticeships this year, which was one more than they'd been able to do last year, mostly because Flint was leaving and because of their restructuring.

"Henry—Marshall," the announcer said, and Angel got first-hand experience for how loud the Marshall family could be. She really felt like adding her applause and whooping wouldn't do anything, but she did it anyway, satisfied when Daddy whistled and applauded as well.

The keenest, most powerful sense of pride Angel had ever felt marched through her as Henry confidently strode across the stage. He shook hands with the four men there, accepted his certificate, and just like everyone else—he wasn't special—he turned toward the crowd and held up his degree.

His family went nuts again, but Angel clasped her hands together and held them at her throat. She'd never been in love before, and she wondered if this was what it felt like. Like his accomplishment was hers, and she suddenly realized that she had not prepared properly to celebrate this with him.

She knew how hard it was to graduate from farrier school. She'd seen countless men do it and double that amount drop out. Even more couldn't even get in. Henry had gotten in. He'd stuck with it and graduated at the top of his class. He'd been their only apprentice last year, and within a year, he'd been promoted from team lead to captain. The man exuded charm and charisma, and everything about him was special to Angel. Her emotions wavered and shook and vibrated through her whole body, almost like she might burst into tears.

Did love do that to a person?

How could she be in love with someone after only three months of dating?

You've known him for a lot longer, she told herself. *How long do you need anyway?*

She worked with Henry every single day. They talked all the time. She knew about his work ethic. She knew about his religious commitment. She'd seen him with his family. He'd seen her with hers.

About the only thing they hadn't talked about was marriage and kids, and she wasn't really sure how he managed his money. She should probably talk to him about those things. But otherwise, Angel wasn't really sure what other crucial conversations she needed to have to decide if Henry was worth sticking with. She sure liked him. She felt comfortable with him. He cared for her.

As he walked down the steps and off the stage, and somebody else took the spotlight, Angel couldn't tear her eyes from him. Marriage was a real commitment. She knew that, but Henry didn't seem afraid of it.

She wanted to talk to him about it. The fight-or-flight reflex inside of her wanted her to jump out of the stands and run toward him right now, leap into his arms, and start asking questions. She put her hands on her knees almost to keep herself in her seat.

As Henry made it back to his, and the names continued to be called. After the four-year degrees, the special certificate ceremony started. They had an additional speaker, and Angel's anxiety started to bleed through in the form of her foot tapping.

Daddy reached over and put his hand over hers. Angel looked at it, the way his skin was older and more weathered. She turned her hand over, curled her fingers into her daddy's, and looked over at him with a smile. He looked at her with plenty of questions on his face, but he didn't vocalize any of them. Angel wouldn't have been able to answer anyway.

When Flint's name was called, Angel jumped to her feet and cheered as loud as she could. Daddy whistled. And of course, Flint's family was there to celebrate with him as well, a few rows back and to her left.

When everything ended, Angel breathed easier. She looked over to Chelsea and said, "Well, that sure was fun."

"Yes, every one of these men has worked so hard for today." Chelsea stood and shouldered her purse. "You guys are still okay if we come back to the ranch?"

Angel grinned at her and said, "I think there'll be a riot if you don't show up with the food."

They laughed, and Angel turned to leave with her daddy. She wasn't sure if she should stay to celebrate with Henry or not. Surely he would meet his family, and they'd hug and take pictures. She suddenly found herself wanting to be in them, wanting to be at his side, simply wanting to be in his orbit because he pulled her in so powerfully.

Before she could decide, she and Daddy went down the stairs, underneath the bleachers, and outside the arena when Henry called her name. She turned back and found him jogging toward her, his blue robes billowing behind him and revealing his black slacks and white shirt—what he might wear to church.

"Hey," he said as he gathered her into his arms. He swept a quick kiss across her cheek and then moved right to Daddy and hugged him. "Thank you so much for coming, sir. Hope it wasn't too much trouble."

Daddy grunted, this time in total surprise. Angel couldn't remember the last time she'd seen her daddy hug a cowboy, and she turned her face away to hide her smile. Henry stepped back, grinning from ear to ear, that powerful charm on full display.

"I'm gonna go meet my parents, but we're still okay to come for lunch, right?"

"Yes," Angel said. "Everyone's counting on it. Tables are set and ready."

He took her hand, his fingers strong and warm. "Do you want to come? I saw you sitting by them."

Angel looked at Daddy. Daddy looked at her. And she met Henry's eyes again. "Yeah, I want to come. Can I be in some of the pictures?"

"Of course, sweetheart." He squeezed her hand, and maybe for the first time, Angel had one of those silent conversations that she'd seen her momma and daddy have. *Thank you for inviting me to be in your graduation pictures.*

"Come on, Daddy," she said, taking his hand with her other one. "We don't have to get back to the ranch anyway."

"No," Daddy grumbled. "But I don't want to be in no pictures."

Angel laughed and said, "That's just fine, Daddy." She released his hand, and he walked alongside her as she hugged Henry's arm and said, "You looked so good up there, baby. You should have seen yourself walking across that stage."

He laughed. "Yeah, you think so?"

"I'm really proud of you, Henry."

He looked down at her, all of his joviality still there, but somehow a sense of sobriety fell over him too. "Thank you, Angel. I did work real hard for that."

"Hey, there he is!" his daddy yelled, and the Marshalls descended upon them. Angel didn't mind because they were so open and so warm. Chelsea chatted with her daddy while Henry introduced Angel around to his siblings one more time.

"All right, all right," Daddy said. "Let's take the pictures and go." He held two phones in his hand and said, "You guys get all together. Everyone together. Then, Henry, we can take you with your momma and daddy and your brothers and sisters and maybe just you and Angel too."

And that was when Angel knew that Daddy had accepted her relationship with Henry.

And if he had, surely the other cowboys at Lone Star would too.

And perhaps it was time for Angel to accept it—and take it out of the shadows.

Chapter Twenty-Seven

Lincoln Glover had had enough of rain, cattle, ranching, and mud. This last week of May had really found Mother Nature angry. In the Texas Panhandle, she'd blown winds that had disrupted their planting, and then she'd sent rain that had washed everything away.

Since Uncle Ward employed rotational ranching and they moved their cattle, turkeys, sheep, chickens, and pigs around from pasture to pasture, something always needed to be done. Seven days a week.

They'd moved the main herd up into the hills already, but Uncle Cactus had reserved some cows and kept them on the ranch, so that he could watch them for medical reasons before he turned them loose into the wilds. He was also training some new cattle dogs, and he needed cattle to do that.

The sky thundered overhead, and Link tipped his head back and said, "Really, Lord?" His clothes bore burrs, seeds, random vegetational debris, and mud. The only good thing he could say was that he didn't have burrowing owls at Shiloh Ridge this year. He and Dawson had built man-made nests for them at the top of the hill just outside of the Rhinehart Ranch property, and the owls had settled there instead of on either one of their ranches.

Link just wanted to go home, and he thought about Misty and what she might be doing that afternoon. She worked at an interior design firm and helped maintain the integrity of historical places. He wasn't sure if she had a client that day or if she'd be home, but no matter what, he wanted to order dinner, shower away everything that had happened this week, and lay with his wife in his arms as they watched something on TV.

The problem was, he still had a couple of hours of work ahead of him, and that lazy evening with just him and Misty felt so far away. He got the last of the sheep through the gate and closed it, tying it off so nothing would come back out and nothing new could go in. He reached down and patted his horse's neck because he wasn't the only one out here putting in long hours in bad weather.

"Let's go take a break," he said. "Get a snack and some water." He headed back to the stable, which took a good twenty minutes, and he didn't make it before it started. The sky opened, and rain began to fall.

"Of course," he muttered, hunching down into his jacket, though it wasn't cold, and stuffing his cowboy hat on as low as it would go to try to protect his face, neck, and shoulders. He and Copper arrived back at the stable, and it took him another half hour to get his horse cleaned up enough to put in his stall.

He could take out another horse to finish moving the turkeys into the field that the sheep had just vacated. After that, he needed to go through some inventory in the equipment shed, and then he needed to check with his momma on the status of a couple of their planters that she had been working on.

Momma had started teaching Sunnie how to be a mechanic just the way she'd taught Sunnie to be a chef in the kitchen. Sunnie was real good with her hands, and she liked little parts and details and things coming together.

All the kids had one more week of school, and then they'd be working around the ranch for the summer. Daddy usually found a ton of projects that needed to be done that kids' hands could do—anyone twelve and older. But this year, that was Link's job.

Link was slowly and steadily taking over everything that Daddy usually did. He had to sit down with his father and make a list of all the things that kids could do.

They could pull chicken wire tight, and the older kids could use a staple gun to put it in place.

Uncle Cactus had work to be done in his barn, and all the groundskeeping needed to be done. All the kids in Link's family could use lawn mowers, weed eaters, and rakes. They tended to the vegetable gardens all summer, and they'd clean True Blue.

Rock especially loved being with the horses, and he worked with Uncle Cactus in their care, feeding, training, and general happiness. Lincoln had started putting together projects weeks ago, and he'd meet with everyone next week once school got out. They'd planned a few days on a vacation schedule, where they would take the kids down to the pool and to play in the river and give them a little bit of summer before they had to start working.

And of course, they had plenty of time to wade in the ponds, go fishing, ride bikes, fly kites, and do all the things kids did in the summer, around the little chores that Link would give them. They weren't full-time cowboys like him. They weren't the junior foreman.

Sometimes the weight of what Link did pulled at him, especially the thought of having to do it his whole life and especially having to be Bear Glover one day. He reminded himself that he had a dozen aunts and uncles and three times that many cousins. He would never be alone at Shiloh Ridge unless he wanted to be.

He had just finished washing his hands when Uncle Ward came in and said, "There you are. I've been texting you."

"Yeah, well, I've been out on the northwest side," Link said darkly. "Not much service down there."

"We're calling it for today," Uncle Ward said. "Where did you get?"

"I just moved the sheep into field four," Link said. "The turkeys still need to be moved, and then the chickens gotta be let out."

"We're gonna do it later," Uncle Ward said. "There's word of some tornado activity kicking up."

Link heard the alarm in Uncle Ward's voice. "Really? Have they put out a warning?" He immediately thought of Misty and where she might be. Was she down in town? If the tornado siren went off, would she be able to make it to the ranch? Did he even want her to? If not, where would she shelter?

A calm, slow voice told him, *Your grandparents live in town. Misty will be fine.* Link took a deep breath, slowly enough to help him calm down.

"Just rumors," Uncle Ward said. "Coming up out of Hondo, but I checked the radar, and it doesn't look good. I want everyone home and accounted for in the next thirty minutes. I'm sending the message now."

His fingers flew across the phone, and in the next five seconds, Link's own device chimed out the tone he had assigned to Uncle Ward. He looked up and said, "Go on, now. Get home to your wife."

"We don't need to try to round up the animals and put them in the barn?"

Ward shook his head. "They'll be better off if they can run." He turned to leave the stable. "You've got the longest drive, so get going."

Link nodded and said, "Yes, sir," and did exactly that. He'd barely made it to his truck when his phone rang, and Misty's name appeared on the screen.

"Hey, baby, where are you?" he asked. "Did you get Ward's text?"

"Yeah, I got it," she said, and she sounded near hysterics. "Are you on your way home?"

"Yep," he said. "I just made it to my truck." He turned the key in the ignition, and it roared to life. "I'm ten minutes away."

"You've got to come up that hill," she said. "It's been so muddy lately."

"I'm gonna make it, Misty," he assured her. "Are you at home?"

"Yeah," she said.

"I thought you were working in town today."

"I did this morning," she said, her voice pitching up. "Link, it's really windy up here."

"I'm gonna make it," he said. "I'm on my way."

Any number of houses sat down here on the main

part of the ranch. He could find shelter for sure. The Top Cottage, where he lived, stood up a dirt road at the top of the hill, just across the border from the Rhinehart Ranch.

They'd had mudslides in the past and some felled trees during bad storms that blocked the road, but Link was absolutely going to make it to his wife. He couldn't imagine her in their house alone during a storm, though he could probably get Dawson or Duke to go check on her. Heck, Dawson lived closer to Link than anyone in his own family, even though they lived on two separate pieces of property.

"I'm leaving right now," he said. "I'm at the stables."

"Okay," she said, and her voice pitched up and broke again. "Please hurry."

Link promised he would, and he ended the call so that he could use both hands to drive. The wind whipped across the ranch, lashing rain against the windows and the top of the truck. No wonder Misty was upset.

At the same time, her emotions didn't make sense. She'd lived in Texas her whole life. She'd lived through hurricanes. She'd been in tornadoes. She had an apartment fire just a couple of years ago. Why was *this* the thing upsetting her so much?

Link pushed it out of his mind as he trundled past True Blue on his right, and then a few hundred yards later, Uncle Ace's house on his left. He started up the hill then, slipping sideways in the mud as a powerful gust of wind blew over the top of the hill and slammed straight into his truck.

"Please, God," he whispered as he righted it. "I have to make it."

Messages came in fast and furious, probably from people reporting on the *Everybody* thread that they were somewhere safe. He hoped none of them needed help because if they did, it would be him and Uncle Ward out there providing it. Then what would Misty say?

Not only that, but Uncle Ward was getting up there in age, and he couldn't do everything that he'd once been able to do. Uncle Preacher had some physical limitations, and though he was the other foreman at Shiloh Ridge, if someone needed physical help, it wouldn't be Preacher out there doing it.

Probably Uncle Ranger or Uncle Judge. Uncle Bishop and Uncle Ace had plenty of strength left in their lives, their legs, and their arms, and they would come to anyone's rescue too. Heck, anyone that bore the last name Glover would be there for anyone else who needed it.

Including your wife, a voice whispered, and Link's grip on the steering wheel relaxed. The wheels spun; the truck slid in the mud; he quickly shifted into four-wheel drive, and the truck kept climbing.

His heartbeat rode on a roller coaster, up one

moment and then plummeting the next. He'd probably have to fix the road later from the ruts he put in the soft mud, but right now, he didn't care.

Inch by inch, foot by foot, minute by minute, Link climbed the hill, and the ten-minute drive from the main part of the ranch to the Top Cottage took twenty.

By the time he turned and came to a stop in front of his cabin, he had over two hundred messages he hadn't read, and Misty had called two more times. She had his location, so she knew where he was, and he wondered if it looked like he hadn't moved or something.

He noticing the wild way the tree limbs moved left, right, back, and forth in all different directions, all on the same tree. He left his lunchbox and cowboy hat and made a mad dash for the house. The two dogs that usually palled around with Link were already there, and Misty held a couple of towels in her hands. She straightened from where she'd been drying Dusty and Rio.

"There you are," she said, and she burst into tears.

Link had no idea what to do with that. Misty wasn't usually terribly emotional, but he had seen her cry over the past year since they'd been married.

"Hey, I'm right here." He gathered her into his chest and held on tight. "It's okay. Come on, let's go inside." His hopes of ordering in dinner and enjoying a lazy evening on the couch withered away. He'd have to make something, but that was fine. He could put a frozen pizza in the oven and call it good. He didn't have anybody to impress, and he and Misty had had plenty of simple meals in their lives.

"Come on, you guys," he said to the dogs. As he opened the door, he let them in first, then ushered in his still weeping wife.

"What's wrong?" he asked. "Couldn't you see me on the map?"

"You didn't look like you were moving."

"Well, it wasn't fast." He stepped out of his boots and then unbuckled his jeans right there by the door. "I'm gonna take everything off here. I'm so muddy and so wet." And he felt so gross.

She laid out the two towels she'd been rubbing the dogs with. "Put it all right here. I'll put it in the washing machine while you shower."

She'd regained control of some of her emotions, but she made no effort to wipe her face as Link stepped out of his clothes and left them on the floor. "Thank you, baby." He swept a kiss along her forehead and said, "I'll be right back out. I promise."

"Okay," she said. "I'm okay." She gathered up the towels and all of his clothes and headed off toward the laundry room while he streaked down the hall to the master suite to take a shower. Nothing had ever felt as good as that hot water, rinsing away the awfulness of this week.

The mud from his hair, and the weeds that he picked out of his beard, and all of the dirt and grime and grossness from his skin. He got dressed in a comfortable pair of sweatpants and a sweatshirt. He took one down the hall to Misty, remembering that she'd only been wearing a T-shirt. She stood in the kitchen now, working at the stove, and he eased up behind her and said, "Mm, making breakfast for dinner?"

"Yeah," she said. "It's about the only thing that sounds good."

"I brought you a sweatshirt," he said, and she turned into him, her eyes already filled with water again.

"Hey," Link took her face in both of his hands. "You gotta talk to me. What's going on?"

She tried to smile, but the gesture shook and crumbled right off her face. She closed her eyes and then opened them again, looking at him with the softest look of love and adoration. Link could drown in it, and he wanted to. If he died right now, this would be the best way to go, with his wife looking at him like he was the only man for her. Because he was.

"I don't want you thinking you're special or anything," she said, her voice tinny and tight. "But you're going to be a daddy."

Link blinked, adrenaline sending waves through his veins, his ears catching on to what she'd said. It took his brain a good long minute to figure it out after that. "You're pregnant?"

Tears spilled down her face again, and she said, "Yep."

Link laughed because that felt like the best thing to do when finding out his lovely wife was going to have his child. He wrapped her up tightly and pulled her against his chest and said, "Is this why we're crying all the time now?"

"Just today," she said. "I just found out this afternoon."

He kissed her ear and down her neck. "I don't care if you cry every day for the rest of our lives." He lifted his head and looked right at her. "I love you so much."

"I'm scared," she admitted. His beautiful, strong Misty only ever told him exactly how she felt.

"You are going to be the best mother in the whole world," he said, taking her face in his hands again. "Absolutely the best." And he meant it.

Because Misty knew how to nurture and care for those around her. She simply hadn't had the opportunity to prove it to herself yet. But God had just granted her that, and Link had never felt more grateful.

Tears pricked at his own eyes, and he cleared his throat. "Okay. Okay, let me finish dinner. You go sit down."

She giggled through her tears and said, "I'm capable of standing, Link."

"I know, but...." His gaze dropped to her flat stomach, and then his hands moved there too. "But I'll finish dinner, okay?" He raised his gaze to hers again. "You're not special or anything. It's just dinner."

She burst out laughing, which made Link's heart so happy, and then he pressed his lips to hers sloppily. As they sobered, the kiss became real, and slow, and beautiful. He pulled away and whispered, "I love you so much."

"I love you too, Link."

Chapter Twenty-Eight

"It's gonna be a madhouse," JJ said as he glanced over to his best friend in the passenger seat. "I can't believe you want to come."

"What else am I going to do?" Tate asked. "Sit alone in the apartment?" He threw JJ a disgruntled look. "I got told no three more times this week. I ain't got no job. I got nothing to do here."

JJ gritted his teeth and nodded. "Well, I hope you're ready for the biggest family party you've ever been to," he said. "There are *seven* Walkers graduating from high school this year."

Tate laughed, his mood brightening pretty quickly, and said, "Just like your Seven Sons Ranch."

JJ could smile too, and he did.

"What are they all doing?" Tate asked. "The graduating Walkers."

"Well, Clara Jean is going to work at the grocery store," JJ said. His younger sister had already been working at Wilde & Organic for the past three or four years, as Momma's family owned it. "She likes being out in the fields with my uncle as well. So she's probably going to do that. I haven't heard anything about her attending college or anything." He cut a look over to Tate.

"What about Ruby? What did she decide?" He had been unable to get his best friend's little sister out of his head since she had shown up outside of their apartment and he'd splashed her with soda. But JJ would never admit it to anyone.

"I think she's gonna come to Amarillo State," Tate said. "She's filling out housing applications now."

JJ pressed his lips together and nodded. "That's great," he said, and he wasn't sure if he sounded like he was about to put his dog down or if he really thought it was great that the gorgeous Ruby Reynolds was going to be at the same college as him next year. It sure would be harder to keep his feelings to himself if he saw her all the time.

"Who else is graduating?" Tate said.

"Let's see." JJ took in a big breath and exhaled it all out. "My Uncle Rhett is the oldest brother—he's just older than my daddy. And he has triplets. They're all graduating this year: Austin, Elaine, and Easton."

"Wow, triplets," Tate said. "These are the ones you

were telling me about that got in trouble with your momma? With the pumpkins?"

JJ laughed, so many memories streaming through his head. "That's them. Mostly Easton. I swear, he exists in a world all his own."

"That's right," Tate said with a chuckle. "And your momma got real mad at him, and the next year, he grew all her pumpkins for her."

That was him, and JJ loved his cousins. Thankfully, he hadn't been the oldest one, carrying the torch for all the rest of them. Conrad was also Uncle Rhett and Aunt Evelyn's son, and he was a year older than JJ. Uncle Tripp and Ivory had a son close to that same age too, and Isaac had left Seven Sons to do a machinery repair course at a trade school in Austin.

Oliver, of course, was older than all of them, and he lived in town with Rory and their three kids. JJ babysat for them a lot while he was in high school and even after, and he did miss Jewel, Lara, and Mason fiercely.

"My Uncle Wyatt and Aunt Marcy have a son graduating—their oldest, Warren. He's probably going to turn pro this year."

"Of course, Wyatt Walker," Tate said with some new swagger in his voice. "The rodeo king."

"Yeah, Wyatt's going to be his manager here at the beginning," JJ said. "I don't know about after that. Uncle Skyler and Aunt Mal's oldest daughter is graduating. Her name is Camila. And, uh...Uncle Micah and

Aunt Simone's oldest son is graduating. His name's Trap."

"A lot of kids," Tate said.

"Yeah, tell me about it," JJ said. "Everyone else at Seven Sons is a teenager. My youngest sister, Hattie, just turned 13. Uncle Wyatt and Marcy have a daughter that age, while Uncle Skyler and Uncle Micah both have kids younger than that by a year or two."

They were all big enough now to run lawn mowers and pull weeds and help harvest the honey from Aunt Callie's farm. They could paint walls and stain cabins, fix porches and back decks, and ride horses to check on fields and round up cattle. No matter what, everybody worked around Seven Sons Ranch.

Tate was so going to regret coming here to work for the summer.

JJ glanced over to his best friend. "I think I'm going to move into the Equine Science and Management program next year."

Tate looked square at him, and it was a good thing there wasn't a lot of traffic on the highway between Amarillo and Three Rivers. "You've decided?"

"Yeah," JJ said. "I think that's what I want to do."

"You're going to do barn management then?"

"I don't know," he said. "Maybe. It's enough that I just know about horses and how to take care of them. Maybe we'll do a little horse breeding at Seven Sons to go along with our cattle ranching. Or maybe I'll become a show ring judge, or maybe I'll want to be a vet." He smiled and then burst out laughing. "Okay, not that last one."

Tate laughed too and said, "Yeah, too much math going on there."

"I could be a technician, though," JJ said. "Or maybe it's just enough that I can monitor all the animals at Seven Sons when I take it over."

Tate made a scoffing noise that sounded like disbelief. "Do you really think you're gonna come back here and take it over?"

"I have never been *really* sure," JJ said. "But the more I think about it, and the more I pray about it, the more I feel like yeah, I'm gonna come back to Three Rivers, to Seven Sons. And that's gonna be my life."

It sounded simple to him, and while JJ had grown up simply and he didn't mind being simple, he also wanted a grand adventure.

Tate didn't say what he was going to move into, probably because he hadn't decided yet, and they drove the rest of the way to Seven Sons with the radio playing country tunes into the silence around them.

He made the turn onto the road that led right along Seven Sons Ranch, saying, "That house right there is my Uncle Liam and Aunt Callie's. This one coming up on the left is Uncle Micah and Aunt Simone's. And then we come around to the fence."

JJ made the turn off that country road and onto a dirt

one, and the enormity of the ranch opened up before them. Uncle Skyler and Aunt Mal had built a second homestead right next door to where JJ had grown up at the main homestead.

Seven Sons Ranch housed four families, and Uncle Wyatt lived in the northeastern foothills, while Uncle Rhett and Uncle Tripp lived about ten minutes away on one of the southernmost roads in Three Rivers just outside of town.

"This is it." He came to a stop, the dust behind his tires pushing up around the truck as they took in the generational trees, the green grass, and the beautiful fence that held the seven stars—one for each of the seven Walker brothers.

JJ sat there, an overwhelming sense of belonging and peace filling him. "Yeah," he said. "I think I'm gonna come back here one day."

"I would too," Tate said, his voice filled with reverence. "Look at this place, JJ. It's incredible."

"I've just got to figure out how to be useful," JJ said. "I got to know more than I know now." And it wasn't like his parents couldn't afford college. They could. In fact, when JJ took over the ranch, he'd probably inherit billions of dollars from his father.

He looked over to Tate and grinned. "Wait till you see the barn with the American flag on the back of it."

"Well, let's go, cowboy," Tate said in his big, booming voice, and JJ pushed on the gas pedal to get the truck moving again. He went past Uncle Skyler's homestead and Daddy's homestead and past some of the old sheds that had once belonged to the Foster sisters. The three of them had owned the ranch next to Seven Sons, and they'd all married a Walker brother. The sheds had been fixed up, and a whole row of cowboy cabins stood just beyond them.

"We're in the middle one," he said, nodding forward. "That green one."

"It's cute," Tate said. "Ruby would love this." He pulled out his phone and snapped a picture through the windshield. "She'd absolutely *love* this place."

JJ didn't know Ruby at all, only what Tate had said about her, so he said nothing as he pulled in front of the cabin and parked the truck. They didn't have a lot to unload—several boxes and bags for each of them—and the cabin came furnished. JJ and Tate could certainly unload their own things, as they had packed them themselves from the fourth-floor apartment in Amarillo and driven themselves here. But JJ wasn't surprised at all to find the freshly painted white door of the cabin opening and Daddy walking out with Uncle Liam.

"Hey," Daddy said as he came down the stairs, his smile as wide as the sky. "Look who made it." He grabbed onto and pulled JJ right into his chest. "How was the drive?"

"Ain't no thing," JJ said. "Passed like nothing."

"Yeah, well, you missed most of the bad weather last

week," Uncle Liam said. He hugged JJ next. "We still got plenty of cleaning up to do around the ranch, though. Don't worry."

"Joy of joys," JJ said. He looked across the hood of the truck as Tate came around it. "This is my best friend, Tate Reynolds," he said. "You've met my dad, Tate. This is my Uncle Liam."

"Pleased to meet you, sir," Tate said, his charming smile in place. He shook both their hands, and Daddy said, "Let's get you unloaded."

That took about ten minutes, and Daddy must have texted Momma at some point, because she showed up with Clara Jean, Emily, and Hattie, his three sisters, and said, "We'll help you unpack, boys."

They did that, Momma hanging up JJ's slacks and church shirts, while Emily and Hattie unpacked the few dishes and food items that he and Tate had brought from Amarillo. Then they moved into Tate's room and did the same thing.

"All right," Momma said only about a half-hour later. "You guys have beds and blankets. The water's all hooked up; AC's pumping hard." She grinned at both boys. "Come on, we don't want to be late for the feast going on over at the house."

JJ looked at Tate, and Tate looked at JJ, and he raised his eyebrows as if to say, *I told you so.*

Tate chuckled and said, "Mrs. Walker, I've heard so

much about the things you do here at Seven Sons. I can't *wait* to go to this family feast."

"Kiss up," JJ muttered under his breath as Momma said something about how glad she was Tate had come to Seven Sons for the summer.

But he laughed as he followed everyone out of his new cowboy cabin and across a field, and then the back lawn to the homestead. Everyone seemed to be making that pilgrimage, as Daddy was the best cook in the family, and he often fed everyone out of the kitchen here at the homestead.

"There you are," Grandma said, and she bustled over to JJ the moment he walked in the back door.

He hugged her back, because he loved his grandma with everything he had. "Hey, Grams."

"Oh, it's so good to have you back," she gushed. "I hate it when you grandkids leave."

"Well, here I am," he said. "At least for the summer." He spotted his grandfather sitting in the living room, and JJ moved away from Grams to go say hello to him.

Grandpa had a hard time getting off the couch these days and walked with a cane or a walker, so JJ sat next to him and said, "Hey, Grandpa." He gave him a side hug and let his grandpa press a kiss to his forehead. "How're you feeling?"

"Doing all right," Grandpa said, though his voice had definitely become older and more gravelly. He moved slower, and while JJ had worked on a ranch his whole life and had seen the life cycle and he knew that new things became old and then died, he still didn't want to lose his grandfather.

At the same time, his daddy was in his early fifties now, with Uncle Rhett sitting close to fifty-five, and his grandparents were pressing up against eighty.

"You got all settled in?" Grandpa asked.

"I sure did," JJ said. "Me and Tate want to come see the mini donkeys as soon as we can."

Grandpa lit up at that and said, "Anytime, JJ. You just text me when you're leaving here, and I'll meet you at the pasture."

"Okay," JJ grinned at him, and then turned his attention to the kitchen when Daddy raised his voice and said, "All right. Everyone's here. We're gonna go ahead and get started."

He looked around the room at everybody, and it was full to capacity. "We've got tables set up in the front den," he said. "And out on the deck, though it is kind of hot and windy today. But then there's a table here and there's a table in the living room. We counted chairs twice. There's somewhere for everyone to sit. No lap sitting."

He looked over to Hattie and Emily and said, "Did you hear me, girls? No lap sitting."

"No lap sitting, Daddy," they parroted back and then giggled together.

JJ wondered how his father put up with so much

sometimes, but he found himself smiling as Daddy shook his head.

"We're celebrating a lot of graduations today," Daddy said. "And the fact that JJ is home with his best friend, Tate." Tate raised his hand and waved around to everyone, and JJ could only imagine how overwhelmed he might be.

As JJ sat on the couch with his grandpa beside him, everyone listened as Daddy ran through the fried chicken feast that he'd made for lunch that day.

It felt like God had opened up his soul and poured His heavenly light right into JJ's mind. He absolutely did belong here.

JJ questioned whether he should even return to Amarillo State next year at all. *Why go back?* he wondered.

He thought about it during the prayer when he should have been listening to the blessing on the food and the gratitude poured out by Uncle Wyatt.

He just wanted to know the path to take through his own life. He wanted to be able to see it for miles and miles ahead, the way he had as a kid.

It felt like the moment he'd become a senior in high school, that road had been broken up and twisted and turned, and JJ had suddenly had no idea what to do with his life. He'd stayed on the ranch for two more years after he'd graduated, saving money, working, babysitting for Ollie and Rory, and even doing a church service mission before he settled on going to college.

"Amen," chorused the house, and JJ lifted his eyes, a twinge of guilt flowing through him that he'd missed the prayer.

"JJ! JJ!" someone yelled, and he turned just in time to see Lara running toward him. Rory's middle child never went anywhere without running, and he barely caught her as she launched herself into his arms. "You're back! You're back!" She grinned at him and pressed her nose to his. "Are you going to come watch a movie with us later?"

"Sure thing," JJ said, his smile real and wide for the first time in months. "And you know what? Maybe you can come to *my* house and watch a movie with me."

A look of wonder came over her face, and she wiggled to get down. "Mama! Mama!" she yelled. "Can I go to JJ's and watch a movie?"

Rory looked at her like she'd spoken another language, and then she glanced over to JJ. "What?"

JJ smiled and shook his head. It didn't matter. He could come pick up the kids anytime. He would take them to the pool or the park, or they could come to the ranch, and he'd show them the honeybees. He'd teach them how to plant carrots and peas, and he'd show them all the horses. Rory spent a lot of time up at Shiloh Ridge Ranch too, as her mama had married a Glover, so the kids had no shortage of opportunity to be outside and around animals.

JJ got up, filled a plate of food, and naturally gravitated towards sitting next to Clara Jean. Tate came to his side and sat by him, and the bubble of comfort around JJ expanded.

"You surviving?" he muttered under his breath to Tate.

"Are you kidding?" Tate said, and he practically glowed from every skin cell. "This is amazing."

"I forgot you're an extrovert," JJ said dryly, as he almost couldn't wait to finish eating and get out of there. But he knew that wouldn't happen because the high school graduation they were going to attend for seven people in the Walker family that day—six cousins and one of his siblings—didn't start until three-thirty. So he still had a very long way to go before he would find himself alone in his bedroom, in the new green cowboy cabin here on Seven Sons Ranch.

Tate's phone chimed, and he looked at it. "Oh, Ruby wants a tour of the cabin," he said. "We can do that later, right?" He looked at JJ, who suddenly felt rough and ragged and jagged inside.

But he nodded and said, "Yep, we can do that."

Chapter Twenty-Nine

Dawson flitted around his house, setting out all the things he and Caroline had prepared for the ranchers' luncheon that day. Caroline was at work and wouldn't be joining them. It wasn't game night; it wasn't couples' night; it was a ranchers' luncheon, and Dawson hosted it at the Rhinehart Ranch a couple of times each year.

He'd left the ranch owners' meeting a little bit early so that he could get back and get things heated up and set out. He wasn't surprised to see Brandon walk in a few minutes later.

"Howdy, brother," Brandon called from the front door.

"Come help me get this salsa out," Dawson replied. His momma made the best salsa in the world, and he breathed in the scent of tomatoes, garlic, and cilantro as he opened the jar.

He and Caroline had planned a taco bar, because Wilde & Organic had little tubs of prepared toppings to make it perfect. No prep, just a lot of opening containers and setting things out.

Ruffin lifted his head from his dog bed at the end of the counter as Dawson put the bag of tortilla chips in line. "I think they're here," he said.

He strode toward toward the front door and opened it. He peered out, and sure enough, Finn had arrived, and he'd brought Paul and Henry with him.

Dawson waved them all in, and they came in laughing and chatting over each other. "Just leave the door open a little bit," he said. "And then everyone can come in when they get here."

Link arrived with Olli and JJ, as they were all related in some way, even if none of them shared a single particle of DNA. Finally, only sixty seconds later, Alex brought up the rear. He closed the door behind him and came into the kitchen carrying a plastic sack over his forearm.

"I got all the mint chocolate chip and all the rocky road," Alex said.

Dawson grinned at him, went to meet him to take the ice cream, and returned to put it in the freezer. Everyone looked to him, as whoever hosted the luncheon usually welcomed everyone and set a topic for the day.

They had finished their planting at the Rhinehart Ranch, their cattle had been driven up into the hills, and they'd moved into that "easier summertime" where they watched things grow. He didn't have a whole lot he wanted to talk about, as they'd discussed watering schedules and pest control last month

"Today." He cleared his throat, suddenly nervous, "I thought we'd share personal news."

The mood in the room changed instantly, and Dawson wanted to backpedal. "I mean, if you have something you want to announce. Might be fun to just have a friend lunch, not a work lunch."

"I like that idea," Finn said, nodding as a slow smile spread across his face. Since he'd been the one to start the game nights and the ranchers' luncheons, a lot of men deferred to him.

"Do we have to say something?" Alex asked, his cowboy hat pushed low over his eyes.

"Not at all." Dawson glanced around at everyone. "But I feel like no one's been texting on the thread very much," he said, the words just falling out of him. "And I thought maybe today could just be more easygoing, more casual." He looked over at Link, and the man had his lips pressed tightly closed. Oh, he definitely had something to say, but Dawson wasn't sure it would come out.

"I think that's a great idea," Brandon said. "Let's get our food, and I'll start." Dawson threw a grateful smile at his brother and picked up a plate too. Each cowboy went through the line, using both sides of the island, to fill his plate with tacos, chips, salsa, and guacamole. They all chatted easily with each other, even JJ, who was a decade younger than Dawson and Finn but somehow managed to fit in with them at the same time. Dawson simply listened to him tell Henry how things were going at Seven Sons and that he might need a farrier to come out.

Henry said, "Let me know. I seem to come to Three Rivers often enough."

"Yeah, how he does that with his new girlfriend," Paul teased. "I don't know."

"Oh boy. Here we go," Finn said just as Ollie said, "Ooh, Henry's got a girlfriend?"

Henry always seemed to have a new girlfriend. Dawson grinned at him as they all took their seats at the table.

"Well, I thought Brandon was gonna go first," Henry said. He looked to Brandon, who sat on his left.

"Yeah, I'm gonna go first. *I* happened to start seeing someone new, and it's going pretty—well." He took a bite of his taco, the crunch of the shell adding a final punctuation mark to his news. Dawson knew his brother, and Brandon would not say more.

Still, Alex asked, "Who is it?"

Brandon shook his head, a playful glint in his eyes.

"He won't tell," Dawson said. "He never tells until he's five or six dates in and feeling good."

Brandon nodded and pointed at Dawson as if saying he was right. Then he simply took another bite of his taco and looked down the table. "Who's next?"

"We don't have a lot going on," Finn said, the chip he'd just dipped in salsa pausing halfway to his mouth. "Edith got another book contract. She's real happy about that. We had a great birthday party for Theo." He laughed lightly. "My mother smothered him with gifts, but it was fun."

It seemed like they'd established a pattern and would go around in a circle now, and Finn looked at Alex.

Alex coughed, reached for a napkin, and wiped his face. "Y'all know that Nikki's had a real hard time getting pregnant," he said. "We've been keeping this close to the vest because we weren't sure if we were going to be able to keep the baby." His smile grew and grew and grew, and his throat worked and worked and worked. Dawson found himself getting emotional at Alex's show of emotion. The man was stalwart and true and hardly ever showed any emotion. His humor was dry and funny, and he was a hard worker and a good man.

"When is she due?" Finn asked.

Alex looked at his brother-in-law and said, "December. She's due in December." He popped a chunk of tomato in his mouth and added, "We think it might be twins. We've got an ultrasound appointment in a couple of weeks."

"Wow-how-how-how-how," Finn said, half laughing and half talking. "Twins?"

"It's a little overwhelming," Alex admitted. "But Nicki's got the yard looking the way she wants, and she's started on the nursery now." He smiled again, and it sure was good to see him exuding happiness. "We're both really excited."

"That's so amazing," Dawson said. "Congratulations, brother." He reached over and held out his fist for Alex to bump. Others added their congratulations to the mix too, and the mood seemed so much softer and better now.

Paul, who sat next to Alex, cleared his throat and said, "Brielle and I are going to get married the first week of November. And she's going to move here to Three Rivers. I'm going to take over Courage Rains from my daddy." His smile came out too, and Henry whooped the loudest.

"I didn't even know that. You've been holding out on me."

"Yeah," Paul said. They hugged one another, causing a ruckus as Henry sat across from Paul and not next to him. The table got bumped more than once, until Henry finally sat back down. And once the congratulations had settled down again, everybody looked at Dawson.

"I ain't got much," he said. "Carolyn's not pregnant

or anything. We're just getting by day by day, enjoying being married."

"Marriage is the best," Finn said.

"Duke's giving me more and more responsibilities," Dawson said. "I'm managing pretty well, but I think I'm single-handedly keeping the sticky note companies in business." He grinned around the table at his friends, so glad he had this safe place where he would find them all smiling back at him.

Not poking fun. Not pressuring him for details. Just love and support and friendship. He ducked his head and glanced at Link. "Your turn."

Link blinked and set down his taco. He dusted his hands. "I don't have much either. Just plugging along. No burrowing owls this year." He grinned at Dawson and went back to his food.

"No burrowing owls," Dawson repeated. He and Misty had been married for a little over a year now. And to be honest, Dawson thought they might start having kids any day now, but Link just bit into his taco and looked to JJ.

JJ wore a hint of redness in his face already, but he said, "I'm feeling real good about coming back to Seven Sons for the summer. I'm still gonna go to Amarillo and try the equine program for a year, and then...we'll see after that." He looked over at Ollie and smiled. "But at least I feel like I have a better hold on what I'm doing now."

"That's great," Ollie said, and he beamed around at everyone. "Rory is going to have another baby too. I told her we have to stop at four, but she's not convinced." He laughed and shook his head. "She's not due till January, and we're both hoping for anyone with less energy than Lara." That caused more laughter to spill across table because his middle child was a real spitfire.

Dawson himself had seen Lara in action when he'd gone to help JJ during a babysitting stint last year.

That only left Henry, but he still didn't volunteer any information.

"What's this I hear about Libby getting married?" Brandon asked into the silence. "I heard she got engaged."

"Oh yeah, yep," Finn said. "I guess I should've mentioned it. Libby and Rusty got engaged. They're gonna get married here in Three Rivers right after they move here to take over the ranch from my daddy. In January."

"You guys got a lot of changes going on out at Three Rivers," Link said.

Finn exchanged a glance with Henry and said, "Seems to be something all the time."

Silence draped over them again, and Dawson just started to open his mouth to say Henry didn't have to speak if he didn't want to when Henry said, "I'm dating my boss at Lone Star. We've been going out for almost four months, and I sure do like her." He spoke in a slow, somber, measured tone, one that Dawson hadn't heard him use when talking about a woman before.

Henry was usually laughter and smiles and playful quips. He'd been on dozens of first dates without a second, but dating someone for four months? That was something for Henry Marshall.

"I sense a story here," Dawson said, and he swiped a chip through the guacamole so Henry wouldn't think he was prying too much.

"There's a story, all right," Henry said. "And I'm really glad that you said we could do personal stuff today." He swallowed. "I'm starting to look at places on the outskirts of Three Rivers toward Amarillo, maybe even Stinnett. I don't want to live permanently at Lone Star."

Everyone watched Henry now, the way they had Dawson, but the mood had shifted again.

"Even if you marry Angel?" Paul asked.

"It's her ranch. We both need a break from it," Henry said. "It's...a lot for her to handle, even with the changes she's made." He glanced around and launched into a short explanation of all the things Angel had done —his promotion from team lead to captain and how a boarding stable as big as Lone Star could devour a person in a single day.

"Sounds like Shiloh Ridge," Link said dryly.

"Or Three Rivers," Paul said.

"Or even my one-man operation," Alex said. "I mean, if I don't do it, there isn't anyone else, you know?"

Dawson nodded because they were all right. They all carried heavy loads. They all did their best every day.

"Anyway," Henry said, "I've been thinking a lot since I graduated. And, well, it would be great if you all could give me some advice about what to do next."

Finn asked, "About moving here?"

"Not all the way here," Henry said. "But I could get something on the outskirts of town, and maybe commute to Lone Star. Forty minutes wouldn't be so bad." He put his last chip in his mouth, chewed, and swallowed.

"But really, see...Angel and I have kept our relationship a secret from everyone at Lone Star, and I'm ready to come out of the shadows. She doesn't seem to be, and it's starting to really irritate me." He glanced around at everyone, pure openness and vulnerability shining in his eyes.

"So I'd love to know what you all would do if you were in my boots."

Chapter Thirty

Henry jogged up the steps to the open doors of the church, something ragged in his soul needing to be soothed. He hadn't made it to church very often in the past several months, but something that Finn had said at lunch a few days ago had stirred him to get up, get ready, and get to the chapel this morning.

Henry didn't like doing much of anything by himself, let alone going to church. He stopped when he entered the chapel. The rows extended forward in front of him, with the pulpit about fifty yards away. It seemed like everyone thought today was a great day to be at church, and Henry had no idea where to sit.

"Coming or going?" someone asked, and the voice tickled recognition inside Henry.

He turned toward Bard. "Coming."

"Yep, us too. Just getting here," Bard said as he

squeezed past Henry and continued down the aisle. Trevor followed him, using only a single cane today

"Hey, buddy," Henry said, and Trevor grinned as he passed.

Henry's pulse puttered around his body when Angel came to his side. "I didn't know you were coming to church today."

He swallowed because he hadn't known either. He also hadn't spoken much to Angel in the past few days since the luncheon. The messages he'd gotten from his friends had run through his mind and taken root, needing to be addressed.

If it's bothering you that much, Link had said, *You need to tell her.*

You guys need to come clean, Dawson had said, while Finn had asked, *Have you prayed about it?*

They'd all had various advice, including JJ, who'd said, *If it's not hurting anybody, why does it matter?*

Henry had been over that a lot. Why did it matter if everyone at Lone Star knew he and Angel were together? As Henry stood there next to her, his fingers itched to be reunited with hers. He slipped his hand closer, and she sucked in a breath. "You're welcome to come sit by us if you want."

Then she walked away. Henry figured that was about as good as he was going to get from Angel. If he sat by her in church, wasn't that public enough for him?

All at once, Henry realized his *pride* needed to be

satisfied. He wanted others to know that he'd gotten the gorgeous Angel White to go out with *him*, that they were together, that somehow that would elevate him and make him more important.

"Which is stupid," he muttered to himself. As another family came up behind him, Henry got himself out of the doorway, strolled down the aisle, and sat on the end of the pew next to Angel. He put his forearms on his knees and let his hands hang down as he leaned forward.

"Are you okay?" she asked, almost under her breath.

"Just thinking through some things," he said.

"Well, church is a good place for that."

The music started only a minute later. The choir sang one of Henry's absolute favorite songs for the opening number, which lifted his heart so much that he returned to his seat with hope running through him.

Pastor Ryan got up, and while he probably had twenty years on Henry, he'd always said exactly what Henry needed to hear. Today, he started with a story about geological terms and directions, about needing a fixed location to measure from.

"It's called a backsight," Pastor Ryan said. "A fixed location that everyone has agreed upon. It's what land surveyors all use—a fixed, known position to move forward to unknown positions around the world."

Henry could see where he was going with this "fixed, known position," and equating it to the Savior.

He sure did enjoy the mini lesson, as told by a great storyteller, about how land surveyors worked to determine property lines.

"I once counseled someone who was having a dispute with his neighbor over where the fence could go and which parcel of property he owned and which his neighbor did. There has to be a legal way to determine that. It's not just what he wanted, and it's not what his neighbor wanted."

The pastor spoke in such an engaging voice, and he surveyed the congregation as he did. "But on the earth, we have established backsights, usually situated at higher elevations, and land surveyors can use those *known marks* to determine property lines.

"So one was called, and he came out and determined where the property line was using this anchored spot on the earth, this backsight, this known and agreed-upon position. By looking back to what has been established, to what is known, a clear boundary between the two properties could be established."

Fascinating, Henry thought. He'd never much thought about such things.

"And that is what the Savior does," Pastor Ryan continued. "When you're not sure about where your boundaries are, when you're not sure of the lines, when you're not sure of the direction you need to go, you turn back to the *one constant thing* that doesn't move and doesn't change—and that is God."

Henry found himself nodding along, his attention solely focused on the pastor up front.

"Go to Him with your questions and your concerns and find out what *He* wants you to do," Pastor Ryan said. "I have one little bit of warning here, and that's about the timing of what you think you want and *when* you want it. Because God very rarely works on men's time.

"He has a plan for you, and He is aware of you. But my friends, my brothers and sisters, speed does not matter if there is no direction."

Speed does not matter if there is no direction.

"We always get our direction from the established backsight, from our Lord and Savior Jesus Christ, and God the Father. So you might be trying to go too fast, and God might feel like He needs to slow you down. It's because He knows the direction that you need to go, and He knows how fast you need to do it. Getting something before you're ready for it does no good, and arriving late could also be detrimental."

"So turn to the Lord in all things, and trust in His timing. Trust in *His* speed. Trust in *His* direction, for *He* is the ultimate backsight."

"Amen, brother," Henry whispered, though the preacher's words also whipped like a chastisement to his soul. He hadn't really been going to the Lord and asking for anything to do with timing. But Henry was a go-go-go man, and he wanted everything all at once.

With the introduction of this new advice, some of his

frustration over Angel's slowness in announcing the relationship to everyone at Lone Star bled away. Speed was irrelevant without proper direction. His mind went through that for the rest of the sermon, though the pastor moved on to say other things.

The meeting ended, and Henry stood to sing and clap along with everybody else. The music finished, and he turned toward Angel at the same time she looked at him.

"He was great," Henry said. "I didn't know that about land surveyors and backsights. Did you?"

"No," she said. "I've never heard of that before."

He led the way out of the pew, wanting to spend more time with Angel that day, but knowing that she spent the Sabbath with her family. He also wasn't sure if she wanted them to be seen together. So he simply moved up the aisle and out of the building, basking in the sunshine as it beat down on him.

Angel didn't come out right behind him, which meant she'd gotten stopped and was probably chatting with someone inside. They hadn't come together, hadn't planned to come together, and hadn't planned to spend any time together today. But Henry still felt a little bit odd just simply walking away from her. He did, because no one could stand outside in this Texas heat for long, but when he got behind the wheel of his truck, he pulled out his phone to text her.

Thanks for letting me sit by you at church today. I

didn't see your momma and hope she's okay. Let me know if you need anything. He sent that, adjusted the vents to blow more directly at him, and turned up the radio before he headed back to Lone Star.

Along the way, Henry wasn't even sure if he passed through green lights or red lights. He had no idea what songs played. He shivered before he realized he was cold from the blasting AC, because he'd been thinking about what the pastor had said.

Speed is irrelevant without direction.

Henry really needed to know what direction to go. He could see himself easing easily into the Whites' way of life at Lone Star. Angel had a cabin; they could get married, and he could move in there with her.

They could raise their family there, shoeing horses and teaching horseback riding lessons for the rest of their lives. His life could definitely go in that direction.

But...Henry didn't see it, and he wasn't sure if he didn't see it with Angel, or if he didn't see it at Lone Star, or if he didn't see it because it was the combination of both Angel and Lone Star.

Could he really just insert himself into their family as if he'd belonged there his whole life when he hadn't?

The questions continued to roar through Henry as he returned to his cabin, grabbed lunch, and then headed out to the stable to go through his paperwork for the week. He didn't often file it on time, and he used his days off to get that done.

He'd put in a request to move his days off to Sundays and Thursdays, so he could attend the rancher luncheons every first Thursday of the month with his friends. He hadn't heard if that had been approved yet.

As he shuffled through paperwork, he finally got a text from Angel that said, *It was nice to sit by you today. Trevor wants to know if you're doing anything with Palermo later this afternoon. If so, he wants to come, and I told him you would text him.*

Henry *was* going to work with Palermo later that afternoon, and he would definitely text Trevor so he could come over. He wasn't exactly trying to make Palermo a therapy horse, but Palermo needed some rehabilitation from an injury, and he had been helping Henry as much as the horse.

He'd mentioned it to Angel, and she must have told Trevor about it. *Second,* Angel said, *I've rearranged your days off to Sundays and Thursdays as you requested.*

For some reason, that made Henry's whole soul light up, and he took it as an answer from God that he needed to be closer to Three Rivers. He needed to be closer to family for some reason. He needed to maintain those friendships with Finn, Alex, Dawson, Oliver, Walker, JJ, and Link.

But why? he wondered as he reread Angel's text. No answer came then, but Henry knew it as well as he knew his own face. He looked up and saw that face partially reflected in the glass in front of him.

"All right, Lord," he said. "I'm trusting in the direction." He hated how he had to constantly step into the dark, but that seemed to be the path God wanted him on.

So Henry prayed right then and there that God wouldn't lead him to the edge of the cliff and let him fall off.

Chapter Thirty-One

Angel turned in a slow circle as Willow galloped around the arena on her horse. "Pull her head up," she called to make sure the girl had her grip on the reins right. Willow wasn't a new rider, which Angel was grateful for because she wasn't sure if she had the patience to deal with a brand-new rider this summer.

The girl and equine continued to move, and Angel enjoyed her time in the sun, calling instructions and watching as horse and human learned to work together. The horseback riding lesson ended, and Angel went to take the reins as Willow got down. "You're getting really good," she told the girl, a fourteen-year-old who lived only a few minutes outside of Stinnett.

"Thanks so much," Willow said. She grabbed onto Angel and hugged her. She always had sunshine and spirit pouring from her, with a wide smile, pale blonde hair, and the skinniest arms and legs that Angel had ever seen on a human being.

"Next week, we'll see how she does with the jumping, okay?" Angel said.

"All right," Willow said.

"In the meantime, make her keep her head up every day when you're riding this week," Angel said, beaming at the girl as she stepped back.

"Okay." Willow took the reins from Angel and led the horse toward the stable. She'd brush her down, and her daddy was probably waiting for her by now. Willow brought her horse with her, but all of Angel's others used horses right here at Lone Star.

Angel cleaned up and headed back to her house for the evening when she got a text from Levi. *Huge shipment for you just arrived,* he said. *I thought about putting it in your office and then realized it was probably too big.*

"A huge shipment?" she wondered aloud. She texted him quickly. *What do you mean a huge shipment?*

Oh, not all of this is for you. Never mind, but there are still a few boxes. It says it's from Sundown Printing.

Angel's heartbeat shot through her body, ricocheting off the sides of her veins as adrenaline pumped through her. "Sundown Publishing," she said to herself. "Those are the employee handbooks.

Oh, I know what those are. Her fingers trembled as she typed out each letter. *They can go in my office if they'll fit.*

Yeah, there are only three boxes, he said. *These others are for something else.*

Angel should care what else was getting delivered to the ranch, but she didn't. It wasn't her job to care anymore, and she had good, competent people over every aspect of Lone Star. She didn't have to know what every little thing was—or where to put it.

I'll put them in your office, Levi said.

Great, Angel said. *Thanks, Levi.*

She did take her training tools back to her house, but she only tossed them onto her back deck. She wanted to see this new employee handbook as soon as possible. Despite the urgency hammering through her to get to her office, she took a few moments to text Henry.

Can you come to my office right now, please?

He didn't text back, which meant he probably had a horse in his bay. Angel forced herself to take normal-sized steps at her usual pace as she went back to her office in the blue and white barn she loved.

Levi had been there and gone, and the boxes stood stacked on the floor near her desk. She grabbed a pair of scissors from her desk and sliced through the tape on the top box, an actual tangible hum filling her ears as she did. She wasn't even sure why. She just knew the arrival of this employee handbook felt like a pivotal moment, and she'd been waiting for it for months.

Only one of them fit in the box, and she turned it, so she could look at it the right way. The cover bore a beautiful aerial photo of Lone Star Ranch that had been taken a couple of years ago. Above that, Angel had put "Lone Star Ranch and Boarding Stable," and below it, "Employee Handbook." The cover had a faded, almost transparent Texas flag behind it. She turned it sideways so the Texas star burst out from behind the words *Lone Star* at the top.

She smiled at it, because she'd worked hard on this booklet over the past few months. She'd give these out to every man who worked at Lone Star and expect them to follow the rules and procedures contained inside. She picked up the book, which had been spiral bound with a blue plastic cover on the back.

This book meant so much more than just new rules and new leadership here at Lone Star—her leadership. It meant she and Henry wouldn't have to sneak around anymore.

Someone knocked on her door, and Henry said, "I'm coming in."

She turned toward him.

"What's going on?" he asked.

She held up the book, feeling fizzy and bubbly inside as she searched his face. He took a few more steps, looked at it, and studied the cover. Then he stopped just in front of her.

"The new employee handbook came," she said. "Just now. Levi texted me right after my lesson."

Henry folded his arms, and he didn't smile. Angel

wasn't sure what he had going on inside, but it looked like something raging and loud.

"How does it look?" he asked.

"I haven't seen everything," she said. "But I know what it looked like before it went to the printer."

He reached for it and took it. "Well, it looks good." He flipped through a few of the pages, clearly not reading them. "She sure has a nice horse."

Angel blinked at him, trying to catch up to what he'd said. "You watched my lesson?"

"I happened by." He glanced over the book to her and went back to it.

"What's going on with you?" she asked.

"What do you mean?"

"I mean, you've been kind of, I don't know...distant." She wasn't sure if that was the right word or not, but Henry definitely hadn't been as *close* as he'd once been. He sighed, slapped the book shut, and tossed it onto her desk.

"I sure did like sitting next to you at church earlier this week," he said. "And Alex and Nicki are hosting an outdoor game night on their ranch next week, and I'd sure like you to go with me."

"That does sound fun," she said. "What kind of outdoor games?"

"I don't know, croquet or something," he said in a disgusted voice and looked away from her. He heaved another sigh as he said, "I told them we might make it, but we might not."

Angel stepped over to him, very aware that the door stood open. "Why wouldn't we be able to make it?"

"Because," he said, "I don't want to go if we can't tell everyone that we're together." He looked down at her, ignoring her touch as she ran her hands up his chest and around to the back of his neck. He'd never simply stood there so still when she'd touched him like that before.

"I thought you told your friends about us."

"I did," he said. "I want *everyone* to know."

"You mean everyone here."

"Yeah," he said. "I mean everyone here."

Sometimes her father stayed grumpy no matter what Angel said or did, and Henry sure seemed like that right now. Still, she smiled at him. "Are you going to be like this all night long?"

"Like what?" he growled.

"All moody and upset that we haven't told everyone here at the ranch."

"I *am* upset that we haven't told everyone at the ranch," he said. "I just hadn't figured out how to tell you that yet."

She stepped back, feeling some of the coldness coming from him. "Well, you just did. I told you I was waiting for the employee handbook." She picked up the one he'd thrown on the desk and put it back on the top of the box. "And now they're here."

"So we'll tell everyone?"

"I'm thinking Monday," she said.

"But why?" He pressed in a step closer to her, moving in behind her. The scent of his cologne mixed with leather and the scent of metal he used in the horseshoes, and Angel loved the smell of Henry.

"Why do we have to wait until Monday?"

"I don't know," she said. "It just feels like a good time."

"Tomorrow's a good time," he said. "Roll call."

"I just thought maybe we'd have a plan first."

"Yeah," Henry said. "The plan is to stand up there and tell them, 'New employee handbook. Oh, and PS, it doesn't have a no-dating rule, so date anyone you want.'"

"That just doesn't make any sense," she said with a smile. "I'm not going to call attention to any of the other rules in the book."

Henry let out an exasperated sigh. "I know, Angel, but this one has to be addressed. Because we *are* dating. Because you told your daddy you would."

"I know. You're right." She leaned back into him, and Henry finally put his arms around her. "I just— maybe we can use the weekend to make a plan."

"All right," he said. "I'll see if I can sneak over tonight."

"You haven't come one night this week." She turned in his arms and looked up at him. "You've been so mad you haven't been able to come over at all."

"No," he said. "I'm not mad. I've just been thinking about a lot of things."

"Yeah, you said that at church too. And when I texted you about it, you never said what was on your mind."

"Sometimes a man likes to work through some things before he tells everyone." A half smile kicked up the side of his mouth. "You're so nosy."

He leaned down and touched his lips to hers. Angel remembered that he had not closed the door when he'd come in, so she didn't kiss him long. "It's not being nosy," she whispered to his collar. "It's called wanting to know what your partner is thinking."

"Oh, is that what we are?" he said, his head ducking as he moved his mouth along her neck. "Partners?"

"Yes," she said stubbornly. She couldn't hide the tremor in her voice from his touch.

He straightened. "Okay. I'll try to get away tonight. And just so you know, it hasn't been my choice that I haven't been coming. The new housing situation is still...." He paused for a moment, obviously trying to find the right word, and said, "Don and I are still trying to figure out how to live together."

A lot of the transitions that Angel had made at the beginning of the month had not been easy for everyone. Henry had a new team with one man who didn't particularly like him, and Levi had moved into Flint's cabin, which meant Henry had gotten a new roommate. Don was one of their summer interns, and he still had three semesters of coursework left at Sherman Academy before he would even be eligible for an apprenticeship. He was inexperienced, and in Henry's words, "whiny and needy." Angel wished she'd known that before the random generator had picked his number.

"Well, I miss you," she said, revealing as much as she dared to reveal right now.

"I miss you too, my angel." He kissed her again, somehow knowing that she didn't want to go on and on. He pulled back after only a few strokes. "I'll text you once I see how things are tonight."

"Okay," she said.

Henry backed up a couple of steps, said, "Okay," and turned and left her office.

She waited until she couldn't hear his cowboy boots against the cements, and then Angel strode back over to the box of employee handbooks and picked up the top one.

She was going to go ask Trevor what he would do, and then Daddy, and show them the employee handbook at the same time. They'd both be interested. And maybe, just maybe, they'd both have some great advice for how Angel could stand up in front of everyone and tell them that she and Henry had been dating since February.

Chapter Thirty-Two

"Nope, you don't have to do anything more than that," Henry said as Trevor leaned into the exercise ball. "Palermo will stand there and wait for you to send it back to him." Henry stood only a pace away. "It's good practice for your balance as well. And Palermo needs the same thing."

"I can't believe he just kicks it back and forth," Trevor said.

"I've got your cane right here if you need it, too," Henry said. "Or you can just reach out and grab onto my arm. The goal is not to hurt you. It's to help you."

Trevor looked at him, something new and bright in his gaze that Henry had not seen before. "I've heard of equine therapy," he said. "I just never thought of doing it for myself."

"It's as much physical as it is mental," Henry said.

"You just go ahead and send that ball back to him anytime you want."

Henry had not told Angel or anyone else that he'd been using equine therapy exercises to help Palermo strengthen his front leg. He didn't see the point. His job was to help the horse get better, and he was doing it. He consulted regularly with Justin, who had a degree in horse care, though he wasn't a vet or a vet technician, and Palermo had been doing really well the past couple of weeks since Henry had started working with him.

Henry loved playing with horses. "This is a different kind of work for a horse than training them to go after cattle or sheep. It's not cutting left or right or knowing exactly where you want them to go with the slightest movement of your body."

"You're right about that," Trevor said.

"This is play."

Trevor straightened and took one hand off the ball. The one that remained shook as if it took a great deal of effort for him to balance himself against the blown-up exercise ball. Henry was sure it did.

"I can see that," Trevor said with a smile. "I like it."

Henry liked it too. "They're playful animals," he said. "I mean, horses are just like great big three-year-olds." He chuckled, glad when Trevor did too. Trevor pushed the ball back to Palermo, and the horse stood there for maybe a moment while both of them watched the ball roll.

Then Trevor reached out. Henry took a lightning-fast step toward him and stood in place when Trevor's hand landed on his shoulder.

"Now you tell him it's his turn to send it back," Henry said. "He's not real great with taking a command from someone who isn't me. But equine therapy horses should be able to obey anyone. They work with kids who have tantrums, or people with mental disabilities like autism. We have horses at Courage Reins who work with nonverbal people who can give hand signals, and the horse will send the ball back."

"Wow," Trevor said. "That's incredible."

"My daddy is real good with horses," Henry said.

"So are you," Trevor said.

Henry didn't answer because he wasn't the greatest at taking compliments. He'd been doling them out left and right the past couple of months, and that had earned him quite a few friends here at Lone Star.

Not Creston though. He'd been assigned to Henry's team, and they'd been working together for a couple of weeks now, but he still relentlessly questioned every-thing Henry said. And about half the time, he didn't do it the way Henry wanted things done. They'd had a couple of talks, and they'd had meetings, both with all four members of their team and then just him and Creston, and things were slowly getting better. Henry didn't mind being challenged, but in the end, he *was* the captain. Just because Creston had been at Lone

Star longer than Henry didn't mean he knew everything.

"Are there any equine therapy programs in Amarillo?" Trevor asked. "Or anywhere closer?"

"I don't know," Henry said. "My daddy will know, though. And you know what? He texted me a couple of days ago and said they're putting in a new road just north of the ranch that will lead almost directly here. It'll only be about forty minutes from Three Rivers to Lone Star." He grinned at Trevor. "That'll make it way easier for me to get home when I want to visit."

"Yeah, that'll be awesome," Trevor said. "I bet any other equine therapy unit won't be as close as that."

"I can get you into Courage Reins if you want," Henry said.

"Can you?" Trevor asked.

"Sure," Henry said. "And I can drive you there too."

"That would be great," Trevor said. "I would really like it."

Henry's chest swelled with pride, because he'd *known* that Trevor would like equine therapy. He had mentioned it to Angel a couple of times before giving up when he realized she was simply not interested in hearing more about it. They didn't really have the space at Lone Star for a new program, and they certainly didn't have the personnel—the required people to train the horses, not to mention any of the counselors or therapists.

"Send it," Trevor called, and Palermo raised his head and looked at him. "Send it," Trevor said again in a super smooth, clear, authoritative voice, and Palermo plodded forward one or two steps and nudged the ball back to him. Trevor laughed as he leaned down into the ball to balance himself. "I just love this," he said. "It's so much fun."

Henry grinned too. Normally, if he was working with a client at Courage Reins, he wouldn't have his phone with him at all. But today, his device rang in his back pocket. "I think that's my momma. Can I take it?"

"Sure," Trevor said, and Henry passed him his cane so that he could balance on it when he sent the ball back to Palermo.

"You can move around the circle with him," Henry said. "He should face you and kick it back to you no matter where you go."

"All right," Trevor said.

Henry pulled his phone out and said, "Hey, Momma."

"Henry," she said, her voice panicked and full of air. "Where are you?"

"I'm at Lone Star," he said. "What's wrong?"

"It's Grandma," she said.

The blue sky in front of Henry splintered, cracking with a jagged line right down the middle of it. "Grams?"

"Malcolm just called and said he thinks she had a stroke," Momma said. "He called an ambulance, and they just arrived when I got off the phone with him. Daddy and I are heading to the hospital right now. We don't know much; we just want everybody to pray."

Praying felt so useless in that moment, and Henry wasn't sure how he could even contribute with something so small and simple as prayer.

"Henry," Momma said.

"Yes, yes," he said. "I'm here."

"I'll know more when we get to the hospital and talk to the doctors. I don't want you to panic."

"*You're* panicking," he said. "How am I supposed to not panic?"

"I'm trying not to," Momma said, but her voice broke, and that only caused everything inside Henry to break as well.

"I'll pray," he said because he didn't have any other choice.

"I'll call you again real soon. I love you." She hung up before Henry could say, "I love you too, Momma," so he said it to the sky and to himself, hoping the Good Lord would be able to take that message to his momma and daddy and most of all, Grams.

He stood there for a moment, not sure what else to do, until Trevor's voice broke into his thoughts, asking, "Is everything okay?"

Henry turned toward his friend and said, "Actually, my grandma is on the way to the hospital."

"Oh no," Trevor said. He sent the ball back to Palermo and leaned on his cane. "Do you need to go?"

"I don't know," Henry said. "My momma didn't know a whole lot. She was on the way in. She won't know for at least an hour."

"Right. Your ranch is pretty far out."

"Yeah," Henry said, surprised that Trevor had remembered such a detail.

"You should still go," Trevor said with that same authoritative voice he'd used on Palermo.

"I need to talk to Angel."

"Nope," Trevor said. "You just go. It's Saturday, and whatever you've got going on today can be covered by somebody else."

"I have horses to shoe," Henry said.

"Not today," Trevor said. "And your day off is tomorrow anyway. We'll give you whatever you need. This is your family."

The way he said that—*this is your family*—as if it came before everything else in the world, struck a major chord inside Henry. He looked at Trevor and said, "You're right. I'm gonna go. I'll text Angel."

"I'll handle it all. You go. It's no big deal."

"I'll be in touch," Henry said, and he started to walk away. Then he turned back and said, "Wait, wait, I gotta put Palermo away. I can't just leave you here."

"No. Go." Trevor held up his phone, his smile just as

sunny and bright as always. Henry marveled at his positive attitude and agreeable disposition.

"I can send one text on this phone and have twenty men here to help me in five minutes. All of them will know how to put Palermo away. Only you can go pack your bag and get to your family's side. So just go."

Henry's mind whirred as if he had poured a bunch of fruit and yogurt into it, then pressed liquefy on a blender. "Okay," he said. "Yeah, okay, I'm gonna go."

"Yep," Trevor said. "You go. I'll handle everything here, and I'll call you tonight to find out how things are going."

"Okay." Henry strode back to Trevor, wrapped him up in a tight hug, and said, "Thank you so much, Trevor. This really means a lot to me."

"We'll pray for you," Trevor said.

And right then, Henry truly understood the culture at Lone Star. Trevor *would* pray for him, and he would tell everyone at Lone Star, and they would pray for him too. Henry suddenly also realized the power of prayer. One prayer was amazing, and God surely heard it, but with the power of many....

Henry's chest fell and then expanded again as he jogged, trying not to panic, trying not to cry, and trying to stay above water until he could find out if he had anything to worry about.

Please, Lord, he thought. *Help me. Help my momma. Help Grams. Help my family.*

* * *

Henry sat in the only available chair in his grandmother's hospital room, listening to the sounds of the machines monitoring her health. One of them wisped every so often when she breathed, and another beeped whenever whatever the IV bag got too low.

No one had been in and out of the room for a while now. As the afternoon turned to evening, Henry shifted. His mama and daddy had plenty to do in the summer, and not all of them could sit in the narrow hospital room anyway. Someone had been sitting with Grams, either from his family or from Uncle Squire and Aunt Kelly's, since she had been admitted over the weekend.

Henry had been gone from Lone Star for five days now, and irritation and frustration pulsed through him with all the texts coming in from Creston. "I'm not even there," he muttered.

Yes, as captain he had a lot of responsibility, and he knew that his horses had been pushed off to other men, probably on their days off, and that everyone shouldered a burden for him not to be there. He also knew that he didn't need it rubbed in his face with every text message that came in.

Angel had called on Saturday night to get an update on Grams, who had had a stroke. A mini one, the doctor said. It hadn't lasted very long, and they'd been doing tests ever since. She hadn't been able to go home yet because the doctors had seen something in her blood-work that they didn't like, and they were trying to get her potassium to go down before they would release her. She slept right now, and Henry, though he'd been sleeping more than ever, looked over to her and wished he could do the same. He had no idea how much longer she'd be here or how much longer he would be needed here.

Finn and Edith usually came in the evening with Theo, after Finn finished on his farm and before Edith started writing in her she-shed, and Henry had stayed to visit with them several times. Finn had started to send him some of the properties around Three Rivers that Henry might be interested in purchasing.

With the new road going in up north, Henry had started looking up there as well, almost along the Oklahoma border. A few small towns had some houses for sale, and he could still commute to Lone Star. He knew with certainty now that he didn't want to live there. He did not see himself moving into Angel's cabin and assuming his role there at her side as if she'd just been waiting for him.

He still saw himself with her, though they hadn't talked about marriage or kids, or even if she'd move away from Lone Star to be with him.

I guess if she doesn't, he thought. *Then that's your answer right there.*

He didn't like the black-and-whiteness of it. He'd learned that most things in life existed in a shade of gray.

Angel loved Lone Star. She ran the place; she definitely wouldn't be leaving that job behind. But she didn't have to *live* on-site.

Henry still believed with a firm determination that she would be happier if she could leave every evening and go somewhere else for safety and solace and comfort. He wanted that to be with him, in a place that they'd built together.

He moved away from texting Creston, because he'd already told him to text Levi. Levi had been handling everything on Henry's team, and he would continue to do so. He navigated over to the text thread he had with a real estate agent in Three Rivers who had helped Finn buy his one-man ranch.

Jerry Bozeman had sent him two more listings, and while Henry wasn't looking for a ranch, he definitely wouldn't mind a pasture where he could keep a horse or two. They could have dogs and chickens and live a good country life, closer to his family while also remaining near Angel's.

Stinnett looks like a good possibility, Jerry had said. *There are two properties there right now that fit your budget.*

Truth be told, Henry had never imagined himself living in Stinnett, a town about halfway between Three Rivers and Amarillo. But if he chose Stinnett and the new road went in as planned, he would be able to get to Courage Reins and Three Rivers Ranch, where the majority of his family lived, in only thirty-five minutes. And he would be able to get to Lone Star in thirty.

It seemed almost too good to be true, like God had made sure that a town had sprung up there specifically so that Henry and Angel would have a halfway point between the two places they both wanted to be.

I'll look at them, Henry said. *Thank you, Jerry.*

Let me know if you want to set up a showing, Jerry said. *The one's been on the market for a long time, so no rush. The other one just came up last week, but nothing's been selling super fast lately, so again, no rush.*

Thanks, Henry said.

Sitting in the hospital made the time go by astronomically slow. Henry leafed through the pictures of both properties. He could see why the first one hadn't sold yet; it needed a lot of fixing up. He played all the games on his phone, answered all the texts coming in with questions about Grams, and he even read a little bit out of a farrier manual. Grams still hadn't woken, and his shift still hadn't ended.

I got everything taken care of with Creston, Levi texted. *That man.*

Henry snorted and chuckled, because at least he wasn't the only person frustrated by the other farrier. *Thank you,* Henry said. *I owe you big time.*

Angel passed out new employee handbooks today, Levi said.

Henry's fingers froze completely while his heartbeat continued at a faster pace.

Oh, yeah? he finally asked. He wasn't sure if he needed to pretend like he didn't know there was a new handbook or not.

Yep, Levi said. *I got you one. Don't worry.*

Anything I need to know? he asked, his heartbeat thundering the way a wild herd of horses' hooves did across dry ground. Had she stood up on the platform and told everyone at Lone Star about their relationship without him? Part of him hoped she had, and the other part really didn't want her to carry that burden.

Nothing of note, Levi said. *I put it in your bedroom. It's sitting on your nightstand for when you get back.*

Thanks, brother, Henry said, and he quickly tapped to call Angel. Her line rang and rang, and she finally picked up, saying, "Henry, hey," in the labored voice.

"Can you talk for a minute?" he asked. He wasn't sure why, but his tongue felt poisoned, and it turned numb as he waited for her to answer. He'd felt like this before—last year when he thought he hadn't gotten an apprenticeship at Lone Star. He bit back on the words threatening to spew from his mouth. If she had time to talk, they'd talk, and if she didn't...then Henry would pray for patience and figure out how to approach Angel when he didn't feel like spitting nails.

Chapter Thirty-Three

"Can you give me five minutes?" Angel asked as she sprinted across the back deck toward her door. She didn't want to tell Henry that she had to go to the bathroom, but she was in desperate need.

"Yes," he clipped out, and Angel said, "Great, I'll—" but then cut off as she heard the beep of him hanging up.

"Just great," she muttered as she whipped open the door and ran through the kitchen. "He's mad about something."

And not just something. The fact that she'd handed out the employee handbooks without him.

Angel hadn't been able to put it off for another day. She had them, and just because Henry had a family emergency didn't mean everybody on the ranch did. She needed the teams and crews to function as teams and crews, and that included following the new guidelines and principles in the employee handbook.

So, she'd met with the master farriers and the foremen on Monday. Henry had left on Saturday before they'd had any time to make a plan at all for how they might announce their relationship.

It needed to be handed out, so she'd simply omitted the part where she and Henry were dating. When she told everyone from the platform that morning that they had new employee handbooks, she said their team leads or captains would be going over any changes and new procedures and rules they needed to know about, and she expected they would do that.

She took care of her business, thinking that someone had obviously told Henry about the new handbook, which didn't surprise her. Angel knew Levi had been keeping Henry up-to-date with everything, just as Levi was supposed to. Angel wasn't mad about that. She was mad that Henry thought she should handle *their* business by *her*self. She didn't want to handle their relationship by herself. He was one half of it, and he should be here when they stood up in front of everyone and told them that they were dating.

She had half a mind not to call Henry back, but she wasn't petty or immature. So, she sat down at her dining room table to enjoy a few extra moments of blessed air conditioning while she talked to her boyfriend. Since she didn't think the conversation would be pleasant, she figured she didn't need to bake while she did it.

"Hey," she chirped happily when he picked up.

"If you're busy, this can wait," he said.

"I'm not busy," she said. "I just needed to get in my house real quick."

"All right," he said, and then he sat there. Classic Henry move, trying to figure out what to say in the nicest way possible when what he wanted to say wasn't all that nice.

"You're mad about the handbook, aren't you?" she asked.

"I'm not mad about the handbook itself," he grumbled.

"You're mad I didn't tell everyone *by myself* that we're together. That's what you're mad about."

Stony silence came through the line, and then he exhaled heavily. "I'm not mad at all."

"Yeah, sure sounds like you're not," she said. "Sounds like you're having a party there. Did your momma bring over cake?"

"All right," he grumped at her.

"I'm not really sure what you want me to do, Henry," she said. "You seem to have an idea of how this is going to go, and I'm not doing it right. So why don't you just tell me how you want it to go, and I'll do my best to do it."

"We both know that's not true," he said.

"What? That I'm not going to do my best to meet your needs?" She scoffed, her own irritation shooting through the roof. "Is that really what you think?" She couldn't sit and have this conversation, and Angel burst to her feet and started pacing in the kitchen. "Because if that's what you think, I think we should—"

"I don't think that," he cut her off, his voice low and dangerous but nowhere near loud. "All right? I'm sorry; I don't think that."

Angel calmed down, but she still spun and walked back toward the sink and then took another lap toward the fridge. "What do you think?" she asked, her voice remarkably calm and smooth.

"I think I'm frustrated with this whole situation," he said.

"Which situation?" she asked. "The one where you're sitting in a hospital in Three Rivers, or the one where I was forced to hand out the handbook so that we could move forward here on the ranch, but you weren't here?"

"Both," he clipped out.

"Yeah, I am too," she said. After a couple of moments where they both sat with themselves, the fire inside Angel started to burn out.

"Henry, baby, I'm real sorry about your grandma." Angel realized the quiet could be incredibly charged with emotions, and this was one of those times. When she'd sat with her momma in the hospital, the quiet had not been this sad or this emotionally charged. Everything about Henry amplified the world around Angel. "I've sat with my mom in the hospital before," she said. "It's never easy."

"No," Henry said, and this time his voice didn't sound like his at all.

"Is that where you are right now?" Angel asked.

"Yep."

"Who's coming in tonight?" An idea started to form in her head, and Angel wasn't sure she could pull it off because it was a long drive to Three Rivers, and Henry had a lot of family surrounding him.

"Tonight is Sammy and Mike," he said. His cousins.

"All right," Angel said. "Well, maybe I can meet you for dinner."

"You don't need to do that," he said. "It's a long drive."

"Yeah, and we would have a few hours together."

He scoffed and said, "Angel, do you know what time it is?"

At least he'd started kidding again, and Angel giggled. "I miss you, Henry."

"I miss you too, sweetheart."

"I'm real sorry about the handbooks," she said. "None of it is playing out the way I imagined."

"Life rarely does," he said. "And maybe it's just God telling me it doesn't matter. We can tell them when we tell them."

"That's right," Angel said. "We'll tell them when we tell them."

"I want to see you," he whispered. "But maybe let's plan on dinner tomorrow. My momma and my aunt have been cooking all afternoon, and she's going to have a feast at the house tonight. And then Paul said he'd go with me to look at a couple places in Stinnett."

Alarms went off in Angel's head all over again, and she resumed her pacing. "A couple places in Stinnett?" she asked, an icy undertone in her voice.

Henry obviously heard it too because he said, "Yeah," in a higher-pitched voice. "Remember, I've talked to you about finding somewhere else to live?"

"The way you phrase that as a question tells me you know that no, I did not remember that," she said. "And number two, no, we've not talked about that."

"We have," he said. "Remember when I mentioned that I thought it would be better if we didn't live at Lone Star? I need a break from that place, and so do you. And the more I've thought about it, the more I think that's true."

Angel hadn't thought about it at all. So much of her life had been mapped out for her, and all she had to do was move box by box, from one thing to the next. Yes, Trevor's accident had caused a major landslide in her plans, and her entire road had been detoured to another one. But still, her life revolved around Lone Star, and she'd never once considered not living there.

"Stinnett?" she asked.

"Baby," he said quietly. "When I imagine the future, it's me and you." He didn't say, *I love you*, but he might as well have with that soft, husky tone.

It's me and you sure sounded nice.

"I know we haven't talked a lot about marriage, or kids, or where we'll live yet, but we need to start doing that."

"Yeah," she whispered.

"And one of those things that I see in the future for us is *not* Lone Star."

Angel couldn't get her feet to move. "Lone Star is my whole life."

"We'll work there," he said. "Heck, we can give a lot of ourselves to that place—our hearts and our souls and our sweat and our blood. But me and you, we've got to give ourselves to each other. And that's going to require a new place for us, a place that *we* find and that *we* make our own. So when I look into the future and I see me and you together, I don't see us at Lone Star."

"Okay," she said. "I think I'm following."

"Are you?"

"I think so," she said. "You want to live somewhere else. Somewhere close where we can commute, where we can work and do all the things that we love, but then have somewhere we can retreat to."

"Exactly that," he said.

"And I'm just wondering if you hear yourself at all," she asked as she collapsed back at the dining room table.

"I hear myself just fine," he said.

"Do you?" she challenged. "Because you used the word 'we' a lot in those sentences you just said, and not once have you invited me to come look at any of the places around Three Rivers or Stinnett or Amarillo or wherever else you're looking."

This silence felt full of truth and tension, and Henry said, "You're right. I guess I just—I don't know. I don't know what I thought."

"If you want us to build that life independent of Lone Star so that we have each other, then I have to look at the places too, Henry."

"Yeah," he said. "I think that's about right."

"So are you gonna go look at them with Paul tonight? Do you have appointments with a real estate agent?"

"No," he said. "We were just gonna drive by."

"Well, Stinnett's not that far from here," she said. "I could meet you there to do that."

"If I'm coming from the ranch, it'll be over an hour to Stinnett," he said. "Let me think about it."

"You'll think about it."

"Wait, that's not what I meant. I just won't go tonight."

"You sound tired, Henry," she said.

"I am tired, sweetheart." His voice wavered. "Grams

is awake and doing well. They get her up to walk every now and then, but her potassium is still too high, and they won't let her go."

"Sorry, baby," Angel whispered. "If I could be there to help you, I would. You know that, right?"

"I know that," he said. "Paul mentioned that we could do an equine therapy session before I told him about the houses in Stinnett. We'll do that tonight. I'll feel better, I promise."

"Yeah," Angel said. "And at the risk of bringing up another thing that we're going to argue about...." She let her words hang there, and Henry chuckled into the silence.

"Baby, just say it. We'll work it out."

She liked his confidence in her, and in them. She'd been feeling real serious and heavy things for Henry, and it sure was nice that he'd been obviously experiencing those things too.

"It's about the equine therapy," she said. "Because I know you've been doing some of that with Trevor."

"You *know*?" he asked. "How do you *know*?"

"He told me," she shot back.

"Okay, first, it's not real equine therapy," Henry said. "I'm not a licensed trainer or anything. Second, equine therapy requires a human therapist aspect, none of which Trevor is doing. And third—"

Angel burst out laughing at his prickly defense. "All right, all right," she said. "But you're definitely having

Trevor work with Palermo as much as you're trying to rehabilitate Palermo. Just admit it."

"I'm not going to *not* admit it," Henry said.

Angel giggled and shook her head. She got to her feet and pulled a bottle of water out of the fridge. "All right, cowboy. I have to get back to work."

"You're not mad about the equine therapy?"

"Oh, so you admit it's equine therapy." Henry clammed right up again, and Angel laughed. "I'm not mad about it," she said. "Trevor gushes about it, thinks it's the greatest thing that's ever happened to him. He's out there every evening working with Palermo. So, I guess you're replaceable."

"Oh, don't say that, sweetheart," he said. "That's my worst nightmare."

And he meant it. Henry wanted to be important, and he didn't want to be replaceable. And so, as Angel left her house, she said, "Henry, you're irreplaceable to me, and all of us at Lone Star are dying without you."

He chuckled this time and said, "You don't have to be a liar on my behalf."

"I'm not lying, baby," she said as she crossed the deck. "We all miss you. But I think I miss you the most."

"You better," he growled. And then he said, "I'll talk to you later. Bye, my angel."

She hung up, and as Angel went back to the blue barn to start going through next week's orders at the feed store, her mind kept wandering down the road to Stinnett and then to Three Rivers.

She and Henry sometimes went together like vinegar and oil. Sometimes like night and day, and other times like rainbows and unicorns and sunshine. As she thought about the conversation they'd just had, they'd moved through three pretty serious disagreements.

He would get mad and blow off steam for literally a few seconds and then come right back down. She did that too, something that usually didn't happen quite so fast. When she got her ire up, it would stay there for hours, and she'd have to vent to multiple people to get herself to calm down. But with Henry, that didn't happen.

Angel didn't know what it meant. And she decided she could do the same thing that Henry had obviously been doing—looking into the future to see what she saw. Was it the two of them together? And if so, where and when? Angel had more than that to consider. She had Lone Star, and she'd always been dedicated to this ranch. So, if she left and lived somewhere else, how would that impact those around her?

She went over to Trevor's every morning and then her parents' house, and while she had reduced a lot of the load on her shoulders, she would not put that burden on someone who wasn't blood.

She glanced over to Trevor's house as she walked by and thought, *You kind of already have.* Trevor had two full-time helpers when he was working on the ranch to make sure he could get in and out of the saddle, to make sure that if he fell off the horse, someone was there to help him immediately, to help him get around. Everybody helped Trevor, and Angel wondered how much of the help she provided was necessary and how much she just simply liked doing.

"And you could still do it," she whispered to herself. She pushed into the blue barn, grateful for air conditioning, and hurried down the hall to her office.

Momma was doing really good right now. Though she'd never be off oxygen and she still rarely left the house, it didn't mean she was bedridden. She hadn't been hospitalized in a couple of years. And besides, Stinnett was only thirty minutes away.

Angel caught sight of a box of the employee handbooks as she entered her office. As she let her mind flow into the future, she did see her and Henry together. She wasn't quite sure where, and that unsettled her. And then the two of them disappeared completely, like a whiff of smoke, there and then blown away by a brisk breeze.

She ran her fingertips along the coil of the book. "Maybe when we tell everyone that we've been together for months," she said. "There'll be more fallout than I'm imagining."

She tried to think of the individual reactions from the men she'd worked with for years, but nothing would come forward. Angel's future was wide open, white, and completely blank.

No matter what she did for the rest of the afternoon, she couldn't make anything solidify on it. She didn't know what that meant. As she liked to plan and had always been able to plan, now she felt like she was marching out into the great wide open, completely vulnerable with armies all around her, weapons pointed in her direction.

She really needed Henry to come home and help her, but she didn't want to add to his burdens by texting him *INACH*. So she did her best to cheer herself and stay busy, and she prayed that God would make up the rest until Henry returned.

Chapter Thirty-Four

Henry read his father's text, a measure of disgust choking in the back of his throat even as he tried to swallow it away. Of course, he could help with the equine therapy appointments the next afternoon. He simply didn't want to. He hadn't come back to Three Rivers Ranch to help with lessons.

I know you don't want to, Daddy said, as if reading Henry's mind from miles away. *But Roscoe quit, and I sure could use your help. We've had an influx of appointments since Grams can't stop talking to everyone at the hospital about how amazing it is to recover with horses.* He added a laughing face emoji, and that did make Henry smile.

Grams had been up and about and recovering really well lately. She should be coming home later today. Henry currently worked at Three Rivers Ranch, lending an extra pair of hands to Beau Peterson, the foreman, who needed some horses fed.

If there was anything Henry could do, it was care for horses. He honestly didn't mind helping with the equine therapy either. All he had to do was greet a patient, get them to the right horse, take care of the horse after, and make sure the person felt like a million bucks. It was essentially the same operation as Lone Star, with some slight variations, obviously.

I can do it, he texted really quick and then shoved his phone in his back pocket. Once Grams got out of the hospital, she and his step-grandpa were planning to come out to the ranch so that Aunt Kelly and Momma could take care of her better.

She had pulled way back from the bakery she owned in town, obviously, since she'd spent the last seven days in the hospital. Grams had the infrastructure, the employees, and the managers to do that. Henry automatically thought of Angel, of course, and how now, if she'd had a stroke or been injured, Lone Star would be taken care of as well.

His heart hurt physically for a moment, because he missed her so bad. Henry had never felt like that about anyone before, and in talking to Paul, he realized that he was falling in love with Angel.

You might already be there, he thought. Love wasn't a destination. It wasn't somewhere he arrived and then stayed forever. He knew it had different layers and different meanings in different situations with different people, and that it could grow and change and expand and protect.

Henry wanted it all, and he wanted it with Angel.

He finished his chores for the morning and went to check in with Beau. "Anything else?" he asked as the man stood against the fence, a trio of mini donkeys in the field in front of him.

"They have the best view on the ranch," Henry said, and Beau chuckled.

"They sure do." They both turned around and leaned against the fence, gazing off into the southern distance.

"You can almost see Finn's place from here," Henry said. It was too far to actually see, but facing in the right direction, Henry felt like he could.

"Beautiful morning," Beau said. "I don't think I need anything else."

"You sure?" Henry said. "If I'm not working here, I have to go back to my momma's." He chuckled as the blueness of the sky threatened to bleed all over Henry's vision. "The jobs she has for me are far less fun."

He'd actually polished silverware the other day, and he certainly didn't want to do another household task like that.

Beau grinned at him. "You can check with Charlotte. She might have something for you to do in the barn."

Charlotte was Beau's wife and the barn manager here at Three Rivers Ranch. They had a lot of horses that they used for roundup and herding, and she took care of all of them. Nothing nearly as large as Lone Star, but enough to warrant a full-time person.

"I'll check in with her," he said.

"We've got a few interns this summer," Beau said. "She's whipping them into shape real good, so there might not be much."

Henry nodded. "I'm sure my daddy has something."

Beau chuckled. "I'm sure he does. He's had a couple of men quit on him recently."

"Yeah," Henry said. "That's what he said." Guilt swept through him that he hadn't wanted to help his daddy with the equine therapy. "All right." He pushed himself back to standing, not really wanting to work at all today. "I'll go check."

He reached to shake Beau's hand. "Thanks for the work, Beau."

"Henry, I'd take you any day," he said.

Henry grinned at him as he left. Since he could, he found a shady spot out of the way where his daddy wouldn't stumble upon him. He texted with Levi for a few minutes, sent a few messages to his crew, and then leaned his head back against the side of the barn.

"Lord," he exhaled, "I love it here, but I don't think this is where I'm supposed to be. Help me get back home." He wasn't sure where home was, but right now it was in a cabin that he shared with someone else at Lone Star, where he was dating Angel White.

"Help me get back to Angel," he said, and he let his mind open completely. Such a thing hadn't happened very many times in Henry's life, but that morning, he felt, heard, and understood so many things about himself, things that had brought him to this point, things that allowed him to be where he'd been for the past year.

He wasn't perfect by any means, but he'd changed a lot, and God let him know that those changes had been for the better. Henry closed his eyes and sighed, relief rushing through him. Sometimes it felt like such hard work to be Henry Marshall—to be good, to think about his family, to compliment others, to take care of Angel, and to stay close to the Lord. Sometimes it almost felt like drudgery. He whispered, "I don't want it to feel like that. I want it to feel joyful."

I can help you with that, God whispered, and Henry smiled.

"Thank You. Could You help me with Angel? How do I feel about her? Should we really be making plans to look at places in Stinnett?" He'd texted more with Jerry, who said he'd be willing to set up the showings anytime and to just let him know. With everything with Grams up in the air and Henry not even sure when he was returning to work—and he couldn't imagine the pile of work waiting for him at the ranch—Henry hadn't been able to take that step.

Heck, everyone at Lone Star needed to know he and Angel were dating before they got engaged. His throat seized at that word anyway. And while he might be falling in love with Angel, he wasn't ready to propose. But again, the Lord enlightened his mind, and Henry absolutely realized that he loved her even if it was on a small scale at the moment.

"Am I good enough for her?" he asked.

While the Lord didn't answer, Henry felt like he got a head nod. "I'll take real good care of her," he promised, and he suddenly needed to see her. He didn't want to leave in the most crucial of hours, perhaps when Grams was coming home, or Momma needed him, or Daddy was in desperate need of manpower at Courage Reins, but Henry needed to see her really soon.

"Okay." Henry worked alongside his dad in the stables the following afternoon. "But I'm going home tonight after this," he said. "I've got to get back to work." He'd been gone from Lone Star for nine days now, and while a part of him had wondered if he would go back, if he and Angel would never be on the same page, if they'd never be able to stand side-by-side and look out at the crowd of men and tell them that they were dating, he knew now that he wanted to work through anything preventing that.

He'd take whatever flak came his way, whatever teasing, whatever consequences, whatever fallout.

He just wanted to be with her.

Henry stopped shoveling and looked over to his father. His broad shoulders rippled and worked as he spread the straw in the stable for the horses they'd already let out that morning.

"That's okay, right?" Henry said. "I told Levi I could be back tomorrow."

"It's fine," Daddy said without looking up. "I know you've got a job to get to. Grams is doing a lot better. She's settled now." She'd actually moved in with Momma and Daddy, as Kelly and Uncle Squire's homestead had stairs everywhere, and Grams couldn't navigate those very well.

But at Momma and Daddy's homestead, she only had to come up two stairs from the driveway to the kitchen, and Momma had a main-floor bedroom prepped and ready.

"It's going to be fine," Daddy said, and he finally stopped working.

"I can stay if it'll help you," Henry said. "I know you're short-handed right now."

Daddy's blue-eyed gaze met his. "If you know I need the help, why don't you just stay? I don't like this conversation of, 'Well, I can if you need me to.' You know I need you to."

He sighed heavily and went back to work. "I also

know you've got a job, and they need you there too. So I'm not going to ask."

"Well, I don't know what to do," Henry said, frustrated.

"You do what's right," Daddy said. "That's what you always do, Henry."

Emotion choked in his throat because Henry didn't know what was right. He desperately wanted to return to Lone Star. They did need him there. But how much of it was that they needed him to do his job, and how much of that was him simply wanting to hold Angel at night?

Henry hadn't felt like crying this much in a long time, and he kept swallowing and swallowing as they finished this stall and moved to the next one.

At the end of the row, Daddy took him by the shoulders and said, "I love the man you've become. You are such a good person. And the problems we're having here at Courage Reins right now are not your problems. So go home. Go back to your horses. Go back to your girlfriend. It's okay. We're going to be okay here."

"I feel bad," Henry said.

"I know you do," Daddy said. "That's just one of the reasons why you're so good. Paul and I have got this handled. Beau has a couple of interns at Three Rivers, and I'm going to talk to him about lending them to us for a few weeks. I think they're just sitting around, and he and Charlotte are inventing jobs for them to do."

"Yeah," Henry said.

"We'll be fine," Daddy said. "We just have a lot of appointments this weekend, and you're gonna stay and help with those through tonight. And then you should go."

Henry nodded in tight little bursts. "I haven't told Levi yet."

"Well, you better call him and tell him right now." Daddy smiled at him and cuffed him under the chin. "Hey, son. Go."

Henry nodded and grabbed onto his dad in a hug. "I love you, Daddy."

"I know you do. Your momma and I love you a whole lot."

Henry couldn't believe he'd ever thought his parents didn't need him, that they could skip from Paul to John without him, that there wouldn't be a hole in his family if he wasn't there. He could see now that if any of them weren't there, they would not be complete, including Grams.

"I'm gonna move closer to Three Rivers," he said.

Daddy released him and looked at him. "You are?"

"Yeah." He nodded as he and Daddy stepped over to the sink and started washing up. "I think Angel and I are pretty serious. We started talking about looking at places somewhere like Stinnett on the eastern outskirts of Three Rivers, and we'll commute to Lone Star."

"She's going to commute to the ranch she owns?" Daddy pushed his sleeves up and scrubbed to his elbow.

"Well," Henry said, "I think it'll kill her if she doesn't."

Daddy studied him for a moment, then started rinsing all the suds away. "Ranches have a way of consuming a person, that's for sure."

"Yeah," Henry said dryly. "Look at you, working twenty hours a day."

Daddy didn't chuckle, because he had been working a lot lately. Grams' illness had come at a terrible time when he'd had men quit and they'd been short-handed.

"Sometimes you have to rely on the angels," Daddy said. "That's how we've gotten through the past week. I don't know how the work's gotten done, I don't know whose hands did it, but somehow it gets done."

"Yeah." Henry pumped the handle on the paper towel dispenser and ripped off the brown paper. "I can agree with that. But I've seen Angel when Lone Star is eating her alive, and it's not pretty. I'm not going to let that happen to her."

Daddy smiled at him. "I sure like seeing you in love, Henry."

"I'm not—" Henry cut himself off. "I mean, it's new," he said, ducking his head.

"Nothing to be embarrassed about," Daddy said. "Love is a beautiful thing. Caring for another person more than yourself is wonderful. Building a family and a life together is something to be admired."

"Yeah." Henry balled up his paper towel and tossed it in the trash can, then got out of the way so Daddy could get to the dispenser.

"So I guess you're going to be a farrier at Lone Star." Daddy grinned at him while he ripped off a paper towel.

"I guess so," Henry said. "At least for now. There's no reason I can't branch out in the future, especially if I'm not living at Lone Star."

"Ah," Daddy said. "Maybe that's why you don't want to live there."

"I honestly don't know," Henry said, turning toward the exit of the stable. "What I do know is that the Lord has shown me a tiny piece of my future, and it's not living in Angel's cabin at Lone Star."

"Well, He'll lead you to the right place," Daddy said. "He always does." He clapped Henry on the shoulder as they stepped outside. "All right. You better get Wide Sky out. Your appointment is almost here."

"Yeah," Henry said, and he took a big breath. "I'll get her out right now." He did that, taking the beautiful cream-colored horse out of her stall in the next stable over, whispering to her how beautiful she was, how smart she was, and how good she was going to do that afternoon for the therapy session.

He went into Courage Reins and chatted with the

secretary at the front desk, who handed him a folder. "Someone new," she said. "Never been here before."

Henry didn't even flip open the folder. He knew the spiel for new people. He'd done it often enough that he could get through one more. "We've had a lot of those lately."

"Yep," she said. "She's here already, actually. Out in the waiting room in the arena."

"All right," Henry said. "I'll take Wide Sky out there." The client was early, but Henry didn't care. He was ready. The horse was ready. And so he headed out to the arena, where he put Wide Sky with a ball and a hula hoop. He prepped her tack so that it was right next to the door, and then he headed for the waiting room that Daddy had built with a a big window for guests to watch whatever was happening in the arena.

"All right," he said as he opened the door, making his voice bright and cheery. He flipped open the folder and found nothing inside. Confusion filled him because he didn't know what to call the guest without an intake sheet. He glanced up. "I don't seem to have—"

He cut off as Angel rose from the upholstered bench. She twisted her hands nervously around one another, her dark blue tank top getting bunched up in her fingers before she released it.

"I thought I'd come see what equine therapy was really like," she said. "For like, a real client, not just someone playing ball for a few minutes."

Henry thought a lot of things in that moment. Somehow, his brain seized onto the words. He crossed the room and swept Angel into his arms.

"I can't believe you're here," he whispered, trying to get every inch of her against every inch of him.

She hugged him back, giggling. "Are you surprised?"

"Beyond." He set her down on her feet and looked at her, cradling her face, trying to gauge if her skin was real or not. He gazed at her and asked, "What are you doing here?"

She lifted one shoulder in a shrug. "My boyfriend has been telling me how amazing equine therapy is for the past few months, and I thought it was time I checked it out for myself."

Henry laughed, so much joy pouring through him. All the angst and worry and work that he'd done in the past several days had culminated into this moment of pure joy.

He looked at Angel and said, "I love you," then matched his mouth to hers and kissed her.

Chapter Thirty-Five

Angel wanted to address what Henry just said, because those three words in that specific order meant a great deal to her. She had a hard time expressing them to other people. While her momma, daddy, and Trevor told her they loved her all the time, sometimes Angel didn't feel very lovable.

Henry kissed her though, and she didn't want to stop that. She kissed him back, hoping that she could say those three little words through actions. Perhaps he would get the message without her having to use her voice. At the same time, she needed to use her voice; she *wanted* to use her voice. He needed to hear her voice.

He pulled away, and they breathed in together. "I'm sorry I'm taking your therapy time."

"That's what you're sorry about?" she asked.

Henry opened his eyes and looked at her. Angel

smiled softly at him. "I want you to have as much time here with your family as you need. But I also wanted you to know that I'm hearing you, Henry."

"I know that," he said.

"No, I don't think you do," she said. "Equine therapy is important to you, and I've dismissed it for months. Us getting up on that platform and telling everyone we're together is important to you, and I've put it off and put it off. I know you're frustrated."

She stepped away from him and tucked her hands in her back pockets. She faced the wall-to-wall window that looked out into the arena. "I'm frustrated too. And I want you to know that the very first roll call you're back, we're going to stand on that platform together. It doesn't matter if we have a plan."

She threw him a dirty look like he'd been the one to postpone the announcement until they had a plan. But that had been all Angel, and they both knew it.

"I don't care, Angel," he said.

"You do," she said. "And it's fine that you do. I guess me coming here today is...." She trailed off, trying to find the right words. "Well, one, it's selfish. I miss you and I want to see you. But two, it's to let you know that what you say is important to me. And what's important to you is also important to me, even if I don't understand it in the beginning."

He approached Angel, and her body tingled in anticipation of being touched by him. He slid his hand around her waist, barely touching her until his hand rested on her opposite hip. She leaned into him, enjoying his warmth, his strength, and his height.

"I should warn you," she said. "Levi's bringing Trevor in half an hour. It's really his appointment."

"Hm...so why did you come early?"

She bumped him with her hip. "Maybe to hear you say you love me."

Henry cleared his throat. The air in the waiting room turned tense and thick. "I mean," he started. "I'm not gonna take it back, but it wasn't exactly how I... maybe it wasn't exactly how I wanted to say it the first time."

"How long have you wanted to say it?" she asked.

"Not long," he hedged.

"Probably not as long as me," Angel said.

"Yeah, except you haven't actually said it."

Angel turned toward him, running her hands up his chest and fisting his collar in her fingers. "When you told me you were looking into the future and that you could see us together, I started doing the same thing—looking into the future."

"Mm hm." He brushed her hair back, which caused a sensation to dance along her skin where he touched.

"And I could see us, Henry, me and you, together. And you know what? You were right. It's not at Lone Star."

Henry blinked a couple of times and then closed his eyes.

"I want to build a life with you," Angel said. "I want to talk about marriage and what you want and what I want, and I want to talk about kids, and I want to talk about where we'll live. And I want to talk about how Lone Star fits into all of that, because if it doesn't fit, Henry, I'm willing to let it go."

His eyes shot open, and "No," burst out of his mouth. "No, we're not letting Lone Star go." He searched her face almost frantically. "Why would you think you need to give up Lone Star? I'm not asking you to do that. I would *never* ask you to do that."

"Because it does consume a lot of me," she said. "And I don't want it to take so much from me that I don't have enough for you and for our kids."

"We won't let it do that," he said. "That's part of us moving off-site, so that it won't do that. So that you have a safe place to come home to at night, and we can leave work at work and have family time at home."

"I just don't want you to be frustrated with me because I'm slower than you."

"Sweetheart, I'm not." He pulled her into his chest the way he had when he had comforted her and rescued her that very first time. "I will always be there to pull you out of the dark water," he said. "And I'm not in a hurry, Angel. Speed is irrelevant when there's no direction."

She pulled away from his heartbeat and looked at him. "The pastor said that recently."

"Yeah," Henry said. "It really meant something to me. It was like God telling me to be patient. I don't know what direction I'm going quite yet, but it's becoming more and more clear every day."

"Is it?" she asked. "In what ways?"

"Well, for one, I know I'm not supposed to be here at Courage Reins. But at the same time, I need to be close. That's been made very clear to me with Grams' stroke and everything going on here now."

"So Stinnett is a great option," she said.

"It is," Henry said. "But it's not the only option, Angel. They're putting in a new road, and I don't mind the drive from Lone Star to here. We could be at the outskirts of Amarillo or the outskirts of Three Rivers. I know I want to be close to my friends and go to their luncheons every first Thursday of the month. That's a direction I know God wants me to take. He wants me to be close to my family, and he wants me to provide a safe haven for you. So it's triangulating," he said. "I'm getting closer and closer."

"I want to look at some places with you," Angel said.

"I've got a great real estate agent," he said. "Finn's used him, and I heard Mitch was looking at some property too. But that's a secret, so don't tell anyone."

Angel giggled. "Who am I going to tell, cowboy?"

He grinned at her. "I just want us to be going in the

same direction, Angel. And it doesn't matter how fast we go, as long as we go together."

She nodded, her throat tight and her lips pressed together. "That's what I want too, Henry."

"All right." He wrapped her up tightly into his arms. "Hug me again. It's so good to see you."

She held onto him tightly, thrilled that her touch could comfort him, and knowing that Henry would need to be rescued sometimes and that she would be the one to do it.

Her phone chimed, and Angel said, "My brother is here."

"All right," Henry said. "Kiss me one more time, and then we'll go meet him."

She took his face in her hands and stroked her fingers down the side of his beard as she said, "I love you, Henry Marshall," right before she kissed him.

Chapter Thirty-Six

Henry had a hive of angry hornets lodged in his throat. They stung down into his stomach, intestines, and bowels, and he seriously thought he might throw up. The clock ticked closer and closer to seven, when Trevor would start roll call. Henry stood near the front of the crowd, Angel at his side—where he always wanted her to be. He looked over at her, everything inside of him calming.

When she looked at him, she swallowed, a sign of nerves. Henry put a brave smile on his face, which was about how he tried to cover up everything that made him nervous. He wanted to reach for her hand, hold it, squeeze it, and whisper that everything would be fine. But the truth was, Henry wasn't sure of any of that. He knew everyone here at Lone Star, some better than others, but Angel was the boss of all of them.

The fallout might be worse for her. Henry gritted his teeth, determined to make sure that Angel didn't suffer after the announcement. Trevor shuffled up the ramp, using his arms to pull himself up. He didn't have to quiet anyone down as he said, "Good morning, everyone."

They all tuned in to roll call, and Trevor went through the announcements for the day, telling them about an exciting new partnership with a saddle maker that would increase their profile with their customers and provide a premier riding experience for everyone who came to Lone Star.

The minutes passed by in a blur when Henry just wanted them to stop. And before he knew it, Trevor said, "And now Angel has an announcement." It took him several seconds to get off the platform, and Angel didn't move.

Henry wasn't sure how this was going to go. They had talked about it, of course, late last night when he'd snuck over to her house after returning to Lone Star. He was tired inside and out, and perhaps they should have waited until another day.

Then Angel's fingers curled through his, and she led him toward the platform. A murmur ran through the crowd because Henry had never been on the platform before, and it wasn't exactly big enough for two people. Still, Angel stepped up, and Henry crowded in right beside her. In that moment, God chose to stop time.

Henry saw every man in front of him for what he

was—a good person, a hardworking soul, a child of God. Bard stood in the back corner, his arms folded, and when he met Henry's eyes, he nodded. That infused strength into Henry's muscles, into his voice, and into his mind.

Since neither he nor Angel had planned who would go first or who would say what, he wasn't sure if he should start or if she wanted to. He looked at her, and she looked at him, and then she faced the crowd.

"In case you haven't figured it out," Angel said, "Henry Marshall and I are dating." The crowd stood deathly still. Henry cataloged the shocked look on Levi's face, Shad's gasp, Cedric's and Clay's wide eyes, and the surprise in every member of his team. Anger flashed across Creston's face, and Henry would have to deal with that later.

"We got new employee handbooks a week or so ago," Angel continued. "The no-dating rule has been removed now that I'm in charge."

"Yeah, no kidding," someone called, and Henry wasn't sure if they were joking or upset. It was a lot to take in—all of their faces, the emotions, deciphering what they might be feeling. He wasn't capable of it.

"We have several female stable hands at Lone Star right now," Angel said. "We've had female farriers from time to time, and we could have a female barn manager or horseman in the future. I'm not my father, and I'm willing to deal with the drama between people who choose to date each other." She squeezed Henry's hand.

"We don't know how long Henry will be at Lone Star as a farrier, but I know he's going to be at my side for a long time."

She nodded and faced the crowd again. Henry wasn't sure what to add to that. He wasn't in charge. She laid it all out exactly the way he'd wanted her to. She'd *claimed* him, and he bent down and pressed a kiss to her forehead.

Someone whooped, and Henry very much thought it was Levi. Applause started, and that only made Henry's face fill with heat. He wasn't sure if it was shame or embarrassment, humiliation, or simply just being in the hot spotlight for too long. No matter what, he didn't like it, and he nudged Angel before he went down the ramp and off the platform.

Others immediately surrounded him, some patting him on the back, and Levi pushing through them all and taking him into a hug. "I can't believe you didn't tell me," Levi said. "How did you hide this from me?"

Henry chuckled and clapped him on the back. "I don't know, brother. I didn't exactly lie." He pulled back and looked his friend in the face, sober as ever. "You know that, right? I wouldn't lie to you."

"I know," Levi said. "My guess is you were out texting on the porch with your family, and then you'd go over to Angel's. You just left that part out." He grinned. "You two sure are cute together."

Henry didn't want to get too far away from Angel, so he tucked her against his side. "You think so?"

"Oh, yeah," Levi said.

"This isn't a problem for you?" Henry asked.

"Not for me," Levi said. Then he turned and clapped his hands. "Alright, I need my crew over here with me." He turned back to Henry. "And that includes you, cowboy."

Henry turned to Angel. "I'll see you later," he said, squeezing her hand. He told himself over and over that Angel was a mature adult and she could handle herself. If anyone had a problem with their relationship, she could handle it, and he would be at her side. He hadn't taken two steps when Creston appeared in front of him.

"You've been dating the boss?" Creston folded his arms. "No wonder you got a captain position."

"That's not true," Henry said at the same time as Angel.

"I got promoted because I deserved it, because I'm a good farrier and a good leader."

"Yeah, right," Creston said. "Just like Angel runs this place because her last name is White. It's not like she knows what she's doing."

"Hey, now," Henry said. "That is totally not true. She knows exactly what she's doing."

"She hasn't been to farrier school."

"Actually," Angel said. "I did attend farrier school.

All the coursework. All the practical hours. I simply never applied for graduation."

"See?" Henry took a step forward, trying to get Creston to back up. "She knows who to promote because she knows who's going to bring the loyalty and team spirit that she wants here at Lone Star. She knows exactly what she's doing."

"Is there a problem here?" Bard asked, stepping into the fray.

Henry looked over to him, suddenly nervous all over again. "No, sir."

"You got something you need to say?" He looked at Creston.

"No, sir," Creston said.

"Because if you do, my office is always open," Bard said. "Isn't that right, Angel? We're open to feedback, criticism, anything we can do to make Lone Star better."

"That's right," Angel said, and together the three of them created a united front. "I just want the best people to work with the best horses here at Lone Star," she said. "I know I'm not perfect, Henry's not perfect, but he didn't get promoted because he was my boyfriend. The three of us—me, Justin, and Daddy—went through all the applications, and we chose the men. I didn't do it myself. In fact, it wasn't me who chose Henry at all."

"It was me," Justin said, stepping next to Bard.

"And me," Bard said. "I seconded it immediately. Henry is a good farrier, and he's a great leader." He looked right at Henry. "And I wouldn't be able to pick a better man for my daughter."

Creston looked like he might blow fire in the next moment, but he simply said, "All right," turned around, and walked away. The tension diffused, and Henry took a deep breath into his lungs. He realized he couldn't just walk away with Levi, so he and Angel stood there and talked to every person who wanted to talk to them until they did finally all move off to start their jobs for the day.

Angel sighed, a totally defeated, deflated sound, and said, "That wasn't so bad."

"That wasn't so bad?" Henry repeated.

"I mean, it could have been worse," she said. "They could have rioted, called for my immediate removal."

"Is that what you were worried about?" He chuckled. "You own this place, sweetheart."

"Yeah, well, you heard Creston," she said. "He thinks I'm only here because my last name is White."

"That *is* why you're here," Henry said. "And you should never be ashamed of that." He pulled her close and whispered, "Besides, your last name will be Marshall soon enough."

She eased into his arms, melted into his chest, and he was glad he could hold her out in the open where anyone could see. Then he stepped back and said, "It's been a real stressful week or so. Let's go to dinner tonight."

She looked up at him, pure hope in her eyes. "Really?"

"Yeah," he said. "I'll come pick you up like a gentleman and everything. Drive my truck to your house and ring your doorbell. I'll even bring flowers."

She laughed and shook her head. "Where are you going to get flowers? You can't drive to town and back."

"You underestimate me. Nice."

She tripped up on her toes and swept a kiss across his cheek. "Just pick me up at six-thirty, cowboy."

"Yes, ma'am," he said and as she walked away, Henry experienced another moment of pure joy with Angel. He couldn't wait for many, many more.

A couple of weeks later, Henry had just finished his work for the day, and he needed a shower and to change into his red, white, and blue shirt for the Fourth of July celebration dinner that evening.

Then, he and Angel and plenty of other cowboys would be headed into Amarillo to watch a mini rodeo with fireworks at the end. It would be a good way to celebrate Independence Day, though he'd worked today, and Henry couldn't wait to get off the ranch.

His phone chimed, and he pulled it out to check it. *I need you*, Angel had said. It wasn't the acronym they'd used in the past, and Henry's pulse bobbed in the back of his throat.

He called her, and she answered without saying anything. But she sniffled over the line, and he immediately turned toward her house. She had to be there, or in her office. She wouldn't be crying out in the open. "Where are you?"

"I just need to get out of here."

"Why? What's going on?" he asked. Since their announcement, things had settled down. No one had quit. No teams had been reorganized. He'd taken a little chiding and ribbing from his friends, and then they'd moved on to other things. In fact, Levi had asked out one of the stable hands, a woman named Leslie, and they'd been out a few times since.

"I'm walking away from my cabin," she said. "I just left through the front door, and I'm just walking."

"Okay," he said, turning in that direction and breaking into a run. "I'm on my way." He caught up to her several minutes later out in the middle of the field across from her cabin. She wasn't crying, but her fingers curled into fists.

"What's going on?" he asked.

"Daddy's pressuring me to teach at Sherman next fall," she said. "I'm feeling so guilty about it, but I don't want to do it."

"All right," Henry said, matching his stride to hers.

"And then I got an email from a couple of the

farriers there who are angry that there's not enough positions at Lone Star for all of them. I don't know what they want me to do—build more stables, get more horses?" She made an angry noise and scoffed. "They have no idea what it's like here."

Henry had been on that side of the equation before, and it *was* frustrating that there weren't enough positions to get the experience that the farriers at Sherman Academy needed. He didn't say anything, because he didn't have to.

This wasn't Angel's burden to carry, but he also understood the frustration from the cowboys on the other side.

She stopped abruptly, and it took Henry another step to do the same. She looked at him, and he looked at her, and he said the first thing that popped into his head.

"I'm going to call Jerry right now. There's a really great place on the west side of Three Rivers. It's a little further to Lone Star than Stinnett, but it's really great, Angel. We should go look at it tonight."

"You've looked at it?" she asked, pure fire in her eyes.

"Only online."

She nodded, softening. "I want to look at it online."

"Okay," he said. "But let's go right now. Let's get off the ranch. Let's just go."

"It's the Fourth of July," she said. "He's not going to be available to look at it tonight, and we have the family dinner tonight, and the rodeo, and the fireworks."

"There'll be fireworks everywhere," Henry said. "Heck, we can buy some of our own and just set them off in the middle of the road." He took her hand. "Please, just come with me right now."

She searched his face and then looked away, scanning something on the horizon.

Henry wanted to ease this burden for her, take it if he could. He wanted to rage at the cowboys who had made her feel this way and tell her daddy to back off and let her make her own decisions about teaching at the academy.

"All right," she said. "Let's go right now."

"I'll call Jerry," Henry said. "If he can't come, we'll just drive by. It'll be fine."

"Will you send it to me?" she said.

"Right now," he said, and he pulled out his phone to send her the link to the listing that he'd been looking at.

"Come on, baby," he said, and he took her hand. "Let's not stand in this field in the middle of the summer day." She turned back toward the ranch and started walking with him, reluctantly in his opinion.

"Let me slow you down," he said. "I got you, okay?"

She nodded. "Okay."

"That's what we do for each other, Angel," he said. "It's what I want to do for you for the rest of my life."

"All right," she said.

"So you tell me what you want for the rest of your

life," he said, hoping this conversation didn't stir up a new nest of worries for her.

"Like kids?" she said.

"Yeah, kids," he said. "Do you want a lot of kids? Not very many kids? Kids right away after we're married, or... something else?"

"I haven't really thought about it," she said.

"Do you want to get married in the spring, summer, or fall?" he asked. "I don't believe you haven't thought about your wedding."

"I've thought about it," she said, and he slowed as they neared the cabin. Henry didn't want her to go back inside, but if they were going to go for a drive and then maybe go to the rodeo after, she might need to grab a few things.

"I think spring would be awesome around here," she said. "The flowers bloom, and it's so green."

"Spring," he said. "Doesn't give you much time if we're gonna get married this next spring."

"Doesn't give *me* much time?" she asked. "Or it doesn't give *you* much time? I mean, it's not like I'm wearing a diamond." She glanced over at him, and Henry almost tripped.

"Do you want to wear a diamond?"

"If it's yours," she said, and Henry was the one who stopped this time.

"I'd marry you in the spring," he said. "Heck, I'd marry you tomorrow. And I'd take a baby anytime God gave us one. I want us to find a place of our own that we can move into when we get married. I don't want to live there before you, and I don't want you to live there before me. I want it to be *our* place."

"I want that too, Henry," she said.

"All right," he said. "So let's go look at this place. And if we have time, maybe we'll still go to the rodeo and the fireworks."

"Yeah," she said. "Or maybe we'll just go out to Courage Reins, see your momma and grandma, and do whatever the cowboys are doing."

Henry knew that was what she wanted, and he'd do whatever he had to in order to give it to her. "How many minutes do you need to put a bag together?"

"Fifteen," she guessed.

Henry took her across the road and kissed her at the bottom of her steps. When he pulled away, he murmured, "You have fourteen minutes."

She laughed, and Henry backed up, deadly serious. "Clock's ticking," he said, and then he hustled home to pack a bag so he could take Angel away from this place.

Rescue her.

Bring her back to the surface where she could breathe—where they could breathe together.

Chapter Thirty-Seven

"We're going to be gone for the whole weekend," Angel said in her team meeting the first week of August. The month of July had passed with heat waves and firecrackers, new teams functioning well, and everything coming together at Lone Star. She and Henry had started looking at several places near Three Rivers and Stinnett, but nothing had really seemed like "their place" yet.

Henry wanted to attend the ranch owners' luncheon with his friends, as he'd been going for the past several months by himself. When she'd asked him if couples go, he'd said no, but she was a ranch owner, so there was no reason she couldn't attend.

He talked to his cousin and his friends, and of course, they had all said she should absolutely come.

They had done some date nights with his friends in Three Rivers, and Angel really liked them.

She and Henry were leaving for Three Rivers in the morning. They would go to the luncheon, and then in the afternoon, they had a couple of appointments with a realtor to show them a few properties in Three Rivers.

Angel didn't want her desperation to choke her, but it was starting to feel like if they didn't find a house or a farm soon, she wouldn't be able to get married in the spring—which was silly.

If they bought a place right now, someone would have to live in it *before* they got married, and neither of them wanted to do that. Henry claimed that wasn't true. They could let it sit—especially if they bought a fixer-upper—and he could work on fixing it and getting it exactly the way they wanted it before they married and then moved in.

Of course, he still hadn't asked her to marry him. So Angel was making all kinds of future plans about marriage and houses, children, pastures for horses, attending ranch owner meetings with their friends, and she still didn't have the diamond.

She trusted Henry, though. She believed in Henry, and she loved Henry, so she knew that was coming.

"We'll be fine here," Shad said. "You've been gone before."

She *had* been gone before, and it had been luxurious and wonderful. "I'll have my phone," she said. "Henry has his phone. I know he's met with his team already." She glanced over to Levi, who nodded. "We don't have many horses coming or going. Everything should be fine."

"We'll be absolutely fine," Justin said. "Trevor's doing great with the meetings. And I hate to say it, Angel." He grinned at her. "But we don't need you here."

"Thanks," she said dryly. She closed her folder, which ended the meeting. "Thank you guys so much." She looked around the room. "Really, I'm going to give mid-year bonuses. They're just a little bit late, but you guys...."

She stopped because her voice had tightened, and she couldn't talk past that. She swallowed and fought for control, finally winning it. "You guys have really stepped up this year, and you've really saved me, and I want you to know that I really love and appreciate each of you." She swallowed hard again, which actually hurt, and let her emotions rage through her. It was okay to feel things; they didn't make her weak or unable to lead.

Justin reached over and covered her hand with his. "We love you too, Angel."

"Yeah," Levi said. "You're doing a great job here."

"Thank you," she managed to push out. "All right, I've got to go get packed up. We're leaving first thing in the morning."

The men started to disperse, but Levi hung back,

glancing at the others as they left. "Angel," he said, once only they remained in the room. "Do you want me to check on your parents while you're gone?"

"Yes, please," she said. "I know Trevor doesn't need it as often, but you're right next door to him too. If you could just, I don't know, pop by for something that maybe you don't need just to see how he is."

"He's always fine when I do that," Levi said.

"I know he is," Angel said, and she was so proud of herself for getting to a point where she could ask a non-family member for help with her family. She thought she'd never, ever do that.

"My parents too. But it just gives me peace of mind to know that someone is looking after them when I'm not here."

"I'll do it then," Levi said.

"Thank you." She gave him a shy look, not sure how else to tell him how much his leadership had meant to her both personally and professionally. "Do you think Henry will ever ask me to marry him?" she asked, her hands suddenly coming up to wind around each other. "Has he said anything to you, Levi?"

Levi chortled and chuckled and laughed. "Oh, I'm not telling you that."

"So that's a yes."

"I didn't say that," Levi said. "I will be in so much trouble, Angel. Don't you *dare* tell him that I told you anything."

"Well, you haven't told me anything," she said. "Tell me what?"

He mimed zipping his lips. "You're gonna have a great weekend." He chuckled as he left the conference room, and Angel had no choice but to head home and do what she'd said: pack for the weekend.

Angel wondered as she packed if she was choosing the appropriate things. Was Henry going to propose this weekend? And if so, wouldn't she want to be wearing a specific dress so that when the pictures got taken—because his momma would take pictures—she would look exactly how she wanted to look?

Angel put a blue dress in her suitcase and then took it back out. "Henry's favorite color is purple," she said. She turned back to her closet muttering, "You can't wear purple every single day, Angel."

And she didn't need to please Henry anyway. She ended up packing what she felt comfortable in, what would be appropriate for the rancher's lunch, and for looking at properties, and for riding horses and doing equine therapy.

She zipped her bag closed and set it by her front door. When Henry came to get her in the morning, he'd load it in the back of his truck for her—which was exactly what happened.

"Ready?" Henry asked.

Angel had chosen a light lavender blouse for today, and she leaned into Henry's strong chest. He wore his usual jeans, and today's plaid shouted in red, white, and black. "I'm ready," she said.

"There's been a change of plans." Henry's eyes skittered around her house, never really landing on anything.

"There has?" Angel straightened and turned to get her purse. It went across her body, and she lifted it over her head while Henry continued to say nothing. "Why aren't you talking?"

"Jerry said he couldn't meet us this afternoon." He cleared his throat. "He's got a couple of places for us, but we have to look this morning."

Angel faced him again, surprise mingling with her doubts. "Do we have time for that?"

"Yeah, if we leave right now."

"Then, let's leave right now."

Henry nodded in a tight burst and spun to leave her house. She followed him, something about him just not quite right. "Are you okay?"

"Yeah," he said.

"I can text Alex about maybe being late."

"Okay." He moved to her door and opened it for her, and Angel smiled at him as she eased into his personal space.

"Hey," she whispered, reaching up to hold his face in the palm of her hand. "Will you look at me, please?"

Henry did, blinking as if he'd just now realized where he was. "Sorry, I'm...tense right now."

"I can see that." She raised her eyebrows, a silent *Why?* passing between them.

"I don't know why," Henry said, but his shoulders relaxed, and the air whooshed out of his lungs. "Let's just go, okay? I think this first place is really nice."

Angel got in the truck, and he walked around the hood to get in beside her. "Which place is first?" she asked. He'd handled all of the communication with Jerry, and he simply forwarded them on to her. Angel loved spending her evenings looking at real estate, and she'd discovered a hidden love of floor plans that she didn't know she had.

"It's the Sagebrush one," he said. "Remember we talked about the cute name of the lane?"

"Sagebrush Lane, yes." She smiled as it came forward in her memory. "That's the one that needs a brand-new kitchen."

"Yeah, it sure does," he said. "But I've never gutted a kitchen, and I think it would be fun."

She giggled because gutting a kitchen was not something anyone would willingly put on their bucket list of "Fun Things To Do."

They settled into the drive, and Angel decided not to pester him or pick at him with questions. His nerves didn't ratchet up again until he started to slow down, about halfway between Stinnett and Three Rivers.

"It's here on the right."

"I've never seen anything here on the right before," she said.

"There's a road," he said. "It goes out to a few homesteads."

"So, ranches?" she asked.

"Well, you looked at it," he said, his tone carrying a hint of irritation. "It's kind of a mini-farm, but I wouldn't really call it a ranch."

She tapped on her phone as he made the turn, but she didn't want to be looking at her device as she took in a possible place where she and Henry would live together, where they'd raise their family.

Trees grew up right next to the road as they did in many places in Texas, and she could only see the brown path ahead of her. It mirrored her life, and Angel simply held on as Henry drove down the dirt road.

"This place on the left is another house," he said, indicating the branching dirt road with a nod of his cowboy hat. "I guess at one time a family owned all this land. They built several houses for their kids, and they all lived here and worked it." The truck bumped over a large pothole, and Henry corrected the trajectory of the truck. "And then when their daddy died about fifteen years ago, they sectioned up the land according to where the houses are, and now there are six or seven out here."

"So we wouldn't be alone," Angel said.

"No," Henry said. "And it's not a full ranch."

"Is there room for your horse?"

"There's room for horses, yes," he said. "And chickens, and even some dairy cows, and some ducks and pigs if you want them."

Angel glanced over at him. "No pigs. We've already talked about that."

He grinned at her. "You're right, you're right." It sure did soothe her to hear him laugh lightly. "No pigs."

He went past another driveway on the left and then turned onto the first one that had come up on the right. "It's this one," he said. "It's on the end, and there are a few more back in there, at least according to Jerry."

They went around another bend in the road to the right and then to the left, and the house appeared. Angel pulled in a breath, because it was the most quintessential two-story farmhouse, something straight out of the pages of a children's book.

"Look at that porch," she said.

"Jerry said they just painted the house," Henry said. "It's blue now; can you tell?"

Angel leaned up and peered through the windshield. "It *is* blue," she said, and that only made the house better. The porch spanned the entire width of the house, and she could see that it had a basement as well. "Three levels."

"Plenty of room," he said. "Five bedrooms already."

She'd looked at the pictures, but everything felt different when she came face-to-face with property, and she could admit she'd semi-dismissed this one because of the kitchen. She reached for the door handle, a sense of wonder overcoming her. *I love this house*, she thought.

Henry had pulled up to a detached garage, which had a cement pad big enough for three cars. The third space extended past the garage, and Angel noted the extra parking. Of course, on land like this, they had plenty of parking for horse trailers or RVs.

"How big is it?" she asked, hugging herself, not quite daring to hope that this might be *their* place.

"It's only six acres," he said. "We don't have to plant anything, but there's plenty of room if you want to grow flowers or a vegetable garden."

He came to her side and took her hand. "Jerry's here already. Let's go meet him."

Angel hadn't even seen Jerry, but he suddenly stood on the porch. She noticed his red truck as they went by it, something she also hadn't seen. The grass in front of the house needed to be watered, and it sure seemed like no one had lived there for a while.

"How long has it been empty?" she asked as she crossed the lawn and started for the steps.

"A few months," Jerry said. "The husband got called to a job in California, and they had to go."

So it's wild, Angel thought, and it kind of matched how she felt inside—and her relationship with Henry. As she climbed the sturdy steps to the porch, the strangest sense of coming home lighted on Angel's shoulders.

She looked at Henry, and he looked at her, and she didn't have to say anything. She hadn't even seen the house, but it possessed a spirit that spoke to hers. As they both turned to Jerry, he said, "Let me show you through it."

"All right," Angel said.

"This door is solid oak," Jerry said as he moved over to the front door. "It's a little bit taller than normal, as you can see. Custom for the house." He continued to talk about the flooring, the new paint, how the kitchen needed to be updated and remodeled. But everything about the place charmed Angel.

It had a beautiful front living room where she could have acquaintances and friends come to sit and visit. Or she could simply sit there and look out the big window at the trees waving their limbs to whoever passed by, or the stars as they came out to greet the night.

From there, a hall moved past the steps that went downstairs, and Angel brought up the rear as they entered a large family room. Everything was empty, so the space looked huge, and that blended into a space for a dining room table and then the kitchen.

"Their plan," Jerry said. "Was to push this wall out a little further into the backyard." He peered through the window over the sink. "You'd still have plenty of room for a trampoline, playsets, dogs, or chickens, but you could double the size of your kitchen."

"Hm," Henry said, mirroring what Angel would've done if she could've gotten her voice to work.

The master suite sat tucked in the front corner of the house with big windows and big closets and a great big bathroom.

"They've redone this," Angel said, taking in the thick carpet beneath her feet and the high-end fixtures in the bathroom.

"Yep, they redid this," Jerry agreed. "It used to be a bedroom attached to an office, and now it's just one big bedroom, one big bath, his and hers closets."

Angel looked at Henry again, and this time he smiled at her. They went through the upstairs, which held bedrooms and bathrooms, and the basement, which contained another large family room, a tiny kitchenette in the corner, and more bedrooms and another bathroom.

"Plenty of storage," Jerry said. "And you have a walk-out basement here as well." He unlocked the door and stepped through it, and sure enough, it led onto a back patio that was sheltered by the deck above.

"That deck comes off the dining room," Jerry said, looking up. "So you've got some outdoor space up there and down here, and then you go right up these steps to the yard."

Some rock steps had been built into the earth, and Angel let Henry and Jerry go ahead of her as she drank everything in. Then she also took the five steps up and stood in the backyard. Trees greeted her from the sides, with a great big copse of them right in the middle of the lawn.

"They specifically left that clump of trees to provide shade for the house," Jerry said. "As your backyard faces west, and it can get hot."

"I love it," Angel said. She blinked, and suddenly the blank canvas in her mind that God had refused to paint on came to life. She could see chicken coops, a storage shed next to the weathered barn that stood there. It had been painted red in the past but needed to be redone. Her quaint, *personal* farm life came to fruition right in front of her, and Angel wanted it badly. She squeezed Henry's hand just as Jerry's phone rang.

"I'm gonna let you guys look around for a little bit," he said. "I've got to take this call. Feel free to explore out here or go back in the house. I'll meet you out front in a few minutes."

"Okay," Henry said, and with that, Jerry answered the call and headed for the steps that went up to the deck. He climbed them, saying things that Angel didn't hear, and went back into the house.

She stood on the back lawn of the house she wanted. And while it wasn't her dream house yet, it sat in the perfect place. Only forty minutes to from Lone Star, it had great views, big trees, and plenty of potential.

"How far do you think it is to Three Rivers from here?" she asked.

"Well, we could take the road to Stinnett and then up to that new road," he said. "I'm guessing forty-five minutes. If we need to get into town, it's probably only fifteen minutes."

"Fifteen minutes to Three Rivers," she confirmed.

They walked through the barn, which needed work. It needed something and someone to exist for. But Angel still loved it. She found the bare vegetable garden beside that, and while she'd never had much of a green thumb, Angel suddenly wanted to try.

They crossed the back lawn again and took the steps to the deck, which needed to be restrained. Henry noted that and said, "I did this once with my daddy. He'll come help."

They re-entered the kitchen, and Angel felt like neither one of them wanted to say what they really thought first. She looked at him, noting that he was scuffing his toe along a piece of the floor that probably needed to be replaced.

"Henry," she said, her courage gathering in her soul. "I love this place. I want this house."

"We have two more we can look at this morning," he said.

"I don't want to." She shook her head. "No, I don't want to. This is it, Henry. This is *our place.*" She rushed to him and planted her palms against his chest. "Can't you feel it?"

He gazed down at her, everything that had been so

tight and tense since he'd shown up that morning softening. "I can feel it."

Joy burst through Angel. "We're going to buy this house."

Henry's smile curved up, and he stepped away from her and into the kitchen. He opened a drawer, and when he lifted his hand, he held a glittering diamond ring. Angel sucked in a breath. Where had that come from?

Henry looked at the ring and then came around the counter. He dropped to both knees and held it up, his expression earnest, open, and vulnerable as he gazed at her. "Every morning I wake up in my bed alone starts a terrible day."

He grinned at her, some of his cowboy swagger returning to his eyes. "Because I want to start my day with you at my side. I want to watch out for you, and I want you to watch out for me. This is *our place*, and we've worked really hard to get here. Will you marry me, and live here with me, and build your life here together with me?"

Angel nodded as tears pricked her eyes. "Yes," she choked out. "Yes, I'll marry you."

"Come on over here, then," he said, and she took the two steps to be closer to him so that he could slide the diamond onto her ring finger. She gazed at it with pure wonder, sure that this had just happened to someone else, and she was only watching it.

And yet, the weight of the gold band on her finger

made it bend, and she felt Henry's lips as they pressed over the diamond, kissing it into her hand. He looked up at her again and wrapped his arms around her waist, pulling her into him. He laid his cheek against her stomach and said, "I love you so much. I am going to work so hard to be the best husband."

Angel held his head in her arms and said, "I love you too, Henry."

Chapter Thirty-Eight

Henry couldn't stop smiling as they drove to Coyote Pass from the place they had just seen with Jerry Bozeman. The moment they'd come out of the front door and seen Jerry waiting by his truck, Henry had said, "We want it. Tell us what to do next." And Jerry had said he'd send the paperwork.

Angel had started a timer to see how long it would take to get to Coyote Pass from their place. They had to go into town, then north, and then a little bit further west. Finn's was to the east, and Henry decided that it would probably take the same amount of time to get to Finn's as it would to Alex's.

"Are you still thinking April?" he asked.

"What?" Angel looked over to him. "Yeah, yeah, April's fine."

He glanced at her. "What are you thinking?"

"I'm wondering how you got that diamond in the drawer," she said, pinning him with one of her boss-looks.

Henry's blood, which had been bubbling since he'd seen Angel's reaction to the blue farmhouse, positively sparkled now. "Yeah, I bet you are." He chuckled. "I gave it to Jerry when you were coming up the steps from the patio."

"You gave it to Jerry, and he just knew what to do with it?"

"Yeah," Henry said. "I told him that if we found a place today, I would ask you to marry me there. And I could tell that this was ours. I sort of felt it from the pictures, but actually physically being there—and seeing your reaction—I just knew." He glanced over to her and reached for her hand, spinning the diamond left and right on that left finger where it had never been before. "I can't believe you said yes."

"Of course I'm going to say yes," Angel said. "We've been talking about marriage and kids and looking at places for two months."

"I know," he said. "It just feels like something that would happen to Paul or Finn or John, not me."

"Well, it is happening to you," Angel said. Her phone beeped, and she looked at it and then glanced up and out the window again. "Also, today's luncheon topic is employee management and staffing," she said. "I guess Alex is thinking of bringing someone on when the twins are born, and he wants to know how everyone handles making sure that they have the personnel they need to get the jobs done."

"It's a great topic," Henry said. "My dad has been really struggling with staffing all summer."

"Yeah," Angel said thoughtfully. She sometimes disappeared into her own mind, and Henry let her, because she always told him what she'd been thinking about.

They arrived at Coyote Pass, and Angel said, "Thirty-five minutes," as Henry put the truck in park.

"It's not bad," he said. "Thirty-five minutes to Alex's, thirty-five minutes to Finn's, probably forty minutes to Three Rivers, and forty minutes to Lone Star. It's literally the epicenter of where we want to be."

"It's perfect," Angel said, grinning. "It's so perfect." She lifted her hand again, and Henry nearly got sidetracked by the diamond there. But they had a luncheon to attend and discussions to have. He hoped that Alex would at least allow a little bit of time for personal news. They'd had their ultrasound last week, but he hadn't said what gender the babies were—surely Alex would have something to share.

Henry got out of the truck and helped Angel down, and he once again positioned himself on her left side so he could hold that diamond-ring-hand. "Sure like this ring on you," he said.

"You didn't even tell me you'd bought a ring."

"What do you think I'd been doing all this time?" he said. "I did talk to my daddy about a loan, and I went shopping with Momma and Aunt Kelly. I've been busy, my angel."

Angel grinned at him and said, "Thank you so much, Henry. I love it."

It had cost him a lot, but Henry didn't care. Angel was worth any price. Besides, his parents had helped him with the ring and told him that he didn't need to pay them back. When he protested, they said they'd done the same thing for Paul, and they'd do the same thing for John and Rich, and to just take the money and not be in debt when he started his new life with Angel.

So he had.

He knocked a couple of times and then simply went inside, as his wasn't the first truck there. Sure enough, Alex stood in the kitchen working, while Finn and Paul waited at the island, chatting.

"Hey," Henry called, and everyone turned toward him.

"Hey," Finn said, and he turned to come greet them. "How was the drive?"

Henry exchanged a glance with Angel and said, "Not bad at all."

Over the course of the next several minutes, everyone arrived. Link came with Dawson, Conrad and JJ Walker, Ollie, and JJ's best friend, Tate. They were all working at Seven Sons that summer, even Ollie, as ranching took a lot of hands, and it sure seemed like cowboys were in short supply around Three Rivers.

Once everyone had arrived, Alex said, "We're ready." He lifted the lid on a slow cooker, and the delicious scent of braised beef filled the air. "Brisket," he said. "Nothing fancy. You can make a sandwich or tacos." He pointed to the chips and the soft dinner rolls. "There's coleslaw, and I ran to the bakery this morning and got mint brownies for dessert."

"All right," Finn said as he clapped his hands in excitement.

"We'll eat first," Alex said. "And then I want to talk about staffing issues." He was a no-nonsense man, as was everyone there. They had busy lives, some of them with wives and children. No matter what, they had big ranches, and their daddies had big expectations for them. They certainly weren't going to sit around not doing anything.

Everyone had met Angel before, so Henry didn't need to introduce her. But once they'd all gotten their food and settled at the table, he glanced over to Alex. "What are you guys having?" he asked.

Alex had just taken a big bite of his brisket sandwich, and he leaned over and held up his hand as if to say, *Give me a second.*

Henry chuckled and said, "Sorry. I didn't mean to do that right when you took a bite."

"Let's do news," Link said, exchanging a glance with

a still-chewing Alex. "I'm pretty sure that's what Alex is going to say."

They had started doing news more and more often at the beginning of their meetings, and no one protested. No one asked if they had to; they all knew they could pass.

"Misty is gonna have a baby," Link said, smiles and sunshine pouring from every cell of his body. "She's due at the end of February."

"Oh, that's amazing," Henry said, adding his voice to the others congratulating Link on becoming a daddy soon.

"No new babies for us," Finn said. "Edith is working on her book. We've got no news."

"You always have something," Paul said, shooting Finn a knowing look from across the table.

"Do I?" Finn asked innocently. Then he broke out into a grin. "Fine, we're adding to our livestock. Edith is getting another cat—hopefully one who doesn't meow constantly—and I'm getting a new horse."

"That's almost better than a baby," Dawson quipped, and that sent a ripple of laughter through the cowboys. "No babies for us either," Dawson added. "But we have a new crow who keeps showing up with Rocks and Nugget."

"Oh yeah?" Alex asked. "What are you going to name this one?"

"Caroline wants to name her Beauty," Dawson said.

"And well, I just kind of let Caroline do what she wants with the crows." He laughed, and Henry did too because Carolyn had wanted crows in their wedding, and she'd gotten them.

"Smart," Ollie said, and the conversation turned to Angel, as she sat next to Dawson.

Panic ran through Henry. He didn't want *her* to tell them they were engaged. *He* wanted to announce it. She glanced over at him, and he found the same fear in her eyes. He quickly raised her left hand.

"Angel and I got engaged," he said.

A second of stunned silence filled Alex's farmhouse, and then Finn whistled through his teeth in the loudest, shrillest celebration Henry had ever heard.

"Holy cow," Link added.

"Look at that thing," Dawson said. He grabbed onto Angel's hand and grinned at the diamond. "Congratulations, you guys."

"When's the big day?" JJ asked.

"Sometime in April," Angel said. "We're going to get married in April."

"April, right," Henry said.

"Not gonna lie, but April is the best time to get married," Finn said.

"I agree," Link said, grinning at Finn. They even high-fived, like they'd had any choice in the month they'd gotten married.

Oliver said, "You know, a holiday wedding is beautiful." He grinned as he scooped up a pile of brisket and sour cream with a tortilla chip. "Easy décor near Christmastime."

Alex said, "Come *on*. Summer is the best time to get married, you guys. You don't have to worry about the weather."

Laughter went around the table, and when it subsided, Ollie said, "Aurora found out she's gonna have another girl. That'll be three girls, one boy. I'm going to try and convince her we're done after that."

Finn chuckled. "Good luck with that, brother."

Henry couldn't even imagine having four kids. But then again, a little over a year ago, Henry hadn't even imagined that he could ever find one person who he could love enough to settle down with.

JJ sat next to Ollie, and he said, "I went on a date last night," with a sly-as-a-fox grin. That started a hullabaloo that took several minutes for JJ to get through, and he finally concluded with, "I asked her out again, and she said yes."

Tate grinned at him and said, "We're going to double too."

"Oh boy," Finn said. "You boys going to the summer dances to meet women?" He eyed them as he ducked his head and took a bite of his sandwich.

JJ nodded. "Why not?"

"Because you're going back to school in three weeks," Angel said dryly.

"Yeah, ain't no thing," JJ said, and Henry could only laugh at the mindset that he'd once had.

Conrad Walker was next. He didn't say much, and he'd only been coming to the luncheons this summer. But he was strong and broad-shouldered, and Henry thought he couldn't be much older than him. Maybe three or four years was all.

"My news is," Conrad said, his voice soft but somehow powerful at the same time. "That I'm thinking of buying my grandma and grandpa's farm and moving in with them."

"You're what?" JJ asked.

"I might move in with them," Conrad said. "Gramps needs a lot more help now, and I'm over there all the time doing things for them anyway. Yard work, things around the house, stuff Grandma can't reach like she used to." He looked at JJ, as they were cousins. "Been talking about it with them and with my parents. I think I'm gonna move in with them. I might buy their place if it makes sense."

"That's great," Finn said with a genuine quality in his voice.

"It is great," Henry said. "Being close to family is important."

Conrad nodded, his news done in only a few words. That only left Paul and Alex, and as Paul sat next to Conrad, he said, "Brielle and I are going to build a house out on the Three Rivers Ranch complex."

Henry stopped eating completely as he gaped at his older brother. "You are?"

"Yeah," Paul said, nodding more than usual, almost like if he kept doing it, he'd believe it too. "We've been talking to Daddy and Uncle Squire about it. Everyone has to be involved—Ethan and Brynn, and the administration at Courage Reins. It'll part of Three Rivers land."

"There's a lot going on out there," Alex said.

"My momma and daddy aren't ready to retire yet. They have a nice place they can still take care of for a good couple of decades. Brielle and I can't live there, obviously."

"You're getting married in three months," Finn said. "Is that enough time to build a house?"

"I don't know," Paul said. "We just started talking about it, and we've agreed that it's going to happen." He looked at Henry. "Uncle Squire is having a land surveyor come out to do some measurements to find a plot of land we can legally annex and buy to build on."

Henry blinked, sure he hadn't heard his brother right. "A land surveyor?" he asked and looked over to Angel. "A land surveyor." This time it wasn't a question.

She grinned at him and said, "It's the best way to make sure that you find the right piece of property and that everyone knows who it belongs to."

"What are you guys talking about?" Link asked, and that only made Henry tip his head back and laugh.

"Nothing," he said. "Something our pastor said a few

months ago." He shook his head, so grateful for his place at this table of good men. "Oh, I have—" He looked at Alex, realizing his mistake. "Wait, you've got news."

"If you've got something else, go ahead." Alex's plate was almost empty as he didn't talk much. He did love hosting everyone at Coyote Pass, Henry knew that. He loved feeding a crowd, and he and Nikki had started hosting game nights just like Finn and Edith.

Henry wondered if he and Angel would do the same when they had their place. He wasn't sure—they both worked around the clock, and it wasn't just one of them. He had no idea what their days and nights would look like once they got married and had to drive home to a big three-story house they had to maintain.

"Angel and I found a place to live," he said when Alex didn't offer up the gender of his coming babies. "Offsite, away from Lone Star."

"You're kidding," Finn said, his words full of disbelief "Where is it?" He became more animated, putting both hands on the table as his grin grew. "It's close, right?"

"Just outside of town," he said. "About halfway between here and Stinnett. It's out on the Miller land."

"Whoo-ee," Link said. "Those are nice."

"You know them?"

"Mitch told me about them," he said. "He said there's what? Seven or eight places out there?"

"Something like that," Henry said. "The one Jerry

showed us today is real nice. We told him we want to buy it."

"That's so great," Paul said, reaching across the table to squeeze Henry's hand. "I'm really happy for you, brother."

"Same," Finn said, and others echoed the sentiment.

All eyes then turned to Alex, and he leaned back in his chair and folded his arms, almost like he was irritated he had to share his good news. "Well, Nikki is going to have a pair of boys."

He finally grinned, and it lit up his face, , the dining room table where they all sat, the entire house, and then the world.

"A pair of boys," Finn said. "That's *so* amazing." He clapped Alex on the shoulder and grinned around at everyone. "He's not going to have staffing problems for long, guys."

They laughed, and the conversation moved on to ranch business. Link had a lot of experience with staffing as he worked a big ranch and had to deal with cowboys moving in and out fairly often. Dawson, not so much though.

They did have someone who worked for them at the Rhinehart Ranch, but just one man, which was what Alex and Finn were looking at doing.

Paul dealt with a ton of staffing, and Henry wasn't surprised to listen to him talk quite a bit about his experience in hiring everyone from secretaries who worked indoors, to licensed and certified counselors to work with people, to horse trainers, to groundskeeping, and everything in between.

Henry had almost no experience at all, but Angel spoke up plenty as she'd managed the staffing across the board at Lone Star for a couple of years now. Everyone treated her with respect and kindness, and she spoke as much as Paul. Every word she said brought more and more pride and love to Henry's chest.

By the time they'd said their goodbyes and left Alex's farmhouse, Henry's heart felt like it might burst wide open. He made it all the way to the passenger door and opened it for Angel before he took her into his arms and said, "You're incredible."

She smiled up at him and giggled. "You think so?"

"Listening to you talk in there with all those ranch owners...." He shook his head slightly and grinned at her. "I love you so much. You're so smart and so beautiful." He reached up and brushed his hand through her hair. Though he knew it was fake, he hoped she could feel something.

"I'm completely in love with you, and I'm so glad you said yes to being my wife." He kissed her right there with others pouring out of the house, and he didn't even care.

She didn't let him go on for too long before she pulled away and rested her cheek against his. Then she did the best thing in the world, the thing that sent shivers all the way down to Henry's heels and back up to his head, the thing he hoped she would do for the rest of his life.

She whispered, "I'm completely in love with you, Henry Marshall."

I think Henry is one of my all-time favorite cowboys. I love the way he helps Angel slow down, and how devoted to her, her stable, and his family he is.

And keep reading for the first two chapters of the next book in the series, THE COWBOY WHO CALLED BACK, featuring the older brother's best friend romance between JJ Walker and Ruby Reynolds!

Sneak Peek! The Cowboy Who Called Back Chapter One:

"All right." Jeremiah Jonah Walker turned in a circle, taking in the entirety of his cabin in only a few seconds. He'd lived in this same one for several summers now, and being back felt like crawling into a familiar bed and falling asleep comfortably.

His daddy finished putting the groceries in the fridge, and Momma currently stood at the front window, fixing the curtain rod so it hung right. Tate Reynolds assisted her, and the two of them chatted easily.

JJ couldn't believe he was back at Seven Sons, though all signs in his life had been pointing him here for a few years now. He belonged in the Texas Panhandle town of Three Rivers, he knew that.

But a small part of him yearned for an adventure. Time spent outside of his family's expectations, outside of Texas, outside of what he'd always thought his life would be.

You're young, he thought, echoing something his mom had told him loads of times. *You have time to do all kinds of things with your life.*

He saw her loving, appreciative smile in his mind when she'd said it to him in the past, and as she turned from the curtains, he found it on her face again.

"You're all set," she said.

"I can really paint the cabin whatever color I want?" JJ asked.

"We saved it for you," Daddy said. "Since you'll be livin' here for a while now, we figured you could choose whatever you like."

"You've complained about the green in the past." His mother came toward him, and JJ just wanted her to fold him into her arms and tell him everything would be all right.

"I've complained?" He frowned and flicked a look at Tate. "I didn't mean to complain."

Momma and Daddy exchanged a glance, and Daddy said, "We just thought you'd like to choose the color. That's all."

JJ nodded, fighting against his inner grump. Being around so many people for so long tired him, and he needed moving day to be done. "All right," he drawled. "Thank you for helping me move."

Again.

JJ had been back and forth between Seven Sons and Amarillo State College every summer now for four years. Relief painted through him—and he wondered if he could find a paint color titled *relief*—that this was his final move.

For now.

"We'll get out of your hair." Momma cradled his face in her hand, though he stood taller than her now. "Let us know if you need anything." His parents left through the front door, and the cabin had one in the back corner too, that led out of the kitchen to a tiny deck. Down three steps and across a field, and JJ could arrive and his aunt and uncle's place.

Aunt Callie often came in that door with something freshly baked, and JJ's mouth watered for some of her homemade honey whole wheat bread.

He met his best friend's eyes. "Let's get out of here."

Tate grinned at him. "Feeling caged?"

"Here?" JJ threw him a dark look. "Always." He turned for the back door and left, pausing at the railing once he'd gained the outdoors. The Texas Panhandle sun hung low on the horizon, painting the evening sky in a breathtaking array of oranges and pinks.

He scanned the vast expanse of land before him, looking past his aunt and uncle's house to the space beyond. Across the street, where the rolling hills dotted with grazing cattle brought a sense of peace to his soul he desperately needed.

Tate joined him, and he didn't have to say anything. He wasn't entirely thrilled to be back at Seven Sons either, but he hadn't been able to find a ranch of his own that he could afford. His family hailed from Lubbock, but Tate had said on more than one occasion that he would never go back there permanently.

He'd fallen in love with Three Rivers, and he wanted to settle down as a rancher here. But property prices had soared in the past couple of years, and that had shut down his dreams.

For now.

JJ had considered telling him that he could buy every ranch in the Three Rivers area, but something always held him back. At twenty-five, JJ's broad shoulders held plenty of responsibility.

Now that he'd graduated with his degree in equine studies and management, he was no longer just the ranch owner's son; he was about to step into his daddy's boots as the new controller and barn manager at Seven Sons. He'd been groomed for this job his entire life, but that didn't make it any less daunting.

"Lord," JJ whispered, closing his eyes for a moment. "Thank You for this beautiful land and the opportunity to steward it. Guide me as I take on this new responsibility. Help me make my daddy proud."

"Amen, brother," Tate said, though the man didn't know how to whisper. Where JJ frowned, Tate grinned. While he stayed silent, Tate couldn't stop talking. They had opposite personalities, but JJ had always gotten along with Tate extraordinarily well, since the very first day of his very first year at Amarillo State.

Before then, even, as he'd met Tate the weekend before classes had started, as they'd been assigned the same apartment on-campus. They'd lived together since, even here at Seven Sons, and JJ glanced over to his best friend.

"How's it feel to be all grown up and important, JJ?"

JJ chuckled, some of the heaviness of his thoughts lifting. He pulled Tate into a quick, brotherly hug. "Feels like I've got a whole lot to learn," he admitted. "But I'm ready for it. How about you? Still annoyed you have to live here with me?"

Tate nodded, leaning against the deck railing. "Yeah, I'm over that. Your daddy pays real good, and I can save up for my own place faster than working anywhere else."

Words piled in JJ's throat, admissions about how much money he had, confessions that he could buy any of the ranches Tate saw online, offers to fund his best friend's dreams. He swallowed against them, because such a thing would need to be discussed with Daddy first, as JJ's money had been gifted to him at age twenty-one, but he didn't have complete control over it until he turned thirty.

Everything had to be done inside a trust, and JJ honestly didn't want to add one more thing to his mental and physical load right now.

As they stood there, soaking in the evening sunshine, JJ's mind wandered to Ruby, Tate's younger sister. The thought of her made his heart skip a beat, and he immediately chastised himself for it.

Ruby was off-limits, plain and simple.

Her close relationship with Tate dictated as much, and besides, she was probably off living her big-city dreams now that she'd graduated from college too.

"You okay there, JJ?" Tate's voice broke through his reverie. "You looked like you were a million miles away for a second."

JJ forced a smile, guilt gnawing at him for his wayward thoughts. "Yeah, just thinking about all the work we've got ahead of us." He started down the steps. "And they didn't paint the cabin?" He scoffed as Tate's boots sounded on the steps behind him. "That wasn't for me, trust me."

Tate laughed, the sound free and loud and filling the sky. "You *have* complained about the green every year, brother. Just admit it."

JJ would do no such thing. He just wanted to see his horses and steal from their gentle spirits. As they walked toward the stables which sat out past the homestead, the storage shed, and the barn, Tate's phone rang.

He pulled it from his pocket, took a look at it, and scoffed before shoving it away again. JJ's interest piqued, but he didn't ask who'd called. Tate obviously didn't want to talk to them, and JJ thought it might be his on-again, off-again girlfriend from Amarillo, Frieda.

Tate's expression darkened, and he let out a heavy sigh. "It's Ruby. She's been calling me non-stop, but I'm not in the mood to listen to her whine."

JJ had never once thought that Ruby had whined about anything, but she wasn't his younger sister. He'd thought that plenty about Clara Jean, his younger sister, so he simply kept his mouth shut. He could listen to Tate complain and disagree with him silently.

His opinion of Ruby wouldn't get tarnished, that was for sure. JJ had had a crush on her since the moment he'd met her, four years ago now.

Four. Long. Years.

Time to move on, he told himself. Now that they didn't have to see each other daily, he might be able to. She'd graduated this spring too, and she had an internship-that-could-become-a-job in San Antonio as part of her interior design degree. He'd been real happy for her when she'd gotten it a few months ago, though it had made his heartbeat sing with sadness.

Truth be told, the pang in his chest still existed. He'd dated other women, but nothing serious, and JJ told himself that once he found his real feet under him at Seven Sons, he'd find someone to date.

All of his friends here in town had found someone, and JJ really wanted it to be his turn. Of course, none of his cousins besides Oliver had gotten married yet, and his momma's words rang through his head again.

You're young.

Tate's phone rang again as they went past the shed, the big, bright, obviously recently painted, red barn came into view. Around the other side of it, the American flag waved, and JJ craved the sight of it. Somehow, it made him feel safe, and protected, and loved.

"Stop callin' me, Ruby." Tate ran a hand through his hair, frustration evident in his voice. He swiped the call away again, while JJ's heart played like a jackrabbit in his chest.

"Come on," JJ said, pushing Ruby out of his mind, hopefully for the last time that evening. "Let me show you the new breeding stock we just got in. Daddy's real proud of 'em."

As they walked toward the stables, JJ tried to focus on the task at hand. He pointed out the improvements they'd made to the ranch over the past year—the upgraded irrigation system, the expanded cattle pens, the repainted barn with its massive American flag proudly displayed on the side.

"You've done all this?" Tate asked, seemingly impressed.

"Daddy involved me in everything in the past year, though I was still in school." JJ came to a fence that contained a pasture with a couple of horses grazing in it.

"He's not going to just hand over Seven Sons in a single day."

JJ didn't even want him to.

"He trusts you, though," Tate said. "That's huge."

A surge of pride moved through JJ with Tate's words. "He seems to, but I've still got a lot to learn." He had dreams to add more horses to Seven Sons, but he hadn't spoken those out loud to anyone yet. Not even his father.

They had space for another stable that could house twenty horses, and JJ wanted to bring horse breeding to Seven Sons Ranch. It was the only thing he got excited about lately—besides Ruby, of course—but now that he'd determined they could only be friends—and long-distance friends at that—he only had the horses.

Tate clapped him on the back. "If anyone can do it, it's you. You've always had a way with horses and cattle that the rest of us only dream of."

JJ nodded, because he did communicate with animals in an extraordinary way. "Let's go see the flag."

He started along the fence, soon leaving that pasture behind, the corner of the barn they needed to round only a few paces away. Just then, Tate's phone rang again.

A yell filled the air.

JJ's boots brought his body to a stop as a bull came charging around the corner of the barn.

Tate had his eyes on his phone still, his head down.

How he didn't hear the thundering hooves, JJ didn't know. Couldn't comprehend.

JJ's instincts kicked in, and he stepped forward, his voice low and soothing as he tried to calm the charging bull.

He should've known better. Bulls couldn't be soothed. They weren't horses.

"Tate!" he yelled as he dodged out of the way. Two cowhands came flying around the corner of the barn, ropes in their hands.

But things moved too fast. Time didn't slow just because JJ wanted to save his best friend.

"Tate," he called again, and the bull seemed to know who JJ was trying to summon. He huffed and trotted toward JJ's best friend just as he lifted his head.

He didn't seem to catalog what was happening, at least not fast enough.

"Move!" JJ yelled. Or maybe he didn't. Maybe the warning only screamed silently through his soul.

Because Tate didn't move.

The bull did, and it caught Tate in the chest, butting him backwards in a violent move that stole JJ's very breath from his body.

JJ watched, horrified, as his best friend in the whole world hit the ground hard—without even trying to catch himself.

He didn't move, and JJ didn't think.

"Tate!" JJ yelled, rushing to his friend's side as the

other cowboys whistled and clapped and yelled at the bull to hopefully distract it from charging again.

Tate lay motionless, a small trickle of blood coming from somewhere on his head.

"Tate, can you hear me?" JJ had no idea where to put his hands, and Tate didn't move a millimeter. JJ's heart pounded in his chest, and thankfully, his daddy held mandatory first aid and safety training every year.

JJ had always found it a tad ridiculous, but that training kicked in as he pulled his phone out with shaking hands. He dialed nine-one-one, rattled off the situation, and where they were on the ranch.

"Stay on the line with me," the woman said, and JJ said he would.

He glanced over his shoulder to find Orion on the phone, probably with Daddy, and the bull moving away in the distance, still free when he shouldn't be. But at least he wasn't over here, continuing to cause problems.

"He's still breathing," he told the operator.

"An ambulance has been dispatched," she said. "They're only six minutes away."

Six minutes felt like six lifetimes, and JJ nodded. After taking a deep breath, JJ picked up Tate's phone, which lay near his hand, as if he'd been able to hold onto it as he'd flown through the air.

He found Ruby's name sitting there, the last incoming call, and silently praying that he'd have good news for her once they got to the hospital, he tapped to call her.

"Lord, give me strength," he whispered. "Help me find the right words." Because then she'd have to give them to the rest of Tate's family.

The phone rang, but Ruby didn't pick up. JJ's mind raced. What would he say to her? How could he tell her about Tate's accident without frightening her too much? And how could he push aside the feelings that threatened to overwhelm him at the thought of hearing her voice?

He looked at Tate, his best friend's face still slack, as Bobby came skidding to his knees beside JJ. "Nothing?"

JJ shook his head, both because no, Tate had not stirred at all—and Ruby had not answered her phone.

Sneak Peek! The Cowboy Who Called Back Chapter Two:

Ruby Reynolds paced the small living room of her soon-to-be-former student apartment, her phone clutched tightly in her hand. The room held a mess of half-packed boxes and piles of clothes, a physical representation of the chaos her life had become.

Sunlight streamed through the dirty blinds, highlighting the swirling dust motes in the air and casting long shadows across the worn carpet.

She glanced at her phone again, willing it to ring. She'd called Tate three times now, and every time, it had gone straight to voicemail. Ruby was probably annoying him, but she didn't know who else to turn to.

Her internship, the one she'd been counting on to launch her career and provide her with housing, had fallen through at the last minute. Now, the future didn't hold excitement and promise after four long years of schooling.

It didn't hold an internship with one of the best interior design firms in Texas—one that came with an additional twelve weeks of schooling and an apartment in a beautiful neighborhood in San Antonio.

"Nowhere to live," she drove home to herself as she collapsed back on the couch. She didn't even own that—she literally only had clothes, knick knacks, and a couple of boxes of household goods to her name.

"Come on, Tate." Her fingers hovered over the call button once more. "Pick up, please." Desperation choked her, making her tongue swell and her eyes fill with tears. The thought of calling her parents and admitting defeat made her stomach churn. They'd been so proud when she'd landed the internship, and the idea of crawling back to Lubbock with her tail between her legs absolutely would not come to fruition.

Ruby closed her eyes and took a deep breath. "Lord, I know You have a plan for me," she whispered, her voice trembling slightly. "But right now, I'm feeling lost and scared. Please, give me strength and guidance."

Her eyes popped open, and the only thing Ruby knew to do, the only safe place she had, was to talk to Tate.

She refused to call him again, though. Frustration bubbled with complete feelings of self-loathing, and Ruby bent over and pressed her forehead to her knees.

"Tate Reynolds, I swear if you're ignoring me on purpose, I'll...." She trailed off, not sure how to finish the empty threat to an even emptier living room. She loved her brother dearly, but sometimes his laid-back attitude drove her crazy. Especially now, when she needed him most.

Just as she was about to throw her phone across the room in exasperation, it rang. Ruby's heart leapt, practically knocking into her skull she sat up so fast.

Tate's name sat on the screen.

"Finally," she said as she looked at the four letters of his name. She wanted to swipe on the call and forgo the hello and go straight to chewing him out for ignoring her calls. But a louder, more devilish part of her wanted him to know what it felt like to get sent to voicemail.

She thought of him on the beautiful Seven Sons Ranch, in the gorgeous small town of Three Rivers. He'd spent every summer here these past few years, living with and working alongside his best friend, JJ Walker.

Her pulse quickened, and a familiar flutter winged through her stomach.

JJ, the cowboy she'd been secretly crushing on for years. It was silly, she knew. He'd always seen her as Tate's annoying little sister, the woman who'd gotten separated from her family on a campus tour, gotten scared, and couldn't communicate.

He didn't know that it was only around *him* that her tongue tied itself in knots. And her heart hadn't gotten the message that they couldn't have JJ. Tate had told her more than once how "weird" it would be for him if Ruby dated one of his friends. So she'd never tried to send any signals to JJ, never flirted with him, never said or did anything to indicate the slow-burning embers she harbored for him.

Ruby's mind raced with images of JJ – his tall, muscular frame silhouetted against the sunset as he worked on the ranch—a picture her brother had unknowingly tortured her with last summer.

His easy smile that never failed to make her knees weak whenever he opened the apartment door and said, "C'mon in, Ruby. Tate's in the living room."

The way his eyes crinkled at the corners when he laughed, though that sure didn't happen a whole lot. Still, he smiled when someone brought cookies to the apartment, and whenever he mixed Sprite with orange juice and offered her some too.

She could almost smell the leather that seemed to come with his skin, and the fresh scent of hay that always clung to him after his classwork in the stables.

Tate's call went to voicemail, and Ruby startled out of her thoughts with the silence.

She'd never known what to do with her feelings for JJ, so she'd ignored them. And life's paths had diverged for them anyway, and in the end, Ruby didn't have to decide. JJ now lived in Three Rivers, miles and miles from where she sat in her student apartment.

Ruby ran a hand through her tangled hair. "You're twenty-three years old, Ruby. Stop thinking like a lovesick teenager." But even as she chastised herself, she couldn't help but let her mind go down the forbidden path with JJ Walker on it.

She flopped back against the couch, surrounded by the remnants of her college life. She closed her eyes, trying to will away the stress and uncertainty closing in around her. She wasn't sure if she dozed or just zoned out, but she jerked to attention and sat up when her phone rang again.

It buzzed against her thigh, and she fumbled it as she tried to pick it up. Again, Tate's name sat there, and Ruby set aside her immaturity and swiped on the call. "You're so busy you can't answer my calls?"

"Ruby," a man said, decidedly not Tate. "It's JJ. JJ Walker?"

Ruby nearly dropped the phone. "JJ?"

"I'm so glad you answered." Concern laced JJ's deep voice, and she imagined it to be for her. Intellectually, she knew it wasn't—and the fact that he'd called from her brother's phone clicked into place in her head.

"What's wrong?" She jumped back to her feet, her nerves shouting at her.

"There's been an accident." JJ spoke in a calm, even tone, about the way he did everything. That, or he growled his thoughts, as he wasn't exactly one to fill the world with sunshine. He'd always been kind to her, though, and she knew his grouchy exterior could be broken fairly easily.

"Tate's hurt." More voices came through the line, then shuffling, and JJ said, "No, he hasn't woken up," which only sent Ruby's pulse through the roof.

"Tate is unconscious?" she asked. The blood drained from her face, pooling somewhere in her stomach, making her sick. Her earlier irritation with her brother evaporated instantly, and she started looking around for her car keys. "Where are you? What happened? Is he okay?"

"He got...hit," JJ said. "The paramedics just arrived, and they'll take him to the hospital here in Three Rivers."

"I'm on my way," Ruby said, already heading for the door. "Text me the details. I'll be there as soon as I can."

As she rushed out of her apartment, Ruby's mind whirled with emotion. Worry for Tate consumed her, pushing aside her earlier problems. She should call her parents, so they could pray, and Ruby did that from the car.

"I don't know, Daddy," she said. "JJ called from Tate's phone. The paramedics had just gotten there."

"I'll call him," her father said, and Ruby set her teeth together.

"He said he'd text me updates." Ruby looked down at her phone in the cup holder. "I haven't gotten any yet." She had no idea how far Seven Sons Ranch sat from the hospital in Three Rivers.

Her dad didn't say anything, and that fueled Ruby's worry. "We can pray," she said, her voice tiny among the vast road in front of her. "I'm on my way, and I'll text you the moment I'm there and know anything."

"Of course you will," her dad said. "We'll pray here, and we'll wait for more news."

Ruby and Tate had two younger siblings, and both of her parents worked. Getting all of them from Lubbock to Three Rivers wasn't something easily done, and Ruby prayed, "Lord, bless Tate that he'll be just fine. That he'll wake up and be okay, so Mama and Daddy don't have to come."

The drive to Three Rivers blurred by, with JJ only texting once that they'd arrived at the hospital, and Tate had woken up in the ambulance. *They took him back in the ER*, he'd said. *I don't know much, but I'll text you more when I do.*

Ruby's knuckles shone a bright white on the steering wheel as she navigated the unfamiliar roads in Three Rivers, her phone dictating to her where to turn. Another text from JJ arrived, the buzz of her phone sending a jolt of fear and anticipation driving through her.

They moved him to a room, he said. *235. You can come up when you get here.*

"Turn right," her GPS said. "And your destination will be on the right."

Ruby peered that direction as she turned, and yep, there sat the hospital. She had no idea how to get up to the second floor, where the patient rooms would be. "Hospitals have information desks," she reminded herself, and she parked near the Emergency Room entrance, because she could see a door leading inside.

JJ hadn't texted again, and he hadn't said if Tate was awake, had broken bones, nothing. Her adrenaline raged through her, and tears pricked at her eyes as she tried to grab her purse and realized she'd left it at home.

"Great," she muttered, swiping at the tears that dared to escape. She turned off the car and headed inside. Her eyes didn't seem to work, and frustration filled her when she got on the first elevator she saw and realized it only went up to the fourth, fifth, and sixth floors.

She went back down and got on another elevator, only to get right off again. Tears flowed down her face freely now, and an elderly man coming off the elevator took pity on her and touched her elbow. "Where are you trying to get?"

Ruby sniffled, her voice always stuck way down in her belly when she got emotional. "The second floor," she managed to squeak out.

"You need the elevators across there." He indicated

the bank across the foyer, and Ruby looked over to them. They bore no signs or anything for her to know that, and she wanted to light the place on fire.

"Thank you," she managed, feeling foolish and angry at the same time. She practically ran across the rotunda and stabbed at the button to call the elevator. When it arrived, she shot forward, only to be greeted by a family getting off.

Impatience stroked through her, but she turned her face away and wiped at her eyes. She didn't want to run into JJ as a total mess, and she certainly wouldn't be able to get anything past Tate. He'd probably laugh and joke and ask her what she was so upset about.

She made it to the second floor, and a huge, triple-wide door stood in front of her, across the waiting room. As she stepped that way, JJ rose from a chair, his tall frame unfolding into all of his gorgeous glory right in front of her. Her heart betrayed her at the sight of him, even as worry for Tate threatened to overwhelm her.

Without thinking, Ruby changed course and threw herself into JJ's arms. She buried her face in his chest, inhaling his familiar scent of leather, and hay, and cool water falling over a ledge as sobs wracked her body.

His strong arms enveloped her, and for a moment, Ruby felt safe, like nothing could hurt her as long as JJ held her against his pulse.

"Shh, it's okay," he murmured, his lips brushing

against her hair, practically touching her earlobe. Her cells sizzled at her. "Tate's going to be fine. The doctors say he has a concussion and some problems with his ribs, but he'll recover."

JJ's mouth ghosted over her cheek, not quite touching her, but leaving a trail of warmth from his breath in its wake. "It's all going to be okay, Ruby. Okay? It's going to be okay."

Standing there in JJ's arms, feeling the solid strength of his body near hers, and the tender brush of his lips against her skin, Ruby believed him. Despite everything going wrong in her life—her uncertain future, Tate's injury, her waiting parents—Ruby felt like maybe, just maybe, everything really would turn out okay.

As she pulled back slightly, Ruby looked up into JJ's handsome, filled-with-concern face. His dark eyes broadcasted warmth and something else she couldn't quite define. For a moment, she allowed herself to imagine what it would be like if JJ saw her as more than just Tate's little sister. What it would be like to be held by him like this every day, to be loved by him?

He didn't step back, and he didn't drop his hands from holding her. They seemed locked in that moment, and Ruby wanted it to go on forever.

Her mind buzzed at her about something she'd come here to do, but in this moment, Ruby did the most un-Ruby thing of her life.

She kissed JJ Walker square on the mouth.

Mm, the unrequited love and secret crushes in this book are going to be delicious! Preorder your copy by scanning the QR code below with your phone!

The Cowboy Who Came Home: A Second Generation in Three Rivers Ranch Romance™ (Book 1): He's been serving in the military for a decade. She's been quietly grieving a devastating loss. When Finn and Edith reunite in small-town Three Rivers where they grew up together, can their second chance romance provide hope, healing, and the happily-ever-after they both crave?

Scan this QR code with your phone to see this series in eBook, audiobook, large print paperback, or regular paperback:

Be sure to check out the other three series set in the beloved town of Three Rivers too!

Meet the cowboys who started it all at Three Rivers Ranch! Scan the QR code below with your phone to check out this complete series.

Scan this QR code with your phone to see and order this series in eBook, audiobook, large print paperback, or regular paperback:

1. Second Chance Ranch
2. Third Time's the Charm
3. Fourth and Long
4. Fifth Generation Cowboy
6. Sixth Street Love Affair
7. The Seventh Sergeant
8. Eight Second Ride
9. The Ninth Inning
10. Ten Days in Town
11. Eleven Year Reunion

Seven Sons Ranch in Three Rivers Romance™ Series

Meet the cowboy billionaire brothers at Seven Sons Ranch! Scan the QR code below with your phone to check out this complete series.

1. Rhett
2. Tripp
3. Liam
4. Jeremiah
5. Wyatt
6. Skyler
7. Micah
8. Gideon

Shiloh Ridge Ranch in Three Rivers Romance™ Series

Become a Glover Lover by reading all the Glover Family romance & family saga at Shiloh Ridge Ranch! Scan the QR code below with your phone to check out this complete series.

1. The Mechanics of Mistletoe
2. The Horsepower of the Holiday
3. The Construction of Cheer
4. The Secret of Santa
5. The Gift of Gingerbread
6. The Harmony of Holly
7. The Chemistry of Christmas
8. The Delivery of Decor
9. The Blessing of Babies

About Liz

Liz Isaacson writes inspirational romance, usually set in Texas, or Wyoming, or anywhere else horses and cowboys exist. She lives in Utah, where she writes full-time, takes her two dogs to the park everyday, and eats a lot of veggies while writing. Find her on her website at www.feelgoodfictionbooks.com.